The Naked Truth

What Reviewers Say About Sandy Lowe's Work

If You Dare

"Grab this little baby and go in with an open mind, it most certainly will be worth it."—*Saucy Reviews on Kinky Korner*

"I love when an author pushes the boundaries, plays outside of the box and writes outside of their comfort zone. Sandy Lowe did this with *If You Dare*. It's sexy, intriguing, and everything this erotica fan is looking for."—*Les Rêveur*

Party of Three

"In the world of erotica, Party of Three is like a day at the fair—cotton candy sweet with plenty of fun rides. It'll leave you exhilarated and a bit out of breath. I sped through this book in one sitting because everything clicked. It's sexy, cool, and funny all at once. If you've never considered reading an erotic romance, this is the perfect novel to get your feet wet. …When you want to spend a quiet night in and need something a little more raucous than a Hallmark channel rom-com, check out *Party of Three*."—*Lesbian Review*

"I really enjoyed this book. It was well written and gripping, and each section had good character development and a strong story arc. …I really enjoyed the author's tone and writing style, and I look forward to her next book."—Melina Bickard, Librarian, Waterloo Library (UK)

"If you're looking for a fun and light read with a few sharp bits, this is it. Of course it's steamy hot, but it's also pretty romantic in its own way. Come for the sex, stay for the romance or come for the romance, stay for the sex, either way you win."—*Jude in the Stars*

"If this is a taste of what's to come, I am excited to see what's next from Sandy Lowe."—*Les Rêveur*

"The book is broken down by each lady's journey and each part gave all the emotions, sweetness, and smoking hot sexiness!" —*Steph's Romance Book Talk*

"One hell of a party!!! …A great read if you want fun, flirty, and a little erotica in an easy story that allows you to really experience the fun being had and the feelings of the characters."—*LESBIreviewed*

Girls on Campus—***Edited by Sandy Lowe and Stacia Seaman***

"[U]nbelievably hot and the perfect book to keep on your bedside table. …This was an awesome book of short erotic stories. I loved that I got to read so many stories from so many of my favorite authors, but also got introduced to a few new ones to follow as well. …They were hot, and sweet, and romantic, and hot! Definitely worth it."—*Inked Rainbow Reads*

"Sensual and sexy! *Girls On Campus* is an anthology of college and university based erotic stories from a variety of authors. A good variety of stories make this a book with a little something for everyone. …I got to discover some new authors, and experience a writing style from some familiar authors that was new and exciting to see what their stories held. I made some wonderful discoveries and had the best time reading this book. If you love erotica, this anthology will give you all you need, and more."—*LESBIreviewed*

Escape to Pleasure: Lesbian Travel Erotica*—Edited by Sandy Lowe and Victoria Villasenor*

"[A] very pleasurable read—especially whilst on holiday!"—Melina Bickard, Librarian, Waterloo Library (UK)

"Irresistible"

"A best friends to romance story line that is not only incredibly loving but also sexy and passionate. Almost like an awakening, this book is going to capture your heart."—*Les Rêveur*

Visit us at www.boldstrokesbooks.com

By the Author

Party of Three

If You Dare

The Naked Truth

The Naked Truth

by

Sandy Lowe

2025

THE NAKED TRUTH

ISBN 13: 978-1-63679-426-6

This Trade Paperback Original Is Published By
Bold Strokes Books, Inc.
P.O. Box 249
Valley Falls, NY 12185

First Edition: January 2025

Credits
Editors: Radclyffe and Cindy Cresap
Production Design: Susan Ramundo
Cover Design By Tammy Seidick

Acknowledgments

I was as green as spring shoots when I emailed Radclyffe to ask if the sex scenes in her romance novels were what sex was *really* like, or if she wrote them that way to sell books. (I know. I can't believe I did that either.) She gave me some advice: "When it's right it's even better. Don't settle." That, dear readers, is the naked truth.

Many thanks go to the whole team at Bold Strokes. You're heroes in pajama bottoms all of you.

Thanks to my editor, Cindy, who catches all my Australian-isms and deeply does not care that I write so many orgasms. I wouldn't have it any other way.

Thanks to Ali, Ashlee, Claudia, and Scotty who read early versions of the draft and provided much-needed encouragement.

Thanks to Ann for her insightful feedback and for inspiring me with filthy bible verses.

Thanks to Radclyffe for basically everything. Everyone thinks I can perfectly structure a sentence, and no one knows you fix all my boo-boos. It's our secret.

Rowan's fantasies were inspired by the nonfiction book *Who's Been Sleeping in Your Head?* by Brett Kahr. If you're as nerdy about the psychology of sex as I am, I recommend it!

Dedication

To Ann, Salem, the North Hero House Inn,
and Abbott's Table wine. All of whom
convinced me to finish this draft.

Chapter One

Genna Fielding's family had her best interests at heart, which had her heart lacing its sneakers to run for its life.

She'd discovered that sometimes in life you laid back to take it. Other times you got on top and rode the hell out of it. Tonight, though, she was flat on her back after taking the stand to defend her romantic apathy to a self-appointed jury of so-called experts. Who, between bites of chicken pot pie and one glass too many of twelve-dollar wine, had cheerfully debated her lackluster options before coming to their unanimous verdict: her love life was bordering on hopeless, and Genna was a short half step from the precipice of eternal spinsterdom. She'd been granted conditional probation, during which she'd have to hurry up and fall in love or her mom and sisters would never forgive her for being perfectly fine on her own. She wasn't getting any younger, external validation didn't grow on trees, and other assorted clichés sealed her fate.

While her heart was running for cover, her libido ran the show. The destination, as usual, was McKinney's.

"Casanova! Over here." Travis Becker's shit-eating grin was the Cheshire Cat and Ronald McDonald's illicit love child.

Genna wound her way around tables to his spot in the corner facing the bar. "God, do I need a drink. Please tell me all the straight people went home and the place is filled with everyone who wants to sleep with me."

McKinney's Bar and Grille didn't need to try, and everyone knew it. Not classy, not cozy, and on a Saturday night, definitely not clean. What it lacked in essentials it made up for with sexy available people looking for exactly what Genna could offer them. Who needed ambiance when you had a rep as the primo spot to pick up a one-night stand?

Travis slid the sweaty IPA he'd obviously ordered for her across the table. "Don't blame you for expecting someone to land naked in your lap. You've such a hard life. Listening to sexy young coeds' jerk-off fantasies. Opining their psychosexual Freudian stirrings, and calling it work. Put your feet up, you deserve a break. I should've brought you a Kit Kat instead of a beer."

Jokes came with the territory when your job was studying sex. No one seemed to be able to talk about it with a straight face. "As fond as I am of Freud, I *coded* six hours of interviews today. My ears are bleeding and my brain's fried. Not to mention an obligatory family dinner."

Travis gave her a sympathetic look. "Ah, family. Can't live with them and wouldn't want to."

She preferred lust-induced amnesia to hashing it all out. "You asked me to detour here. Spill."

"Have I ever let you down?" Travis swigged his beer and sent the sexy-side-eye to a svelte woman in a leather vest two tables over. A software engineer who'd left Silicon Valley for a slower pace and a lower price tag, Travis had his pick of partners. He was attractive in that generic way some men were. Classically handsome due more to his symmetrical features, deep blue eyes, and full head of hair than to actual effort. Men had it so easy. He got to show up in nothing more spectacular than a collared shirt, while Genna was in a dress, heels, *and* makeup. She probably should've done her hair, but just couldn't be bothered. Travis wore jeans. The injustice burned.

"Do I need to remind you of the time you convinced me to leave with the giggle twins? I needed therapy," Genna said.

Travis waved a hand dismissively. "Honest mistake. I can't be held accountable for the relative immaturity of anyone under thirty. The woman I have in mind for you hasn't seen thirty in at least a decade."

She and Travis had been regulars at McKinney's for longer than was healthy. One night, a woman Genna dubbed Mistress X had shown up in red leather, five-inch heels, and Texas-big hair with her metaphorical whip swinging. Travis's dream girl had just entered the building. So, she'd done what any friendly acquaintance would do and texted him to haul ass over to McKinney's and score. He had too. Ever since, when someone who fell into the zip code of her *type* walked in, Travis returned the favor.

Sweet really. A pimp, a wingman, and a decent friend in a three-for-one deal.

"Who is she?" Genna looked around.

"Black dress, reddish hair, far left at the bar," Travis said.

If she'd been a misogynist, she might've whistled. The basic description didn't come close to doing the woman justice. Yeah, her dress was black, but it toed the line between accentuating her many curves and providing an abode they spilled from. Not quite brown and not quite red, her hair caught the light and shone a thousand shades of in-between, so damn pretty Genna's fingers itched to tangle in it. Her skin all but glowed ivory under the designed-to-be-flattering half-light.

"Why is a soccer mom that hot still alone at ten p.m.?" The reason was usually unwelcome.

"Sam came by to gripe about her," Travis said.

Tall, lanky, and non-binary, Sam had ended up in her bed a time or two. Genna wouldn't have called Travis a gossip, exactly. But his kind eyes and affable nature had invited more than one person to spill their guts.

"Are they here?" Genna asked. "I should say hi." *Hi* being code for *I wouldn't mind a repeat if you're interested.*

"They left ten minutes ago with a woman who looked tough enough to take us both down without breaking a sweat," Travis said knowingly.

Maybe next time. Genna turned her attention back to the woman still alone at the bar. "What's Sam's intel on her then?"

"She's been sitting there for an hour, turning away everyone. Turns out she's a *pillow queen* and wants the night to be one-sided as long as it's her side having all the fun. That doesn't go over well with these equal opportunity Gen Xers. So, obviously, my pal Casanova is the only woman for the job."

"How do you know I'm right for this job?"

"People gripe." Travis shrugged. "What else do you call it when you want to give someone pleasure but refuse to let them touch you?"

Her lovers had complained? Genna's stomach nosedived.

"Wait, there's a word for that, isn't there? Rock something?"

She wanted a rock so she could throw it at him. "I'm not stone. And I'm not Casanova, either." Clearly, or she wouldn't be getting one-star reviews.

Travis shrugged. "She's hot and I suggest you use your stone-rock wiles to convince her of what you both want. Someone you don't have to persuade not to touch you sounds like just your brand of masochism. You're welcome."

Genna said nothing, because damn it, he was right, and that the regulars at McKinney's knew it pissed her off. Apparently, being transparent was also her thing. Even so, she had no desire to explain her preference for not being touched, and Travis didn't ask.

"Alright. Can't hurt to try. Statistically she's probably straight though." She set her empty bottle to one side and stood, offering her chair with a flourish when leather-vest lady approached the table.

Time to get out of Travis's way. She had a pillow queen to worship. Maybe.

❖

"What do you do?" Hot Soccer Mom asked, tugging her full bottom lip with her teeth.

"I'm a graduate student at SCU. Working on my PhD," Genna added in case the woman mistook her for a coed. She hadn't been *that* young in…never.

"Sexy and smart." Hot Soccer Mom smiled flirtatiously. "SCU is a bit of a ways though. What are you doing all the way out here?"

Trying to get laid. How about you?

Genna took her hand, sliding their fingers together. Small talk was getting nosier by the second. She had a rule: decide in the first twenty minutes or move on to more eager pastures. She despised talking about the weather.

Since she wasn't charming enough to get away with lines that sounded like lines, she played to her strengths and went for nice but direct. Stepping a little nearer, she cut as close to the chase as she dared. "What are you looking for tonight?"

Hot Soccer Mom winced. "Oh, well, I'm married." She waved her left hand unnecessarily between them, then gestured down the bar to a forty-something guy in blue jeans and a black sweater. The dude version of dressing up for the evening. Genna couldn't help glancing down at herself dolled up in her one and only do-me dress. Damn the patriarchy.

"That's my husband, Kenneth," Hot Soccer Mom continued. "We're committed." She leaned in. "But allowed to *stray*."

New to the whole straying business then if the whispered confession was anything to go by. Genna tried not to smile.

"That's no problem. Would you be interested in my leading you astray?"

Hot Soccer Mom bit her lip. "Are you into BDSM? The last three people I spoke to were, but I'm afraid that I just can't with all of that." She pronounced BDSM with a pause between each letter and a faint air of incredulity, like she couldn't understand why anyone bothered.

Genna lifted a shoulder. "I just like sex."

Hot Soccer Mom nodded. "I like, just, you know, regular. Basic. The things women do."

This wasn't Genna's first time with a bisexual, or maybe it was pansexual, woman in a long-term relationship. She didn't disparage guys' skills simply because they had a cock that called the shots. There were some things women were plainly better at, and pleasuring the fairer sex was one of them.

"If we agree BDSM is off the table, can I tell you what I'd love tonight?" Genna gave the words a conspiratorial twist, as if she had a scandalous secret on the tip of her tongue.

Hot Soccer Mom's eyes brightened. "Please."

"I'd love to go down on you. I know that's not very adventurous of me, but there's just something about oral sex that makes me so hot. I love having my mouth on a woman. It's so intimate and sexy, don't you think?"

Hot Soccer Mom sipped her drink and nodded. She tucked her hair behind her ears in a nervous gesture one part coy and sixteen parts sexy. She might've been a little too soft around the edges to make it to a runway, but Genna guessed she'd been the prom queen in high school and now that the girl next door had matured, she was nothing short of a knockout. Hot Soccer Mom took care of herself, and Genna took care to notice.

She took Hot Soccer Mom's nod as permission to continue. "I like to take my time. Licking and stroking, making it so good for both of us. I hate to rush. It's not really about getting to the orgasm, it's the experience. A woman all hot and wet for me is the sexiest thing ever."

She *was* trying to move them from the bar to the bedroom, but she drew the line at lying. And she wasn't. Messy, nose-deep, oral sex was a huge turn-on, and if Hot Soccer Mom was into this basic thing women did together, she was only too happy to oblige. Crazy hot sex or being politely cast aside as not quite the right fit, were equally plausible outcomes, and only Hot Soccer Mom and her gorgeous pouty bottom lip could decide.

Picking up strangers wasn't as easy, or as popular, as all the movies made out. People were usually more worried about being liked than actually fucking. She'd learned two things in her time at McKinney's—don't try to convince anyone they're into you, and figure out if you were willing to give them what they wanted and not the other way around. No matter how attractive someone was, if you weren't into the same things, the sex was going to suck in a not-good way.

Genna slid her fingers away. "I'd really like a night with you, but I understand if you're not ready to leave with me." *Here's an out if you want it. But time to decide because your twenty is up.*

Hot Soccer Mom gave Genna a once-over she probably imagined was subtle. "You like to take it slow?"

"I have all night just for you."

"I can take a while. I like to *relax*." Hot Soccer Mom drew out the word like a world-weary, work-life-balance veteran. She and Kenneth probably had two point five kids at home, and a night on the town was a rare luxury. Who'd blame her for being picky.

"My favorite thing in the world is giving pleasure. I'd love to help you relax for as long as it takes." Truth without having to dodge questions about her own needs was Genna's version of a relaxing evening, and hell if she wasn't dying to be taken up on it.

Hot Soccer Mom drained her glass. "Let me just tell Kenneth I'm leaving."

Thank you, Travis. I owe you one.

❖

Of all the places Rowan Marks could've woken up, Mrs. Penellie's twin bed wasn't a top-ten location. That she'd rented the room, and Mrs. Penellie was two doors down snoring like a freight train, was only a marginal improvement. Rowan tossed back the hand-crocheted quilt-thingy and her feet hit the too-cold, hundred-year-old floorboards before her eyes were fully open. It's not as if she wanted to look around. The bed was hideous, the walls slicked with little daisy wallpaper, and every piece of furniture the drab brown of ugly antiques. Between work and classes, she had no time to spend here anyway.

She slipped into the bathroom, then dragged on a pair of faded sweatpants and a sports bra to go with the T-shirt she'd worn to bed, stepped into her sneakers, and was out of the house and on her way to Pete's Gym in under three minutes.

"Morning," Pete called out from the broom closet he'd promoted to an office.

She lifted a hand in greeting and kept going, dumping her stuff into a cubby and heading to the back of the building. She suffered two thirty-minute runs every week as an offering to the cardio gods, but lifting wasn't about the exercise. And not about looking good naked, either. Lifting was meditative. The sounds and scents of the gym, the repetition, the tremble and burn when she was almost spent. Nothing cleared her mind faster, and she needed industrial-strength Clorox and a crew of twenty to scrub away the thoughts that'd kept her up last night. Tossing and turning, restless and edgy, until she'd given in.

Again.

Nope. Not thinking about it. Time to put it away. She couldn't take it back now. Life had no do-overs. She'd just move forward and vow never again.

Again.

She bit her lip to stop from groaning out loud at the women crowding the free weights, chatting while surreptitiously checking themselves out in the floor to ceiling mirror. One at least dangled a five-pound dumbbell from her brightly manicured fingers. The other hadn't bothered.

Pete's had plenty of glossy-haired, lululemon-wearing, so-female-she-couldn't-look-or-she'd-stare clientele, and loads were ripped. She'd once dropped in on a Saturday morning Pilates class and hadn't been able to take the stairs without wincing for a week. These two, though, the ones currently gossiping and in her way? Breaking a sweat would've ruined their makeup.

"Mind if I squeeze by you?" She waited for their nod before moving between them.

The one attempting to have a reason for standing there zeroed in on her arms. "I love your ink." The woman held her gaze a beat too long.

Rowan willed away the heat on her cheeks. The last thing she needed was come-and-get-me eyes from a total stranger, even if she did look pretty great doing absolutely nothing. "Thanks."

Rowan took her dumbbells over to a bench and started on some easy bicep curls to warm up. *One. Two. Three—*

"So, anyway, it's weird, right? I mean, she's *paying* people to tell her their sex fantasies. That's fucked up."

"I don't know. Professor Turner wouldn't have to pay me to talk sexy to him. I'd do it just to see the bulge in his pants grow."

The one who'd smiled at Rowan shoved her friend on the shoulder. "That's gross. He's so old."

"Fifty-whatever isn't old, and who cares anyway, it's not like I'd marry him. No reason not to put all his experience to good use right between my legs."

"Jessica!"

Rowan cursed herself for leaving her headphones in the cubby. Some noise cancellation would be handy right now. She closed her eyes and focused on breathing out on the curl, in when she released. *Four. Five—*

"Shame it's not Turner's study, that's all I'm saying. What's it about, anyway?" Jessica asked.

"Sexual fantasy and feminist discourse. Whatever that means," not-Jessica said. "I hate it when they say *discourse* like they're trying to be intellectual. Why do academics study things that are actually fun and make them completely boring? I'm not signing up to ruin my fantasies. Does anyone need to know *why* they have them? Sexy-boardshorts-guy and just-the-right-amount-of-facial-hair guy in a threesome is my go-to. Don't care why."

Rowan couldn't see the woman's face, but her tone dripped eye-roll. *Please. Six. Go. Seven. Away. Eight.*

"I wouldn't talk to some bra-burning, man-hating, hairy-pitted feminist about sex. Did you read about the one that's giving away cookies? That's my idea of a study," Jessica replied.

Hairy-pitted? Seriously?

Rowan headed back for her headphones.

Ninety minutes later, she was drenched with sweat, but the bulk of the uneasiness churning in her gut had disappeared. Small mercy. She wiped down the gear she'd used and put everything back. At nearly nine a.m. on a Sunday, the early morning fitness crowd was hitting the exit. Football games, picnics, and yard work were much more appealing than being inside under fluorescent lights with the latest angsty girl-band pounding the eardrums. Jessica and her pal had left more than an hour earlier.

She slid the weights back into their cradle and noticed a slightly crumpled printout on the floor. Her mom would be horrified at such blatant littering of a public place, of *any* place that wasn't a trash can. If cleanliness was next to godliness, Doreen Marks was the patron saint of Lysol.

She bent to pick it up and caught the words "sexual fantasy" in bold type. She blinked, sure her not-quite-all-the-way-gone arousal was messing with her head. What the hell? She smoothed the paper.

The Intersection of Sexual Fantasy and Feminist Discourse in Adult Women.

Dear Invitee,

I am a doctoral student at Silver Creek University conducting research on sexual fantasy and feminist discourse. The intention is to assess the impact, if any, that psychosocial feminist discourse plays in adult female sexual fantasy development, content, interpretation, access, response, and duration. The study involves collection of data to determine eligibility for participation, a survey of sexual history, and six one-hour, one-on-one, verbal interviews conducted at the Sexuality and Gender Studies division on campus over a three-week period (sessions flexible with student schedules).

Participation is voluntary and you may withdraw from the study at any time. All data will be recorded and stored indefinitely. A one-time payment of $500 is offered upon full completion. If you wish to participate, please review the informed consent and confidentiality agreement attached. To determine eligibility for the study, contact:

Genevieve Fielding
Sexuality and Gender Studies Division
Preston Grant Building
Ph: (311) 555-2812

What was it not-Jessica had said?

She's paying people to tell her their sex fantasies.

Reading between the academic mumbo, that's exactly what it sounded like. Rowan swallowed and read the letter a second time, more slowly. *Female sexual fantasy development, content, interpretation, access, response, and duration.* What *was* all that, exactly? How someone came up with their fantasies? What they were about? How hot they got thinking about them? How often and for how long? How fast they came? *Jesus.* Sex fantasies were a hell of a thing to base a PhD on. Six one-on-one interviews, over three weeks. All recorded.

But unlike Jessica and not-Jessica, Rowan instantly wanted to meet Genevieve Fielding. The future Dr. Sex-Fantasies-Are-My-Specialty. Dr. I-Know-What-Makes-You-Orgasm. Dr. Let's-Talk-Dirty-For-Research. Bet she was a blast at dinner parties.

Rowan stared at the flyer. She should toss it in the trash. Sexual fantasies were unequivocally the very last thing she needed to be thinking about. Hadn't she just turned her muscles to applesauce to forget about them? She needed to stay the hell away from a study like this, and from the kind of person who found sex interesting enough to investigate.

But…

What if Genevieve Fielding could help her? Lifting until exhaustion was a decent coping mechanism as such things went, better than booze or coke. But it was just that, *coping*. Temporary. A glorified Band-Aid. What if Dr. Tell-Me-Your-Sexy-Thoughts could provide more permanent relief? What if she didn't *have* to cope? She'd be better off going to a licensed professional. There were sex therapists in strip malls next to dog groomers and nail salons. Except she couldn't afford to pay out of pocket, and the crappy-ass insurance that came with her part-time gig at Alessandro's Family Restaurant likely wouldn't cover sex therapy. Did she really want to call a complete stranger to find out? Did she want to risk her boss knowing she had *lady problems*? Fuck no, and precisely why she'd chosen dumbbells over therapy in the first place.

But maybe participating in the research was a way to figure out why she was so drawn to certain *content* that elicited such an uncontrollable *response*. Maybe some *interpretation* would, as not-Jessica had put it, ruin the fantasies altogether. Couldn't hurt to call and see if she was eligible to be ruined by the good doctor.

What do you say, Genevieve? Want to chat about the most fucked-up fantasies you'll ever hear? I've got dozens.

Megan stared at the [illegible]. She [illegible] tomatoes were [illegible] the very last thing she needed to be thinking about. [illegible] she just turned [illegible] to forget about them? She [illegible] the hall [illegible] the kind of person who found [illegible] enough to investigate [illegible]

But [illegible]

What if [illegible] was a [illegible] as such things went, better than nobody [illegible] But it was [illegible] glorified Band-Aid. [illegible] they were [illegible] of the [illegible] and the [illegible]

[illegible]

[illegible]

Chapter Two

Whatever you do, don't drop the vodka.

Not for the first time, Genna dreamed of becoming a 1950s housewife. Such a dirty little secret for a feminist scholar, but right now a hunky—preferably strong and dashing—partner to bring home the bacon would be a lot more useful than... Subservience? Inequality? Not being able to marry a woman because queer rights meant no rights? The housewife gig wouldn't pan out. But housewives didn't have to deal with a backlog of research papers, six bags of groceries, *and* the ominous check engine light on her 2004 Dodge Neon that wouldn't go away no matter how fervently she believed in magic.

She heard the unmistakable clink of her keys hitting the sidewalk. *Fuck.* Balancing her grocery bags and the bottle she'd tucked under her arm, she lowered cautiously into a crouch, and scooped them up. Don't drop the vodka. She teetered back to standing and shuffled along the sidewalk to her building. Managing to loop three of the environmentally friendly, biodegradable, circulation-restricting bags onto one arm, she freed a hand to fit her key into the lock. It slid in on the second try. There wasn't leverage to swing the door wide enough for her *and* all her stuff to fit through at once, so she flung one bag-laden arm inside and wedged herself into the gap.

Oh, this was graceful. She could just see tomorrow's headline: Modern woman too stubborn to live, killed by her own front door.

She squeezed the rest of the way in and was just about to start on the stairs when Lady Gaga's "Rain on Me" blasted at full volume from the depths of her purse, scaring the bejeezus out of her. The Grey Goose slipped and fell in slow motion. No, no, no!

Gasping like it was her last breath, Genna dove, managing to catch the bottle on the tips of her fingers only by sacrificing half her groceries.

Lady Gaga was still hollering about misery raining down, and fishing her phone from her purse, Genna understood completely.

"Yes, hello?"

Silence on the other end. She'd just dumped fifty dollars' worth of food on the floor for a crank call. Brilliant.

The offender coughed politely. "Uh, hello. May I please speak to Genevieve Fielding?"

She stopped inspecting her bruised fruit long enough to close her eyes. A work call, and she'd just answered it like an ass. Doubly brilliant.

"This is Genna. Sorry about that. I'm a little preoccupied on my knees in the lobby of my building."

More silence.

Did she really just say that? "My phone rang, and I dropped my stuff. I didn't mean to be so rude."

"Oh, right," the woman said, like this was perfectly understandable. "I hope everything's okay. Would you like me to call back?"

She'd have preferred the woman had waited five minutes to call in the first place.

She threw a bag of destroyed ready-made chicken tenders into the lobby trash can and managed to haul herself and everything else up.

"That depends on what you need." She sure hoped everything she said would stop sounding like innuendo soon.

"I need…I'm calling about your study? Sexual fantasy and feminism? I'd like to know if I'm eligible to participate."

"Of course. Can you give me twenty seconds?" Genna jogged up the last few steps and turned the corner toward her apartment.

"If it's an inconvenient time, I'm happy to—"

"No, no," Genna said with the same I-can-do-it-all-no-problem logic that had, of course, caused all the problems. She opened her door and set everything on the kitchen counter. Fishing the pint of Ben and Jerry's Cherry Garcia from one of the bags and tossing it into the freezer, she asked, "What did you say your name was?"

The woman hadn't introduced herself. Probably debating whether she ought to hang up.

"Rowan Marks. I'm a student at SCU and saw your flyer."

Free of distraction, Genna noted the soft timbre of Rowan's voice. She didn't sound like a college kid. "What's your major?"

"Social work." Rowan's voice had an almost imperceptible rumble, like the engine of a brand-new car, little more than a hum but oddly reassuring. And, hey, a new car, or at least a new engine would be really useful.

She sat on the couch and pulled the study's intake survey up on her laptop. "Social work, huh? You must be in it for the stress-free lifestyle." The joke was bad. Like, dads-at-a-cookout bad, so flat it could've doubled as a pancake, but it didn't sound like innuendo, so *yay*.

"Nah." Rowan had a smile in her voice. "I'm all about the flexible hours and easy money."

She's nice. Genna had met enough strangers that she could tell genuinely nice people by the way they handled an awkward situation, and Rowan was making her feel like her dead-on-arrival quip hadn't been quite so bad. Not to mention exceedingly polite and kindly ignoring all the stupid things she'd said so far. Damn if talking to someone nice wasn't the highlight of her day.

"What do you know about the study?" Genna asked. "I attached an introduction when I dropped off the invites, but most faculty don't bother with it."

"Just what's on the invite. I'm missing the consent agreement it mentions."

"I'll get that to you to review and sign when you come in to complete the history and instruments."

"I didn't know your research required instruments."

"Oh, it's pretty standard—" She cut herself off when the teasing in Rowan's voice penetrated. *Rowan's a social work major. She isn't going to know what an instrument is*.

"A psychological instrument," Genna clarified, trying not to picture what other kind of instrument Rowan had imagined for a study on sexual fantasy. "Tests, surveys, questionnaires, all used to measure psychological variables. Have you ever taken the Meyers-Briggs?"

"Yes," Rowan said.

"So, that's a psychological instrument used to measure personality traits. The ones I use will help me measure sexual esteem, preoccupation, motivation, control, openness, and the like. They provide a benchmark standardization from which we can dig deeper in one-on-one sessions."

"As long as I don't have to take the Love Languages one again, I'm in."

Genna laughed. "Gary Chapman's Love Languages? Uh, no. I'm afraid that hasn't been validated."

"Thank God," Rowan said with feeling.

"What's yours?" She immediately scolded herself. It wasn't relevant, not to mention none of her business.

"Physical touch." Rowan didn't seem put off by the intrusion. "Yours?"

"Acts of service." *The path to my heart is lit by my check engine light.*

She'd crossed a line and didn't quite know how to hop back over it without being even more awkward, so she just kept talking. "I'm conducting research on the impact of feminism on the sexual fantasies of adult women. Has feminist discourse served to regulate, or liberate, sexual fantasy, and if there's been change, is it equal across fantasy categories? Additionally, I'm interested in both positive and negative affective responses to psychological sexual stimuli and why they occur, viewed through a feminist framework."

There was a short pause before Rowan swallowed and said, "Right."

Not a psych student, Genna. Use English. "What I mean is—"

"I understand. You want to know if equality has changed women's fantasies. And if they feel good or bad about their fantasies and why," Rowan said.

"Fancy a career in psychology? You're a natural."

"Too many statistics," Rowan said seriously.

Genna talked to people all day, but talking to Rowan was different. Somehow both effortless and nerve-wracking at the same time. She was smiling and she had no reason to be all smiley except that Rowan Marks was easy to play with. Verbally. That's why she kept getting sidetracked. Now she had to stop chatting and get to the survey before they both turned a hundred.

"I have a set of standard questions designed to rule out anyone who may not be a good fit which I'd like to ask you now. Some may pertain to your sex life, current and historical. I am the only one who will know your identity. For the purposes of the published study, if you're accepted, you will remain anonymous. Sound okay?"

"Go ahead," Rowan said.

"Your age?" Genna scrolled her list.

"Thirty-two."

"And you're an undergrad?" She couldn't mask her surprise.

"Yes."

Silence.

Okay then. Not going to talk about being a mature-aged student. Interesting.

"Ethnicity, sexual orientation, and sex and gender identity?"

"Caucasian, lesbian, cis-female."

She typed and ignored the way her pulse picked up when Rowan said *lesbian* in her sexy voice. So what if she was nice, and around her age, and attracted to women? Participants in the study were off limits for reasons so obviously important her libido had gotten an official memo in triplicate. Sexy voice tingles were not allowed.

"Are you sexually active?"

"Oh geez." Rowan's breath huffed out as static against her ear.

"I know it's tough sharing that information with a stranger over the phone. I'm sorry if it's awkward. This study is about sexual fantasies, and the information is relevant."

Talking about sex was second nature to her, but difficult for a lot of people. Normally, she'd be irritated with someone who'd volunteered to participate and couldn't answer a simple question. But she felt a tug of compassion instead. Rowan was nice. The least she could do was be nice back.

"Right. Sorry. What do you mean by that, exactly?" Rowan asked.

Genna sat back on the couch. Under other circumstances, the fluster in Rowan's voice would've been adorable. But under *these* circumstances she definitely didn't note any adorable fluster. "Sexually active means you've engaged in sexual relations in the recent past."

"Do you mean with a partner, or does solo count too?"

She could almost feel Rowan's embarrassment and gave her points for having the guts to state her question plainly. "Not technically, but solo is important for the purpose of the study. Shall I mark no for sexually active and yes for masturbation?"

"Yes," Rowan said.

Masturbation. Check.

"In a relationship or seeing anyone?" She knew better than to assume no sex with a partner meant no relationship.

"No." Pause. "Why is that relevant?"

"Intimate relationships can have significant impact on sexual fantasies, from basic frequency to the more complex questions of whether you share your fantasies or engage in fantasy while intimate with a partner."

"Makes sense," Rowan said.

"How long ago was your last relationship, if any?"

"A year or so, a little more."

"And were you—"

"Yes, we were sexually active."

"How long were you together?"

"Two years. She moved for work. The split was amicable."

But she didn't ask Rowan to go with her, or she did, and Rowan said no. People broke up for all kinds of reasons, but it was surprising someone as nice as Rowan had been single for over a year.

"You live locally?"

"Baker Street, just off campus. I could be available whenever you needed me."

How's tomorrow night?

Why was she interpreting everything they said as poorly disguised flirtation? There was just something about Rowan. Some mixed message that she couldn't quite put her finger on that intrigued the hell out of her. Rowan was hesitant but not shy, funny but serious too, nice yet reserved. How could someone be all those things when the combination made no sense? And let's not forget her soft rumbling tones that reverberated through Genna like a made-for-sexy-times luxury locomotive.

Before she could respond with the same I-didn't-hear-that-the-way-it-sounded politeness that Rowan had gifted her, Rowan said in a rush. "I don't know why I said that. It's not true. I have classes and a job and everything. I'll try to be available, but…"

But you're not that easy?

"It's no problem. I can work with your schedule as long as you're free two hours every week for the next three." No need to mention this was her entire life outside of her family so she'd be available for Rowan whenever.

"Okay, great. All this interview stuff is weirder than I thought it would be. I'm glad we'll be face-to-face."

"Take a breath," Genna said gently, wanting to ease the weird neither of them seemed to be able to shake. If Rowan thought a few standard questions were awkward, she was going to find the one-on-one interviews arduous.

To Genna's amusement, Rowan did actually take a long slow breath. "Okey dokey."

Okey dokey? Where did this woman come from? Planet Sugar?

"Do you have sexual fantasies?" Genna asked.

Rowan's breath whooshed in her ear again. "Yes."

"When did you last fantasize?"

"Saturday night, late, or early, I guess. About two a.m."

She wanted to ask why Rowan had waited until the witching hour to indulge but bit her tongue. If Rowan fit the study criteria, why might come later. *Only* if it was relevant.

"How often do you fantasize?"

"Often."

She paused, waiting to see if Rowan would elaborate. That one word sounded loaded. But like a witness on the stand, Rowan kept to the facts.

"Do you achieve orgasm when you fantasize?"

"Sometimes." And then, "Does that matter? Will I be disqualified from the study if I don't always come?"

The rumble in Rowan's voice caught, and Genna wanted to hug her. Why did she want to hug her? How ridiculous. Her answers were adequate.

"Not necessarily. Do you have difficulty achieving orgasm?"

"It's not that." Rowan paused, then sighed in a way that made her seem a lot older than thirty-two. "I don't always come because I stop before I get there. Sometimes."

Genna was *dying* to ask why. Was it an edging thing? An I-like-to-walk-around-turned-on thing? She doubted it. Rowan had a hard time talking about it, and that usually meant the answer would be hard too. Not an area to explore over the phone.

Insatiable inquisitiveness had driven her toward a career in research. The why of things being more compelling than who, what, or when. But curiosity didn't only kill cats. She definitely couldn't go there.

Going with her gut instead, Genna said, "I'm getting the sense you don't want to talk, and I want you to know that you don't have to. You can hang up. Just end the call if you want to. You don't even have to be nice about it or make an excuse. The study is voluntary, and I won't be offended." She would've said the same to any study participant. Consent and confidentiality were cornerstones of research with human subjects, but with Rowan, Genna got the sense she really *didn't* want to talk. So why had she called?

"Thank you, I appreciate that, but no. I have to do this." A little resolve crept into Rowan's tone.

I have to do this. That was an interesting tidbit Genna had no right to push on just now.

Rowan sounded tired, as if she'd reached an internal limit and it would all be downhill from here. That was concerning considering they'd only been on the phone for fifteen minutes.

She scrolled through a bunch of questions that were important but that could be added to the sexual history she'd have Rowan complete during her first visit.

She set her laptop on the coffee table and asked the only remaining question that might give her some insight into this intriguingly contradictory woman's lack of enthusiasm. The question that would form the basis of her decision to accept Rowan into her research. "Why do you want to take part in the study?"

❖

Rowan paced Mrs. Penellie's doormat-sized back patio with the phone glued to her ear. Now would be an excellent time to take up mindfulness and start channeling the Buddha.

"It sounded interesting." Rowan did a mental facepalm. Could she be any vaguer? She needed Genevieve—*Genna*—to accept her into the study, and so far, she'd come off like a high school freshman on her first day in sex ed.

"What about it sounds interesting?" Genna asked patiently.

Rowan sank into a lawn chair so rickety she said a prayer it would hold her weight. "I think I'd be a good fit. I'd like to learn more."

Replace *interesting* with *disturbing* and she'd approximate the truth, at least when it came to herself. The actual truth, the honest to God variety she rarely indulged in, wasn't something Dr. Friendly Sexy Distraction needed to know.

She wasn't usually prone to distraction, but from the second Genna had barked, *Yes, hello,* into her ear, things hadn't gone as planned. Interest in sex was normal, biological even, and she wasn't immune. She'd spent a good twenty minutes in the shower after her workout wondering about Genevieve Fielding. Who was she, this woman who wanted to make a career out of other people's most private thoughts? Despite giving it ample consideration, she hadn't realized she'd been leaning toward any one conclusion until Genna had answered the phone and her Cleopatra-crossed-with-Marilyn-Monroe pretend person tumbled from its pedestal. She'd imagined powerful and remote, extremely seductive but out of her league and unapproachable. She'd assumed a whole identity for Genna without even realizing it. The trouble was, she'd been dead wrong.

"What do you find interesting about sex fantasies?" Genna asked like a dog with a bone.

Rowan smiled. *Not going to give me a break, are you?*

Eventually, she'd have to tell her some sanitized version of the truth, but that day wasn't today. "I'm training to be a social worker. Sex and relationships are a big part of people's lives. I can't say if it would ever come up in my work, but a fuller understanding can't hurt."

As lies went, it wasn't great. She was tough as a marshmallow.

The barest of pauses on the other end was noticeable only because Genna's responses were usually so quick. "I'd imagine a fuller understanding of yourself can't hurt either."

Rowan's pulse beat in her ears and her mouth went dry. How had Genna guessed it was all about her?

"Self-awareness is key in social work." She was surprised her voice came out steady because her insides were training for the Olympic gymnastics team.

"In psychology too." In a softer tone Genna asked, "Does the study of sexual fantasy interest you on a personal level?"

There was no censure in her voice, but the follow-up question indicated Genna wasn't satisfied with her earlier bullshit. For some reason, she wanted to satisfy Genna, to *be* satisfying. She needed to tell the truth, but not the whole truth, because not even God would be able to help her out of this one, and she just…*couldn't* yet.

"I've always been flummoxed by how different some of my fantasies are from the real sex I have. I wouldn't ever want to *do* the things I fantasize about. I'm wondering why I find something I wouldn't do so hot." *Boilingly, blisteringly, burningly hot. Tell me why, Dr. Sexy Daydream. Save me from myself.*

Genna laughed.

Rowan froze, the light and contagious sound so at odds with the discussion that she couldn't process what was happening. Her laughter became muffled as Genna presumably covered her mouth in a futile attempt to keep her mirth where it belonged.

"I'm so sorry. I promise I'm not laughing at you. It's four hundred percent okay to have fantasies you wouldn't want to enact. That's a universal human experience."

"And yet…" She let the rest of her sentence dangle. She wasn't miffed, exactly. Clearly, Genna wasn't laughing at *her*, but she was laughing at the first truly personal thing Rowan had revealed. Would she laugh at her fantasies too? Surely that wasn't allowed, by politeness if not official rule.

"I've never heard anyone outside of a seventies sitcom use the word flummoxed before. I just lost it for a second."

Okaaay, slight overreaction. Genna was laughing because she was a dweeb not a pervert. Not a vast improvement but she'd take it.

"My family is kind of old school, and some of it stuck."

"Oh no," Genna said quickly. "I like it. You're really sweet."

Oh, good grief. If Dr. Sex-Me thought she was sweet, there was no way she could tell her the truth about what really went on inside her head, and she *had* to tell her the truth…some of it…eventually. She absolutely, positively did not want Genevieve Fielding to think she was sweet. The further they strayed from reality, the further she had to fall when it all came out.

"Do you have any other questions?" Rowan asked.

"I've offended you. I'm sorry," Genna said in that cashmere voice that'd somehow wrapped itself around Rowan like a hug.

She wasn't offended, she was… Mired in self-loathing and existential torment. "I'm not sweet. You have that wrong, that's all."

"I never should've said that. I was trying to explain there was no need for you to be sorry. I'm the one who should apologize. I overstepped."

Rowan rubbed at her forehead like she might be able to wipe away the thoughts she couldn't seem to keep straight. "Can we both agree not to be sorry?"

"I don't have any further questions. If you want to participate in the study, we'll set up a time for you to complete the paperwork and instruments."

Rowan instantly missed the tenderness in Genna's voice, but it was for the best. Interviewing people about their sexual fantasies probably gave a person a highly efficient bullshit barometer, and Genna was way too good at persuading her to be honest. She'd have to be careful not to reveal too much. Enough, *just* enough, for her to figure out why she had the fantasies she did, and how to make them stop, but not so much she humiliated herself.

After setting up a time to meet, Rowan hung up. Leaning back in the death-trap lawn chair, she closed her eyes and tried to conjure her made-up Genevieve—the consummate ice queen—but instead recalled the too fast and energetic way the real Genna had spoken, the comments that could've been interpreted as flirting but obviously weren't, the abrupt greeting followed quickly by a sincere apology, *on her knees*. The questions and questions and still more questions that made Rowan's stomach churn and her heart pound in equal measure. Genna's soft tone that had spun around her demanding honesty. The way Genna had admitted to crossing a line. The way she'd called her sweet.

Genevieve Fielding was no Cleopatra.

Sincere and honest in a totally approachable could-talk-to-you-all-damn-day way, Genna was compelling as hell. With Cleopatra or Marilyn, pretty to look at but too aloof to be real, Rowan's secrets would be safe. But with Genna? She would have to tread very carefully.

Chapter Three

"You look like hell," Dr. Alice Sullivan said when Genna walked into her office.

"Nice to see you too, Teach." Genna dropped her tote on the floor by Alice's desk and stifled a yawn. Somehow, the middle of the week was already here, and she'd never caught up from her sleepless night. *Totally worth it.*

"Busy weekend?" Alice asked pointedly, as if reading her mind.

"Why would you think that?"

"I was your professor, then your thesis advisor and friend. I know you. You need more sleep than a python. You only *think* you can stay up all night and spend the next week asleep on your feet."

"Recovering just in time to do it all over again." Genna went to the Keurig and brewed herself a cup of truly awful coffee. Pod coffee was the worst. She always drank it anyway.

Alice shook her head. "I'll never understand why you don't date. You're pretty. You're smart. You know more about sex than Kinsey ever did. You're a catch. Be a proper queer and rent a U-Haul with someone nice."

Genna stifled another jaw-breaking yawn, flopping into the chair facing Alice's desk. Compared to Alice anyone would look like hell. Fashion had never been Genna's thing. Clean and reasonably coordinated were her only standards. Alice was a walking advertisement for Stylish Professors 'R' Us. Even her jewelry was classy. A simple diamond pendant hung just under the hollow of her throat, precisely in the vee of her collared white shirt, both standing out beautifully against her black skin. Genna could wear every outfit she owned and never look that good, so she didn't bother trying.

"I'm not looking to be caught." Genna tuned back into their conversation. "Did you read that article I sent you on the prevalence of choking fantasies among millennials? Fascinating."

Alice gestured with her pen. "I mention U-Hauls and you go right to choking? You're subtle."

Genna shrugged. "You're funny."

"Kinsey didn't know squat about choking fantasies." Alice refused to be deterred.

"Kinsey was a zoologist who didn't care about squat that wasn't observable. Fantasies weren't his jam." No way Teach was going to win this one. Genna had at least ten thousand hours experience obfuscating her personal life and was a bonified expert. She'd start the morning with an easy win. "Anyway, why did you want to see me?"

Alice sighed and put down her pen. "Seeing how they're your jam, get me up to speed so I can sign off on your progress and do my duty as your advisor. You have a new participant coming in today?"

Teach had called for a meeting out of the blue to discuss a new participant? Strange, but okay. Genna pulled her iPad from her bag, brought up Rowan's info, and handed it to Alice. "Yep. She fits the criteria."

Alice scanned the screen. "I hear a *but* in there somewhere. What's her story?"

"I have no idea. She wasn't very forthcoming. Gave me some line about being interested in the study to help future clients."

Petty of her to find it frustrating. Lots of people had defense mechanisms when it came to sex. She had a few doozies herself. But it'd irked to be on the receiving end of Rowan's. Shut out, fed a line, the door closed in her face. She was being overly sensitive; Rowan was a total stranger who owed her nothing. But it *irked.*

Alice smiled. "Because social workers assist their clients with sexual fantasies all the time?"

"I suppose if she wanted to specialize in therapy, it might come up once in a blue moon, but…"

"She's avoiding her true motivations," Alice surmised.

"At a guess." Genna shrugged again, weirdly uncomfortable discussing Rowan as if, well, as if she were a study participant. "It might be a waste of time to interview her if she can't be open."

Alice leaned back in her chair and steepled her fingers, regarding Genna with a probing stare that would've done the CIA proud. "Did you get any sense of what might be going on?"

She wanted to pace but stayed where she was. No need to let on that thinking about Rowan had her edgy. "She comes across as reserved, but I think that's more nerves than anything. She's reluctant to provide details and evaded the question about why she wanted to participate. She fits the criteria, but it seems like she's hiding something. Do you think…" Genna couldn't finish the sentence, but from the way Alice's face tightened they were having the same thought.

"Let's not jump to conclusions. You don't know anything definitive. Keep your list of referrals close by just in case. We both know how prevalent assault is."

God, she hoped that wasn't it.

"I'd be interested to see the results of the instruments," Alice continued. "Add the Multidimensional Sexuality Questionnaire as well. That'll give you a score for sexual anxiety and shame."

Genna sat up straighter. Had she been too distracted noticing how sweet Rowan was to do her job? "Do her responses indicate anxiety and shame? How did I not pick up on any of this?"

Alice shook her head. "They don't indicate anything yet. She could simply be particularly modest or repressed. If she scores highly on the MSQ she'll round out your data nicely. So long as you can get her to open up and refer her if necessary. Brush up on your interpersonal communication. It would be good training for you to interview her thoroughly and further develop your communication skills."

Genna felt her shoulders start to bunch up around her ears. "I know how to talk to people." Kind of. Well enough. Pretty much.

"You know how to draw conclusions from your observations too, but we still have metrics to ensure the data is valid. This is no different." Alice glanced at the iPad, "Participant 47C may need coaxing to divulge her affective responses. That's going to require more than ask and answer style talking. Let's see if you're up for the challenge." She handed the iPad back to Genna.

Just then Poppy, Alice's TA, tapped on the door and stepped into the room. She looked from Alice to Genna with meaningful slowness, tilting her head as if to ask, "So?"

Genna shoved her iPad back into her bag. "What's up?" Poppy wasn't often seen standing about waiting for something to happen. She might be twenty-three, but Poppy was ambitious as hell and usually the one *making* things happen—including scoring a sweet TA gig for one of the most popular professors on campus.

"Someone's waiting for you in the lobby," she told Genna.

"We're nearly done," Alice said in a tone that resonated go-away-if-you-know-what's-good-for-you.

Poppy brushed her hair out of her eyes and rolled them for good measure. She rocked a pixie cut, dyed bubblegum pink that set off her gorgeous blue irises and complemented her heart-shaped face. The miles of black eyeliner she'd managed to apply ought to have qualified her for an art degree. Poppy was *flawless.* Genna could barely use mascara without stabbing herself in the eye. Who knew what her own face had looked like that morning, but her skin hadn't been flawless in a decade. Washed out and pasty was more like it. She sucked at all the girly stuff, which wouldn't have been so bad if she wasn't surrounded by women who seemed to have aced the class, or inherited the gene, or whatever it was that made some women good at things like makeup. Probably hours of TikTok tutorials on how to apply lipstick, or something equally annoying. Why did looking good have to be so boring?

"Thanks for letting me know," Genna said. "I wonder who it is? My next appointment isn't for another twenty minutes. I love those boots by the way. Only you could pull off purple Doc Martins with tights and a leather bomber."

Poppy grinned and gave a little twirl. "It's a look. I'm a sexy biker chick lost in a cotton candy factory, you know?"

Genna laughed because that was *exactly* Poppy's look. "You nailed it."

"Thanks. Bye." Poppy disappeared from the doorway as quickly as she'd arrived.

"What was that about?" Genna asked, rising.

Alice sighed. She motioned for Genna to sit back down. "Your mystery caller can wait a few minutes.

"Okay." Whatever the meaningful stare had communicated it somehow involved her.

"I have news. Flint came back with their recommendations."

Not bad news. Teach hadn't said bad news and she wouldn't bullshit her. The Flint was the biggest and most prestigious grant afforded to sexuality research, but also competitive as hell and they'd never been able to nab it. Scoring that funding would mean years of additional resources, cutting-edge equipment, maybe even an assistant to help with the paperwork. "That's good, right? They're interested. What are they looking for?"

Alice nodded. "We have an excellent chance this year. I have several promising PhDs, including you. But they want us to go in a slightly different direction."

Genna had been in academia long enough to know when *us* meant *you,* none of Alice's other students had been called to this meeting. She frowned. "Different how?"

"I'm not sure your work has practical application." Alice held up a hand to ward off the slew of objections on the tip of Genna's tongue. "Your research is a step toward understanding how modern-day sexuality fits in a post-feminist world."

Genna kept her mouth shut. When rape culture was still up for debate on a college campus, the world could hardly be called post-feminist, could it? And don't even get her started on reproductive rights.

"But Flint wants practical application *now*. We need a way for practitioners to apply your findings in a clinical context."

"That's not how research works. Without investigation into the context of sexual fantasy, how can you know how to apply the findings to help people? That's jumping ahead of the facts," Genna argued.

Alice nodded. "I don't disagree, but we still have to sell the potential for practical application to get the funding. I *want* that grant, Genna."

Genna wanted that grant too, damn it. "I'm halfway through my research. I can't just change direction."

"Not change—tweak, maneuver, fine-tune. All we need is to make your research more relevant to clinicians and less…"

"Theoretical?" Genna suggested dryly.

"Right. Something a sex therapist can use to improve patient outcomes. You knew this might be an issue. I did urge you to find a clinical pathway earlier."

Genna fought not to roll her eyes. She wasn't twenty-three. It wouldn't be cute like it was on Poppy. Teach *had* said her purely theoretical framework was a weakness, but Genna sucked at therapy. She'd completed an internship in a mental health clinic as part of her master's and had been bumbling and blank-brained the entire way through. She had no idea what to *say* to people when they came to her with problems, with feelings and tears and faulty logic they insisted on believing regardless of what actually made sense. She wasn't good with emotions, so she'd gone into research. Data. Hard facts. Neat and tidy answers. *Safety.*

"Can I have a few days to think about it? I need to finish coding everything I have so far to see if there are any emerging clinical implications."

"That's all I ask," Alice said, even though she hadn't asked. She'd all but demanded Genna change her approach halfway through her research to head in a direction that gave her the heebie-jeebies.

But…the Flint grant.

Getting that would be next level. It would put Silver Creek on the map as a premier sexuality research institute. It wasn't just about Alice, or Genna, for that matter. This grant would set the stage for *years* of pioneering research. No wonder Poppy was desperate to get Genna on board. She'd be starting in on her own research soon enough. It made total sense, and the more sense it made, the worse it sucked. Genna had to take one for the team.

Alice rose, signaling the end of the meeting. "Keep me up to date. I'm still waiting on your factor analysis of subjects 27A and 35C too."

"You'll have them by the end of the week." Genna's backlog of work made her want to curl up like a cat and sleep for a month. She pulled herself out of the chair and grabbed her bag.

"Add getting some rest to your to-do list. I worry about you," Alice said mock-sternly before turning to her laptop.

Something else she didn't have time for.

Genna left Alice's office and stifled another of her endless supply of yawns as she strode into the tiny lobby of the Gender and Sexuality Division. She stopped abruptly, feeling as if she'd somehow tripped and fallen backstage at a rock concert. Her mystery caller lounged against Poppy's desk, one hand resting casually on the wood, the other holding a dog-eared textbook. They should've been just another student, but they exuded badass in a rebel-with-a-cause sort of way. Their lean five-foot-eight frame showcased muscle just visible under their navy T-shirt, and black ink wound all the way up their arms, disappearing seductively under the cotton. Blond-haired toughness wafted off them like expensive perfume. They weren't intense enough to be the rock band's lead guitarist. No tortured artist vibe. A drummer, maybe? Weren't drummers always the most attractive? They sure fit the profile.

Hello, gorgeous. Would you mind signing up to star in my fantasies from now on?

Of course, in real life, tortured wasn't her type. All those dark and twisty emotions with no outlet. Too much angst and drama. She'd said good-bye to anyone with serious issues years ago and didn't regret it. She would've sworn Poppy was straight, but maybe she'd been wrong, and Poppy had a new lover? She'd grill her for details ASAP. *Tell me everything and don't leave out the sexy parts.*

Genna's it's-not-real-so-what-the-hell fantasy looked up from their textbook and smiled, revealing a row of perfectly white straight teeth. "Good morning. Are you Genevieve Fielding?"

Genna tried frantically to reboot her brain, unexpectedly frozen mid-download, the instant they said her name. "Um, yeah, hi. You're…" *Stupidly hot.*

They stepped forward, holding out a hand. "Rowan Marks. We spoke on the phone?"

If the rumble in her voice hadn't given her away, Genna never would've believed it. *This* was sweet, shy, and secretive Rowan Marks? The woman she'd need to coax into answering her questions?

"My lifecycle theory class let out early. I'm happy to wait if you like," Rowan said when Genna didn't immediately reply.

She swallowed past the dryness in her throat and shook her head. "It's no problem."

No problem at all. She just needed a second to stop picturing Rowan naked. Like, pronto.

"You had some forms for me to fill out?" Rowan prodded her when Genna just stood there blushing.

Rowan was talking about the consent agreement, the sexual history, the instruments, but from the way Genna's blood sizzled, Rowan might as well have been asking if she wanted to go to her office and get naked all over her desk.

She shoved aside her rogue hormonal response, summoned whatever remnants of professionalism she had, and took Rowan's hand. "Call me Genna. It's nice to meet you."

Rowan's fingers slid between hers and Genna focused on all the tattoos trailing up Rowan's arms, circling her forearms like imprints of a lover's caress. Weren't tattoos just the hottest of all varieties of sexy?

She dragged her gaze back to Rowan's face and used every ounce of willpower she had to keep it there. Rowan's gold-green eyes glinted with a smile. She could probably tell exactly what Genna had been thinking and was doing her a favor by not mentioning it. Surely women checked Rowan out on a daily basis. An hourly basis. An every damn minute basis. Genna had to get it together before she embarrassed them both.

Fortunately, her phone buzzed in the outer pocket of her blazer, jolting her back to reality. At least the version of reality in which Rowan Marks was a human subject in her research and not a woman intent on pleasure. Why hadn't she met Rowan at McKinney's? Meeting her on the job meant any attraction had to be squelched with a ferocity she normally reserved for flying cockroaches.

Genna released Rowan's hand, pulled her phone out, and glanced at the screen. Mom.

Rowan said, "At least this time it's not me calling at an inopportune moment."

Right. When Rowan had called about the study and her sweetness had left Genna reeling. She ignored the twist in her stomach and dropped her phone back into her blazer without answering. "It's my mom. Is this an inopportune moment?"

Rowan held Genna's gaze. "Moms seem to have a radar for sex, don't they?"

Genna leaned back on her heels, unable to stop replaying the way Rowan said *sex*.

Was it possible to maneuver the conversation so Rowan said "fuck" or "God, yes" or even "yes, please"? Those were everyday words in a different context, right? How much innocent dirty talk could she get Rowan to say in her rumbling phone sex operator voice?

Stop it. Be professional.

Fortunately, Genna had boatloads of experience compartmentalizing the personal and the professional. "I spend much of my life thinking about sex, so the odds are good Mom will be interrupting any time she calls. Let's get started. My office is down the hall."

Genna spun on her heel and led the way. Not looking might be her only defense against the bizarre impulse to step closer and circle Rowan for a better view. One decent three-sixty and she'd never need a vibrator again.

"Too much is a relative term," Rowan said mildly from behind her. "Thinking about sex all day sounds pretty amazing."

"It's not dull." Genna brushed aside the comment, years of such conversations kicking in a default response. For some reason people assumed her fantasy life mirrored her participants, and she got off on their stories. Not even close.

She was nothing more than a clinical observer and reporter of others' psychosexual stimuli. She engaged, she listened, she took notes and drew conclusions, but she wasn't *involved.* She had her work, and her occasional indulgences. Sex was something that happened around her, sometimes because of her, but not to her.

What were Rowan Marks's fantasies?

She'd find out soon enough.

"Let's get you set up. How's your day been? Busy?" Genna said.

She'd hoped small talk would settle her, but she was too far inside her head to hear Rowan's reply. If she was on her way to some semblance of normal human behavior, that's all that mattered. She just had to remember Rowan wasn't only a very attractive and intriguing woman, she was 47C, a study participant, so off-limits she came with a warning label, a consent form, and an ethics committee that all encouraged Genna to keep her hands to herself. Lusting, while harmless in private, could easily lead to trouble.

Genna held open the door to her office and gestured Rowan in. "This is where the action happens."

The door shut behind them, closing with a click that echoed like a gunshot. Sealing them in. Alone. A muscle twitched in Genna's jaw and something like anticipation rolled through her.

For a split-second, as Genna's comment hung in the air, Rowan's reaction was unguarded. Her lips parted and her gaze flicked up and down the length of Genna's body, fast and urgent, like she knew she shouldn't be looking but couldn't seem to help herself. As quickly as it appeared, that hot and hungry expression was masked with a polite smile.

"I'll keep that in mind."

A thudding pulse came to life between Genna's thighs. She closed her eyes, realizing too late she'd barreled into another unintentional innuendo. "Not that kind of action. Obviously." *Hear that, inappropriately turned-on nether regions? Hard no.*

Rowan nodded slowly, as if convincing them both. "Obviously."

"Please, sit. I need a minute or two to compile your instruments." Genna determined she would restrict further communication to only what was necessary. She was no stranger to attraction. Hell, to survive the meat market of the casual sex scene, you had to really want it. But lusting after someone at work? Completely unlike her. Somehow, her professional barriers had been cleanly vaulted. Pretty amazing didn't cover half of it, and she *really* had to stop.

She'd felt a pull right from the start, even over the phone, and that made no sense. It's not like she didn't have adequate opportunities for sex. She was far from desperate. So, okay, none of those opportunities looked quite as wonderful in simple jeans and a T-shirt, but so what? Insta-lust was surely outweighed by all the reasons sex was a terrible idea. *You're forgetting she's nice, and she's pursuing a career helping people, and she looks reeeally good. Stop fooling yourself. You're human—beating heart and all that. Accept it and move on!*

Genna sat and started furiously pulling up documents on her iPad. Not looking just might keep her out of trouble, because not wanting appeared to be impossible.

While Genna seemed to be gathering her instruments or whatever they were about to do, Rowan sat in the chair across from her and gripped the armrest tightly, trying to work out the tingle in her palm. Since when did she get sparks shooting up her arm from shaking a woman's hand? Since never. Her muscles tightened, and she shifted in her chair. Could this be a sign she was losing control? Bridging the gap between fantasy and reality? She hadn't fantasized about Genna. But the room was too warm, Genna too close, and her response to Genna too much of a response. *Sexual. Admit it. God, that's wrong. You don't even know her. She's probably not even queer.*

Genna was talking, explaining all the forms, and she hadn't been listening. She'd probably been staring. Genna's gaze went from her iPad to somewhere just past Rowan's right ear. Looking anywhere but at her. Rowan tried to think of some not-weird thing to say. Some sorry-I-just-cruised-you-and-made-you-uncomfortable thing. She needed the perfect thing to ease that sexy laugh out of Genna.

"You look tired."

That was *not* the perfect thing.

Silence thundered.

"I'm sorry," Rowan said quickly. "Talking to Women 101. Never tell them they look tired. I have a sister. I should know better. It's just…you do, and…are you okay?"

Genna gave her a bland stare, making eye contact for the first time since they'd entered the office. "I am a little tired. Thank you for noticing."

Rowan smiled at the deadpan delivery. "If it helps, you carry it well. Some people cry pretty, all sparkly eyes and tears falling from their lashes. You're tired pretty, as if you've been up all night searching a deserted moor for your one true love."

Genna looked at her like she was a lunatic for a full five seconds and then burst out laughing. "Not hardly."

"Why so weary then?" Rowan was irrationally pleased to have made Genna laugh after all.

Genna bit her lip, her teeth sinking into the red of her mouth in a way that had every muscle in Rowan's body seizing up again.

"Up late studying." Genna's gaze darted back to the iPad.

Studying was an entirely plausible explanation. Half the students on campus subsisted on caffeine and Adderall. It was a lie, though. Studying wouldn't have made Genna catch her breath or bite her lip. Studying wouldn't have ignited that glint in her eye that suggested she had a thousand enticements to stay up all night.

Genna already knew so much about her, and all those *instruments* would only tell her more. She wasn't entitled to it, but Rowan wanted this one thing. A small fact. A chink in Genevieve Fielding's professional armor. *What keeps you up at night?*

Why did she even care? Because she wanted to be the reason Genna was tired? Because Genna was about to discover so much and she wanted to even the playing field? Or was it the voice in the back of her head she was trying to ignore encouraging her to look closer, to pay attention because Genna affected her in a way she didn't want to analyze. A voice that was more to do with how cared for Genna's warm tone made her feel. Which was obviously crazy. Rowan didn't even know her.

But Genna had opted out of the insignificant truth of why she was tired and in doing so had put Rowan firmly in her place.

"Up late studying sex fantasies. That sounds brutal." Rowan injected enough levity in her tone to let Genna know she was kidding.

So, she had a tiny little crush. The likely explanation for her response. But, really, could she be blamed? Genna looked as if she belonged on the cover of a natural beauty catalogue, her dark hair swept into a knot so messy strands fell haphazardly around her face, her brown eyes framed by thick lashes. Her cheeks were paler than they should've been, the dark circles under her eyes making her seem dangerous and forlorn at the same time. She looked amazing in black jeans and a blueish-purple blazer. Put it all together and Genna was goddammed beautiful, like a dark violet blown about by the breeze. Beautiful wicked fragile perfection.

"It's not brutal." Genna gave her a wan smile before turning her attention away again.

Rowan leaned back in her chair. Interesting. This was the second time she had made a comment about Genna's research and both times she was met with an answer that wasn't an answer at all. "Can I ask a question?"

Genna glanced up, a frown line digging its way between her brows. "Of course."

"Why sex fantasies? Why base your PhD on something so… so…"

"Intimate and vulnerable?" Genna offered with another half-smile.

Rowan nodded. Asking a researcher about her research was perfectly legit. But damn if she wasn't hoping Genna's answer would be intimate and vulnerable too. That part had more to do with her tiny little crush. Best she not examine it too closely.

Genna spoke carefully, as if choosing each word exactly. "We develop and maintain relationships based on shared cultural norms that regulate behavior. Even with those closest to us, even in a sphere as personal and vulnerable as sex, we may choose to modify the expression of our needs or desires to preserve others' impression of us, or so as not to drive others away and risk the relationship, or a myriad of other reasons. But when it comes to fantasies, all that is stripped away. They're entirely our own. Entirely private and separate, unless we choose to share them. Reality no longer exists. They don't have to make sense, they don't have consequences, the individual controls every possible variable. They're entirely safe, physically and emotionally, and so all that's left is what arouses. What that is, why it is, where it comes from, and how it fits into the all-too-real context of actual life? Well, that's a fascinating puzzle, and at the heart of what it means to be sexual."

Genna shrugged, then grinned four thousand watts brighter than the half-smiles. "I find the juxtaposition between fantasy and reality fascinating."

Rowan's stomach dipped. Her tiny little crush was pumping iron and bulking up real fast. Genna's measured intellectual tone would've suited a lecture hall full of students. But it wasn't so much the hot teacher vibe as the glow of her eyes and the laser focus of her attention. Attention Rowan wanted focused on her a little too much. Genna was clearly passionate about her research and couldn't help beaming when she talked about it. So then why did she fob off questions with meaningless responses?

"So, basically, you geek out about sex, and stay up late at night thinking about it." Rowan was joking, but she was kinda-sorta flirting too. Flirting with the woman she'd need to carry her deepest secrets was an exceptionally bad idea. Even given the remote chance Genna might be interested in her, her deviant fantasies were sure to kill any glimmer of hope at romance. Still, she couldn't seem to resist temptation.

Genna lifted a shoulder in a half shrug, as if to say, *Well, obviously.*

Rowan's heart fluttered a little. Her heart was fluttering. Her *heart*. But she was grateful to be female, because if she were a guy, her attraction would be obvious. The flutter south of her heart was dancing the rumba.

Genna spun the iPad toward Rowan. The document on the screen read *Multidimensional Sexuality Questionnaire*. "These will take about an hour. Let's get to work."

CHAPTER FOUR

Not-Jessica had been right. Answering questions about your sex life wasn't much fun, especially when they came as an avalanche of paperwork and an infinity of checkboxes. Rowan tapped the screen to check *strongly agree* on a question about whether emotional intimacy and love were important to sex. She'd answered the same one, phrased differently, at least four times already. Was Genna trying to change her mind?

A text box popped up. *Instruments complete. Please call for assistance.*

She slumped in her chair exhausted, but finally, blessedly, done. She tilted her head from side to side trying to dispel the tension curled like a sulking snake at the base of her neck. Whether the pain stemmed from too long craned over the iPad or too much pressure answering probing questions, she wasn't sure. The instruments had been standard as far as she could tell. General questions about her values and experiences. Certainly nothing that would prompt her to reveal why she was really here. If only she hadn't anticipated accusations every time she was led to a new screen.

Please rate your sexual perversions on a scale of one to five.

Would you consider your sexual fantasies morally reprehensible?

Do you experience embarrassment? How about self-loathing?

Describe your attempts to be normal and why you've failed.

Living inside her own head wasn't always a picnic. Those questions hadn't come. But they'd bounced around anyway, and now she was strung tighter than a violin. Surely, she'd skew Genna's data. The person her answers represented wasn't her. She hadn't lied, but there was a mile of ambiguity between a truth and a lie. Who she really was, and how she really felt, lay somewhere inside all the questions she hadn't been asked. *Yet.*

She sent Genna a text to let her know she'd finished and, a minute later, the office door opened. Genna smiled as she walked in, but her expression quickly turned concerned. "Uh-oh. Was that difficult? Can I get you something? Water or maybe coffee?"

Rowan tried to smile back. "Do you offer hugs? I'd take one."

Genna bit her lip instead of replying. Rowan hadn't meant to flirt. She'd been more than halfway serious. Okay, dead serious. A hug would be really nice. *Really unprofessional too.*

"I'm good, but thanks," she said to cover the slip.

Genna dragged a chair around her desk to sit close to Rowan, their knees almost touching. "Were the instruments problematic?"

"No," Rowan said honestly. Her answers were nothing to be embarrassed about. She was team love and connection. Who'd be ashamed of that? She *believed* that love made sex better. But for some reason, believing wasn't always enough to get her off. That fun fact opened the door to secret-agent level interrogation, aka self-flagellation, but it was all on the inside.

Genna touched Rowan's knee for a microsecond. "Can you tell me what's put that expression on your face? Is there someone you'd like to me to call?"

Rowan shook her head, straightening her shoulders and doing her best to pretend she didn't want Genna to keep touching her. "I'm fine. I don't need anyone. I need…"

"What?" Genna asked softly.

"You. I guess."

That line appeared between Genna's brows and burrowed deeper as she frowned. "Me? Why?"

Go ahead. Tell the sexy woman why, you nincompoop. And while you're at it, plummet all the way to the Earth's core. She'd progressed from flirting to stalker in less than two minutes. What was next, taping Genna's student ID photo to her sex toys?

Because you're sexy as hell, and who wouldn't need you would be honest, but another evasion. Not a lie, but not the whole truth. If she was going to get what she came here for, she'd have to stop beating around the bush. If her issues messed with Genna's study, best they both knew upfront. Rowan took a deep breath and steeled herself for a foreign concept—the truth.

"You're a sex expert, and I need help." She was training to be a social worker, for God's sake. It shouldn't have been so difficult to ask, but Genna was sitting so close and looking so concerned.

Genna didn't move away but her expression remained worried. "I'm not a doctor or a therapist. I'm a student researcher. I may not be equipped to help you, but I can refer you to a sex therapist, or perhaps your GP could help?"

Rowan gripped the armrests of her chair to center herself. Okay, so admitting she'd needed help had elicited a *don't ask me*. But even if Genna said no, what did she have to lose?

"You're exactly who I need. You're a researcher, and not just a sex researcher, you study sexual fantasies. That's what I need help with. Fantasies, understanding them. I need to—" She faltered, swallowing the lump threatening to cut off her air supply. "I need to know how to make my fantasies stop."

"Why do you want to make them stop?"

Rowan sighed. The answer to that question was more truth than she had the strength for today. "They're bad. Like lock me up and throw away the key kind of horribly, terribly, embarrassingly bad. Not very tough of me to be here crying on your shoulder, but I don't know what else to do."

"If you're looking to understand something that's troubling you, then you're brave and tough. Not many people have the guts," Genna said.

The pretty lady thinks I'm brave! She ignored the caveman beating their chest inside her head. "I'm usually stoic. Got anything heavy that needs lifting? That's my go-to skill."

Genna's gaze darted to her arms for a millisecond before snapping back to her face. "Not all strength is physical. Sometimes strength is facing something that hurts."

Rowan barely resisted rolling her eyes at the platitude that should've been stitched on a pillow. If this was strength, it sure felt a whole lot like weakness. "Please. I understand this is unconventional. I'm not looking for therapy. I'm looking for exactly what you do, research, getting to the bottom of a question. Analyzing until things make sense." She shrugged hoping to downplay it a bit. "I just want my fantasies to make sense. They don't. That's what is problematic for me."

Problematic. Ha. Just a tricky equation that needed solving, and not the bane of her existence. Easy-peasy lemon squeezy.

"You want to understand them, make sense of them, because you think that will help you stop them?" Genna asked in a dubious tone.

"Pretty much exactly that, yes." She held her breath. Genna was going to say no. She could see the no in her eyes, in the line of her jaw.

"What makes them horribly, terribly, embarrassingly bad?" Genna asked again instead of saying no.

Rowan did her best not to squirm. "I know that's important, but it's, well, it's horribly, terribly, embarrassing, I'd really rather not get into it if you're just going to send me away."

Genna nodded and eased back in the chair. An invisible barricade flew up in the space she'd created as they were suddenly separated by a wall of ice. "Okay. I'm sorry, it's a no. The study is designed for students interested in the research topic, not to solve sexual fantasy problems. Thank you for your time, but I don't believe you're a good fit."

Rowan's stomach dropped into her shoes. She'd been expecting it ever since Genna said it wasn't her job to help her and to go somewhere else. But, *damn*. Hearing the no was ten times worse than thinking it. Her inner caveman dropped the macho act. "I realize I'm asking a lot, and making it difficult by not telling you everything, but I really do want to participate. My own stuff is secondary, I promise."

Was Genna susceptible to begging? Begging could happen.

Genna shook her head. "It's not an indictment of your character. I need participants who can be open and honest about their fantasy lives. I'm not trained to help with what you perceive as a problem. It would be irresponsible to allow you into the study, knowing it may be distressing for you."

Genna stood, not looking at her and clearly done with this conversation, but Rowan refused to move even as Genna towered over her. If begging wouldn't work, pure stubbornness might. "I understand. I just need to ease into it. I've never told anyone before."

Genna closed her eyes and dropped back into her chair, quiet exasperation radiating off her. But when she opened them, her eyes were soft. The contradiction was fascinating. Maybe Genna wasn't as by-the-book as she seemed? Because she seemed *very* by-the-book. She probably wrote the book. "Do you want to tell me even though it's hard? Are you here because you want to tell someone? If you don't want to talk to me, you really can't be in a study that requires hours of talking."

"I just…" Rowan wanted to disappear the rest of her sentence like a magician's trick, but she knew Genna would have no qualms about tossing her out if she wasn't totally honest. "I need to know you'll still be here after I do."

God. She may as well have just shouted *Don't leave me* right in Genna's face. She was making a fool of herself, but that didn't change anything. She needed to be sure her confessions would result in answers, otherwise none of this was worth it.

Genna brushed strands of hair out of her eyes and tucked them behind her ears. Rowan could all but hear a clock ticking as she made her decision. "How about this. You do your best to be completely honest with me, and I'll allow you to participate in the study. We can explore your sexual fantasies, and the reasons you want them to stop. I'm not here to make judgments, and I'll help you as much as I can, which may not be as much as you hope."

Rowan worried her smile might explode off her face her relief was so huge. “Thank—”

“But, if after you tell me, I think seeing a therapist would be beneficial, you’ll go to campus counseling and set up an appointment.”

Rowan groaned. “Come on. Campus counseling isn’t equipped to deal with sex fantasy problems.”

“A sex therapist then. I can give you a bunch of numbers. That’s the deal. If I think you need to talk to someone qualified to help you, you will. I won’t have your psychological well-being on my conscience.” Genna folded her arms and delivered her sexy eyebrow raise, the one that said, *take it or leave it, cowboy.*

“Are you always this much of a hard-ass?” Rowan asked, half curious, half impressed, and emboldened by Genna’s acquiescence even if it was conditional.

“If I were a hard-ass, I’d have dismissed you from the study like I intended to. Don’t make me regret it.” Genna’s tone was stern, but her eyes were smiling.

Definitely a hard-ass. Rowan fought a grin.

Seeing no way out, she nodded. “If you think I need a therapist, I’ll go, as long as you allow me to continue in the study simultaneously. Please, Genna.”

Please, Genna. Genna wanted to laugh. Just the dirty talk she’d longed for less than two hours ago. Too bad it wasn’t the least bit sexy now.

“It’s a deal.” She held out her hand to shake on it, and Rowan enveloped her fingers. She’d only meant to seal the agreement, but Rowan was holding her hand and looking at her with so much gratitude Genna wanted to shove her headfirst out the door. Why had she agreed to this? Rowan might need counseling, and the last thing Genna wanted was to be responsible for someone else’s well-being.

Emotions were not her thing. Emotions were why she was still single at twenty-nine, why she kept intimacy to one-night stands, and why other people stayed at a safe distance. Too much responsibility. Maybe that made her a jerk. Her mom certainly thought so, but she didn’t care. She wasn’t hurting anyone. Only, somehow, she’d agreed to help Rowan without even knowing what the problem was, and certainly without being qualified to fix it.

Rowan squeezed her hand and let go. Genna nearly jumped up from her chair. She had to get her out of her office. The space seemed to shrink with Rowan in it, making her feel as if they were pressed up against each other and breathing the same breath. Her heart not quite steady, she backed away. She needed space to come up with a game plan. Interviewing someone she was attracted to would be difficult enough, maintaining appropriate boundaries a constant refrain. But Rowan was asking for more. She wanted to spill her secrets. She wanted help. She wanted *Genna* to help.

Genna walked to the door and opened it. "I'll be in touch to set up the first interview next week. That's all for today. Thank you for coming in."

Rowan's eyes were full of questions as she brushed past her on her way out. "Thank you. See you soon."

Watching Rowan leave, Genna winced. She'd been abrupt. She should've asked about her fantasies again, encouraged Rowan to open up. At the very least, made polite conversation until the tension radiating off Rowan was a distant memory. But her phone hadn't stopped vibrating all morning. She barely had the energy to deal with her own problems, and she'd just signed herself up for Rowan's as well. She'd ask her about it in their first session and make up for her terseness.

Genna checked her missed calls and contemplated throwing her phone into the trash can when she saw the red *five* next to her mom's number. She'd spoken to her only yesterday and everything had been fine. She hit redial and pulled up the file of Rowan's instruments on her iPad. If she distracted herself while they talked, she'd be less annoyed. Maybe.

"Hi, Mom."

"Gen!" Her mom was breathless. "I've been calling you."

"I'm aware," she said dryly. "I'm working. I had a couple of meetings. I can't answer the phone whenever I feel like it."

"I know that," her mom said, like she hadn't been the one to call.

"What's up?" She typed Rowan's answers into an analytical program on her laptop that would give her a comparative report.

"Bob Brown next door—you remember Bob, right?"

She hoped that might be a rhetorical question, but her mom waited for an answer.

"Yes, I remember Bob."

"His wife Francine just had surgery, *plastic* surgery. You remember Francine? She used to give you a card and a five-dollar bill for Christmas. You called her the five-dollar-fairy."

"That was Grace." Genna didn't bother to confirm that, yes, she also remembered Bob's wife Francine the five-dollar-fairy.

"Right." A metaphorical forehead slap was evident in her mom's tone. "Grace is the most creative of the three of you."

Or the greediest. "What about Francine?"

Genna split her attention between her iPad, her laptop, and her mother.

"She's having the surgery Friday, and Bob wants to know if you could pick her up from the hospital. They won't discharge her without a ride. He has an important business meeting he can't miss."

She doubted that Bob had asked the kid next door who didn't live there anymore to give his wife a ride. More likely, he'd asked her mom, and she was regifting the task like a pair of candlesticks that didn't match her decor. No way would she tell him no and risk his asking why not. "Mom, you can pick up Francine. Just explain your situation. You won't have to get out of the car."

Her mom didn't respond for what felt like an hour but was probably ten seconds. Her inaudible, yet somehow still palpable, hurt barreled across the phone line, into Genna's ear, and beelined for her brain. *How could you refuse to do such a simple favor for your own mother? So selfish. After everything she's done for you.*

"They need someone to sign off on her care plan." Then in a smaller voice her mom continued, "I'd have to go in, Gen. You know I can't."

"Not if you called to explain," Genna argued. "A hospital of all places will understand."

"I'm not telling a stranger my business."

Getting Gloria Feilding to admit she had an anxiety disorder had been a feat. Being open about it outside of close family hadn't happened yet.

There had to be forty-seven people Bob could've asked, but he'd asked her mom, and asking Mom was asking Genna. Leaving the house was an ordeal. Leaving the car wasn't an option. Ever.

She'd been to a handful of carer support groups over the years and had never managed to dislodge her resentment. Her mom couldn't help it. No one asked to be constantly fighting their own brain, but this was her second trip home this week, and it was only Wednesday. She'd hoped moving an hour and a half from home would ease her sense of responsibility, but all she'd done was earn herself a long commute.

"Can you ask Gabby?" She made a last-ditch attempt to save the Friday she usually spent meeting with three of her study subjects. Maybe meeting with Rowan if she was available. "I have meetings I can't miss too."

"I did ask her. I tried not to impose on you, you know," her mom said, like Genna ought to be grateful for the effort even when it amounted to nothing. "But she has a date with that lovely young man she met at an outdoor concert. Do you remember me telling you about him? He's just lovely. So polite."

"Surely they're not discharging Francine at night?"

"Well, no. But Gabby doesn't want to be rushed. This is an important date. She really likes this one. He's studying finance. She could end up a rich banker's wife."

She couldn't help but smile at her mom's certainty. Although she would cheerfully strangle her blissfully boy-crazy little sister who *really liked* just about every age-appropriate guy. "I need to work this week. Gabby can rush her date prep. Or ask Grace."

Her mom scoffed. "Grace drives like a madcap. I wouldn't trust her to drive the dog home if I wanted it to arrive in one piece."

What's a madcap?

Genna didn't reply, already preoccupied figuring out how to adjust her schedule to make an unplanned trip home Friday afternoon. Arguing was pointless. She'd save the day. Like always.

"Fine," her mom said in a tone that wasn't at all fine. "I just thought you might want to help out the lady who was so kind to you as kids, but you have your *research*."

She fought not to grind her teeth. All fine and dandy for Gabby to blow off an unwanted chore by getting ready three hours ahead of time, but she got guilt-tripped for having to work? Her meetings weren't *important* like Bob's? Of course, it was never actually about the work. She'd moved, and that was unforgivable. The three-hour round trip was her own fault and sympathy a luxury she didn't deserve.

"What time is Francine being discharged?"

Chapter Five

Rowan shoved her pillow over her face. Life wasn't fair. She should've been dead on her feet after working a double at Alessandro's, then dropping by Pete's and using her twenty-four-hour access card to sprint five miles uphill on the treadmill. She had her midmorning gym routine down pat. Why she'd run at night, at twice her normal speed, up a goddamned mountain, as if daring her heart to burst from her chest, she had no idea.

Running from Dr. Seriously Sexy, perhaps?

She'd lasted almost five days not thinking about Genna. Well, not thinking about Genna *naked,* anyway. She'd done plenty of thinking about Genna in other ways. Genna had been warm and kind on the phone, but Rowan was forever thinking the best of people and being disappointed. Not with Genna, though. She'd listened to her fumbling explanation of what troubled her, even sat back down and, hell, touched her just to make her feel better. She'd bent her own rules for her—and that hadn't been easy. Rowan knew she'd pushed her pretty hard, and Genna had agreed to help her. She'd made Rowan feel special. Like this wasn't something she did for just anyone. So, yeah, she'd done plenty of thinking about just how special Genna Fielding was. And just how much she wanted the chance to see her again—talk to her again. Even if it was about her worst secrets.

On day four, she'd actually congratulated herself. *Well done. You're not a sleazebag. Good job.* She'd obviously jinxed herself, because at close to midnight on day five, she was wet. Not just wet but *drenched*. She didn't even know how she got to be so wet. Twenty minutes ago, she'd been fast asleep and now need pulsed insistently between her thighs, distracting, provoking, seducing. Warmth chased over her skin as anticipation clouded out reason and longing rushed into her bloodstream. She moaned without wanting to.

She really shouldn't go there. But Genna filled her mind anyway. Genna striding into the tiny waiting area that was little more than a desk and a few mismatched chairs. Stopping and staring as if she'd been expecting someone else. Hoping for someone else? Some women tended to be unsure of her. She didn't possess the brand of femininity they were used to. Had she made Genna uncomfortable? God, she hoped not. Surely working in the Gender and Sexuality Division, Genna met all kinds of people. But it's not as if she actually knew her well enough to say. She didn't even know if Genna was queer. Not entirely implausible, but likely more wish than reality. And even if she was—why would she be interested?

Rowan rolled onto her stomach and pressed her thighs together in a fruitless attempt to will away her arousal. She'd stop thinking about Genna and go back to sleep.

Not thirty seconds later, something heavy thudded unapologetically onto her ass, pinning her hips to the mattress. She glanced over her shoulder and could just make out Clementine's olive-green eyes slowly blink in the darkness. "Gotta work on your grace, Clem. You'll never make the Olympic team with a landing like that."

Mrs. Penellie's ridiculously chonky ginger cat began to knead, turning in three tight circles before curling up on her butt like he was Goldilocks and Rowan's ass the just-right bowl of porridge. One false move and Rowan's boxers would brush against her clit. Jesus. Way to help a woman out. Clementine began to purr passive-aggressively, his claws dangerously close to bare skin. Rowan shoved the cat off and flopped onto her back.

"I'm sorry," she said when Clementine glared. "You're going to have to find somewhere else to sleep. My backside is off limits to anything with claws and a tail."

Clementine swished said tail disdainfully as if punctuating his rebuttal, before executing an almighty leap to the floor, landing with a thump worthy of a baby elephant and stalking haughtily out of the room.

"You're going to break the floorboards," Rowan warned him, as if the cat gave a damn.

She closed her eyes. Genna was kissing her. *Fuck.* She opened them again. But it was hopeless, the scene played out like a movie projected in 3D animation inside her brain.

Genna entered her office after Rowan had completed the instruments. "Uh-oh. You look like you need a hug."

She attempted a smile. "Are you offering?"

"Sure." Genna took her hand as Rowan got to her feet.

One moment of comfort wouldn't hurt. One small hug she could keep safe in her memory for later.

Rowan guided Genna toward her. Genna fit perfectly, her curves and valleys matching Rowan's as if they'd been made for each other. Rowan held her breath for endless seconds as they stood folded into each other, holding on. When was the last time she'd had someone to hold on to? Too long. Hugging Genna was no small pleasure, but in the privacy of her mind she was free to indulge.

Genna's chin rested lightly on her shoulder, her arms wrapped securely around Rowan's waist. Cocooned within Genna's embrace, warmth radiating out from every place Genna touched, Rowan was engulfed in a simmering heat that seemed to start on the inside and spread outward. Somehow, Genna's body spoke directly to hers and convinced her swirling head, her aching neck, her tired heart, that everything would be okay. *She* was okay because wrapped up with Genna was exactly where she needed to be. Just for this moment nothing else existed.

Her tension melted away, her muscles released their vice grip, and the thoughts ping-ponging inside her head began to float, happily adrift, growing fainter and fainter until they disappeared completely. Until all that existed in the universe was Genna—Genna's arms wrapped around her, Genna's chin on her shoulder, Genna's heartbeat a steady rhythm against her chest.

Rowan encircled Genna in an embrace that was pure contentment, her palms coasting the angles and plains of Genna's back just to touch and be touched. Just closeness. Just being *wanted* for such simple intimacy. They hugged the old-fashioned way. Part hug, part hold, part cuddle.

At first, close was enough. Then Genna shifted, her pelvis inadvertently brushing the zipper of Rowan's jeans. "Oh, sorry."

She slid her hands to Genna's hips, holding her in place. Heat flared, then burned through two layers of denim and branded Rowan's thighs. "Don't be sorry. I like it."

Genna whispered, "We really shouldn't. You're participating in my research. It's unethical."

"Not yet. It doesn't count until the first session."

A sexy smile coated Genna's voice. "I'm pretty sure it counts, cowboy."

"It definitely doesn't count." Rowan slid her thigh between Genna's, pulling Genna into her until she gasped. "God, I want you."

Genna's eyes fluttered closed as she rocked slowly against her. "We're going to get caught."

She cupped Genna's backside. "I don't care. Kiss me."

The curve of Genna's mouth guaranteed illicit pleasures, and the curve of her backside promised more. "You make it really hard to say no."

Before Genna could say another word, before Rowan voiced her decision to do what they both knew was a bad idea, her mouth was on Genna's. She tangled her fingers in Genna's dark hair, angling her head to take more of her mouth. She kissed with only a brush of her lips. Gentle, featherlight strokes against Genna's lips. Softly, quietly, she submerged them both in slow, honeyed kisses that were as lazy and languid as Savannah sweet tea on a Sunday afternoon. "Why say no when it feels so good to say yes?" she whispered against Genna's lips, not wanting to move her mouth away for even a second.

Genna gripped Rowan's shoulders and pressed up on her toes to deepen the kiss. "Maybe we should undo that zipper."

Rowan groaned. She wanted things exactly as they were, tender and honest, heartfelt and comforting. Close and sensual, but still on the white hat side of ethical. She did. She really fucking did.

But when Genna slipped her tongue into Rowan's mouth, barely restrained need kicked sharply between her thighs, refusing to be denied. Rowan wanted to be good, but the seductive lure of bad, the tempting lustful vixen of forbidden passion was the devil she knew best.

Still, she resisted.

"I want to make it good for you." Even in her fantasies, Genna deserved more than being thrown down on her desk and consumed like drive-thru takeout. *Wham bam. Have a nice day!* Genna deserved all the care and patience she had. Rowan only hoped hers wouldn't snap before she'd exhausted them both with pleasure.

Genna laughed quietly against her mouth. "It's already so good. I want more. Why are you denying us?"

"You're so damn sexy."

"Oh, you haven't seen sexy yet." Genna smiled coyly and backed away from her.

Rowan was about to protest when Genna shrugged off her blazer, letting it drop to the floor and the words died happily on Rowan's lips.

Fuuuck.

Genna's camisole came off next, leaving her in a black lace bra and dark jeans.

"Maybe I'll keep going if you're good," she teased her, toying with the clasp between her breasts.

Rowan was prepared to swear a lifetime allegiance to the Almighty God if only Genna would take off her bra. "Define *good.*"

Genna smiled wickedly, her eyes locked on Rowan's, her fingers wandering to the waistband of her jeans. "You'll have to work for it."

All the air in her lungs evaporated and blood began to roar in her ears. "Anything you want." She meant it too. Anything Genna found hot she'd be up for, because, well, *Genna.*

Was Genna wet already? Had kissing turned her on? Rowan wondered vaguely if it was normal to be concerned with someone else's pleasure in your own fantasy. Or, more to the point, to create a fantasy in which she inserted worry she had the power to remove. She'd ask real-life-Genna sometime.

"Are you wet?" Rowan asked, because even in her fantasies she wasn't cool.

Genna gave her signature eyebrow raise. She popped the button on her jeans and shimmied them down her hips. "Why don't you find out? On your knees, cowboy. Let's see if you know what you're doing."

Rowan fell to her knees, closed her eyes, and immersed herself in pleasuring Genna.

Rowan kicked off the sheets, slipped a hand into her boxers, and circled her clit while she imagined making Genna come with her mouth. She fought to hold on to her thoughts, but their witty repartee was eclipsed by the desire pulsing over her skin, in her veins, between her legs, at the very center of her need. God, she needed to come. She hadn't even gotten far enough into the fantasy for Genna to touch her and already she was so close to the edge, oblivion less than half a step away. Genna stripping for her, demanding she get on her knees to make her come was so ridiculously hot her brain was about to detonate. No. Scratch that. Her body was about to detonate, like a homemade bomb going off on a hair trigger.

Rowan slid two fingers up the base of her clit to hold off as long as she could. But it felt too fucking good, and she pumped her hips into her hand instead, Genna's smile playing in her mind. Genna's moans filling her ears. Genna—

Light burst like fireworks behind her eyes, and Rowan groaned as she came into the empty darkness of her bedroom. *Genna. God. Genna.* Her hips rocked as the tremors crested and then slowly ebbed away, leaving her hollow. Her body finally calm, but some unexplored region in her chest left wanting. Reaching for something. For someone with soft eyes and a wicked smile. For a hug that was never offered, and a lust she couldn't satisfy with her own hand.

She was running from Genevieve Fielding all right and getting absolutely nowhere.

❖

Genna stared at her iPhone the way contestants on *The Bachelor* stared at the other gorgeous supermodels: with pure resentment. Not that Genna stared at them that way. She had no problem with gorgeous. She never watched *The Bachelor* anyway. She watched CNN and MSNBC and…oh, fine, *okay,* she watched *The Bachelor*. So what? It *did* have women in bikinis. Watching the news was dumb anyway. It changed every day, so what was the point of trying to keep up?

Her taste in TV wasn't going to get her out of calling Rowan.

She tipped her face up to the water stain on the ceiling she stared at sometimes when she was trying to think. It wasn't like her to procrastinate over an enjoyable task, but talking to Rowan again seemed like a really bad idea when she had no clue what to make of her instrument results. Rowan didn't fall into one clearly defined sexual type. Many people bridged two, sometimes even three, but Rowan was an oddball mix of half a dozen categories that contradicted each other. She had a hefty dose of lover, a strong belief that sex should be emotional and romantic, but was also part scheduler, willing to sacrifice some rose petals in the name of having regular intercourse. Rowan was little bits novelty seeker and voyager too, at odds with both lovers and schedulers. It didn't make sense.

Had she lied? Genna remembered the utterly defeated expression on Rowan's face, the way she slumped in the chair as if she were a leaky tap and everything had slowly seeped out of her. No. Rowan hadn't lied. But with results like these, her fantasy life had to be all over the place. A lot about Rowan was unexpected. She looked as if she'd be right at home in a street gang with all that ink and muscle. But her looks were deceiving. Rowan was earnest and nervous and uncommonly nice. Just… Genna tried to put her finger on it and couldn't.

What did all this mean for Rowan's fantasy life? Rowan's words had been playing over and over in her head. *They're bad. Like lock me up and throw away the key kind of horribly, terribly, embarrassingly bad.* She should've told Rowan straight away that it was unlikely her fantasies were as awful as she thought. Lots of people fantasized about stuff they wouldn't want to actually happen. Stepmother fantasies, captive fantasies, exhibitionist fantasies, the list was endless. She should've explained that fantasies were fantasies, not real, and with no consequences. Fantasies were just an idea, a made-up series of events in which the fantasizer controlled every variable. Entirely safe. Of course, fantasies diverged, sometimes wildly so, from what a person sought in other areas of their sexual lives. Partnered sex was more complicated than an orgasm, even in the most casual circumstances. Most likely Rowan had some mildly kinky, toe-sucking fantasy and Genna could cite a bunch of articles to reassure her she was entirely normal. Why hadn't she thought to do that when Rowan was in her office last week? They could've resolved the mystery immediately, and Genna wouldn't be sitting around obsessing about Rowan Marks's fantasies and all the reasons she couldn't help her.

She pulled up Rowan's contact and hit call on her phone. She'd set up their first interview and they'd get the whole you're-totally-normal-don't-worry part squared away. Then she'd be off the hook.

"Hello?"

"Hi, Rowan? This is Genna Fielding." She heard a baby wailing in the background and added, "Is now a good time to set up your first interview for the study?"

"Hang on." There were muffled sounds of movement before everything went quiet. "Sorry. I'm at my mom's house."

"Babysitting?" Genna imagined Rowan with a baby in her arms and quickly squelched the image.

"No. He's…never mind. What time were you thinking for the interview?"

Of course, the baby wasn't her mom's child. Was the baby Rowan's kid? Genna had a bad habit of assuming everyone was just like her and didn't want children just as fervently. But Rowan was at the right age for a baby. No partner, though. Not that that made any difference.

"Genna?"

"How's Thursday afternoon around three?"

"That works. Where do we meet?"

"In my office if that works for you."

There was a pause. Rowan cleared her throat, "Sure, okay. Sounds great."

Genna tried to think of something else to say. Something that wasn't *so is the baby yours?* "I'm sorry I was abrupt last time we met. You caught me off guard with your request."

The knee-weakening hum in Rowan's voice came out in full force when she said, "Hey, no problem. No one would've expected that, and you were tired." Rowan waited a beat, "From all that late-night studying."

Genna instantly went hot at the gentle teasing. Rowan knew she hadn't been studying. Don't ask her how Rowan had guessed because she had no idea, but it seemed she had. Did Genna somehow radiate, *my social life is comprised of one-night stands*? That was just excellent, totally the impression she wanted to give to a research participant. Rowan probably thought she got off on her participants' fantasies too. No wonder she was hesitant to talk to her.

"I was kidding," Rowan said when Genna didn't answer. "What you do at night is none of my business."

Genna stared at the ceiling again, wishing she didn't want to make it Rowan's business. "I can handle a little teasing. You're right, I wasn't studying and am clearly a terrible liar."

"You don't need to, you know," Rowan said against her ear. "Lie, I mean. You can just be you."

Queasiness churned in Genna's stomach, making her grateful she'd skipped lunch. Everyone judged and no one was ever just themselves.

"Thank you," she said, because *talking about my sex life at work violates a boundary* would've been too complicated. "Same goes. No lies, okay? You might be even worse at them than me."

Rowan laughed and the sound made Genna smile for no reason. "You're right about that. No lies. There's something about you that makes me want to be honest."

Butterflies launched into flight inside Genna's chest. Geez. What was she supposed to say to that? *Stop looking so closely. Stop noticing me. Stop wanting too much from me.* "Thank you. See you tomorrow."

"See you then," Rowan said before they hung up.

Genna had only just pressed end, the butterflies still coasting drunkenly, when her phone rang in her hand. She didn't have to look at the screen to know her mom was calling.

Chapter Six

"You're strong enough to haul my butt outta here. Do a friend a favor. Throw me over your shoulder and make off to Tahiti."

Rowan rose from her stool at a table the size of a generous Frisbee and pulled Maria in for a quick hug. "You need to be carried away, because?"

"I'd have to protest for form. If I go of my own volition, I'd have to bring Fiona, and if I bring Fiona, who'd look after the smallest humans while we're drinking mai tais and cruising women?" Maria grinned.

"Of course. Abduction is the only way. Though, I'm not sure I know where Tahiti is."

"It's an island in the Pacific, between the US and Australia." Maria dropped onto the stool opposite Rowan and stole a sip of her beer.

"That's specific," Rowan said.

"It's been on my bucket list for years. Sand, sunshine, and women in grass skirts. It's heaven, only you're not dead yet."

"Stare at those skirts for too long, and you might end up dead." Rowan signaled the passing server for another round as Maria polished off her beer. They often ended up in conversations like this, entertaining for entertainment's sake, bordering on ridiculous, and going exactly nowhere.

"You're not wrong. Monogamy is a small price to pay for the everlasting devotion of the love of my life."

The server set their round on the table, tossed Rowan a smile, and hurried away. Happy Hour, the ubiquitously named campus bar was bursting with students. Rowan was a regular.

She sipped her beer, grateful for the distraction as the words *everlasting devotion of the love of my life* began to swim laps inside her head. Back and forth, like the energizer bunny in a Speedo. God, she wanted that too. Wanted it and was terrified it might happen in equal measure.

"I'll research flights to Tahiti. If we both ditch classes for the rest of the week, we could manage a five-day getaway. You can drink as many mai tais as you like, and the only person bothering you will be me," Rowan said.

Maria sighed wistfully. "Don't call me Mommy, and I guarantee that you won't bother me. Not that you'd ever skip class, you Goody-Two-shoes."

Rowan ignored the jab. Her shoes were unquestionably goody. "Does Fiona call you Mommy? Kinky."

Maria snorted and wacked her playfully on the arm. "Hardly. But a woman says *baby* with the right mix of lazy and wheedling, and it sounds a hell of a lot like Mommy."

Rowan could totally hear Fiona saying baby in just that tone, but you left that kind of comment the hell alone if you knew what was good for you. "Thanks for meeting me. I know it's tough to get time away from the little ones."

She and Maria were unlikely friends. Maria was teetering over the brink of thirty with a fledgling part-time business, an everlasting love of her life, and two kids she adored even though she reserved the right to gripe about them. Rowan was…well, she was alone, basically. Her aloneness more acute in contrast to Maria's full life. But they'd clicked the first day of orientation as the only two students over twenty-five in most of their classes.

For half a second, before Rowan had discovered Maria was married, she'd considered asking her out. The whole sexy, curvy, hotness thing came naturally to Maria. With her deep tan complexion, she was equal parts womanly and nerdy in jeans rolled at the ankles and ripped at the knees, a black shirt in some kind of silky material, and large dark-framed glasses that covered half her face yet somehow managed to look chic.

"Drinking is necessary." Maria was already halfway through the beer she'd stolen. "Susan is coming over for dinner tonight. If a person can't get tipsy before their mother-in-law shows up, when can they?"

Before Rowan could think of a scenario more dire than Susan, Genna walked into Happy Hour, her hand on the arm of an older woman. Every thought fell out of Rowan's head and scattered across the floor like she'd just dropped a bag of Skittles. Genna was laughing at something her companion said and looked amazing, brighter and more together than when Rowan had last seen her. Evidently, she'd made an effort for the…date? Rowan's stomach contorted itself into intricate sailor's knots as they smiled at each other.

Upside: Rowan's hopes were, for once in her life, likely dead-on. If that smile was anything to go by, Genna was attracted to women. Downside: she was clearly already taken, and to add insult to injury, her date was Rowan's polar opposite. Not just because she was extremely feminine and Rowan wasn't, but because she was *elegant*. Ridiculously elegant. Like Olivia Pope in a bespoke suit level elegant. You didn't see that too often in a college bar. Maybe Rowan could conjure a smidgen of elegance? She grimaced. She was about as elegant as a gorilla at the opera. Stupid for her to think she'd have a chance with someone like Genna if stunning, classy sophistication was her type, and how could it not be?

Genna and her date took seats at the bar, rather unfortunately in Rowan's direct line of vision, and Genna turned her unfairly sexy smile on the bartender, saying something to make him and the frat boy on her right laugh in unison. *You're a charmer aren't you, Dr. Sex?*

As if sensing a story brewing, Maria asked, "What's new with you? Seeing anyone? You need to date more. It's boring to live vicariously when you're having even less sex than I am."

Rowan dragged her gaze from Genna holding court at the bar. "How do you know I'm having less sex?"

"I got lucky last night between diaper changes and midnight temper tantrums. Did you?" Maria asked, all smugness.

Instantly, she flashed back to fantasizing about Genna. Hugging and stroking and making her come while she touched herself and exploded faster than a shaken can of soda. But, according to Genna, it only counted if someone else did the touching. Fantasies were as worthless as they were hopeless. That should've pleased her. She wanted her fantasies to be worthless. Insignificant and downright hollow. Watching last night's fantasy all but sitting in the lap of another woman, Rowan's desire making absolutely no difference to the reality, should've been comforting. It should've been a miracle. The key to unlock the handcuffs imprisoning her sexual psyche. So why wasn't she pleased? She was less of a terrible person if her fantasies were meaningless, right? Yet she couldn't muster any enthusiasm for the idea.

"Earth to Rowan." Maria waved a hand in front of her face, frowning. "Who are you—" She cut herself off and whipped around in her seat, scanning the bar.

"It's nothing," Rowan said hurriedly.

Maria made an overly suggestive sound of appreciation as they watched Genna and her date practically glued to each other, both reading something on the iPad she never seemed to be without. "Oh, she isn't nothing. The one in the middle, right? Long dark hair, kind of looks like a less skinny version of Keira Knightley. Totally your type."

Rowan took a too-large gulp of her beer before asking, "Who's Keira Knightley?"

Maria spun back around, an aggrieved look on her face. "Seriously? She's an actress."

"Does she star in chick flicks or something, because if it's chick flicks you should know better than to make the reference."

Maria pulled her phone out of her jeans and tapped before showing Rowan an image of a tall, dark-haired woman in a long dress with a sash thing tied around her middle.

"Okay, she's hot. But that dress is awful."

Maria rolled her eyes so hard Rowan worried they'd never make it back to their original position. "It's a period dress, you complete Neanderthal. This is Keira Knightley in *Pride and Prejudice.*"

"Just because it's based on a classic doesn't make it not a chick flick." Rowan leaned closer to Maria's phone. "Might be worth watching though. Does she get naked?"

Maria put her phone away. "Or you could go talk to the sexy-pants Keira lookalike and explore some real-life nudity."

Against her will, Rowan glanced at Genna again. Sometime in the last two minutes, her date had disappeared and Genna was chatting to the frat boy, who looked like Santa had just given him all the gifts on the nice list at once. Lucky bastard.

"I'd rather watch the movie." Rowan heard the unhappiness in her tone and vowed not to care so much. Genna could flirt with everyone in the place. She had a right.

"Well, that makes you a bit of an idiot," Maria said cheerfully. "She's hot. She's not my type, but I can appreciate hot when I see it. Why not take a chance? She looks friendly."

Seeing no way around coming clean about the whole thing, Rowan drained her glass. "I know her a little. She's a PhD student. I'm participating in her research. She's off limits."

Maria was stumped for a second. "Well, only for the duration of the study, right? And flirting wouldn't be off limits."

"I really can't. It's not a Psych 101 study. She's studying sexual fantasies."

Rowan waited for that ticking bomb to explode and wasn't disappointed.

"*What*?"

A few people turned around to stare when Maria shrieked the word.

"Shut up, or she'll hear you," Rowan said, the grumpy back in full force.

Maria hissed, "You're participating in a study on *sexual fantasies*?"

"Yes. The intersection of sexual fantasy and feminist discourse."

Maria looked gobsmacked for an instant, then cracked up. "Perhaps you can act out your fantasies. You know, for *research*."

Rowan had expected the joke but couldn't seem to find it funny. "That's not a good idea. Affective responses to psychosexual stimuli are serious business." Don't ask her how she'd managed to remember Genna's spiel about the study and pull it out of thin air, but it *was* serious. To her at least.

"Come on. I mean, yeah, totally sign up for the sex study with the super-hot researcher. I'm all over that. But you're only doing it because she's attractive, right? Who'd want to tell a total stranger what makes them come?"

Time seemed to slow, the crowd in the bar moving sluggishly as Rowan's limbs grew heavy, gluing her to the spot. *She* wanted to tell a total stranger the things that made her come, even if *wanted* was too simple a word for it. She believed that Genna's study would be important to a lot of people. Rowan was first in line for answers. "I guess I do," she said quietly.

"Oh shit. *Sorry*." Maria slid off her stool and rounded the table to fling her arms around Rowan. "I'm an idiot. I was only kidding."

Rowan patted her on the back. She was overreacting to what would otherwise be a hilarious conversation trying to guess the craziest fantasy Genna had ever heard. So funny and so not serious if only Rowan wasn't about to be the punchline of the joke.

"It's okay. It's pretty out there, I guess. Obviously, I'm just curious about how sexual fantasies relate to feminism."

"Of course you are," Maria said without a hint of the sarcasm that would usually accompany such a response. "You couldn't pay me to talk about sex with a stranger, and I'm projecting. You do you. I'm sure it'll be great."

Maria was trying to smooth things over the way any friend would, and Rowan wasn't really mad at her. Maria only said what most people felt. What Jessica and not-Jessica had felt. That's the way a normal person reacted. But Rowan wasn't normal, and tomorrow around three, Genna would know that.

"What are you cooking for dinner with Susan?" Rowan tried distracting Maria while pretending not to be gazing at Genna. Wistfulness piling high in her heart, Rowan longed to walk over and talk to her, maybe just touch her hand for a second, make her smile. Ask about her day. Was that dumb? An overwhelming desire to simply be a part of someone's day? To be there for all the mundane moments that weren't worth mentioning? It *was* dumb. But she couldn't seem to stop herself wishing. *If wishes were horses, beggars would ride.* Genna was taken, and as soon as tomorrow rolled around, even the fantasy of making Genna hers would be dust.

Rowan had to focus on fixing herself so that one day, somehow, she could maybe not be so broken and have the kind of relationship she ached for. But not with Genna, *who was taken.*

Genna paid her tab and reached down to grab her tote from between the legs of her stool. The hem of her sweater inched up and revealed a strip of tantalizing skin.

Rowan swallowed. She wouldn't think about licking that exposed skin. Nipping at it with her teeth, cupping her hands around Genna's hips. Sucking…she wouldn't.

Would. Not.

Her clit began to throb.

Fuck.

She was so completely screwed.

CHAPTER SEVEN

The lot outside Happy Hour could've set the stage for *Dateline Murder of the Week.* Rain that'd been sulking in the clouds threatening a tantrum now drummed so hard against the asphalt it barely resembled water. The dark, secluded, nearly empty lot held only a smattering of cars too far apart to do her any good. Genna just knew a creepy dude in an oversized hoodie lurked somewhere in the shadows ready to stab her. And here she was, completely helpless. She thunked her head against the steering wheel as the check engine light mocked her in glaring red. A warning she hadn't heeded. She'd end up really gruesomely dead, and it would be her own damn fault.

At the knock on the passenger's side window Genna gasped, shrunk back, and searched wildly for something to defend herself. She came up with lip balm from the cup holder. Really, really gruesomely dead clutching a half-used juicy grape. What a way to go.

The assailant pulled down the hood of their raincoat and offered an apologetic smile. "Sorry," Rowan shouted over the roar of the weather. "Didn't mean to scare you. Let me in?"

Genna tossed the Chapstick and unlocked the door, still shaking. "Don't you know not to sneak up on people while they're imagining being violently murdered? Not cool."

Rowan slid in, obviously doing her best not to bring a tidal wave of water with her but failing to protect them from the wind that whipped around the interior of the car like an angry bird. She slammed the door and the wind died, a morbid chill in its wake.

"Imaging your own violent murder? How do you die?" Her tone was totally casual, as if she'd said, "How are you?" and not, "How do you die?"

Genna stared.

Rowan smiled. Shrugged. Smiled again. "I'm curious."

Genna harumphed, her heart still hammering. "Can I help you with something?"

"I was thinking I might be able to help you. Are you okay out here?"

Rowan rested her fingers lightly on Genna's wrist for less than a second. The touch was wet and cold. It shouldn't have warmed her, but her skin heated the tiniest bit. "I'm sorry I scared you. I was heading to my truck and noticed you. No one sits in a parking lot in the rain unless…"

"Unless they're about to die?" Genna asked.

"That's an option. Not one I'd recommend but, sure, an option."

Rowan smiled again, and Genna's fright slunk away, dragging its heels on the way out. Without anything left to distract her, tears threatened. She widened her eyes and blinked hard. Crying would just add to the fucking helplessness. "The car won't start. I'm stuck in a deserted parking lot in the dark and the rain and it's been…a not-so-great week." A terrible week, piled on an awful month, crammed inside a dreadful year that wouldn't be getting any better on January first.

Rowan said lightly, "Can I take a look?"

"Do you know anything about cars?" She asked as if her crap pile of a motor vehicle was a priceless classic. Why was she being so snarky? She hated that Rowan was seeing her like this.

"Some." Unperturbed, Rowan turned on the flashlight on her phone. "Pop the hood."

"Uh…"

Genna could just barely make out Rowan's features in the darkness, but saw her grin.

"I guess *you* don't know much about cars?" Rowan said.

She scraped together her dignity. "I study sex, not engines."

"Pretty sure my sex drive has an engine."

Rowan threw open her door, inviting in another gust of wind, and not giving Genna a chance to respond. Good thing because the words on the tip of her tongue weren't professional. Rowan came around the driver's side, opened Genna's door a few inches, then crouched and pulled a lever that Genna hadn't even known existed. Nearly drowned and pummeled by rain shouldn't have been a good look on anyone, but Rowan was a sleek otter in her raincoat. The hair not hidden under her hood had turned a deep caramel and, when she glanced up, Genna had to look away, her heart hammering for an entirely different reason. Lovely. She'd just add attraction to otters to the ever-growing list of things she ought to see a therapist about, right above woeful procrastinator. She'd been frightened, that was all, and Rowan was coming to her rescue.

Genna wasn't a swooner. Only her heart clutched its little chest and all but fainted as Rowan disappeared under the hood. Her stupid heart was loving this damsel shit.

Rowan was gone less than five minutes, shouted "try to start it," then closed everything up and got back into the car.

"Well?" Genna asked.

"You have engine trouble. Gotta get this baby to a professional."

Genna sighed. "It's not going to help. My *baby* is worth less than two grand, and that's when she runs."

Rowan nodded. "Do you have someone on their way to help?"

She definitely wasn't going to admit she didn't have a Triple A membership. Or that she didn't really have anyone to call. *In case of emergency contact absolutely no one because I always take care of everything.* "No. The check engine light has been on for over a week. It's going to be bad. I was…processing when you arrived and almost made me pee my pants."

Rowan glanced down at Genna's lap as if by reflex.

"Almost." She fought a smile.

Rowan took longer than was necessary to pull her gaze away and she did it slowly, dragging her eyes up Genna's body like she was resisting a magnetic pull. "Well, okay, probably. But you still need it looked at."

Genna was getting her fill of being looked at right here and now. Rowan had an unreadable expression on her face, but Genna managed to convince herself she'd just made up the heat in her stare. Her frazzled brain was trying to make a bad situation a little more pleasant. Only she hadn't made it up, and even as her brain was busy rationalizing, her heart was hugging itself and spinning in giddy circles. *She looked at me! She looked at me!*

Genna appreciated that Rowan hadn't given her a hard time for not getting the car seen to before it died and left her stranded. She'd have given herself a hard time in Rowan's shoes. Hell, in her own shoes. A hard time was on her agenda for later. *Rowan's so decent.* The thought popped into her head to remind her she hadn't even said thank you. Despite her giddy heart, she definitely wasn't being very nice. Maybe a week ago the car wouldn't have been so bad, but now? Now, she'd need to raid her meager emergency fund to buy another crap pile and start the whole annoying process over again. Not to mention almost getting stabbed by a sexy otter who'd just been staring at her crotch. Let's not forget that.

And yet, Rowan radiated bone-deep decency, a kindness that went further than merely polite. She was one of the good ones. A catch. So why was she single? Alice had made a similar observation about Genna not so long ago, sans the kindness and niceness and decency. Sometimes people had very good reasons for being single, and what appeared worth catching ended up being a major disappointment. Certainly true in her case. Tears threatened again, and she curled her shoulders inward, hoping Rowan wouldn't notice.

Rowan reached out and tucked a loose strand of hair behind Genna's ear. She blinked, not quite sure what to make of a gesture so small and tender, but so…so…*big* at the same time. Rowan really shouldn't have done that. What did she mean by it? Was it just a reflex, or did it indicate something more? Was she reading into it because she was attracted to Rowan? Or should she pair it with the intense looks Rowan was shooting her? Did she *want* it to be what it looked like? Like, flirting? Rowan wasn't the type to take advantage of a woman in a vulnerable situation. She wasn't flirting, she was—

"You look so sad. I wish you weren't," Rowan said simply. No longer touching her, but her voice a caress that stole Genna's breath.

Caring. Rowan was caring for her.

Suddenly, everything she didn't know became too much. Right now, with Rowan, in the dark confines of her car going nowhere, everything she had to do, everything she didn't want to face, everything she *felt* was so overwhelming she just *couldn't*. If it had been just the car, she'd have managed. But it wasn't ever just one thing. Not with her never-ending pile of work, or her mom's incessant guilt trips, or the dalliances at McKinney's that never quite satisfied. There were always so many somethings, and this small and tender something she didn't know how to categorize broke her. Her bottom lip trembled and even though she bit down hard to hold onto her composure, tears slid down her cheeks that had heated with embarrassment. The warmth spread up from her jawline until even her eyes were hot. Rowan had to think she was a basket case sitting in the rain crying, but as embarrassing as it was, she couldn't help it. She just needed one damn minute to fall apart. Instead of addressing the touch like the adult she was, she laid her head back against the seat and closed her eyes, blocking it all out until she'd calmed down enough to deal with it. Deal with Rowan. Deal with *life*.

She could feel Rowan's eyes on her. It sounded like she was riffling in the glovebox. She called someone, said some things, recited Genna's license plate, all while Genna just sat there fighting tears.

"I know a guy. Phil's got a garage around the corner, and he's on his way. He'll tow this for you and take a look. It might not be as bad as you think."

Genna peeled the back of her head off the seat and opened her eyes in time to catch Rowan tucking her phone back in her pocket. "You called someone for me?"

Rowan looked puzzled, and why wouldn't she. It was a stupid question. Genna had just heard her doing exactly that. She replaced the registration in the glovebox. "Of course. That's what you do when your car breaks down."

Genna bit her lip, not about to mention that Rowan swooping in to save her wasn't exactly *what you do*. Not in her world.

"Thank you. I really appreciate you helping me out." There, that wasn't so hard. She hadn't choked on the admission. Much. "I'll call Alice and she'll drive me home." Genna contorted herself into a pretzel to reach into the back seat for her bag, at the very bottom of which was her phone. The added benefit of avoiding Rowan's gaze didn't hurt either. Why was it that every time she was alone with Rowan there never seemed to be enough space? Who could she call to make a complaint? More space, please.

When she turned around again, Rowan was studying her. The look was…resigned? "I can take you anywhere you need to go. I might even let you live."

She smiled at the joke, but Rowan was looking at Genna's phone like it smelled bad.

"Oh, no. That's okay," Genna said automatically. The last thing she wanted was to inconvenience Rowan any more than she already had. "I'll call Alice."

"Okay." Rowan turned away, her posture stiff, and looked out the window at the water about to wash them away.

Genna hesitated. "I appreciate your offer. I do. I just…" She fought for an explanation. "I don't like to rely on people."

Her stupid heart pouted.

A muscle twitched in Rowan's jaw. "You don't need to explain. I'm nearly a stranger and getting into a car with a stranger is against all common sense. You're upset. You should absolutely call your girlfriend."

Genna would've been less surprised if Rowan had told her to call Fred Flintstone for a ride in the footmobile. "My girlfriend?"

"Alice isn't the woman I saw you with in the bar earlier?"

Rowan had seen her in Happy Hour? Had paid enough attention to make an assumption about who she was with? "She is. But what makes you think she's my girlfriend?" Genna hadn't given off relationship vibes. She'd never even crushed on Alice. Alice was beautiful, but not in the sexy way Rowan was. Alice was fine art: classic, refined, completely untouchable. Genna liked touching way too much to deprive herself and, honestly, if she touched Alice, she'd probably leave smudgy fingerprints all over her.

Rowan shook her head and gestured to Genna's phone. "Forget it. Call Alice to come and get you."

Instead of calling Genna said, "She's my thesis advisor. My friend." *Currently also my pain in the ass boss.*

"Oh," was all Rowan said in response.

"I'm attracted to women. Well, to all genders. But I'm not dating anyone," she said for no reason at all. Rowan didn't need to know her sexuality or relationship status. In fact, she really shouldn't have corrected her. If Rowan thought she was somebody's girlfriend maybe this *vibe* between them, the simmering chemistry she couldn't seem to shake, would disappear. Rowan was too good-looking, too good *everything,* to waste time chasing after women already in relationships, and that's assuming she'd have wanted to chase Genna in the first place. Which she didn't. Probably. Her heart needed to stop offering up potentially damaging—and positively embarrassing—information.

But somehow, even though it had been a colossal mistake, the too-much-honesty was worth it when Rowan's distant expression relaxed, and she gave a small nod. "That's good information."

"I shouldn't have said anything, I just…"

She just what? She just wanted her to know she was available in case Rowan was interested? Never mind her research, never mind that Rowan clearly had a secret, never mind the fifty-five billion ethics violations, never mind she'd just humiliated herself falling apart over a stupid car. *Just announce you're single hoping she'll wanna jump you. Brilliant strategy.*

"You already know I'm unattached." Rowan held her gaze, and Genna's stomach flip-flopped. Rowan had really green eyes. It was a silly thing to keep noticing. But truly green eyes weren't very common, and Rowan's were the most remarkable gold-green. Wolf's eyes. Pure intensity. Rowan's eyes seemed to sink beneath her skin and wrap around her heart. Her traitorously giddy heart that was currently doing cartwheels waving an "I Heart Rowan" flag. Little idiot.

"It's really not relevant," Genna said, at the exact same moment Rowan said, "Want to talk about what's on your mind?"

Genna tried for a smile and felt it wobble on her lips. "That's my line."

Rowan's fingers were back on her wrist. Not holding, not even moving, just resting there like a flame against her skin. A little shot of electricity zipped up Genna's arm. "I can't promise to know the answers to your pain any more than you've promised to know mine, but if you want to tell me, I want to listen."

"Oh, no I—" The car suddenly felt claustrophobic. Why did Rowan seem to take up all her air? More air, please.

"Genna." Rowan squeezed her fingers. "I'm a person. You're just a person. We can just be people, not researcher and participant. Just two students stuck in a rainstorm trying to pass the time."

"I'm stuck in a rainstorm. You're…why are you here, exactly?" Genna asked.

"It's where you are."

The words hit her like fists to the gut, her breath caught, and her mind went completely blank. She forgot how to swallow and couldn't speak. She had no idea what to say to that. She wanted to believe Rowan was just being nice but couldn't find a way to convince herself. Rowan was here helping her because *here* was where Genna was. And that whispered of feelings a lot more complicated than altruism. The only feelings Genna allowed herself were ones that started and ended below the belt, and even that was off limits with this particular sexy otter.

She risked a glance at Rowan and found her relaxed against the seat, half-turned to face her, looking as if she hadn't just stopped Genna's heart and then sent it sprinting into overdrive with four simple words.

"That freaks you out, doesn't it? That I might want to get to know you," Rowan asked.

"It would freak out the ethics panel I'd have to make a case to if anyone found out I was sleeping with my research participant," Genna replied in lieu of actually answering the question because *um, hell yes.*

Rowan shifted even closer. "Is it unethical? We're consenting adults."

"There are campus-wide policies preventing sexual or romantic relationships between professors or instructors, and their students."

"Okay. But you're not grading me. It's a voluntary study."

Genna sighed. "It's a study on sexual fantasies. The power differential applies. As the researcher I'm responsible for your safety and all sorts of things can go wrong if we cross the line, even if we don't intend them to. Is it an *official* policy? I don't think so. But it would be a black mark against me that could impact my career and Alice would likely drop me as one of her students."

Rowan nodded slowly. "So, it's basically a policy even if it's not. I get it. But I said get to know you, not fuck you."

She thought about it. Rowan *hadn't* said sex. But she didn't need to. They'd both said it plenty often without words. Now Rowan wanted out on a technicality? "So, the way you've been undressing me with your eyes isn't sexual then? Don't play games. I study this for a living."

"I have no doubt you're skilled," Rowan said calmly.

Genna choked out a laugh. "Why do I feel like you're insulting me?"

"I don't know. Why does my interest feel insulting?"

"Because we *can't*. It's against every rule in the book. Rules designed to protect both of us. You know this."

Rowan shook her head. "You're not listening. I want to spend time with you, get to know you. Not everything is about sex."

"Not about sex?" Genna asked in a tone she normally reserved for anti-vaxxers and flat-earthers. "I'm researching sexual fantasies. You want my insight for personal reasons. You've been flirting with me since the day we met, and you definitely did not just look at me in a let's-be-gal-pals way. Stop fooling yourself."

Rowan tilted her head to the side like a confused puppy. "You're irritated."

Genna couldn't help it, she threw her hands up and let them crash into her lap. "You think?"

"You're irritated I want to know you?"

Genna dragged air into her lungs in an attempt at curbing said irritation. "You're lying to us both by stating your interest in me has nothing to do with sex."

"I never said it has *nothing* to do with sex. If you weren't conducting this study, if I didn't need your help, then, yes, I'd absolutely ask you out in the hopes that sex would fall somewhere into that equation at some point in the future. I can't deny an attraction."

"Then you understand we can't go there." Good. It was settled. Rowan might want to be *here* but *there* wasn't a destination on any map.

"I understand we can't have a personal relationship right now. But I don't understand why that precludes me from getting to know you."

"I—What does that even mean? Is there a difference?" God, she wanted to kiss Rowan. The thought launched into her brain out of nowhere and lit up like a neon sign. *Kiss her. Just kiss her. Kiss her. Kiss her. Kiss her.*

Rowan looked at Genna without speaking for a beat too long and then sighed. "I think so. There's plenty of ways we can get to know one another without crossing lines."

She was only irritated because she wanted what Rowan was offering and that made it even harder to say no, but that she looked like a fantasy come to life and was as tempting as sin wasn't Rowan's fault. So Genna gentled her tone and tried a little reason.

"Tomorrow you're going to tell me what makes you believe your fantasies are terribly, horribly, embarrassingly bad. That revelation makes you vulnerable, or you'd have told me right away. That I will know, that you want my insight coming to terms with it, puts me in a position of power *emotionally*. You have to trust me as the keeper of your secrets, to be non-judgmental, to try my best to support you. I can't betray that trust by indulging a selfish desire to lay my problems at your feet. Getting to know me, my run-of-the-mill dramas, my sordid history, is going to undermine the trust we build tomorrow, and if we do that, you won't get the answers you want."

Rowan's eyes bored into hers in the semi-darkness and that space and air shortage reached crisis level. She willed her heart to stop racing. Everything she'd said was true. But for some reason, telling the truth didn't stop her wanting to lean across the console and press her mouth to Rowan's, slide her fingers into the damp hair at Rowan's nape, fog the windows as they kissed a kiss that'd make her wetter than the downpour.

Instead of replying to her highly logical and well-reasoned explanation, Rowan said, "You have a sordid past?"

Genna rolled her eyes. "Thank you for making my point for me better than I ever could. If you don't see how having access to that information is problematic, you're not ready to be a social worker."

The barest hint of a smile played on Rowan's lips. "Firing at my professional integrity, that hurts."

Genna just raised her eyebrows and waited for Rowan to admit she was right.

"You think I want to even the score, don't you? That I want to know a history you consider sordid because it will make me feel less vulnerable tomorrow if I know your secrets too."

"Aren't you?" Genna asked, impressed Rowan had the insight to hit the nail on the head.

"What's your favorite home-cooked meal?" Rowan asked instead of answering the question.

"What does that have to do with anything?"

"Can't you just answer without analyzing it to death?" Amusement rode Rowan's tone.

"Not really," Genna muttered. "It's shepherd's pie. But I haven't had it in years, and I don't see the point of the question."

"The point is now I know you like mashed potatoes. Shepherd's pie is an easy recipe and that you haven't made it for yourself suggests you don't like to cook, so I know that too. What's your favorite TV show?"

"Maybe it's not about the mashed potatoes," Genna said, unhappy with this not-as-innocent-as-it-seemed version of twenty questions. Knowing random facts about someone wasn't really knowing them.

Rowan gave her a droll look. "Now who is fooling themselves? Shepherd's pie is *always* about the mashed potatoes. If you were in it for the beef, you'd have picked something else. I like mine with half-and-half and sour cream."

Genna wrinkled her nose. "Sour cream in mashed potatoes? That's one way to ruin them, I guess."

"How do you make yours then?" Rowan asked.

"Milk, butter, and a generous handful of ground parmesan. Potatoes should taste like potatoes, only with cheese."

"Tell that to French fries."

Genna leaned forward, drawn into the debate despite herself. "Uh-uh. French fries are about the grease and salt. Ever had an unsalted French fry?"

Rowan nodded slowly. "Unsalted French fries are bad."

"See? You'll never win. I'm a famous potato connoisseur." Genna pointed at Rowan. "You, my friend, are merely an amateur."

Rowan grinned. "I see a mashed potato grand championship battle in our future. Fifty says mine are the best you've ever had."

Our future. The best you've ever had.

What were they doing? She shouldn't have let Rowan maneuver them into this conversation. It was unprofessional. Except, it wasn't, not really. Cracking jokes about potatoes, a little friendly rivalry, that wasn't unprofessional. It just wasn't something she usually did at night with a sexy woman. Rowan wanted to get to know her and now she knew how Genna liked her mashed potatoes. That wasn't significant.

As if she could read her mind, Rowan asked, "So, what's your favorite TV show?"

Genna shouldn't reply. She needed to cut this off. But fifteen minutes ago, she'd been in tears and now she couldn't seem to remember what was so upsetting. Potatoes and TV shows and whatever else Rowan might throw at her was completely harmless. Maybe this *wasn't* about sex. Rowan understood the boundaries, and she could trust her to keep them, couldn't she?

Part of Genna knew it was a lie. Getting to know someone you were attracted to only made temptation stronger. But fuck it, they weren't crossing any lines.

"*The Bachelor*," Genna answered, curious to see what Rowan would say about her choice.

Rowan's eyes widened. "That's some heavy hitting women's lib, Dr. Feminist Discourse. At least watch *The Bachelorette*. A woman in power is hot."

"Do you find powerful women hot?" Genna asked without thinking. *Fuck.* Visions of the kind of erotic powers she wanted to wield over Rowan flashed into her head, and she hurried on before Rowan could answer. "See, *The Bachelorette* has one woman, and as powerful as she might be, *The Batchelor* has thirty. Some of them don't wear a lot in the way of clothes. There's really no competition."

"I guess I'm more of a one hot and powerful woman kind of person."

Rowan was cut off from further explanation by the blinding flash of high beams in the rearview mirror. The tow truck had arrived. Genna had never wanted to see a vehicle less in her life. Damn.

"Stay here where it's warm. I'm already wet. I'll go." Rowan took her keys.

Before she had a chance to open the door, Genna caught her arm. "I'd love a ride home, if the offer is still valid."

So, she wanted to chat a little longer. It wasn't against the rules.

"I'd like that." Rowan smiled and slipped from the car.

Genna stayed where she was, letting her head tip against the seat again. She couldn't possibly explain why, but her smile was hurting her face, so she expected it rivaled Rowan's. All because Rowan had been in the right place at the right time when she'd needed someone. Rowan had calmly helped her without Genna having to ask. All without being even the tiniest bit condescending. Because Rowan hadn't backed down when Genna tried to prevent her getting closer, but instead had found a way to make getting to know her okay. The more she thought about it, the more she wanted to kick the tow truck driver where it would hurt and start the night all over again.

As Genna sat in the now not-so-scary lot of Happy Hour, only one thing was for sure. Rowan wasn't the only one who was wet.

Chapter Eight

"You're being overly chivalrous," Genna said as Rowan peeled off her raincoat. "A little water never hurt anyone."

"It's not far," Rowan said as if the distance only applied to her and not to Genna. She hopped out of the car, leaving her raincoat on the passenger seat.

Genna watched her get instantly drenched as she jogged to her truck.

It *was* overly chivalrous, but nice too, in that way of old-fashioned manners. Genna slipped the raincoat on and pulled down the hood, barely resisting burying her nose in the collar. Strawberry jelly was a weird scent for a raincoat, but homey, somehow. She got out of the Dodge and made a run for Rowan's truck, swinging herself into the passenger seat.

Rowan didn't look like someone who owned a strawberry jelly smelling raincoat with her gray T-shirt plastered against her skin, water dripping from her hair, and her jeans dragging down her hips. And suddenly Rowan *not* wearing her raincoat was a stellar idea. The best idea Rowan had ever had. She should only ever walk around soaked.

Genna risked a few sneaky peeks at Rowan's rower's shoulders, small breasts, and impressive biceps. The woman was sitting right there being all gorgeous, and androgenous, and tough-looking. What was Genna supposed to do? Squeeze her eyes shut and count sheep in her head to keep herself from noticing? Rowan had looked at her just as blatantly, hadn't she? Fair was fair.

"Genna?" Rowan asked.

Genna jumped. She'd been too busy leering at Rowan to catch whatever it was she'd just said. "Sorry, what?"

A smile crept into Rowan's eyes, crinkling them at the corners. "A little distracted?"

Genna made a show of shaking her head and frowning very hard. "If I'm distracted it has nothing to do with," she waved a hand in the general direction of Rowan's wet hot sex appeal, "and everything to do with the giant estimate your guy is going to call me with tomorrow. Not to mention the bill to tow the heap of junk we all know it's not worth it to fix."

Rowan's face instantly fell, and she reached for Genna's hand. "Oh geez. I'm sorry I didn't think of that."

"I was kidding." Genna shoved Rowan gently on the shoulder. "Lighten up, Thor."

"Thor?"

"The god of lighting and thunder." Genna tilted her head toward the window. "And in the Marvel remake, Thor is quite strong. Impressively heroic. There are some minor similarities I can't deny."

"So, you were checking me out then?" Rowan grinned.

Genna sized Rowan up like she was going to sell the wet T-shirt look to millions, "*Very wet* is a good look on you."

Rowan swallowed audibly, the grin falling off her face as her eyes went all hot and sexy wolf. "Fuck."

Genna winced. What was she doing tossing sexual innuendo around like it meant nothing? Flirting felt good, and she couldn't seem to help herself. Faced with all this unbelievable gorgeousness, she was only human. But that didn't make it okay. There was absolutely no way to justify this, and that was exactly the problem with the whole *getting to know you* charade.

She looked down at their hands, their fingers woven together. "We both know I shouldn't be doing this."

She felt Rowan nod more than saw it. "It's been a long night. We'll put Thor back in the Marvel remake and pretend you didn't suggest I'm a god."

Genna laughed despite herself, both relieved and guilty that it was *Rowan* who was strong enough to keep the boundary and not step through the door she'd just flung open. "That would be for the best." She let go of Rowan's hand. "I'm not far. The corner of Delray and Third."

"I know it." Rowan shifted the truck into gear and backed out of the lot.

"Now I know you've lived here a while." Genna did her best to ignore the sexual tension that made the damp interior of the car steam. *More air, please. More space, please.*

"All my life," Rowan replied. "I grew up in Fort Donovan."

"That's a nice area," Genna said. Fort Donovan was thirty minutes south, a middle-class neighborhood full of homestyle diners and bicycle lanes that drove commuters nuts. Up-and-coming but still affordable. If she got her wish and scored a permanent position at SCU, she'd buy a house in that neighborhood.

"It's nice now. When I was a kid, it was seedy as hell. Before gentrification." Rowan's tone had changed slightly. Genna was starting to recognize the nuances now. Rowan's nervous tone, her pleading tone, her teasing tone. That hot-and-bothered one she'd used to whisper *fuck* not five minutes ago. But this tone was new. Tight and stretched thin.

"You don't approve of the redevelopment?" Genna asked.

Rowan turned onto her street. "No. I don't."

Her words were flat. Clipped. End of story.

"I'm halfway down, the oldest, ugliest apartment building." This line of inquiry wasn't going to lead to potato banter. What could Rowan possibly have against her neighborhood becoming safer with more resources? "Do you still have family in the area?"

Rowan nodded and Genna thought that was the end of the conversation until Rowan tossed her a bone. "My mom still lives in the same falling-down Victorian I grew up in. No backyard, though."

Desperate to move them away from whatever was bugging Rowan, but unsure which direction to push, Genna said, "What was that like? I can't imagine not having a backyard as a kid."

Rowan's shoulders relaxed a little. "There was a community playground a few blocks over. The neighborhood kids claimed it as theirs, and we were kings of the jungle gym. They knocked it down a few years ago and turned it into a dog park, but Mom takes Sawyer and Cameron there sometimes."

Rowan pulled to the curb outside Genna's building. For the first time, coming home to an empty apartment held little appeal. She liked living alone. She liked being alone. She liked sitting in Rowan's truck talking more. "Who are Swayer and Cameron?"

Genna wished Rowan would look at her, but all she got was profile as Rowan stared out the windshield. "My sister's kids. Three and eighteen months."

"Your sister has her hands full," Genna said for lack of any better response. She was sure she was supposed to ask some developmentally appropriate question like whether Cameron was reading or if Sawyer had learned to walk, but it'd been forever since she'd spent time around small children. She didn't want to get it wrong. *Look at me, Rowan. Tell me what's bothering you. You wanted us to get to know each other. This is safe.*

"Something like that," Rowan's gaze was glued to anywhere-but-Genna.

She shoved down her disappointment. She would know plenty about Rowan soon and better they kept it as professional as possible. Casually friendly. The third degree over family memories that clearly sucked wasn't either. If there was one thing Genna knew about, it was not-at-all-casual family drama. She brushed her fingers against the damp cotton of Rowan's sleeve before reaching for the door handle. "Thanks for the ride. I'll see you tomorrow?"

"You bet, see you at three." Rowan gave a wave as Genna hopped out of the car, and she caught Rowan wincing as she shut the door.

Genna hid her smile until she'd turned her back and was jogging up the path to her apartment. Rowan was still a fascinating contraction. Kind, considerate, helpful, funny, stubborn, distant, sexy as all hell. But her sweetness lingered like the smell of rain on the night air. That dorky little wave all but melted Genna's heart right out of her chest.

She was inside and locking her front door behind her when she realized she was still wearing Rowan's raincoat. She hung it carefully on the hook by the door, resisting the urge to wear it around her apartment dripping water. Too tired to do more than feed the slowly dying African violets on her windowsill, she wandered into the bedroom and flopped, fully clothed, onto the bed. God, she needed sleep. She could feel her eyes sinking into the back of her head as she closed them and let herself relax. She shifted. Squirmed. Sighed. Tried to harness the power of…whatever the fuck had the potential to turn her unsated arousal into sleep. She didn't have time for an orgasm. She really couldn't be bothered. She needed to rest more than she needed to come.

Bullshit.

Genna could feel her clit pulse, and it was going to take about a nanosecond for her to come. But there was just no way she could without thinking of Rowan. It would be so easy to slide her fingers south a few inches and imagine Rowan's mouth, Rowan's hands, Rowan's body on hers. What would Rowan be like in bed? Would all that sugar turn to heat and caramelize on her skin? Genna played with the button on her jeans, her resistance nothing more than teasing anticipation. Something told her Rowan would be oh-so considerate in bed too. Eager to please. So easy. So fast. Just one little orgasm then she could sleep. Rowan—

Lady Gaga saved her from herself.

Genna rolled over and grabbed her ringing phone. "Hello?"

"How's it going?" Gabby said into her ear by way of greeting.

Genna flopped back onto her pillow, willing her body to settle down. "It's fine."

Rule number one of the Feilding Survival rulebook: answer meaningful questions with arbitrary responses. She was always just fucking fine.

"Great," Gabby said, just like Genna knew she would. "So, can you come over a week from Saturday and help us move? We got the *best* off-campus apartment."

"What makes it the best apartment?" Genna asked warily. Almost anything would be more exciting than living on campus for two sophomores, but at least the state college was only twenty minutes from home, and Gabby and Grace could visit on weekends between parties. They managed to stay in Mom's good graces, which was more than she'd done.

"It has a hot tub," Gabby said, glee infusing every word.

Genna would've groaned, but she'd expected as much. Gabby and Grace weren't exactly prepared for adulthood. With her mom unable to leave the house, Genna had done her best to raise them to survive in the outside world, but she'd been in school, then college, and had barely made it to adulthood herself. All nineteen-year-olds were a little bit senseless, but Genna was pretty sure Gabby thought the lights always turned on no matter what, and fairies imbued her laptop with the internet. Moving out of the dorm and having to take care of themselves was going to be an uphill climb for her sisters. A good thing. She couldn't protect them forever.

"Are there any holes in the ceiling? Do all the appliances work? Does everyone have their own room? You know you can get bacterial infections from hot tubs, right? You have to sanitize them. And use chlorine." Genna tried to think of, and thus somehow prevent, everything that could possibly go wrong.

"Oh yeah, of course," Gabby said with way too much confidence.

"Gabby." They were never going to clean that hot tub.

Gabby sighed dramatically. "Like, the dishwasher leaks, I think? But it's fine. No one cooks anyway."

"Have you signed a lease? Will anyone else be living there?"

"Bianca's dad owns the place. It's totally legit. It's just me, Bianca, and Grace."

"Who's Bianca?" Genna asked.

"A *friend*. I have them, you know," Gabby said like Genna had insinuated Bianca must be Ted Bundy in drag. "Can you help us or not? We have to move everything out of the dorm over the weekend or they fine us or something. I don't really know, but like, we need to move."

"Sure," Genna said, because she'd have to check the place out anyway. Whoever Bianca's dad was, he'd better be legit if her baby sisters were going to be renting from him. "Email me a copy of the lease and make sure Bianca's there on moving day so I can meet her. Her dad too, if it's not too embarrassing."

"You're the most embarrassing person ever," Gabby said instead of thank you.

"I love you too," Genna said wearily.

"I do, you know, like, love you. But could you not give Bianca the third degree? She's cool."

"I'm not cool?" Genna said, mock offended.

Gabby scoffed. "You're not *not* cool. But you're, like, parental. It's different."

"It means I have to haul my ass to your dorm a week from Saturday."

"Pretty much," Gabby said, brightening. "Thanks. Oh, and can you bring a truck? Some of the furniture is ours, and Grace has that dumb memory foam mattress she can't live without."

"Gabby! Where am I going to find a truck?" It was just like her sister to tack the most important part of the request onto the end like it meant nothing.

"Dunno." Gabby turned the word into a shrug. "But parentals always figure it out. Love you. Bye."

Genna set the phone aside and closed her eyes. At least the conversation had killed her arousal. She'd worry about all the rest in the morning.

Chapter Nine

Rowan snuck into cell block D with the keycard and passcode she'd stolen from a sleeping guard. She tugged at the too-stiff collar of the Silver Creek Penitentiary uniform she'd ordered online through a dummy account. Her too-new standard issue black boots squeaked like terrified mice on the linoleum. To say she was ill-equipped for a prison break would be an understatement. She'd spent weeks obsessively going over every possible contingency and still was pitifully unprepared. But Sara was in the minimum-security unit. Her choice was now or never. Not a choice at all. Sawyer and Cameron needed their mom. She had to get Sara out, even if it cost her everything. She walked faster down the dimly lit, narrow, horror-movie corridor with the numbered doors of cells on her right and a thirty-foot drop over a short railing on her left. How many inmates had been thrown over? Why on earth would anyone design a prison with such an obvious mechanism for harm? Or was it on purpose?

Counting the cell numbers as she passed and lost in her own thoughts, Rowan only noticed someone behind her when a heavy hand landed on her shoulder.

"And who the hell are you, sweetcakes?" The voice was rough, as if a pack a day smoker had swallowed sandpaper.

"Marks. New guard." Rowan's voice was high and tight, a livewire stretched taut. She willed it not to quaver and bent a little at the knees to prevent a tremble. "Light check." All the overhead lights in the cells of the prison were operated via central control. "Lights out" was literal. But inmates still had matches and flashlights and God knows what else.

The guard spun Rowan around with a twist on her shoulder and studied her like a hunter sizing up prey through flat, narrowed eyes in a broad, heavily-jowled face. She stood with legs spread, tipped back on her heels as if preparing to strike, and a tilt to her lips that could've been a smile with more effort. "There's no new guards on the roster."

Rowan shrugged, instinct making her hyperaware of every breath Rough took. She watched the rise and fall of the woman's chest. Counting the breaths. "Someone must've called in sick then."

Rough laughed, the sound sharp and mean as feral cats. "You think I'm dumb enough to buy that?"

Rowan stared straight ahead saying nothing. What the hell was she going to do? Rough was so close she could see a shadow of hair on her upper lip just above surprisingly full lips that curved in a sensual cupid's bow. She looked away, flushing.

"I know how you got in here, and you aren't getting out without payment. I own you now, sweetcakes."

Rowan swallowed, her skin beginning to tingle with a familiar rush. "I'm just doing my job, ma'am."

"Yeah?" Rough asked conversationally, grabbing Rowan by the upper arm and perp-walking her to the end of the corridor. "Because a code yellow just came over my fucking radio, you complete fucking idiot. Someone stole Jerry's keycard and waltzed in here like they owned the place. Wasn't you now, was it?"

Rough had a vice grip on her arm and Rowan couldn't have run even if she wasn't trapped between the woman and a steel reinforced door. "No, ma'am."

Rowan's voice cracked. She'd end up in jail just like Sara, and then who would take care of her mom? Of Sawyer and Cameron? How had she fucked everything up so badly?

Rough swiped her keycard against the door at Rowan's back. "Inside. Now."

With little choice, Rowan stepped inside the shadowy room. Would she ever walk out again? Was her life really in the hands of this stranger who looked like she could do some serious damage with little more than the flick of her wrist? Grateful that her body responded to both panic and excitement in the same way, Rowan hid the rush that clouded her mind and the pulse that beat between her thighs behind the respectable veneer of fear. Anyone would be afraid. She should be afraid.

She wasn't.

Rough stepped in behind her and locked the door from the inside. "Yours has been deactivated."

Rowan dropped the useless card and looked around her cell. Some kind of breakroom with a sterile-looking stainless-steel kitchenette and a sagging couch tainted by patches of brown-colored *something* in the corner. She bit her lip, her stomach seizing at the thought of what she might have to do to get out. "Please. I'm sorry. Don't turn me in."

Probably useless to beg, but what choice did she have?

Rough pulled a pair of heavy-looking handcuffs from her belt. "*Don't turn me in.*"

She mimicked Rowan in a singsong voice, walking toward her and forcing Rowan to back toward the couch, toward…Oh God. Rowan felt the wetness begin to gather between her thighs and turned her head away.

"Please. I'm sure we can come to some kind of arrangement, ma'am. I'm very skilled."

Rough swung the handcuffs around on three fingers, barely missing hitting Rowan in the face. "Sure you are, sweetcakes. You're good for lying on your back and taking what you're given."

Rowan shook her head vigorously, eyeing the cuffs. "I'm gay. I've never given it up for a guy in my life, I swear. But you…" Rowan trailed off as the cuffs stopped swinging and Rough's eyes turned intense. "A woman like you, I can please. I'll show you if you let me go. Maybe…" Rowan sucked in air, her heart beating so fast she could only manage shallow gasps. Pushing her luck maybe, but the sneer had fallen off Rough's face for the first time. "We could make it a regular thing if you help my sister. If I meet your expectations, of course, ma'am."

"Is that why you broke in? For your sister?"

Rowan nodded. "She has two little kids. It's my fault she's here."

Rough's face contorted in a full-throated belly laugh that was somehow more demeaning than her words. "That's the dumbest thing I've heard all week, and the stupid bar is pretty fucking low around here." Still laughing, Rough's gaze slid down Rowan like the slimy tentacles of an octopus. "You know how to get a woman off?"

Rowan nodded again. "If you let me go, if you help my sister, I won't fight. You don't need those." She motioned to the handcuffs. "You don't have to force me. I want to please you, ma'am. Willingly. Don't you want to be with someone who likes it and doesn't fight you?"

Rowan could see the flame in Rough's eyes ignite and stifled a sigh of relief. Thank God Rough wasn't the type who liked to force. That would have been so much worse. This she could do. For Sara.

Yeah, right.

Rowan moaned. Rough's hard grip against the back of her head, drawing her down and between her legs, was almost real in her half-conscious state between sleep and waking. She willed herself back into the fantasy that she could pretend was her subconscious dreaming. Need tore at her skin and slipped into her soul. Chipped away at her bit by bit until she no longer recognized herself. This wasn't her, was it? This woman who dreamed of prison breaks and being blackmailed into sex by a woman who laughed in her face and treated her like an object? She had to be better than this. She had to…

Fuck it.

She didn't care. She didn't want to think, she wanted to ache and burn. To slip unnoticed into the pure, selfish pleasure of her own worst self and wallow heedlessly.

Rough's hands were on her skin, calloused palms snagging on the softness of her breasts. Rowan got on top, she wanted to watch Rough's face, watch the sweat drip from her own skin and land on

Rough. Watch what she could do to her. Rowan felt as if a jackal at a feeding frenzy lay beneath her, moaning and bucking, scrabbling and keening. Laughing like she couldn't believe her luck. There was a hot sticky mess on her thigh where Rough jerked against her. Fuck, this felt good. A finger of nausea poked into Rowan's stomach. Pleasure and sickness whirled in an angry tornado, destroying everything in its wake and leaving her helpless with wanting.

"You fucking love this, sweetcakes," Rough told her, a whining quality to her voice.

"Yes, ma'am," Rowan breathed. Rough's blind self-assurance made the outcome seem inevitable and that calmed her. Out of her control. She couldn't be held responsible for something out of her control.

Her head snapped back, and she felt the grunt before she'd heard it. She'd reached that heart-stopping instant where the world was ripped out from under her and she had no choice in the fall. Pleasure dove its merciless fingers into Rowan's soul, and she came on a cry that tore the breath from her throat and sent cascades of bone-chilling pleasure shivering down her spine.

Rowan lay as still as a corpse in the dreary room of Mrs. Penellie's house. If she didn't move, then what had happened hadn't actually happened. If it hadn't happened, she wouldn't have to think about it. If she didn't think about it, she could be the person she hoped she was. She could survive the interim between this fantasy and the next.

When the aftershocks of her orgasms subsided, and her heartbeat finally slowed, tears slipped down her cheeks and into her ears. Would she ever dare move again?

Genna ignored her buzzing phone as it danced its way across her desk and focused on the spreadsheet from hell in all its zillion column glory on her laptop screen. Only reflexes honed from years playing catcher on the Silver Creek recreational softball league had her swiping her phone mid-fall as it toppled off her desk. "Hello?"

"I can't believe you made me call you like some middle-aged Gen Xer," Grace said accusingly. "We need to talk to you."

Genna frowned. Was Mom okay? Were the twins safe? Had someone been hurt? "What's wrong?"

"Like, *everything*," Grace said unhelpfully. "Please?"

"Okay, okay."

Grace disconnected the call without saying good-bye as if phone calls made aging contagious.

Genna flicked through her home screen until she found the bright green app she'd downloaded because the twins refused to use anything else and hit video. Grace and Gabby came on screen together, sitting side-by-side against a blurred background. Genna's heart instantly backflipped into her throat. Gabby's eyes were red-rimmed, and Grace's usually perfectly straight brown hair could rival Bert and Ernie's for bedhead. "What's wrong? What happened? Is Mom okay?" Genna had risen half out of her chair and only the quizzical look on Gabby's face stopped her from racing to get an Uber.

"Of course, she is," Grace said like their mom was the kind who looked after them instead of the other way around. "We're calling you about *us*."

Genna slowly sat back down. "What's going on then?"

Gabby said in a tremulous voice thick with tears, "We just, like, *can't do anything*."

Grace rolled her eyes at her sister. "You're such a baby, Gabs." She turned to Genna, all business. "We need references for the landlord and proof of employment and the security deposit and, like, boxes to move and stuff and we have to get it all there somehow. Plus, they want us to clean the dorm room or we lose *that* security deposit." Grace wrinkled her nose delicately. "How do we even get all that stuff by next week with no money?"

Genna cursed the video gods that she couldn't close her eyes and bang her head against the wall like she wanted to. Instead, she reminded herself that learning how to be an adult was hard, especially when the adults in your life were struggling with it too. "Ask your resident advisor to write you a reference, they'll have a standard form. Go to your online account and download the transaction receipts from your last few cell phone bills. If you don't get a paystub from Fashion Forever, there are tons of online templates to make your own. I can lend you the security deposit until you clean the dorm and get that one back. Go to the campus food court for boxes or try the bookstore. You guys can do this stuff." Genna tried to sound encouraging, but her brain was screaming, *does Grace even know how much she pays in taxes at her minimum wage job at Fashion Forever?*

Gabby burst into actual tears and Grace just stared at Genna with pleading eyes. "The RA is a misogynist, the food court doesn't have clean boxes, and we can't make our own paystubs. It has to look *official*."

Genna succumbed to the inevitable. "I'll help you."

The twins smiled in unison, tears instantly forgotten, clearly having angled for this response. "Thank you, thank you, thank you. You're the best big sister in the entire world." Gabby flopped backwards out of range of the camera moaning "Thank God" loud enough for Genna to hear. Grace ran her fingers through her mussed hair. "Thanks."

Genna couldn't help but smile, her love for her sisters crowding out the hundred reasons she didn't have the time or money for this. If only she could call and have someone swoop in and save *her*, running their fingers through her life and smoothing out the tangles like Grace smoothed her hair. Everything back in place like nothing had ever happened. Rowan drenched with rain crouching down to open the hood of her car popped unbidden into her mind like a wet and sexy handywoman. Genna snorted. That was an anomaly. She'd been so pitiful that Rowan felt sorry for her. That wasn't the same as caring about her. Genna had never had anyone who cared for her like she cared for Grace and Gabby, which was exactly why she gave in to the twins' dramatics on a regular basis. They *could* do this without her, but everyone needed someone to rely on. Rowan's raincoat was still hanging neatly on her coatrack. She'd give it back to her at the first opportunity and forget it ever happened. Genna's best skill was needing people who had nothing to give, and she'd made that mistake too many times to count.

"Start packing and all the cleaning is on you guys. College dorms are gross."

"So gross," Gabby agreed. "Thanks, Gen. Love you."

"Love you too," Genna said to the blank screen. The twins had already ended the call. On to their next adventure. She glanced at the time. It was 2:55 p.m. Just enough time to splash water on her face and give herself a good old-fashioned don't-think-about-fucking-her pep talk before meeting Rowan.

As Genna walked down the hall toward the restroom, she ignored the bubble of anticipation at having her next adventure waiting in the lobby.

Chapter Ten

Rowan was going to puke all over Poppy's desk if she had to wait much longer for Genna to come get her for the first interview. Poppy had a cute desk too. She'd brightened the throwaway Ikea with a polka dot cupholder, a keyboard lit with rainbow lights, and a desk calendar that demanded one *seas the day* above an orange cartoon octopus. It'd be a shame to disgrace all that winsomeness with vomit, so she dealt with her queasiness by pacing back and forth across the waiting area of the gender and sexuality division. She had to *move* before she panicked.

Poppy was doing a very bad job pretending to work, and after a minute of hunt-and-peck typing, she gave Rowan an evaluating look. "There's no need to be scared. Genna's not that bad once you get to know her."

"I'm not scared," Rowan said automatically, even though scared was exactly what she was and *not that bad* was hardly a ringing endorsement.

"You're pale. You should sit before you fall on your face."

Rowan laughed despite herself. Poppy reminded her of Sara. Well, Sara twelve years ago. Young, smart, and just a little bit full of herself, but charming with it. That's where the similarities ended. Sara had been deep into her goth phase at that age and Poppy, well, her beauty was in your face. Her skin was so translucent she could be mistaken for a porcelain doll, especially with her sports car red lips and pink hair set in curls just like Frenchie in *Grease*.

Poppy was no beauty school dropout.

Most people would say Poppy was prettier than Sara, prettier than almost anyone, but to Rowan she didn't seem real, like an airbrushed advertisement for a quirky college student. *Not as beautifully real as Genna.* Rowan sighed. The more she tried *not* to think about her, the bigger the Genna-shaped elephant in her mind became. She took a deep breath to center herself and let the thought wash over her without resistance, trying to get rid of the Genna in her head before she had to face the real deal.

"I'm fine. Just…this feels weird."

Poppy rested her chin in her palm. "What does? Being nervous talking about your fantasies?"

Rowan leaned a hip on the corner of Poppy's desk. "You must talk about this kind of thing all the time. Me, not so much."

"Not really. Talking about sex in the psychological abstract is one thing, but personally about your own stuff? Not often. You got this, though. You've made it through the instruments, and Genna is a good researcher. You'll like her once you loosen up a bit." Poppy lifted one shoulder in a lopsided shrug.

"I already like her." *A lot, too much, inappropriate over-liking, if you know what I mean?*

Poppy raised her eyebrows, surprised. "Well, there you go. Just go in there and tell the truth. With the truth and your stunning good looks, you'll sail through."

Rowan raised her eyebrows right back. Did some people *not* like Genna. Why? "What do my looks have to do with anything?"

"Nothing at all." Poppy batted her eyelashes.

Rowan laughed. "Thanks, I think I needed that. God knows why, but I did."

"Making people less nervous is my superhero skill," Poppy said.

Rowan was just wondering if Poppy was queer or if she flirted with every poor schmuck who showed up on Genna's doorstep when Genna herself rounded the corner.

"Rowan?" Genna asked.

Rowan jumped from Poppy's desk like she'd been caught with her hand in the cookie jar. "Hi. You look great. Beautifully real."

Genna blinked. She looked at Poppy. Poppy just shrugged. Seemingly at a loss for how to respond Genna asked, "Shall we get started?"

Rowan nodded and followed Genna to her office in silence, lest anything else pop unbidden from her mouth.

Genna's office was the same as last time she'd been in it. A cramped hole-in-the-wall with a sturdy desk in tiger oak, two chairs that leaned more toward comfort than style, and a bookcase so full it overflowed a literary avalanche onto the floor. The blinds on the narrow window cast horizontal rays of sunshine on Genna's desk as she took the chair behind it and motioned for Rowan to sit opposite. "How're you feeling?"

"Like an idiot," Rowan said before realizing Genna was talking about her upcoming interview and not her comment. "I mean, a bit nervous, I guess."

"That's to be expected," Genna said. "I'll try to make things as comfortable as possible."

Rowan nodded. Anything Genna did to try to make her comfortable would likely have the opposite result. The problem was that Genna just being Genna had her squirming in her seat, nervous and excited and a little bit terrified. Genna's deep burgundy blazer, thrown over a silky-looking something with a deep V, wasn't helping at all. Rowan took another breath. Her attraction wasn't breaking news. She could deal. To be honest, one of the most exciting things about Genna was the way Rowan's response never seemed to normalize. The rush of want startled her with its intensity as raw today as when she'd first met her.

With her ex, her desire had eroded over time, familiarity chipping away at it, the person behind her expectations emerging as more ordinary than before. That was the thing about fairy tales. They never fully satisfied. When Claudia was offered a promotion requiring a relocation, she'd asked Rowan to follow—a passenger in Claudia's master plan. She wished she'd stood her ground, said no. But she hadn't had the guts. She'd said nothing and that had been answer enough. A boring finale to a relationship that had once held so much promise.

With Genna, just being in the same room had her tingling, she couldn't imagine ever being bored. *Any chance you could be less sexy for the next hour while I reveal my depravity? Pretty please?*

Genna placed her iPhone on the desk between them. "I'm going to start the recording, is that okay?"

Rowan nodded. "Sure."

Genna tapped the screen. "Three p.m. Week one, interview one, participant 47C."

She smiled at Rowan. "Would you be open to telling me what you were just thinking? You don't have to."

Rowan bit her lip. "Just now? Isn't this interview about your research?" *Aka you so don't want to know what I was just thinking, Dr. I'll Ask Anything.*

"It is. But we'll practice first. You assured me you'll be honest with me, and we'll work up to the harder stuff. You just had the most pensive expression, so I'd like to start there if that's okay. Tell me what you were thinking."

Rowan swallowed. How on earth was she going to be honest without making it all about Genna *on the record*? "Uh…I was thinking about my fantasies." She paused, trying to pull thoughts together faster than her brain could compile them. "I was thinking how physical attraction, even in fantasy, tends to fade kind of quickly. Does everyone experience that, or just me?"

Genna picked up a pen and twirled it between her fingers thoughtfully. "Often the truth lies somewhere between what everyone experiences and complete uniqueness. What do you think? Does physical attraction ultimately fade for everyone?"

"It changes, maybe. But it doesn't always fade. My friend, Maria. She and her wife have been married for years, and they're still having sex even after kids."

Genna nodded. "So, what about you? You've been in at least one relationship. How did your physical attraction change?"

Rowan hadn't expected a brain teaser right off the bat, but she wasn't nervous anymore, so that was something. "At first, it's easy, spontaneous. We ripped each other's clothes off and didn't have to try. That's the stuff of romance novels, right? A grand passion?"

Genna lobbed the question back at her again. "You tell me."

Rowan laughed. "Come on. Answer at least one. Anyone who watches *The Bachelor* must read romance novels."

"I've read a few where the spunky but clueless heroine gets taken hostage by an unhinged stalker and is rescued by a rugged cop who broke all the rules to save the day and steal her heart." A twinkle sparked in Genna's eyes, but Rowan couldn't tell if she was joking.

"No way." Rowan leaned forward, mock outraged on these fictional characters' behalf. "Your favorite trope is rogue first responder meets too stupid to live?"

Genna shrugged. "Hopefully not that stupid. As *Romeo and Juliet* teaches us, there's a fine line between romance and tragedy."

A thousand questions battled for supremacy in Rowan's brain. Genna liked romance novels about damsels in distress being saved. Odd considering she'd been so resistant to the smallest offer of help last night. Odd too that someone as confident and capable as Genna, as presumably *feminist*, would find damsels damseling attractive. Or maybe her taste in fiction didn't mirror her romantic preferences? One of those fantasies she'd never want to act on? Or was she the cop in this scenario and not the damsel? Annoying to have to answer all the questions without permission to ask her own.

"So, back to the topic." Genna's voice got that professional undertone again. "For you a relationship usually starts with spontaneous passion. Then what?"

"Then…" Rowan thought back on her relationship with Claudia. How easily turned on she was in the early days and how after a while it took work to get there. "That instantaneous physical response dims a bit. Not all the way, and not all at once, but over time sex is less about mind-blowing orgasms and more about being close, being in love, maintaining the emotional connection through sex. With a side of orgasms." Rowan shrugged. "I'm not sure that makes sense. But it's because Claudia and I weren't right for each other."

Another twirl of Genna's pen. "A common theory in sex research suggests uncertainty and novelty enhance desire. That sex is spontaneous in the beginning of a relationship because it's new, and you're unsure how your partner feels about you. Your connection is growing and inherently unstable. Over time, as the relationship solidifies, and sex becomes habitual. Desire fades."

Rowan took a minute to process…that truckload of bullshit. "Are you saying we can have either great sex or a great relationship, but not both?"

Genna shook her head. "As you've already established, plenty of people have great sex in great relationships. But that doesn't mean there isn't work involved. It's all about reintroducing uncertainty and novelty back into the bedroom."

Rowan bit back her instinctual denial. Trying not to argue, but also really wanting to argue. "You're talking about hate sex."

Genna tilted her head to the side. "Am I?"

"You know what I mean. You're having a fight with your girlfriend, and they're just so damn frustrating, but somehow that gets tangled up in how beautiful they are when they're angry and you just have to fuck them. It's so much hotter."

Genna breathed out in a rush like she hadn't quite been expecting that, but then pointed her pen at Rowan. "Perfect example. When a couple has a disagreement, there's a sense the relationship is on shaky ground. The negative emotions you're feeling are atypical, giving the sex novelty."

Rowan frowned. "But if that's all true, don't you find it depressing? That something so crucial to a relationship is so hard to maintain and so easily influenced by just about anything?"

"I don't find it depressing, no. Sex isn't crucial to everyone and a lot of things in life are hard to maintain and subject to outside influences. Doesn't mean they aren't worth it. Why do you find it depressing?"

Rowan sat back, thoroughly deflated. None of this felt right. There was some truth tucked away in there somewhere, for some relationships that weren't meant to be, but that only made it worse. If they weren't all striving for the grand passion promised in romance novels, TV commercials, and *The* fucking *Batchelor*, what was the point? She had to believe true love made sex fantastic because, well, why bother otherwise?

"I don't know," Rowan said. "I just do. It makes me sad you believe this. I want grand passion, not just in the beginning, but forever. I want a soul mate. Spending your relationship trying to restore what was once so effortless sounds miserable."

They didn't speak for a few moments. Rowan had just lost something that she'd taken for granted and never knew she ought to have treasured. The silence confirmed Genna really believed what she'd said and had nothing left to explain. Long term, sex drive dies unless you resuscitate it on the regular. Bed death for everyone. It couldn't be true. Sure, Rowan had experienced it herself, but that's because Claudia wasn't the one. Didn't everyone have that one special person they were meant to be with? The one who made passion effortless?

Rowan met Genna's eyes as they each stood on the precipice of their beliefs with no bridge to meet in the middle. The sinking in her stomach signaled she was dealing with more than physical attraction. She hadn't been lying when she'd said she wanted to ask Genna out once the study was over.

Genna was by-the-book and guarded, doing everything in her power to keep Rowan at arm's length. But she was also beautiful and smart, with a wary sort of vulnerability behind her charming but prickly exterior that hinted at hard knocks and hard work. Rowan couldn't help being intrigued. But could she date her when Genna fully expected their passion would fade and she was *fine* with it? Just throw in a new restaurant and a blindfold every so often to keep things interesting? Was Genna even monogamous? How could someone who liked sex *be* monogamous under those circumstances? Did she just settle for boring? Did everyone?

Genna wasn't her Cleopatra/Marilyn fantasy, but maybe everything Rowan thought she knew about her, had *assumed* about her because she'd wanted it to be true, was a fantasy too. The worst kind.

Genna sighed softly. She dropped her pen. "Do you want to continue?"

Rowan didn't want to talk to Genna right now. *Why aren't you who I thought you should be? My perfect somebody?*

When she didn't say anything, Genna leaned over and tapped the screen of her phone to pause the recording. "Would you prefer to leave? The door is right there, and the choice is yours."

Seriously? Genna had tromped all over her admittedly way too soon—and clearly unfounded—hopes for a date, and now she was kicking her out?

"I don't want to leave," Rowan said, more to argue than because it was true.

"Okay. Then we have a couple of choices. We can stay off the record, and you can tell me why your fantasies are a problem for you, or I can turn the recorder back on, and we can proceed with the interview the way I would for any other participant, keeping to the standard questions. What's your preference?"

What *was* her preference? To leave? To be Average Jane study participant? Or to bare her soul to Genna? Why was everything suddenly complicated? Maybe because she was the one making it complicated.

Rowan rubbed a hand over her face. "I'm sorry. I'm being unfair, aren't I? We don't agree on this…sex thing, and I'm making it personal when it shouldn't be."

Genna gave a tilt of her head that basically said *yep, pretty much that exactly*. "Now you see why it's a problem for us to get to know one another outside of the study." She smiled wryly. "Hopes get dashed."

Rowan grabbed onto that last part like a lifeline. "Wait. *Your* hopes are dashed?"

You had hopes? About me?

"Well, it does throw a bucket of ice water over things for us to disagree on something so fundamental."

For some reason, Genna admitting that she too was disappointed helped. A lot. At least Rowan wasn't alone. That proved she cared just as much as Rowan did. Maybe this wasn't a total catastrophe. "Sometimes a little disagreement isn't such a bad thing. I bet you're even more gorgeous when you're angry. I hear arguments help to keep the passion alive."

Rowan held her breath and the metaphorical olive branch as she waited for Genna's reply.

Genna gave her that look she was growing to love. The *did you really just say that, cowboy*? look.

Rowan's stomach climbed up into her throat. *Come on, Dr. Stupid Sex Theory, meet me in the middle.*

"It's up to you. But if you want to stay and tell me more about your fantasies, I'd like that," Genna said eventually, her tone cautious.

Rowan leaned forward and grabbed Genna's hand where it rested on desk before she could move it out of reach. "I'd like that too. I shouldn't have taken that so personally. I'm sorry."

Genna nodded, gave her fingers a quick squeeze, then unceremoniously dropped Rowan's hand, and squared her shoulders. "You ready?"

Was she ready to tell Genna everything right when they'd discovered a chasm that could make anything more between them impossible? Rowan was about to find out.

"I've been ready since the moment you agreed to this."

The look again. Always with the look.

Chapter Eleven

Genna wasn't at all sure she was making the right decision. Rowan's reaction to a perfectly legitimate theory had been intense. Intensely passionate. Intensely personal. Intensely over the line. But Genna was just as responsible for putting them here. That she had more experience keeping her reactions to herself didn't exactly let her off the hook. She'd felt the same punch to the gut that had spread across Rowan's features. God save her from women who'd grown up on too many Cinderella stories and expected happiness to be custom wrapped in a single person. *Soul mates*, really? That crap was too corny even for romance novels. As if love would solve every problem. Or any problem. In her experience love created them. You know what was actually depressing? How many people weren't willing to work on a relationship. They just dumped and ran, moving on with all their rose-tinted expectations and demanded their next victim be the superhuman their last wasn't. It just completely, totally sucked that Rowan might be one of those people. Couldn't she see she was being unreasonable?

Okay, so maybe Genna was also being a bit intense. She had no idea if that was even why Rowan and her ex had split. The ex had moved for a job, hadn't she?

They were in this now, and she'd agreed to help. So that's what she'd do.

She absolutely had not agreed to continue because Rowan's graphic description of hate sex was blow-her-brain-cells hot. Not that hate sex even existed. No couple who loved each other ever really *hated.* But she and Rowan agreed on something. Intense emotion, be it joy or frustration, made sex so, so good. She absolutely wasn't thinking about frustrated, how-could-you-believe-that sex with Rowan. A relationship would never work, but frustrated not-hate sex…

"Genna?"

Genna flushed. *Get your head in the game.* "Sorry. I need to record the part that is for my research, so before I turn the recorder back on, I'd like to discuss the fantasies you'd like help with."

Genna didn't glance at her iPad with all its questions, her attention one hundred percent on Rowan.

Rowan swallowed the balloon rapidly swelling in her throat. Genna was looking at her in a completely normal way, but she still squirmed under the scrutiny. She'd wanted this. One-on-one sessions with the *super-hot researcher* as Maria had put it. But now that she was here, she couldn't quite meet Genna's gaze. "I know you have a job to do, so my stuff can wait."

As long as you want. Forever was an option. *Why* had she pushed Genna into this again?

Genna gave her a can-we-skip-the-bullshit look. "You sought me out for this. I'm not going anywhere, and I have all afternoon. If I can help you, I will." She looked away briefly before bringing that focus back to Rowan with a sheepish smile. "Honestly, I'm a bit nervous myself. I need more experience talking to people beyond ask-and-answer style, and my advisor thinks this is a good opportunity to hone my skills. So, let's do the hard part first, and then we can enjoy the easy part."

Genna had talked about her with her advisor? Well, of course she had. That's what PhD students did. And, oh God, wasn't Genna's advisor the elegant woman from Happy Hour? Rowan wanted to curl up and die. She was a subject to be talked about. Discussed. Analyzed. Psychologically dissected. She'd somehow forgotten that Genna was *studying her*. "Easy for you maybe."

Genna leaned forward and rested her elbow on the desk, her chin in her palm like she wanted to inspect Rowan under a microscope.

"Wasn't it you who said we're just people? Just two students? It doesn't have to be intimidating. Tell me like you'd tell a friend."

Sure, easy-peasy, if only she'd told a friend. Or anyone. Ever. "I don't know where to start."

"What makes you feel your fantasies are so bad?" As was her way, Genna struck right to the heart.

"They're…" Rowan fought to find the right words. "They're just not okay. I fantasize about things that would be illegal, would be *hurtful* if they were real, and it gets me off. I'm flexible when it comes to what makes me hot. But the bad fantasies get me off the hardest. Put me in a relationship, and I want all the romance I can handle, but my fantasies? They're disgusting. The opposite of romance. But, hotter."

The line between Genna's brows formed as she frowned. "Disgusting is a strong word."

Rowan shrugged. She *was* disgusting. The irony of having to tell Genna, who sent her want-you-o-meter into the stratosphere, wasn't lost on her, but what choice did she have? If Genna and all her research couldn't help her, no one could.

"Give me an example."

And this was the part she'd really been avoiding. The exampling. Somehow saying it out loud brought it all into the real world, when it had only ever existed in her mind. Rowan took a long, careful breath. She was more than a little terrified Genna would laugh at her again, but she *had* to figure this out. She could trust Genna, couldn't she?

"A few nights ago, I fantasized I had broken into prison and had gotten caught by a guard. A large, not particularly attractive guard, who threatened me, demeaned me, and blackmailed me into having sex with her on the floor of a questionably clean break room."

"Submission and humiliation fantasies aren't uncommon," Genna said.

Rowan let out the breath when Genna looked completely unfazed. Not even a brief flicker of surprise. She shook her head. "It's not about being in *her* control. If anything, I am the one in control, at the end anyway. On top. Making her come. But it doesn't feel like it's about power, even though that's the setup."

"You said you broke *into* the prison? Why?"

Heat curled up Rowan's neck. Why was everyone so hung up on that? "I was trying to get someone out. A prison break. I failed."

"Someone?" Genna asked.

"Someone." Rowan had agreed to share her fantasy secrets, not every terrible thing that had ever happened. Maybe she really could trust Genna with this stuff, but Sara was off limits.

Genna waited another beat and then moved on. "What's it about then? What turns you on?"

"Just how fucked up it is. I'm not attracted to her. But not being attracted to her, being repulsed by her even, and doing it anyway, is the appeal. I know that sounds stupid, but it's like the more horrible my brain can make it, the harder I come. When she orgasms it's almost like she's an animal. Like we're both just animals, acting on our instincts."

Genna nodded slowly. "Isn't there a whole genre dedicated to basically this? Humans embracing their animal instincts by turning into them? Like, Dracula or Frankenstein?"

Rowan tried not to laugh. Genna had the entire paranormal genre at her fingertips, and she'd picked Dracula? The 1800s were calling and wanted their undead back. "I think you mean Edward… or Jacob."

Genna looked blank. "Who?"

Genna read romance novels and really didn't know? "*Twilight*? Although maybe Spike from *Buffy the Vampire Slayer* is the most popular vampire. I'm not sure."

"*Buffy the—*" Genna cut herself off. "The tiny blonde who fights demons before homeroom?"

"After homeroom," Rowan corrected. "Vampires come out at night. Sunlight being deadly and all."

"Why are we talking about Buffy?"

"Because apparently the only TV you watch is *The Batchelor*. Did you live under a rock as a teenager? We're going to have to remedy this. Buffy is iconic. I'm jealous you still have all eight seasons to watch for the first time." *Maybe we can watch it together after our mashed potato grand championship. Snuggle on the couch.*

A shadow passed across Genna's face, and Rowan instantly regretted whatever she'd said to cause it. Here she was planning their first date, and Genna clearly wasn't interested in watching TV. Curiosity pulled at her. "Hey, I'm sor—"

"Give me another example." Genna redirected the conversation away from herself.

And they were back to exampling. Didn't Genna realize how damn hard this was—how humiliating, how stripped naked Rowan felt? If Genna could just talk to her like a real person it would be so much easier. Like friends, Genna had said, but it didn't feel that way.

Another long breath. The second time would be easier. She wished Genna was sitting next to her instead of behind the desk.

"My parents have rented their condo from the same married couple for over thirty years. I know because they've always made their rent check out to Mr. and Mrs. David Sutton. Sometimes I fantasize that Mrs. Sutton, who I've never met in real life, becomes obsessed with me. Full on stalker. Follows me everywhere. Installs cameras in my home to watch me. In the fantasy, I'm still in a relationship with my girlfriend and Mrs. Sutton watches us have sex on the hidden cameras. She learns what I like. She uses the information to seduce me." Rowan lifted a shoulder to signal her distaste. "I cheat on the woman I'm supposed to love with a crazy psycho, and the sex is *good.* A lot better than with Claudia. I fantasize about how good it is to cheat. What kind of stupid-ass fantasy is that? Am I so insecure I have to pretend people are obsessed with me?"

"Do you think you're insecure about your attractiveness?" Genna asked.

Rowan held Genna's gaze without saying anything. *We've already admitted it's there between us. So between us, we need this desk as a barrier. Isn't that right, Dr. Sex?*

A muscle twitched in Genna's jaw, but her gaze never wavered. "Rowan?"

God. Her name on Genna's lips did things to her. So did her take-no-prisoners interrogation.

"Isn't everyone a bit insecure about their attractiveness? It's not like women go around comparing me to gods."

The corner of Genna's lips tilted in a tiny smile but she didn't crack. "Regardless, I don't get the impression you routinely feel a high degree of insecurity. Would that be accurate?"

"Regular amounts of insecurity only."

Genna nodded, picked up her pen again, and started twirling it between her fingers, thinking…who knew what. That was the problem.

"It gets worse," Rowan said in a morose tone that was only partly for effect.

"Tell me."

"I call her Mrs. Sutton when I fuck her. *Mrs. Sutton*, like I'm a kid, and not a thirty-two-year-old having very adult sex with a woman who has a first name."

To her credit, Genna didn't laugh. "Have you tried calling her something else?"

Rowan nodded. "It feels wrong."

"Is the sex similar to the sex you have with the prison guard?"

"No. The stalker is completely into me. The sex is everything I like and she's very…attentive. It's not candlelight and soft music, but it's not rough either. She's just, you know, a manipulative bitch. Which I guess I must find hot." *Why do I find that hot? Why would anyone?*

Genna nodded. "Why does she stalk you? Is there a reason?"

Rowan sat back, never having thought about that before. "When the fantasy starts, she's already obsessed. I never ask her why."

"Do you find it strange that she decides to stalk you so intimately out of the blue?"

That was the part Genna found strange?

Rowan had no answer.

There was silence as Genna thought. Tapping the pen against her iPad distractedly.

"So, what's the verdict? Am I a hopeless case?" The words sounded much smaller than they would have if Rowan were able to pull off the cavalier tone she'd intended.

"Not a hopeless case. But I don't see enough similarities in these examples to have any clear indication of what attracts you to them yet. I'd like to think about it some more. There's a book I want to find that has a case study that's niggling at me. It's interesting you chose your parents' landlord's wife, a woman you've never met, as the focus of your fantasy. That's quite a few degrees of separation and unusual. Do you know the prison guard?"

"No." It hadn't ever occurred to Rowan to wonder why she'd chosen either woman.

"Interesting," Genna said, and Rowan believed she meant it.

"Do people usually fantasize about someone they know?" Rowan asked.

"There's no usually. Some people do exclusively, some never do. Many will fantasize about someone they find attractive, both in appearance and/or personality, if they haven't acted on the attraction. First dates. Secret crushes. Your best friend's wife. That kind of thing is more likely to lead to a higher occurrence of fantasies starring someone you know, according to self-report data."

"So, if two people are attracted to each other, but can't act on it, for ethical reasons related to a research study, they're more likely to fantasize about each other than about a stranger?" Rowan asked, all innocence.

Genna sat up straighter, her expression revealing her total sense of humor failure. "We can't discuss that."

Rowan knew her quip had just crossed a line, or maybe crossed the desk, and even though she hadn't meant it all that seriously, she didn't care. She was too exposed. She needed Genna closer, and if Rowan had to drag her, so be it. "You're saying the instability of our attraction, its forbidden nature, not being able to act on our desires, is what makes it hot. And if we could act on them, our feelings would, what, just *go away*?"

Genna closed her eyes briefly. "Are we back here again? That is *not* what I said. I was talking about people in general and their made-up fantasies."

"Twice now we have agreed that we are people. Do *you* have fantasies? Or are researchers immune to the commonalities that afflict regular humans?" *Did you fantasize about me after our rainy encounter, Dr. Sex?*

"Researchers ask the questions," Genna said curtly, her eyes going to ice. "I'm sorry, but you need to stop this. Most especially here and now, when we should focus on what you've just shared."

Rowan had known she was pushing too hard even as she was asking, but she didn't have the energy to cast aside her irritation in favor of her better judgment one more time. She was supposed to sit here and spill her guts about the very worst things about herself, and Genna got to hide behind her walls? No, not walls, a freaking moat. Rowan had better just forget about ever getting inside Genna's castle. Silly of her to forget she was the one being studied like a lab rat in a cage, and Genna had the power to deny her every question.

Anger swirled sour bile in her throat. That she was overreacting was obvious even to her. But she couldn't let it go. She *agreed* with Genna that their flirting had to wait. But what was the point of waiting when they weren't compatible long term anyway? They weren't going to date once this was all over because Rowan needed something Genna didn't think was possible. Rowan wanted that one person she knew was out there, and no one who believed that sex in relationships was some kind of homework assignment would be right for her.

Rowan didn't care what self-report data said. True love and true passion could coexist. She had to believe that. "Turn on the recorder. That's why we're here."

Genna rubbed a hand across her face in a fuck-my-life gesture and suddenly looked about as tired as when Rowan had first met her. "Let's back up a minute. You have questions about what your fantasies and your beliefs might mean for you in future relationships. I'm sorry I snapped at you. I took your questions personally. I did warn you I wasn't good at this."

"From my perspective, you didn't take them personally enough."

Genna was looking at her like she was a two-year old throwing a tantrum in the candy aisle of the grocery. Like she just didn't *get* whatever there was to get. "This can't be about me. I'm sorry that bothers you, but I could get in hot water for revealing that kind of information to a study participant. I thought we were on the same page about that."

Revealing that kind of information. Like she was CIA or something. "Your recorder isn't on. Right now, I'm not a study participant. I'm a *person* who shared personal and shameful *information* with you and just wanted to know you understand what it's like to have fantasies and desires too, even if you expect them to evaporate. I didn't mean to ask you to reveal anything inappropriate. I just need to know you get what I'm going through. That you get me."

She wasn't being entirely fair. Her questions *had* been about them. But was it so hard for Genna to admit she had fantasies? That she understood what it was like to *want* the way Rowan wanted her? That she was human too?

"I…" Genna opened her mouth and closed it again.

"Just turn on the recorder. Let's get this done."

"I'm sorry. Really. I can't give you what you want."

"I know. I won't ask again."

Genna turned on the recorder.

Chapter Twelve

Genna slid onto a stool at McKinney's and nodded her hello to Daryl the bartender, whose bald head shone like an ocean pearl in the overhead light. He'd have been at home with the Hells Angels and was the nicest guy in the room. When he set her usual down in front of her, Genna asked, "How's Amy doing?"

Daryl shook his head. "She's doing very, very pregnant. I'm supposed to stay the hell away from her except for when I don't pay her enough attention and should stick like glue. We're counting the days until she pops."

"It's the hormones," Genna said, making it sound like a question because what did she know about pregnancy.

Daryl nodded. "The hormones. I'll get my wife back once the little bundle makes it out. You alone tonight?"

"So far. Quiet for a Friday."

Daryl looked up at the industrial-style loft ceiling like he could see through the roof. "It's the weather. No one wants to drive in the rain."

The storms that'd been rolling through on and off for days now suited Genna's mood. "That's just lazy."

Daryl laughed and toasted her with an empty shot glass before sliding it back onto the stack. As he moved down the bar to serve someone else, he added, "Have a safe night, Casanova. I hope you find what you're looking for."

What *was* she looking for? Not sex. She'd been holed up listening to her recordings and coding data since Rowan had walked out of her office days ago. Trying to forget the disastrous interview. The hurt on Rowan's face. The *I shared shameful information with you and just wanted to know you understand* soundtrack that had been playing on repeat in her head. God.

She'd done *nothing* to reassure Rowan. Too caught up in the puzzle of it all, in her disappointment that Rowan believed in *the one*, to remember she was there to *help*. She was starting to realize Rowan believed a soul mate would somehow make her fantasies go away. As if finding the right person would cure her. And what had Genna done? Not only fail to reassure Rowan her fantasies weren't wrong, but she'd also shot down the only thing giving Rowan hope at the worst possible time. All because Rowan had thrown some personal questions at her, and she hadn't had the objectivity to see Rowan's pain. And all of that because she fucking *wanted her* and couldn't seem to stop. She was terrible at responding to Rowan's emotional pain, couldn't manage her own boundaries, and never should have agreed to try in the first place.

By the time nine o'clock rolled around, she couldn't stand herself anymore. So, it was either McKinney's or her mom's for company.

The stool beside her scraped the old wooden floor, and Genna's heart sank a little as she turned with her best friendly, small-talk smile.

"Save your smiles, it's just me." Travis nodded to Daryl and was presented a beer without asking just as Genna had been. Travis's acorn brown hair, usually well-behaved in a preppy classic crew cut, had been tousled by the weather, giving him an attractive windblown look any woman would've killed for.

"Oh, thank God." Genna hadn't realized how much she really didn't want to make sexy small talk until she didn't have to.

Travis gave her a quizzical look. "Did I just save you from some dude who doesn't know you can't stand macho?"

"No one can stand macho. But no. Just happy to see you."

Travis took a long pull from his beer. "What gives?"

"What do you mean?"

"I mean, you're sitting alone in an almost empty bar, nursing a drink you haven't even started, and when a hottie *doesn't* sit next to you, you thank God. So, what gives?"

I didn't want to be alone.

"We're friends. Are we not friends?" Genna tried not to be hurt that Travis thought her being glad to see him was so out of character it warranted a *what gives.*

"Sure," Travis said. "We're as friendly as you want us to be."

"What is that supposed to mean?" She hadn't meant the question as a grenade, but it came out as one. Now she wasn't *friendly*?

Travis shot a hand up to shield his heart. "I wasn't saying anything. Just that you're not usually looking for a friend. Don't get me wrong, this place is a *joint,* but some people, they just want someone to be close to for a while, whether that's sex or friendship or whatever. You, though. It's physical and transactional. That's all I meant."

"Wow." Genna infused the word with more sarcasm than necessary. "That's all you meant?"

Was she the world's worst human suddenly?

Travis stopped looking at her and began peeling the label off his beer. "You going to sit there spitting fire at me for calling it as I see it, or are you going to tell me what's wrong?"

Genna found she couldn't look at him either. "I'm a nice person. A hell of a lot nicer than most people who come through here."

"I never said you weren't nice. I'll even add interesting and motivated to give people what they want. That's more than *anyone* who comes through here."

"And yet, I'm transactional." Her bitterness weighed the words down.

"What would you call a one-way street? You *are* nice. But it's hard to get to know you."

Genna shook her head. "That's not true." *Was it?*

"How long have we been coming here?"

"Almost a decade."

"Name five personal things you've told me about yourself," Travis said.

Genna frowned. They'd been friends for *ten years,* and he wanted five things? Too easy. "You know what I do for a living and that I'm in school."

Travis nodded. "They're the same thing, so that's one."

"You know my type," Genna said, because everyone seemed to.

"You didn't tell me that. I put it together myself from who you left with and what people said about you."

"No, you didn't. I told you. Didn't I tell you?"

"No." Travis said bluntly. "I'm not saying it's a problem, because it isn't. Not for me. Not until now when it seems to be a problem for you."

She'd been going to the same bar as Travis for a decade, and she hadn't even told him her *type*? She didn't believe it. Except she couldn't remember ever telling him. God. Her friends weren't even friends, because she couldn't share something so completely trivial. Genna's throat swelled to signal tears, and she stared holes into the bar top trying to get herself under control. *Do. Not. Cry.*

She could feel Travis looking at her and then his chair legs scraped again, and his arm came around her shoulders. "Is it okay if I do this?"

She nodded.

"I'd like to upgrade our friendship, if you'll let me," Travis said more gently. "What gives, Casanova?"

Genna took a breath. So much of her wanted to shrug it off. Make a bad joke about Travis hitting on her, shove him away, and go home to deal with her personality crisis herself. Alone. Like always. But Rowan, and now Travis, saying she was basically a robot was too much for her to handle alone.

"I had a rough interview at work. The participant, she wanted my advice about some personal concerns, and I agreed to help her if I could. But once she had told me everything, stuff that was difficult for her to reveal, she asked me something personal along the same lines, and I…I was cold. I basically said it was none of her business, and that I would be asking the questions."

Travis squeezed her shoulder. "Well, devil's advocate, you're not obligated to tell her. She's the one who came to you asking for help, right?"

Genna nodded. "Yes, but…"

Travis waited.

"I fucking want to do a whole lot of physical, not-entirely-transactional things with her and wasn't even in the neighborhood of objective researcher."

Travis started to laugh and coughed to try to hide it.

"No, no, go ahead and laugh. It's a comedy. From the second I saw her, she hit all my buttons. Sex on legs, and sweet and nice to boot. Kryptonite."

"She sounds divine," Travis said.

"It gets worse." Genna stole Rowan's line and the tone she'd used. "She wants me too, though God only knows why. We've been flirting, but not flirting, since day one even though we absolutely shouldn't, and she…pushes."

"Pushes?" Travis asked.

"If you ask me a question and I change the subject, you just let it go. She nudges and maneuvers and pushes until I get irritated with her, or I give in to whatever stupid thing she wants to know. I couldn't give in this time, so irritation won."

"What stupid thing?"

"Like what my favorite meal is."

Travis used his hand on her shoulder to turn her toward him. "She had to push you to tell her what your favorite meal is?"

"I told her. I ended up telling her a lot of stuff I didn't intend to."

"Oh, Casanova."

"So, my telling her that something personal…something about my fantasies—which really *should* have been off-limits considering the circumstances—was none of her business was harsh. She'd wanted reassurance that she wasn't alone. That I understood how she felt because I had fantasies too. But what she actually asked felt personal and accusatory and now here I am sniping at you."

Travis let his arm slide off her shoulder and turned fully to face her. "Alright. You get some asshole points. But I've been to enough of these rodeos to know that when a woman you've been flirting with says *Do you fantasize?* what she really means is *Do you fantasize about me?* Can we assume there was that subtext?"

"Yes," Genna conceded. Rowan had teased her with the quip about them feeling attracted and not acting on it. "But it's not like I had to say *Hell yes, I fantasize that you're the lead drummer in a chart-topping mega band and I'm the groupie of the week.*"

Travis grinned. "As the second personal thing you've told me about yourself, that's a good one. Groupie, huh? Nice. What happens next?"

Genna ignored him. "I didn't have to say that. All I had to say was *Yes, like most of the population, I fantasize too, so I understand what that's like. You're not alone.* And it didn't even cross my mind she needed that."

Travis drained his beer. "The way I see it, you both made a mistake. Considering what she revealed, you perhaps should've clued in that she was feeling vulnerable, reassured her, and given her a pass on the rest. But if she wanted reassurance, she shouldn't have asked for it in the context of your fantasies about her. She had to know you couldn't tell her that."

Had Rowan known? Genna had *thought* Rowan understood they couldn't take their attraction any further than they had already. But maybe she'd been wrong.

"This is *exactly* why I can't get involved with participants. Even if there isn't a power imbalance, which there can be when someone makes themselves vulnerable that way, and it wasn't treading the edge of unethical even when it's not a therapeutic situation, it screws things up."

"Not arguing. But you can't help who you're attracted to. And be honest with yourself. If she wasn't the type to push, you'd be sitting in a bar with her years from now bitching that you're not friends."

Genna poked him in the ribs. "We upgraded that."

"She pushes, and that's the only reason you even know her well enough to like more than her boobs, or whatever it is you like on women."

"Definitely boobs." Genna laughed.

"So, wait until she's done participating in your research, but maybe then you'll ask her on an actual date. She might just push you into a feeling or two."

Genna thought about that. It sounded…not as terrifying as she expected. But could she go there when they had totally opposite views? Well, they'd no doubt argue and make up, because Rowan would be so damn frustrating. But then that would get all tangled up with how gorgeous Rowan would be when she was angry, and she'd just have to fuck her. Genna swallowed, completely sure she'd never get untangled from Rowan's description of hate sex. "You know, I really do want to date her. Even though I'd be a major disappointment."

Travis looked at her for a long moment. "Perhaps try the date and let her decide how she feels."

He rose to leave, but Genna put a hand on his arm. Something else was bothering her. "You and I, we've never had sex with each other."

"Sherlock, your observational powers amaze me."

Genna brushed that away. "Does it bother you that we're ten years in and this is the longest conversation we've had? That we've never been more than each other's wingman?"

"I wouldn't say it's bothered me. I nursed some mild disappointment in the beginning, but that went away once your preference became clear."

"I'm not only attracted to women."

"Your preference for not being touched. That would bother me."

Genna nodded. That would probably bother most people. "I'm glad we're friends. We could talk more sometime if you wanted to."

Travis stood and pushed his stool in toward the bar. "Anytime. Maybe one day you'll tell me how your desire not to be touched is connected to your fear of being a major disappointment."

The bottom fell out of Genna's stomach. "No. I—"

"But right now," Travis interrupted her, "I have to hustle if I want to chat up gorgeous Ms. Blue Eyes before she leaves with Sam instead."

"Have a safe night," Genna echoed the phrase they all used to remind themselves of the inherent dangers of being alone and vulnerable with near-strangers.

"Casanova?" Travis said.

"Yeah?"

"Make sure you tell Rowan you want to date after the study. Everyone wants to be wanted for more than their boobs."

❖

Genna's brains were going to start leaking out her ears. She was about to have an iPhone covered in gray matter and an empty bank account. "What do you mean it'll be three hundred dollars? That's highway robbery."

"You want a Ram and you don't prebook, it's three hundred a day." How-Can-I-Help-You-Today-Toby wasn't helping her at all, frankly. Working customer service at Rent-a-Ride probably came with a whole lot of problems that had nothing to do with cars, and Genna's budget was surely the least interesting. She didn't have three hundred.

"What do you have that's cheaper?"

"I can do you a Chevy for two fifty." Toby continued to be enormously unhelpful.

Genna groaned. "Will it fit a mattress do you think?"

"I'm not sure, ma'am." Toby had no fucks to give and Genna couldn't blame him.

The buzzer on her apartment's intercom saved her from blowing all her cash on the world's second most expensive rental truck. "I'll have to call you back."

If she was going to get to the twins' dorm by midmorning, she'd have to hustle. She pressed the audio on her intercom. "Hello?"

"Genna, it's Rowan. Can you come down for a moment?"

Genna's stomach summersaulted and then flopped back into place. *Rowan.* She couldn't think of a single reason Rowan would be at her place at eight o'clock on a Saturday morning. Not a single good reason, anyway. "Is everything okay?"

"Yes, of course."

Genna hesitated. Was Rowan upset? Did she want Genna to come down because she didn't want to come up? Was she trying to say *I don't want to be alone with you so close to a bedroom*? And if she was saying that, was it because she was resisting temptation, or because she was still pissed? Ugh. Why was *her* first thought that her apartment had a bedroom? Rowan probably hadn't thought that at all.

"I'll be right there."

Genna jogged down the stairs as a boa constrictor wound itself around her chest. She had no time to prepare for seeing Rowan again, so anxiety kicked off its shoes and made itself at home. She found Rowan standing next to the Dodge in the lot reserved for residents.

"Hi."

Days of obsessing about everything she should have said and *hi* was the best she could do. Words were impossible when Rowan was so tall and solid in straight dark jeans broken in at the knees and scuffed brown boots, her blond hair mussed like she'd just rolled out of bed. Her white T-shirt stretched across her shoulders and hinted at a body honed by hours in the gym. Genna wanted to press her mouth to the smooth skin beneath the hollow of her throat. Sex on legs was right. Looking that good just wasn't fair.

Rowan clearly wasn't having similar thoughts. She gave her a nod and held out her car key. "Hi. It's fixed. Sorry it's so early. I asked Phil to tow it over before the shop opened."

Genna stared at the key. "When I spoke to Phil, it was a write-off. He was going to try to sell it for scrap."

"Now it's good as new. Or, good enough it should last another few years. He sold me some parts at cost. I did the work myself. You're lucky it's so old. If you'd had anything with fancy electronics, I'd've been sunk."

Genna took the key cautiously. "You did this. Why?"

"You were worried about affording a replacement." Rowan shrugged. "I've been working on cars since I was a kid."

"How much do I owe you?"

Rowan frowned. "Nothing—the parts were cheap, and I wanted to do it."

"You didn't have to do that." Genna bit her lip. She didn't want to seem ungracious, but who did this kind of thing? And why?

Rowan's eyes went from distant to a far-flung island off the coast of Timbuktu. "You're welcome. Have a nice weekend."

She turned to go.

Blind panic surged and shoved her anxiety off its cozy lounger. Genna grabbed Rowan's hand before she knew what she was doing. "Wait. Please."

Rowan stilled, letting her hand rest in Genna's without holding it.

"Thank you. I…I don't know what to say. This is amazing. So, just, thank you. You're always doing things for me, and I don't say that enough. I appreciate it."

Rowan nodded. "Happy to do it."

Things weren't right between them, but she didn't know how to make it okay. "I owe you for all of this anyhow." She waved a hand at her car. "Maybe you'll let me buy you a beer at Happy Hour sometime?"

They absolutely should not be hanging out at Happy Hour, but making things right again seemed a lot more important than some rule she was now pretending she couldn't remember.

Some of the frost melted from Rowan's eyes, but her smile was sad. "You don't owe me anything. I wanted to help you. You don't need to even the score."

You, though. It's transactional. Genna mentally punched Travis and his words of wisdom in the nose. It *wasn't* transactional with Rowan.

"No one has ever done something this nice for me before." She hated how pathetic that sounded. Why was Rowan always doing nice things for her?

Rowan frowned. "I'm sorry to hear that."

"I'm just saying I want to pay you back somehow. I'm not used to taking from people." This whole opening up thing sucked. No wonder she never did it. But if it made things better with Rowan, she had to try. She had no choice. Rowan being distant wasn't an option.

Rowan slipped her thumb along the back of Genna's hand. "It's not taking if it's given to you. But I won't say no. Do you have plans today? We could—"

"Oh." Genna pulled her phone out of her jeans and glanced at the time. "I'm late. I have to call Toby back."

"Toby?"

"How-Can-I-Help Toby from Rent-a-Ride."

Genna looked up from her phone to see Rowan suppressing a laugh. "What?"

Rowan merely raised her eyebrows in a way Genna did sometimes. Genna shoved her lightly on the arm, which brought her up close and personal with Rowan's very sexy bicep and the ink that encased it. Fuck, she was hot. And she had to stop thinking about that. She had bigger problems. "It's a rental car place, Ms. Mind in the Gutter."

"Why do you need a rental now? Yours is right here."

"The twins, my sisters, are moving out of their dorm, and they need a truck. I'm supposed to drive one down today and help them. Only trucks are gold-plated, and I didn't get the memo because it costs a fortune."

Rowan looked at her like she had two heads. "Not to drag out the oldest joke in the book, but you could try a U-Haul."

Genna blinked. Jesus, she was an idiot. "I didn't think of a U-Haul. Would that be less expensive. Never mind—I'll Google them."

"I have a truck."

Of course, Rowan had a truck. But it's not like she could ask her to borrow it.

Rowan's truck would solve everything.

She couldn't ask.

Rowan stared her down playfully. "Well?"

Genna scowled, but on the inside, her heart was dusting off its *I Heart Rowan* flag. They were back to teasing. "If you were a nice person, you'd offer so I didn't suffer the humiliation of having to ask."

Rowan lifted a shoulder. "I've already been nice today. If you want the truck, you'll have to ask. Maybe when you do, you'll realize it's not as humiliating as you think."

The heat on Genna's cheeks went from warm summer day to Arizona heatwave. "I can't."

Rowan stepped into her space and put one finger under her chin, bringing their eyes level. "You can. Just ask. I'll say yes."

Genna tensed with Rowan so close. So touchable. So kissable. She tried not to stare at the smooth skin just above the vee of Rowan's shirt where she wanted to press her mouth as temptation pulled slowly at her sanity. "If you'll say yes, why are you making me ask?"

"Because you need me." Rowan's voice had gone hoarse. She was staring at Genna's mouth.

Genna's belly dipped, and a rush went through her. She wanted her—which was a hell of a lot safer than needing her.

"Rowan?" Her voice came out breathy, as if she'd just run a up a flight of stairs.

"Hmm?"

"Can I borrow your truck?"

Rowan brushed the pad of her thumb across Genna's bottom lip, leaving it tingling. "Say please."

Genna moaned.

Out loud.

In front of Rowan.

She'd be reliving this moment and dying from embarrassment on repeat later. "Can I please borrow your truck?"

"I have a better idea."

The words made every drop of Genna's blood sizzle. So did she. A whole compendium of naked and dirty ideas. All of them involving her bed.

"You still want to do me a favor?"

Genna wet her lips. Was she asking for what Genna thought, hell, what she *hoped* Rowan was asking for? She could do that favor all day and all night long. Fuck ethics. "Yes."

"Then let me drive you."

"Let's..." She stopped speaking as Rowan's words parted the haze of lust obscuring her better judgment. Genna deflated. What had she been thinking? Or more accurately, had she been thinking at all? Fuck ethics? "You want to help my sisters move? Moving sucks. Moving someone else sucks worse."

Not going upstairs with you sucks worst of all. Did you know my apartment has a bedroom?

"If I'm with you, it won't suck." Rowan stepped back. "That's the deal. You can have the truck, if we're a package."

"That's not doing you a favor, that's you doing *me* a favor." Genna could hardly remember what it was they were even talking about anymore. Rowan's control was a *lot* better than hers. She'd just prevented them from making an awful mistake.

"I want to spend time with you. Away from your research. Away from my issues. Just two people helping your sisters move. It would be doing us both a favor." She paused. "I hope, us both. Unless this"—Rowan gestured in the space between them—"is all one-sided?"

What would you call a one-way street?

I'd call it none of your fucking business, Travis. Get out of my head.

"It's not one-sided." She shoved her anxiety and arousal on their asses before she became too tongue-tied to say what she should've said days ago. "The truth is, I like you."

Rowan sucked in a breath, her eyes widening. "I like you too, Dr. Sex."

Genna choked on air. "Dr. Sex?"

"That's what I call you in my head sometimes. Dr. Sex."

As nicknames went, it was better than Casanova. "You know I'm not a doctor, right?"

"You will be."

Genna looked at her phone again to hide the smile that she could feel playing around the edges of her mouth. Dr. Sex. How ridiculously corny. And sweet. And so like Rowan. "You really want to help out today?"

"I really do."

"Then we have to leave five minutes ago."

Rowan swept her arm toward the truck. "After you."

Genna could feel Rowan's eyes on her as she climbed in and had to resist the urge to take her time. She'd never been an exhibitionist, but she liked being watched if Rowan was doing the looking. Rowan held the match that could burn her whole life down, and Genna could barely resist fanning the flame.

But they liked each other.

Chapter Thirteen

"Tell me about your sisters. They're twins?" Rowan concentrated on merging onto the interstate toward the large state college Genna's sisters attended.

"Yep. They're ten years younger than me. Grace is book smart but still young enough to think that makes her uncool. She's really into art. She makes the most amazing abstract paintings just by throwing things, or blowing things, or shooting things at a canvas. Grace can take spray paint, a hair dryer, and a colander and make a gallery-worthy piece. She's so talented."

"Is she studying art?" Rowan asked.

"Mom convinced her to go the design route for the career prospects, which was probably wise. I hope she can make it as an artist though."

"And the other one?" Rowan asked.

"Gabby is the social butterfly. You know, those people who just know everyone? That's Gabby. She's majoring in journalism, but she's barely scraping by. I'm pretty sure her actual major is makeup application, hair styling, and dating boys not good enough for her. But she makes you feel like the most interesting person in the room. Everyone loves her."

"I'm looking forward to meeting them." Rowan focused on the road and not gaping open-mouthed at Genna, who'd just told her more in the last sixty seconds than she had in ever.

"What's it like having sisters so much younger? There's two years between me and my sister. Ten seems like a lot. Did you have to do a lot of babysitting growing up?"

Silence sauntered in with its suitcases and looked like it might be staying a while.

Rowan sighed and counted off the seconds until Genna changed the subject, or answered her question with a question, or any one of the dozen tactics she had to avoid the topic of herself. Talkative streak: officially over.

"This is hard for me. I'm trying, but it's hard."

Rowan glanced at Genna. "What's hard?"

"Talking about myself. That's why I can sometimes come across transactional. I don't mean to be."

Rowan kept her eyes on the road, so she didn't drive over the median. This was new. "I don't think you come across transactional. You're…task oriented. By the book. In a sexy, ice queen, power suit librarian-on-a-mission kind of way."

Genna snorted.

"Who said you're transactional?"

"My friend Travis. He said I'm hard to get to know."

"Perhaps he hasn't tried very hard. There's dignity in being choosy about who you share yourself with. Trust needs to be earned."

"I could do with being less choosy," Genna said, a little bit sadly.

"Do you want people to know who you are?" Rowan asked. *Do you want me to know you?*

"I'm what other people want me to be. Who I am, really? I have no idea." Genna said nothing further and for once Rowan didn't push. For Genna to share this much was a victory—something special had just passed across the console. Rowan wanted to keep it safe.

"The twins and I have different dads. Mine was never in the picture." Genna's gaze was fixed out the passenger side window. "Mom got pregnant as a teenager, and my dad wanted her to get an abortion. She didn't want that, so they agreed that she'd keep me, and he'd have no obligation beyond child support payments."

Genna's sadness, that she'd probably deny, swirled between them, and Rowan ached to touch her. "That must've been hard."

Genna shook her head. "It wasn't. Mom was fantastic and my grandparents helped a lot. I'm glad she gave him an out. Not everyone wants to be a parent, especially at sixteen. He did the right thing, and so did she. They both ended up happy."

"That's a mature way to look at it," Rowan said, not really sure Genna meant it. Sometimes what seemed like maturity was a front to hide being hurt.

"She got pregnant again when I was nine, and that guy stuck for a few months until things got hard, and they split. She doesn't have the best luck with relationships."

"Seems she used all her luck to have great children," Rowan said.

"Something happened. I don't know whether it was the pregnancy, or postpartum mental health, or caring for two babies on her own, but…" She stopped.

Rowan couldn't see Genna's face and wished she'd look at her.

Genna fisted a hand on her thigh. "This is hard. Why is it so hard? Why can't I just say it?"

"There's always tomorrow," Rowan said. She wanted a tomorrow, hoped Genna did too. She pushed the thought away. She was getting way ahead of herself. Now was not the time for a romantic daydream.

"I don't want to stop. I just want it to be easier." Genna's tone had gone from frustrated to grumpy.

The tension in Rowan's chest eased a little. Grumpy was better than sad, but she wished she could do *something* to make this easier for Genna. Anything. If Genna could just tell her what she needed.

"Someone once told me that facing something that troubles you makes you brave and tough," Rowan said.

"Whoever said that clearly had no idea what she was talking about."

Still grumpy. Good. Would Genna be able to push past the hard with her?

"What happened after the twins were born?"

Genna took Rowan's hand and held it in her lap, tracing the lines of her palm with a fingertip. A bubble of hope inflated in Rowan's chest. Genna wanted to touch her. She wasn't alone in needing that.

"She developed an anxiety disorder," Genna said. "There's no definitive diagnosis, just generalized anxiety which is what they say when they've run out of alternatives. She has agoraphobia."

"Fear of spiders?" Rowan asked, confused.

"That's arachnophobia. Agoraphobia is fear of leaving a safe environment."

Oh, man. Rowan's heart seized right back up. "What was that like?"

Genna shrugged. "Not terrible. There are a lot worse things. Like I said, Mom is fantastic."

Sure. There were always worse things. That didn't make the hard things any easier. Especially at ten years old. "I can't really imagine it. What was it like?"

"When you asked me if I babysat my sisters, well, there were some things that Mom just couldn't do, you know? Like grocery shopping before there was Instacart or after-school activities, or taking us anywhere for any reason."

Rowan started connecting the dots. "You did those things for your sisters when your mom couldn't."

Genna nodded. "As much as I could at the time. Things were easier when I got older."

"That's a lot for a kid to take on."

"It wasn't enough. They missed out on so much. No one to watch them play soccer, or take them on playdates, or teach them to drive. They didn't even go to preschool because we couldn't get them there."

We as if the twins going to preschool had been her responsibility. Rowan's heart broke for all of them, but especially for little Genna. Genna wasn't saying it, but there must've been a lot *she* missed out on too. Who taught her to drive? "Did your mom get help?"

Genna nodded. "I took the twins to a pediatric appointment when they were six months old. I'm not sure what we were thinking, just that they needed to go. So, mom put me in a cab, and we went.

Of course, we weren't even there twenty minutes and the doctor called CPS. I get now that he had to do it, but at the time I didn't understand."

Rowan squeezed Genna's fingers.

"They came, they got mom into therapy and on meds, and then they left. We were healthy and happy and not being abused. They gave mom a number to call if we needed to go places, and someone would take us wherever, but mom only ever called if it was an emergency or a mandatory reporter." Genna shrugged. "The twins grew to love White Sedan Lady because it meant French fries and cheeseburgers."

"I know about mandatory reporters. Medical personnel, therapists, school officials, and all the rest who must report child endangerment," Rowan said. She was going to be a social worker after all. How could anyone leave three little kids in that situation? "They should've done more."

"We were fine," Genna repeated.

"You were a kid taking babies to a doctor's appointment. That's not okay." She should shut up. Genna didn't need this right now. She was just so damn *heartbroken*.

Genna shrugged. "It's more okay than the kids being sexually abused by the people they should be able to trust the most. Being kicked and punched and burned with cigarette butts. Being neglected in favor of drink or drugs. Better than a hundred different outcomes. Mom did everything she possibly could to ensure we were safe and loved and happy. Not every kid gets that. We didn't need CPS."

Rowan bit the inside of her cheek to keep from arguing. From banging her fist against the steering wheel in impotent rage that *any* child should ever be harmed but especially, *most especially,* Genna. Because even if Genna was right and she had it better than a lot of kids, she was still a child taking on adult responsibilities with no one to look out for her. Were there even cell phones when they were kids? Rowan didn't think so.

Genna squeezed Rowan's knuckles one at a time until she unclenched the fist, she hadn't realized she'd made. "You're mad."

"I'm not mad at you," Rowan said quickly. "Never at you."

"But you are upset."

Rowan took a breath and actively worked on not being upset, however one did that. "The system failed you, and Grace, and Gabby. That makes me angry. You shouldn't have had to do everything by yourself. Your mom should've had more support."

Genna turned from staring out the window to look at her curiously. "No one has ever been angry about it before."

Her heart seized for Genna now, and Genna then. The little girl who'd had no one to care that she'd lost her childhood and had been carrying the burden of looking after everyone she loved since she was ten years old. Rowan understood her a lot better now. Knowing what she'd been through, and everything she'd accomplished despite it, she respected her even more than she had before.

The GPS told her they were two miles from their destination when she pulled over to the side of the road. She took off her seat belt and turned to face Genna, refusing to let the moment pass without acknowledging the enormity of what she'd just been trusted with. "I'm going old school and giving you a hug."

Genna laughed. "You stopped the car because you want to give me a hug?"

"Yes. Can I?"

Genna paused and Rowan thought she'd say no, spout some nonsense about her research and ethics, but she nodded and took off her seat belt. When she bit her lip and ducked her head, Rowan's heart filled. The super-hot, fantasy researcher was shy about a simple hug. She tucked that little tidbit away for later.

Cursing the manufacturers for making the center console so wide, Rowan still managed to wrap her arms around Genna. When Genna rested her cheek on Rowan's shoulder, it didn't matter that the hug was awkward or that traffic was flying by just outside. All that mattered was this, was them. Was showing Genna how much it meant to her that she'd opened up. To her. For her. Rowan tried to pour all of that into the hug.

"You're not mad anymore," Genna mumbled against her neck.

No, she wasn't mad anymore. Not with Genna in her arms, feeling so right.

"You smell good," Genna said, her words a caress.

"Genna," Rowan warned her.

"I don't really do hugs," Genna mumbled again, inching closer and wrapping a hand around the back of Rowan's neck. "This is a nice one though."

"Genna." The warning was nothing more than a whisper of smoke this time. Rowan shuddered when Genna's fingers brushed the back of her neck. God, she wanted to kiss her. Now was *so,* not the time but she wasn't made of stone. Genna might've been shy about the hug, but now that they were inside it, she had no problem cuddling as close as humanly possible.

Genna pulled back far enough that Rowan could see her eyes. Deep brown and endlessly sexy. "This is what you needed, wasn't it?"

Rowan needed a lot of things. "Needed what?"

"In my office when you asked me if I fantasized. You needed comfort. Because you'd just shared something hard."

Inwardly, Rowan groaned. That was the last thing she wanted to talk about. "Yes, but it's okay. That day we were researcher and participant. I realized later that you couldn't have given me a hug even if you'd wanted to. I was feeling vulnerable and took it out on you. I'm sorry about that."

"I could've given you common human decency. I'm sorry I didn't."

Rowan kissed her very lightly, very gently on the tip of her nose. "You're forgiven."

"Just like that?"

"Just like that."

"If we hug any longer, I'm going to kiss you," Genna said so matter-of-factly Rowan lost all the air in her lungs.

"I want you to." Heat began to curl around Rowan's nerve endings like silken smoke. Their hug turning to foreplay.

"I know," Genna whispered, not moving her mouth any closer. "But if we do, I'll get in trouble, and you'll have to tell a sex therapist all about sexy evil Mrs. Sutton."

Rowan half laughed, half groaned, "That's not fair."

"I know," Genna said again. "But it's the truth."

"You're going to pull away now, aren't you? Please don't. I don't think I can take this anymore."

Not kissing Genna might just split her open. She couldn't possibly resist what felt like insurmountable temptation an unending number of times. For the first time, she understood the fundamental difference between fantasy and reality. She might've thought she'd been tempted by her fantasies, but in the end, they left her hollow and unsatisfied. Fantasy was two dimensional and shallow. But *reality*. That had the power to drive her to the brink of insanity. Kissing Genna wouldn't leave her wanting. Giving in to this temptation would only bring pleasure.

Genna brushed her fingers across the back of Rowan's neck again, and Rowan moaned softly. "Fuck. You have to kiss me. You just have to."

"I'm not going to. Do you want to know why?"

"You don't mean that." Rowan's mind hazed at the edges as Genna caressed her neck.

"I do mean it." The lust clear in her eyes belied Genna's words. "Because I want something better, and if we kiss now with everything we're risking hanging over us, we'll fuck it up."

Better? What could be better than her mouth on Genna's, kissing her, taking her, having her, finally, fucking filling the void in her chest she'd never been able to satisfy. Genna could do that.

Genna cupped Rowan's cheek bringing their faces so close all Rowan saw, all she knew, was her. "I want to go on a date after you've completed my research. I don't care that we see long term relationships differently. That will sort itself out if we get there. We have this connection, and it's sexy as hell, but I want more. I want to get to know you better. I want a chance at more than kissing. Is that okay?"

If you'd have asked her thirty seconds ago, Rowan would've sworn there was nothing that could've prevented this kiss. It seemed as inevitable as blue skies. But now. Rowan stared at Genna, trying to see past even her skin and bone to the very core of her. Did she mean it? Hope sprouted a seed in her belly and started growing faster than Jack's beanstalk. "Really? You want that? An honest to God date?"

Genna smiled. "Really. If you'll say yes, of course."

Even though it ran contrary to every instinct, Rowan made an exaggerated display of moving away from Genna until they were both safely back on their sides of the center console. She started the truck with shaking fingers. "I already have the perfect date in mind."

Genna shot her a signature eyebrow raise, her cheeks a little flushed and her eyes sparkling. "Been thinking about it, have you?"

Rowan took her hand and squeezed as she merged back into traffic. "I've been thinking about you a lot."

Chapter Fourteen

"So, what's the deal with you and my sister?" Grace asked as they packed books into boxes that Genna had magic'd up from a storage room somewhere.

Rowan was the first to admit she'd been the tiniest bit nervous when Genna had left them all to fend for themselves while she tracked down the dorm RA for a reference. She didn't want to screw up in front of these hundred-pound, mini-Gennas and that made the two minutes actual-Genna had been gone seem like millennia. Rowan could talk cars and workouts all day long, but from the look of all the clothes and makeup they'd been packing for the last hour, Grace and Gabby weren't into either of those things. They were, however, very into gossiping about their big sister, ambushing Rowan with the strategy and finesse of trained militia. It must've been their plan from the outset.

"Uh, there isn't any kind of deal." *Yet.*

"You must like her though, because if not, what are you doing here?" Gabby smiled at Rowan encouragingly and rolled her duvet and sheets up into one giant roll, then karate chopped them down the middle, and stuffed the whole mess into a box.

Rowan winced. She caught herself before she gave in to the temptation of a lesson on folding a fitted sheet, lest she be deemed too *millennial.* "I'm just here to help."

"Moving is *not* fun." Grace nailed Rowan with a pointed stare. "No one *helps* unless they're getting laid."

"Or they *want* to get laid." Gabby pulled her hair, the same dark chocolate, but wavier than Grace's and Genna's, into a loose ponytail.

Rowan didn't respond.

"Ouch. She just wants to be friends?" Grace gave her a slow up and down. "I'd do you, if you want."

Genna, please come back. I'm getting pummeled here.

"We met through her research, so there isn't any kind of deal, but we definitely aren't friends, and to the last part, absolutely not." Rowan couldn't count the ways she didn't want to be *done* by Grace. For the love of God.

Gabby looked pleased. "It's not every day you get turned down with an *absolutely not*, Grace."

"Whatever. Gen would maim me anyway, but it still doesn't mean they're dating." Grace sulked.

What the actual fuck? What was going on here? Rowan had missed something.

Gabby shook her head but didn't say anything to Grace. She zeroed in on Rowan again. "It counts if you're interested in dating. Genna's never brought anyone she wasn't dating to meet us before. Is this serious?"

"Meeting Mom is serious." Grace jumped in before Rowan could answer. "Meeting us is just adjacent to manual labor. No one else could carry these boxes." Grace got up and started going through the drawers of her desk without packing anything.

"Did she bring you to meet us?" Gabby asked Rowan, ignoring her sister.

Genna's interrogation skills were a family trait. Gabby was relentless, but she preferred it to the weird and sulky come-on from Grace. *Genna, where are you? Is this serious?*

"I don't think that was her intention exactly. She needed to borrow my truck and…" Rowan paused, trying to figure out how to tell Genna's sister she'd basically blackmailed her. But, nice blackmail. Not the stalk you in the dead of night kind. "I told her she couldn't have the truck unless I drove because I wanted to spend time with her."

Great. Now she sounded like a creep.

Grace scoffed. "Why would you sign up for this?" She gestured around the total chaos of the dorm room.

Fair question. Rowan was starting to wonder the same thing.

But Gabby was looking at Rowan knowingly. "She likes you. I can tell."

"You can?" Rowan and Grace said together.

"Yep." Gabby sat on the box she'd stuffed with bedding. "When she looks at you, she goes all sparkly. It's easy to miss because Genna's sparkles…"

"Glint like shards of glass?" Grace suggested.

"That's so mean." Gabby made it sound like a compliment. "She likes you. And you wouldn't let her borrow your truck without you, which means you like her too. Which is *pre-dating*."

Grace rolled her eyes. "It's not dating until it's dating. Pre-dating is BS."

Gabby held Rowan's eyes. "Do you care about her?"

Rowan's palms got sweaty. Of course she cared about Genna. But they'd barely managed to acknowledge that themselves and telling her sisters was a dick move.

Grace clapped her hands. "I *told* you. It's going nowhere just like all the other people Genna fucks around with that she thinks we don't know about."

What people? How many people was *all the other people*? But that could wait a minute because something else had just fallen into place for Rowan.

Finally getting what this inquisition was all about, she sat opposite Gabby on the bare mattress and risked the dick move. "I care. But maybe we can keep that between us until I've had a chance to tell her myself?"

"Gen doesn't just…let people drive her around," Gabby said. "We just…"

"Want to make sure your intentions are pure." Grace paused. "Well, maybe not *pure,* but—"

"I get it." Rowan cut her off before Grace said something else no one wanted to hear. "I really like Genna. Whatever it's been with *all the other people* it's not going nowhere with me." Rowan leaned toward Gabby. "Just between us? I'm planning our first date for when her study ends."

"I knew I liked you." Gabby launched herself off the box and into Rowan's arms before Rowan knew what was coming. Hugging her tightly, Gabby whispered in her ear, "Ignore Grace."

Rowan patted her on the back and eased away. "I'm thinking a home cooked meal and a few episodes of *Buffy*. What do you think? Would she like that?"

Grace crossed the room and sat a bit too close by Rowan's side. "If you can cook, I hope one of us gets to marry you."

Rowan figured that was as much approval as she'd get from Grace. Would there come a time when she could tell the twins she cared about them too? That she was sorry for everything they'd been through? Maybe. But not today.

Gabby bit her lip. "But, like, you're not too nice, are you? She'll walk all over you. She can be kind of…"

"Stressed out and bitchy?" Grace supplied without missing a beat, and Rowan realized this was a thing they did. Gabby trailing off and Grace interjecting something snarky. It wasn't a very endearing comedy act.

Gabby shook her head. "Not bitchy. Angry."

"Genna isn't angry." Grace took the words right out of Rowan's mouth. Why did no one but her seem to like Genna all that much?

Gabby shrugged again. "Obviously, she's not the going around all *angry* angry. But under it? She's a decent amount pissed off."

"What does she have to be annoyed about?" Grace asked, looking annoyed about it.

Gabby walked around Rowan and pulled her sister into a hug, sitting on her lap with the casual intimacy of sisters.

"Why doesn't she talk to us? If anyone gets what there is to be pissed off about in life, it's us. She can tell us stuff," Grace said, contradicting her previous comment.

"No, she can't," Gabby said. "We're the stuff. That's why she needs someone like Rowan who's more than a good time."

"I care," Grace said in the same grumpy tone Genna sometimes used.

Rowan smiled. Grace's sparkles were hidden under some shards of glass too. With killer edges.

"We're the stuff," Gabby said again. She smiled at Rowan. "Your date idea sounds magical."

"I guess I could be team Rowan. If she does actually like you," Grace agreed skeptically.

"I don't think she planned for us to meet so soon," Rowan said, more to convince herself than Gabby. Meeting the twins was adjacent to manual labor after all. She shouldn't go reading into it. Genna had a knack for dashing her hopes.

"Who didn't mean what?" Genna asked, coming back with a handful of printouts.

Thank God.

"Oh, nothing." Gabby said, completely unconvincingly, sliding off Grace's lap and tugging her a couple of inches away from Rowan.

Rowan just shrugged. Ratting the twins out wouldn't do her any favors, even if Grace did make her a bit uncomfortable.

Genna eyed them all sitting on the bed like the three bears. She held Rowan's eyes for a second. Genna was wondering what had happened while she was gone, but she said, "You know that mattress came with the room, right? The semen of forty thousand guys is all over it. What you're all doing could get you pregnant."

Rowan breathed a sigh of relief. She didn't want to explain anything that had just happened.

Grace jumped up and twisted around to look at her butt as if she had grown a tail. "Eww. I didn't think of that."

Gabby just smiled like all that semen wouldn't be so bad really.

"Wait until we see the infamous hot tub," Genna said menacingly. "You'll be almost *naked* in that one."

Gabby groaned. "Please don't call it *the infamous hot tub* like a thousand babies have been conceived in it or something."

"If I told you a thousand babies had been birthed in it, would you clean it?" Genna asked.

"Oh my God. No one had a baby in there."

"Gabby," Rowan interjected before the argument escalated. "Let me show you how to fold those sheets."

❖

"They're going to be okay." Rowan pulled the truck into a parking lot downtown. After driving all the twins' stuff over to their new rental, checking the place out, squaring the details with Bianca's dad, and mercifully leaving the unpacking to everyone else, food was now a top priority.

"They'll make it," Genna agreed. What choice did they have? It'd always been sink or swim for the twins. Somehow, they stayed afloat.

"They'll do more than that," Rowan said. "They're great kids. I mean sisters. They're great sisters. They really love you, you know."

Genna rubbed a hand across her face tiredly. "They are kids in a lot of ways. Big know-it-all kids."

"Who love you," Rowan reminded her.

"I know. I love them too."

"Grace is team Rowna." Rowan was grinning as she hopped out of the truck.

"Who's Rowna?"

"Rowan and Genna. Rowna."

"*Grace* wants us to be a couple? Gabby, I could see. But not Grace."

"She was taken in by my charms," Rowan joked as they walked the two minutes to the best burrito place in Silver Creek.

Genna laughed. "She was taken in by you doing all the packing for her. But your charms aren't half-bad. Did she offer to sleep with you yet?"

Rowan stopped walking. "Is that a *thing*?"

Genna grimaced. Fucking damn it, Grace. "She did, didn't she? That's fast even for her. I guess you're pretty hot, Thor."

Rowan had gone pale. "I thought she was joking. Probably joking. Hopefully just joking. You're telling me she was serious?"

Genna wasn't sure how to say that her little sister, who was thirteen years younger and thirty years less mature than Rowan wasn't joking, but not to take her seriously. It's not what it seemed. "Let's get our food and find a table."

Burritos and an order of guac and chips later, they found a picnic table tucked behind a row of hedges on the outside patio. Rowan still looked a bit like she wanted to puke. "Grace would actually sleep with your girl—with a woman you were interested in dating? Why?"

Genna opened her burrito and started eating the insides with a fork. "I rarely date so it's never really been a problem. But yeah. If Grace thinks I'm into someone, she usually finds them attractive too."

"Why would she?"

Genna sighed. How could she explain this level of fuckedupness to someone like Rowan. Someone so good and sweet, whose biggest problem was a couple of twisted fantasies. She didn't even need to ask if Rowan had turned Grace down. There was no chance Rowan had said yes, even though Grace was younger, prettier, and a hell of a lot braver. Genna didn't know when she'd come to trust Rowan, but she did. Now she'd have to trust her with the truth. "Grace has always tried to emulate me. It's tough being the little sister. It's tougher being the little sister *and* a twin to someone who's naturally better with people. It's the toughest of all to grow up the way we did, insulated from other role models and relationships. All my life, if I had something, then Grace wanted it too. And when she's five and I'm fifteen, it's lip gloss. But when she's nineteen, it's people and sex. She'll grow out of it."

Rowan bit into her burrito, chewed, and swallowed before saying, "And if she doesn't? Doesn't it seem disrespectful to you?"

Genna's heart lurched. Taking Rowan to help the twins had been a risk, and she'd agreed with her lusty sex-brain instead of her common sense. Now Grace had hurt her. "I'm sorry you felt disrespected. I'll talk to her. There's no need for you to see her again."

Rowan took her hand. "Disrespectful to *you,* and you don't even seem upset. You're her sister. She should want you to be happy, not try to get between any relationship you might pursue."

Oh.

Genna had never really thought about it like that. Yeah, it was awkward to have to explain, but Grace was more important to her than any romantic relationship had ever been. "It's not her fault. You don't understand how it was when the twins were growing up. I was so much older, so much freer. I'd had Mom when she was well. They struggled. They still do. Grace wants what I have because she lacked so much that I didn't. I was older and wiser and luckier."

"Genna—"

"I need you to back off from this, Rowan." Genna did mostly trust her, but she didn't want to argue about something she'd experienced, and Rowan knew nothing about. Her relationship with her sisters might be a hot mess, but it was *her* mess.

The unhappy line of Rowan's mouth fell into a frown. "Is it possible that what she needed was someone who turned Grace down cold and still managed to convince her that team Rowna was the better option? Now you're free to pursue a relationship without worrying about Grace's choices."

Genna swallowed a bubble of pleasure. She absolutely, unequivocally, without a doubt did not want Rowan involved, but she could get on board with needing that.

Rowan blew out a breath. "I know I'm overstepping. I don't understand what you all went through. I can't. I can only try to be here for you now. But Grace piggybacking on your attraction seems unhealthy, for you, and for her too. She'll never find someone of her own if getting what you have is what makes the person attractive."

Genna's stomach twisted like she was upside down on a roller coaster. Well, fuck. That *was* a problem. Now Genna had something else to worry about. But secretly, another part of her was just as happy for Grace to crush on the people she crushed on every now and then. It was mostly harmless and kept her out of trouble. Gabby on the other hand… "I hear what you're saying. I'll think about it."

Rowan nodded, apparently satisfied. "While we're on the topic of things said in your absence. Who are all the other people?"

Genna licked salsa off her fork. "What people?"

"Grace mentioned you sleep with other people. She made it sound like there had been a lot. Is that something I should be concerned about?"

The question rankled. "We aren't even dating, Rowan."

Rowan's eyes did that distant thing she hated, and her jaw tightened. "And when we are? Does sleeping with other people stop?"

"You're jealous I slept with people before I met you? So have you. Remember Claudia?"

"I'm not jealous, and Claudia was my girlfriend. I'm asking about the future, not the past." Rowan came around the table to sit beside her and took Genna's hand. She seemed huge suddenly, and Genna felt her space and air supply start to evaporate.

She could barely think about tomorrow let alone some indefinable future, and she definitely didn't want to think about what not going back to McKinney's might mean. "So, it's okay for you to have sex with your girlfriend, but I'm, what, promiscuous if I have sex with someone who isn't? Is this nineteen fifty?"

Rowan looked annoyed and never having seen that expression from her before, Genna flinched.

"I didn't say that. I don't even think that. I'm not currently having sex with anybody." Rowan shoved a hand through her hair. "I like you. I want time with you to see where this goes, and I'd like us not to see other people while we do that. I'm not asking for a commitment. But I think it's reasonable to prioritize the *potential* we have and not see other people. So, you have to decide if you want me enough to give the rest up."

Genna's throat began to thicken with impending tears. Rowan's words slid under the armor she'd spent so much time honing and punched her right in the chest. She'd never consciously expected Rowan to share her. But monogamy came with expectations she'd never be able to meet. Hell, even the regulars at McKinney's thought she was strange. What would Rowan think? "You want me to decide who I will and won't sleep with before we've even kissed? That's arrogant, not to mention unreasonable and moving way too fast."

"If it is, then I guess I am arrogant. If we're going to date, then it's only going to be me for as long as it lasts. Even if the sex gets boring as hell, and you're watching the clock."

"Now you're picking a fight," Genna said flatly. "That will sort itself out. Either you're right and this grand passion never fades, or I'm right and we work on the relationship to ensure the sex *isn't* boring. Either way it's a non-issue unless *you* decide to leave."

Rowan cupped her chin to tilt her face up to hers. "My passion for you will never be a non-issue, Dr. Sex."

Genna yanked her chin out of reach. "You believe that now. But it doesn't always work that way. If it starts to fade, you'll decide I'm not *the one* and move on."

Rowan shook her head. "So now you want me to decide if you're the one, before we've even kissed?"

"It makes about as much sense as your suggestion does," Genna shot back.

Rowan looked away, as if taking her gaze head-on was too much. The fight visibly drained out of her. "If a kiss is what it takes, then we'll decide it right now."

Genna tried to respond but her tongue had forgotten how to move, and she didn't make a sound. She didn't like arguing any more than the next person, but it was better than the defeated way Rowan had turned away from her.

"Rowan—"

Rowan turned back, the frustration still there but something bleak had taken root in her eyes, something old and dark that had nothing to do with her. Rowan pulled Genna toward her, her hands none too gentle. One cupped Genna's cheek, the other twisted in her hair.

This was all so wrong. She'd been thinking about this kiss for weeks and no fantasy had prepared her for the desolate expression on Rowan's face. Were they really going to have their first kiss to win an argument? Didn't they deserve better than that?

"I'm going to kiss you, *then* you can decide if I'm worth not fucking other people."

"I never said—"

Rowan took her lips in a hate-kiss that had no hate at all.

Chapter Fifteen

Rowan kissed Genna hard, using her mouth to convince her she was worth whatever paltry sacrifice casual sex was to Genna. Genna froze for a split second with a sound in the back of her throat that shot electricity through every synapse. She held Genna tightly and raked her teeth along Genna's bottom lip, demanding access. *Let me in. Let me show you exactly what you'll be gaining by giving up everyone else.*

Genna pressed both hands against her shoulders. "No."

Rowan couldn't stop. *Why don't you want me as much? Why don't you care that Grace wants to sleep with me?*

"I said no."

Rowan eased away, fear mushrooming in her heart. Well, there was her answer. A kiss hadn't made a bit of difference. Acid burned a hole in her belly, the pain so acute she couldn't get up and walk away. All she wanted to do was walk—run—away.

She'd kissed her. Genna had said no. Close the book. End of the story. She'd never felt so worthless, and life had handed her more than a few soul-crushing moments.

"I think, perhaps, it's time I shared one of my fantasies with you," Genna said with so much gentleness it only heightened Rowan's fear.

Probably a threesome. Or foursome. Or twelvesome, depending on how many other people *all* comprised. Would she join the cast to make a baker's dozen? No way could she handle knowing. "I don't want to hear it."

Genna shook her head. "Well, that's too bad. I want to tell you, and since you decided it was fine to manhandle me to prove a point, you'll do me the courtesy of listening."

"I didn't." *Fuck.* She had. She'd kissed Genna too fast. She'd broken their rules and their trust because she was terrified Genna wouldn't choose her. That Genna would leave her…*alone*. A word scary enough to hold within itself the terror of its meaning.

She was the shmuckiest of shmucks.

"My fantasy," Genna soldiered on, "starts with us grabbing burritos after helping my sisters move. It's a beautiful afternoon, and we've snuck into a private corner. You're dropping truth bombs on me about Grace, which I mostly don't want to hear, but I'm distracted thinking about the way you hugged me earlier. The feel of your body pressed to mine. Your skin hot against my fingers. The sound you made when I touched you. It's a really sexy sound."

Fear loosened its chokehold on Rowan by a quarter inch. She sucked in air.

"You dunk a chip in the guacamole and, as you take a bite, a little fleck of green goop lands on your lip. I'm mesmerized."

"Genna—" Rowan wasn't just a shmuck, she was the goddamn mayor of Schmucksville.

Genna frowned at her. "Shut up. I'm not done."

Rowan guessed she deserved that.

"I lean in toward you." Genna leaned in. "And I kiss the guacamole off your lips."

Genna brushed her lips against Rowan's in a touch so featherlight she'd have missed it if every nerve in her body wasn't screaming *Genna.*

"And, once I've had a taste, I just want more." Genna kissed her again. Soft. Light. Nibbling at her lips.

Rowan moaned, dragging the sound out through her throat from the gaping wound of loneliness such sounds bred in.

Genna hummed against her lips. "There it is. So sexy."

She brushed her mouth back and forth across Rowan's lips, unhurried.

"What happens next?" Rowan asked, breathless.

"I think this is the part where you kiss me back."

Rowan embraced longing's dangerous edge, the need to wiggle her toes over a death-defying precipice to feel alive. She knew exactly what this meant, and she invited peril with a welcome heart. She kissed Genna the way she ought to have kissed her in the first place.

Rowan closed her eyes, inhaling clean sweat, spring breeze, and some indefinable female scent. Genna let out a little sigh, accepting Rowan's kiss, her lips softening as she allowed Rowan access. The tension in Genna's muscles unfurled beneath her fingers as Rowan gathered her up. The kiss was sweet and savoring. A true first kiss. Rowan let herself fall into the moment, into every inch of her body as their kiss enveloped her senses. Finally. For all the times they'd misunderstood each other, they synced in touch, and she discovered Genna anew.

Genna as she dreamed she'd be. More than a dream. More open. More honest. Unflinchingly present. Genna melted into her, hands roaming her back, threading through her hair, touching and teasing. Rowan layered slow kisses along the curve of Genna's neck, tasting the salt of her skin. She could spend the rest of her life relishing every touch, every sigh, every texture. They were breaking the rules again, but in the perfection of the kiss, it didn't matter. Sometimes doing the wrong thing was all that felt right.

"Rowan." Genna made her name into thick cream, causing a rush of liquid heat to Rowan's center. She wanted Genna's hands on her. Inside her. She sucked Genna's bottom lip into her mouth, running her tongue along its edge, her fingers tracing her collarbone just visible above the opening of her shirt. Another rush whipped through Rowan as Genna's fingers began to inch under her T-shirt.

Her body went taut. She'd fucked this up once already, she wasn't about to get them arrested. "Baby, we have to stop."

Rowan tried to pull away, but Genna followed her mouth, mummering nonsense words against her lips. Words stopped making sense and so did her thoughts as Genna dialed up the kiss. Exploring her mouth with lips and teeth and tongue until Rowan began to tremble with all she was holding back. Genna slipped a hand around the back of her neck and took control. She slanted her mouth over Rowan's, and their tongues twined in a dance that had Rowan's every molecule humming. Somewhere along the way, the kiss had changed. Now fierce with something other than passion, as if Genna was afraid Rowan would evaporate if they stopped. The guillotine hanging over their heads echoed with judgment.

Fuck. Rowan eased back.

"No," Genna breathed, "don't stop."

"Baby, we're in public."

Genna blinked at Rowan as if she'd completely forgotten where she was. She slid her hands out from under Rowan's shirt, ducking her head. "Oh. Right."

Rowan ran a thumb along Genna's bottom lip, swollen from her kisses. "That was worth the wait."

She waited for what was coming, For Genna to freak out. They'd screwed up the timing. There was no way around it. Rowan had played with fire and burned them both. She'd known it before the kiss. She'd done it anyway.

Genna just sat there her chest rising and falling unsteadily, her hair mussed from Rowan's fingers, her cheeks flushed with arousal. Or was it stress?

"Wow."

Rowan stared. That was it? Just *wow*? No lecture about how they couldn't and shouldn't and mustn't?

"You're okay," Rowan said slowly, not quite believing it.

Genna laughed. "I don't know what kind of kisses you've had, but if that one rates as just okay, you need to give lessons."

Rowan shook her head. "The kiss was unbelievable. But you, you're really okay? We broke the rules."

"We did. I won't say I'm not a lot worried about that. But wow. It's difficult to regret it."

Rowan kissed her brow, the bridge of her nose, the dip in her chin. "Don't regret it, please."

"I couldn't."

Rowan swallowed the lump Genna's declaration had created. Not so long ago Genna couldn't answer a question about herself without running, or hiding, or falling victim to the frustration that bubbled closest to the surface. That decent amount pissed off that Rowan had thought she'd caused until Gabby had said otherwise. But with a kiss, Genna had turned them away from anger and fear and toward the truest form of pleasure. She'd forged a link far beyond sensation, one of connection and discovery. She'd given Rowan a gift beyond any dream.

"Who'd have guessed the sex researcher's fantasies would be so tender," Rowan teased her.

Genna smiled. "You bring it out in me, but don't tell anyone. I have a reputation to uphold."

"All your secrets are safe with me."

Genna started bussing their table. "I need to get home. The sex researcher must get some work done."

Rowan pulled her back down. "One more minute. I need to apologize."

"For what? Do *you* regret the kiss?"

"I regret the first one. I'm sorry. I was scared that you…" Rowan hesitated, the terrifying abyss of her psyche overwhelming her.

"That I would prefer to sleep around?" Genna asked, just a bit dryly.

Rowan nodded. "I'm sorry. Your sister hit on me, and it didn't seem like you really cared if we were monogamous. I got scared."

Genna bit her lip. "I have casual sex. Routinely."

"Okay." Rowan placed the word carefully down between them. "I don't want to share you."

"I understand."

Rowan waited for reassurance that the wow of a kiss had convinced Genna that kissing anyone else was inconceivable.

It didn't come.

"I *don't* understand. If you want sex, I'd be delighted to provide as much as you need. You know that."

"It's not about sex. If all I wanted was an orgasm, it would be cheaper, faster, and a hell of a lot easier on my ego to stay home and indulge my fantasies with Wiggles, my battery-operated companion."

"What is it that you want then?" Rowan asked, pretty sure whatever it was, Genna was convinced a real relationship couldn't give it to her.

Genna didn't reply right away, staring off into the row of hedges, thinking. "I just want the space to be me," she said eventually. "But I need to figure out who that is."

❖

"Good. You're here early. Stop by a minute, I want to talk to you."

Alice stood in the doorway of her office looking like old money in gorgeous blush-colored pants and an expertly tailored silk crème shirt with lace detail on the cuffs that matched the accents on her pointy-toed shoes. This was the level at which Alice did life, perfection down to the smallest detail. Just looking at her was exhausting. Genna's morning had been a blazing dumpster fire, and she'd thrown on a "Girls Do It Better" T-shirt and a pair of distressed jeans and called it done. She hadn't been able to eat anything for breakfast and still her stomach swirled.

For all her brave talk of not regretting kissing Rowan, the morning after was a bitch. Before Rowan had dropped her off, she'd pointed out that no one had to know. But *she* knew, and when it came down to it, she couldn't act as if it hadn't happened. She had to come clean and face the music.

What would Alice say when she admitted to kissing a participant? A *human research subject*? Would she have to make a case to the ethics panel? How could she possibly defend the indefensible? *Sorry, folks. I lost my sanity because this sexy woman I can't stop thinking about is insisting I give up the only outlet I have, and that's fucking with my head.*

Genna brushed past Alice without saying hello and took the seat in front of her desk.

Instead of sitting behind it, Alice leaned against the desk, looming over Genna like a fashionista mob boss about to introduce her to Jesus. "Is everything okay at home?"

Caught up in trying to think of a way to tell Alice she'd fucked up, Genna took a second to register the question. "Mom's fine. It's all fine. Same old, you know."

Alice nodded. "Then tell me what's wrong. You look like someone just died."

Just my career, and possibly our friendship. No biggie.

Genna opened her mouth to tell her but closed it again. She froze. She *had* to tell Alice. She was a lot of things, many of them unpalatable, but she wasn't a liar. Her hands began to tremble, and she couldn't quite breathe a full breath. As soon as she said it, the snowball would start rolling toward the avalanche that could not only stall her career and her hope for a future on her own terms, but her friendship with Alice too. She could lose it all. Over a kiss. A kiss she could've had free and clear if only she'd *waited.* But, no. She'd had to get all handsy with the sexy otter and destroy her life.

"Does this have anything to do with Rowan Marks?" Alice asked as Genna sat there silently angsting.

It was worse than Genna thought if Teach already knew. Only she and Rowan knew. Unless someone had seen them. They *had* been in public. God. Could she be any stupider? With her luck, they'd snapped a worth-a-thousand-words shot and she was already on Insta and canceled. Genna almost laughed. "Yes, it's Rowan Marks."

Alice nodded. "Sometimes these things happen. I wouldn't take it personally. Certainly nothing to get so upset about."

Sometimes these things happen?

"Teach, Rowan and I…" No matter how much she needed to say it, the words just wouldn't come. When push came to shove, she couldn't do it.

Alice knew her, saw she was struggling. She waved her emotions away. "Rowan's already been here. She explained everything. While you *do* need to work on your communication, Rowan simply isn't able to talk about her sexual fantasies. She's hardly the first person to be reticent. It's not your fault."

Genna shook her head very slowly, as if any sudden movement would cause the nausea churning her insides to make a run for freedom. "I don't understand. Rowan came to see you?"

"Earlier this morning. She wanted to let me know she was withdrawing from the study and was very sorry for wasting your time." Alice shrugged. "It's the risk you take with student volunteers, and you have plenty of other participants with several more in the wings. It shouldn't delay you too much."

Rowan had withdrawn from the study.

She'd made an excuse for Teach.

She'd left so Genna wouldn't have to blow up her life.

Of all the kindnesses Rowan had shown her, this was the biggest. Without the sessions, Rowan would never know why she fantasized the way she did. She was giving up that chance so Genna wouldn't have to face the consequences of her runaway libido. She *deserved* those consequences, but she'd never been more grateful to anyone in her life.

Could she just not tell Alice? What they'd done had been wrong. No question. But the ethical dilemma didn't exist if Rowan wasn't in her study. *No one has to know*.

Well, not telling Alice hadn't been an option because any further sessions would be impossible, but with Rowan out of the study… Maybe, she didn't have to tell? One might even say it was the *correct* choice for them to agree that Rowan ought to un-volunteer herself. Of course, Rowan's reasons had nothing to do with not being able to talk. But Alice didn't need to know that. Alice didn't need to know anything. Not yet. If things worked out with Rowan, and God she hoped they did, she'd tell Alice once Rowan had been unvolunteered long enough for it not to come up.

"She's not the only one who struggles," Genna said, to move them away from Rowan. "I only need three sessions for the data, but so many participants find it hard to talk about their fantasies that it takes six, and these are people who have volunteered. I can't imagine how difficult it must be for everyone else."

Alice nodded. "Sex and shame often go hand in hand."

Genna leaned back in her chair, her brain was switching on now the oppressive dread was behind her. "It's deeper than that. I mean, yeah, people have a shame-based response to sex sometimes without even knowing it. It's ingrained in phrases like 'dirty talk' and 'doing the nasty.' But sexual fantasy brings a whole new element into the picture."

Alice walked around her desk and sat down. "I'd have thought sexual fantasy would be a work-around for the shame-response. It's so private. If no one knows, then no one feels shame."

"You'd think so, but it's not true. Actually, it's the opposite. Sexual fantasies tend to be *more* shameful. The privacy, the infinity of options, the lack of consequences, strips away socially imposed behavioral modification and so fantasies tend to be riskier, kinkier, more morally questionable than sex. Attracted to the same sex but live in a country that prosecutes queers? There's a fantasy for that. Want to dress in women's panties but worried you'll be ridiculed? There's a fantasy for that too. People do in fantasies things they wouldn't in partnered sex."

Alice looked thoughtful. "But that's also helpful. If a person cannot, or would not, act on their desires, then fantasy gives them an experience they wouldn't otherwise have, which for some, such as in the LGBTQ example, can be lifesaving."

Genna nodded. "People need their fantasies. But many are also guilt ridden and sometimes even repulsed. If only we could have one without the other."

"I read Nancy Friday's *My Secret Garden* as a freshman in college," Alice said with a sentimental smile. "That book took away a lot of shame for me. Just to know there were other people who had similar thoughts. Or completely different ones, but to my young mind, far more deviant than my own."

"It gave you perspective," Genna mumbled, only half listening to Alice. A lot of what they were saying showed up in the data she'd collected and could be traced historically to the systemic oppression of women and to American puritanicalism in general. Genna was no Nancy Friday, but her research could be used to help people get the perspective Alice was talking about.

"I'm sorry, I have to go." Genna rose.

"I thought we might grab lunch."

Genna shook her head. "Not today. I just figured out how to apply my research in a clinical context. Flint is going to eat it with a spoon."

Chapter Sixteen

Rowan's mom handed Cameron over to Rowan while Sawyer zoomed dizzying circles on the toddler tricycle Rowan had gotten him—and almost instantly regretted buying him for Christmas the year before. "We'd better take Sawyer outside before he breaks all your aunt Mary's china."

Rowan said a little prayer that Sawyer would crash right into the crusty old cabinet bursting with Waterford knockoffs that had been passed down through generations of reluctant heirs and would probably raise the princely sum of fifty bucks at a yard sale. Even then someone would haggle. She hoped it would go to Sara next, and she'd be spared.

Rowan rubbed her nose against Cam's tummy, making him laugh. She turned him around, snaking an arm around his middle and resting his pudgy little backside in her other hand so he could see the great wide world and his favorite person in it—his big brother. She followed her mom and Sawyer out the door and down the stairs to the front porch where the residents of 34 Windemere Lane gathered in good weather to watch the world go by.

Bertie Johnson in apartment three had been somewhere around a hundred and thirty years old for as long as Rowan could remember. She was three iced teas deep, going strong, and had settled in for the duration. "Hi, Bertie."

"Rowan." Bertie's tone was infused with aren't-you-a-good-girl. "It's good to see you. I wish my daughter visited as often as you do. I hope you don't mind if I don't get up. Damn knee replacement wasn't worth the copay."

Rowan leaned down to kiss Bertie's papery cheek. "You stay right where you are, young lady. It's good to see you too."

"I should go relieve Mom for a bit," she said as her mom walked down the front porch steps, one hand holding the bike and the other in Sawyer's.

Bertie patted her hand. "Doreen's looking a bit worse for wear. It's not easy keeping up with two small kids at her age."

"I know."

"That Sara is good for nothin'." Bertie shook her head.

Rowan didn't say anything. As hard as Mom had it, Sara had it worse.

Before she could trade places with her mom, Talia Trenton from number thirty-two jogged across the street and scooped Sawyer into her arms, spinning him in the air with the confidence of someone who'd done it a thousand times. Rowan didn't know much about the Trentons, but Talia was a sixteen-year-old jewel who helped her mom with babysitting.

"I got him, Mrs. M.," Talia said. "Wanna race, Sawyer? I bet I can run faster than you can ride, what do ya say?"

"Be careful now," Doreen said halfheartedly and relinquished Sawyer to his superior playmate. She joined Rowan, Cameron, and Bertie Johnson on the porch, accepting an iced tea gratefully.

Rowan watched Talia and Sawyer in a race that was wide open until the final leg where Sawyer beat out Talia by a hair's breadth, inching his bike over the finish line moments before she caught up to him, panting a bit too hard for someone who had lazy-jogged the whole way. Between visits she somehow always forgot just how *active* a three-year-old could be.

"I'm sorry, Mom," she said as she handed Cameron an empty plastic iced tea bottle to play with.

"What for?" her mom asked.

"It's too much for you to always be looking after them. I need to take them more and give you a rest."

Her mom gave Rowan the look she always gave her. That imperfect mix of patient love and mind your own business. "I love them. They keep me young. You have your own life. As you should."

They had this conversation about every third time Rowan visited, but this time she was reminded of Genna. Of Genna's love for Gabby and Grace and the shackles family had placed on her. She and Genna shared that familial responsibility. But Genna had done what love and duty had asked of her for two-thirds of her life. Rowan had been a coward.

"Mom, do you think everyone has a soul mate?"

"Well, I was married to your father for thirty-five years, and I didn't stay for his charming personality, let me tell you."

Rowan let the sadness wash over her the way it always did when she thought of her dad. Graham Marks's personality had been drowned in booze for more than a decade. He'd passed a year earlier. Rowan wasn't sure whether her mom saw it as a tragedy or a mercy. Both, perhaps.

"I've met someone," she said. "But I don't know if we're right for each other."

"You want a family girl," Bertie Johnson, who had ears like a bat, advised her. "Not one of these career-obsessed vegans who don't want children."

Rowan smiled. "What's wrong with vegans?"

Bertie shook her head. "It's namby-pamby, hipster nonsense. No one can live on kale and quinoa. You need some meat on your bones."

"Is your daughter dating a vegan?" Rowan asked.

"My *son* is dating a vegan," Bertie said in a tone that let it be known this outcome was even worse. "How is she ever going to cook him a proper meal?"

Rowan looked to her mom for help.

"Daniel is happy. Be satisfied with that. It could be worse." Her mom looked pointedly at Cameron who was happily banging the plastic bottle against his thighs.

Bertie pressed her lips together and said nothing more.

"You've met someone?" her mom said. "That's wonderful. When do I meet her?"

"We're not actually dating, so I think it might be a while."

"But you want to be dating? You should ask her to dinner, life is short," her mom said kindly, as if Rowan didn't have two brain cells to rub together.

"I'll do that. But do you think everyone has one special person out there somewhere?"

Her mom pulled a pacifier from one of her many pockets, uncapped the hygiene seal, and stuck it in Cameron's mouth when he began to fuss. "I hope that everyone who wants to can fall in love, but it seems unfair for there to only be one chance. What if they get hit by a bus or perish in a famine?"

A famine? Well, okay, if your soul mate *died in a famine* then it seemed God's benevolence ought to bestow a second chance. But her mom was missing the point. "But if you do meet someone, who is, you know, *the one* for you, that love can overcome anything, right?"

Her mom looked amused. "It can change your heart, sweetie. But I don't think love, even once-in-a-lifetime love, can overcome everything."

"You and Dad never got over losing the deli, and you still loved each other."

Her mom's mouth set itself in a pinched line. "Your *father* never got over losing the deli, and it put a big ol' dent in our marriage. But I managed. Someone had to hold this family together."

Guilt fell on Rowan like a ton of bricks, keeping her stuck in the past. "I should've done more. I should've…"

"Should've what?" her mom asked tiredly. "Should've gotten yourself involved with the wrong kind of people? Should've robbed hard-working families? Should've ended up with two babies to different daddies and then been arrested for a third time and left them motherless for years?"

"Mom—"

"Should've ended up in jail? Is that what you should've done? Sara thought she needed to help us too, and look where it got her. Where it got all of us." Tears gleamed in her mom's eyes. "You were both too young to do anything. We were your parents. It was our responsibility to take care of things, and I did the best I could. All I ever wanted was for you to get good grades and stay out of trouble."

Stubbornly, guilty still, Rowan insisted, "It wasn't enough. Things were never the same after the deli went under. I could've gotten a job, helped financially. I wouldn't have ended up like Sara, you know it. Maybe if I hadn't been so selfish, Dad would—"

Her mom placed her hand on top of Rowan's. "Your dad was responsible for himself. He chose to dwell on the past and drink himself to an early grave. What's done is done. I love you, and I want you to build a happy life for yourself." Her mom took a breath. "Now, tell me about this woman. You must like her very much if you're thinking about soul mates."

"I do, maybe too much. I'm not sure she feels the same way."

"Why do you say that?"

Rowan sighed. "For starters, she thinks relationships are hard work."

Her mom and Bertie laughed at that.

Bertie helpfully added, "If you think relationships *aren't* work, you ain't met much of life."

"Of course, I know they aren't always easy. But are they always hard? Isn't there some middle ground?" Was a great relationship really too idealistic, or was everyone too cynical?

"When I was growing up, you and Dad were so happy. So perfect. It didn't look like work at all, not until the deli fell apart. That's what I want. I know it exists, because you had it. It's why you stayed with him, isn't it? Because your love was strong enough to weather anything?"

Her mom shook her head. "No relationship is perfect, so you can get that notion right out of your head. But I won't deny we were happy."

"She's sleeping with other people. We aren't dating and I have no right to ask, but I can't imagine dating someone who's also getting it on with God only knows who else. That's not unreasonable, is it?" Rowan probably sounded a bit desperate. She *felt* desperate. Her mom *had* met a lot of life. She'd tell her if Rowan was being an idiot.

Her mom looked thoughtful. "Usually, you would wait for that kind of thing, but you have feelings for her already. So, no, it's not unreasonable. If she would rather have sex with other people, she might not feel the same way you do."

A small part of Rowan shriveled up and died as her mom confirmed her fears. She liked Genna a lot more than Genna liked her, despite the flirting and the tenderness with which Genna had kissed her. Maybe for Genna, she really was just one in a string of all the other people. She felt sick thinking about it.

"Have you asked her about it? You might wear your heart on your sleeve, but you're a straight shooter. If you have feelings, then she's something special."

"I asked," Rowan said, "and she said it wasn't about sex, and she had to figure out who she was. How can sex not be about sex?"

"That's a question for her," her mom said. "But it sounds like it might not be because she *prefers* it to you. Maybe you have her questioning her choices."

"What if I'm not enough to change her mind?" Rowan put her worst fear into words.

Her mom fingered a locket she always wore, one Rowan's dad had given her on their wedding day. "All you can do is try to understand her. When you know who she is, you'll know if you're enough."

"You're right," Rowan said. "That's good advice. Thank you."

She hugged Cameron and watched Sawyer ride circles around Talia, urging her to chase him. They were both laughing like lunatics, and Rowan couldn't help but smile too. "Talia's really good with him."

"That girl is the miracle in my life. I don't know what I'd do without her." Her mom sipped her tea.

Rowan hugged Cameron, comforted by family when she needed it. Genna might never trust her enough to let her learn more, or perhaps Rowan wouldn't like what she discovered, but she was determined to find out. Maybe her mom was right, and she did wear her heart on her sleeve, but sometimes you had to believe in miracles.

❖

Genna walked through the front door of her apartment in the late afternoon after a campus-wide internet outage made inputting the notes from her last two interviews impossible. Who was she kidding? Even if Spectrum hadn't taken a sick day, working was a dubious proposition when all she could think about was Rowan. She had to thank her, but she had no idea what *else* to say. *You saved my bacon, I appreciate it,* just didn't seem like enough. For some reason, Rowan was always helping her, like some walking, talking safe harbor. The concept was so foreign she was at a loss for how to deal. What did she have to offer Rowan in return? Nothing but a bucket full of mommy issues.

Hold up. Rowan *had* asked her for something. Help with her fantasies. What if she could still help her with that? They didn't need the study. Would Rowan still want to?

She pulled her phone from her purse and texted Rowan as she headed to the shower.

I owe you, big time. Name your price.

Rowan: *Dr. Sullivan told you I left the study?*

Genna pulled out the tie keeping her could-never-be-bothered-to-cut-it way too long hair off her face and peeled her T-shirt over her head before she texted Rowan back.

I went to confess only to find out you'd quit. For me.

She stood shirtless, staring at her phone.

Rowan: *Knew you wouldn't be able to keep it a secret. But not for you. For us.*

For us. Genna closed her eyes, the words warming deep within her. Rowan really was the nicest human on the planet. She didn't deserve her. Before she could reply, another text came through.

Rowan: *Now, about that payment...*

Genna's breath hitched. She slid her jeans down her hips as heat built between her thighs. *I'm listening.*

Three dots appeared on her screen as Rowan typed a reply, then disappeared. Genna turned on the water. The dots reappeared and soon after Rowan's text.

Rowan: *I liked the way you slid your hands up the back of my shirt yesterday, biting into my sides like you were three seconds from ripping it from my skin.*

She could almost hear Rowan saying the words in her rumbling voice, as if whispering in her ear. Fuck. Her skin began to tingle.

Tracing all the muscle beneath your T-shirt. Got it. What else am I adding to this invoice?

Rowan: *This game takes two. Your turn.*

Genna thought, which was hard to do with every cell busy fanning the embers of arousal. *I liked the way you kissed me, especially when your tongue dipped into my mouth and stroked mine—making promises I expect you to keep.*

Genna stripped off her bra and panties as the bathroom filled with steam.

Rowan: *What sort of promises, Dr. Sex?*

She owed Rowan for all the questions she'd dodged lately, and she could answer in detail. *Promises like, this is how I'll lick you, and this is how slowly I'll slide my fingers inside you, and maybe even this is how my hips will move against yours when I fuck you.*

Genna paused to reread the message. Jesus. She'd meant to text Rowan to say thank you, to tell her they should talk more about her fantasies, and instead she was standing naked in her bathroom, tripling her monthly water bill, and *sexting.*

She hit send.

Rowan: *You're killing me. I picked a terrible time to squeeze in a workout.*

Genna couldn't help laughing. Rowan was at the *gym*? Some perverse part of her liked that. *Poor baby. Did I turn you on?*

Rowan: *So much. I'm starting to worry it shows.*

Genna opened the shower door. *I'm naked and about to get in the shower to take care of what you just started. Have a good workout.*

Rowan: *Are you making that up to fuck with me?*

Genna stepped away from the shower. She took a photo of the steamy empty stall and sent it to Rowan. *Sucks to be you, Thor. I'll be thinking of you.*

She tossed her phone onto the bathmat and stepped inside, the hot water nothing compared to the fire between her legs. She brushed her clit and her center clenched. God how she wished Rowan was here so she could wrap her legs around her. Beg. She stroked her most sensitive spots, curling her fingers inside herself, the sound of her own wetness obscene. Then it was Rowan behind her, an arm wrapped around her waist, Rowan's hand working between Genna's legs, thrusting inside, stroking her clit, owning her body. The pulse between her thighs reverberated through her body. Thoughts melted away as Rowan touched her, the stroke of her fingers inside leaving her clenching and desperate for more. Her arousal shot up to eleven and her vision went hazy, her body shifting all its resources to the orgasm that was about to engulf her. She couldn't hold back. Couldn't stop the pressure from building.

"I want to spend every day with you," Rowan whispered in her ear. "So hot and wet for me, so needy."

Ohmygodyes. "Please don't stop."

"Every day. Just like this." Rowan bit her ear, sucking the sensitive lobe into her mouth.

"I need you so much. Please."

Rowan squeezed her clit, and her orgasm whipped through her like an EF5 tornado and emptied her brain.

Genna rested her cheek against the tile until the water cooled and she shut it off. She stepped out on shaking legs. What was that? The quickest of all orgasms? If a few sexy texts could inspire an orgasm that left her blind and half drowned, Genna wasn't sure she'd survive anything more.

She grabbed a towel from the hook on the back of the door and picked her phone up off the floor. A text waited for her.

Rowan: *First time I've been jealous of a bar of soap. I hope it's a good fantasy. Enjoy.*

Genna smiled, completely smitten with Rowan's signature combination of sweet and sexy. *So good. If you still want my help with Mrs. Sutton and company, meet me at Happy Hour tomorrow around 11.*

She wondered what Rowan would say if she knew Genna's terribly, horribly, embarrassing fantasies were about every day until forever.

CHAPTER SEVENTEEN

You fucked her over text? Dude. Get some game. That shit is for teenagers." Maria wrinkled her nose.

"I felt like a teenager." Rowan had asked Maria to meet her at Happy Hour when they opened at ten thirty so she could bring her up to date on all things Rowna. She *had* to tell someone and certain details were TMI for her mother. "It was just some hot texts. She took a shower to *take care of business,* and I finished my reps with a hell of a lady boner."

Maria laughed. "Tell me you're going to sleep with her soon. It's been *forever*. You two are the hottest slow burn in history."

"I hope so." That part she wouldn't be sharing with anybody.

"What's she like outside of *business*?" Maria asked when Rowan fell silent.

"She's…" How could she sum Genna up in only a few words? "She's really nice if you can get her to relax. She's loyal. She'd do anything for her family. She's smart and works hard. She gets shit done, but she also has so much on her plate. It's probably sexist of me to want to help her, but I do. She's not afraid to say what's on her mind and share an opinion that contradicts mine, which is also hot when it's not annoying. I just wish…"

Maria took a sip of her diet Sprite. "You wish?"

"I wish she knew that someone caring for her is *normal*. She treats it like it's never happened before. She has a hard time accepting even the smallest thing I do for her."

"Maybe she *hasn't* had anyone to care for her before."

"Not without strings attached," Rowan said. "For Genna, loving someone means looking after them." Rowan popped a potato chip into her mouth and thought about what she'd just said. "I think she secretly likes it. She reads novels about damsels in distress and watches *The Batchelor*."

"I thought you said she was smart," Maria said, deadpan.

Rowan threw a chip at her. "Everyone needs their fantasies."

"Yeah, but *The Batchelor*—"

"Is awesome," Genna said from behind Maria.

Rowan and Maria jumped.

"I didn't see you there." Rowan checked her phone. Ten fifty a.m. She was early. That was good, right?

"I gathered." Genna smiled.

Rowan breathed a sigh of relief. She wasn't required to also like *The Batchelor*. Thank God. How much had Genna heard?

Maria swiveled on her stool to face Genna. "Hey. Um, sorry. Obviously, you're smart."

Genna laughed. "You must be Maria. It's nice to meet you."

Maria nodded, plainly still embarrassed.

Genna sat next to Rowan at the table. "Reality TV is too lowbrow for you, huh? Let me guess, you stream *Ozark*." She paused. "Or maybe you're one of those Discovery Channel nerds."

Maria relaxed. "Wrong on both counts. All I watch is *Sesame Street* and *Mickey Mouse Fun House*. Talk about lowbrow."

"How old are your kids?" Genna asked.

"Three and six. I can't wait until they're old enough for an iPad and headphones. Let the internet mommy-shame me, KIDZ BOP is the worst."

"If I'd have had YouTube when my sisters were young, life would've been easier," Genna said wistfully.

Rowan ate her chips and watched Genna charm Maria. She was killer at the small talk thing. Probably came in useful finding casual dates. After five minutes, Maria grabbed her stuff, gave Rowan a hug, and made her excuses, leaving them alone.

"That was nice of you," Rowan said.

Genna grabbed the last chip. "What was?"

"Talking to Maria for a bit so she didn't feel bad about her joke."

"She wouldn't really judge. She's friends with you, and you like *Buffy the Vampire Slayer*. Vampires aren't even real."

"And *The Batchelor* is?" Rowan asked, incredulous.

"There aren't any night horrors lurking in the shadows."

Rowan just shook her head. "I like you in spite of your awful taste in TV shows, Dr. Sex."

"Right back atcha." Genna smiled.

Happy looked good on her. Maybe Rowan had played a small role in that. She hoped so. "Speaking of terrible, you wanted to talk about Mrs. Sutton?"

Genna nodded. "I know you're no longer in the study—and thank you again—but I thought you might want to talk more about your fantasies? I'd still like to help. And it *was* the only reason you signed up."

Rowan laughed. "What gave me away?"

"Could've been you trembling in your boots at the prospect of talking about sex for six hours. Poppy said you almost ran out the door."

Poppy had ratted her out? Traitor. "I can talk about sex. How was your shower yesterday?"

Genna raised her eyebrows, a hint of pink staining her cheeks. "Look at you being so brave. It was very satisfying. Thank you."

"Good." Rowan left it at that. If Genna wanted to tell her about her fantasy, she would have. She was finally getting that not pushing and letting Genna come to her was also very satisfying.

Genna glanced around and leaned closer. "Since we're alone, give me another fantasy. I have a couple of theories, but nothing is really gelling yet."

"Then I guess I'd better tell you about Penelope." Telling Genna her fantasies wasn't so hard anymore. Not only had she not judged her, but she liked Rowan despite them. As if her fantasies were just like her taste in TV, something that didn't really matter.

"Sexy name," Genna said.

"She was one of the developers who handled the paperwork when my parents' deli went under, and they had to sell the building."

Genna winced. "That sounds hard."

Hard wasn't even the half of it. Some wounds never fully healed. "I was fifteen, so just at the right age to get all the wrong ideas about buxom blond-haired Penelope."

"Buxom?" Genna smiled.

"What's wrong with buxom?"

"Nothing if you're a kindly grandpa. It goes in the sweet category, alongside flummoxed."

"It's not sweet. It's literally a description of the size of a woman's breasts."

"Fair point," Genna said. "Please go on."

"Anyway, buxom Penelope comes into the deli with some papers for Dad. He's not there. She's annoyed and too important to pay attention to me at first, until I start yelling at her. Her company is putting Dad out of business, and she doesn't care. She's all about profits and shareholders. I sort of…prevent her from leaving."

Her self-disgust enveloped her like a weighted blanket, hot, itchy, and full-bodied. Why did she strip perfectly nice people down until they were basically no longer human? And somehow it turned her on. Genna was right after all. She did hate talking about sex.

What. The. Hell. Brain.

"It's perfectly normal," Genna said, as if reading her mind. "Go ahead."

"I try to intimidate her but I'm not very successful. All she sees when she looks at me is a kid. Somehow, someway, in the fantasy, we end up kissing and she wants it. I don't force her. It's not a rape fantasy." She needed Genna to believe that.

Genna just shrugged. "Wouldn't be unusual if it were. The largest study on sexual fantasies ever conducted found that force was the third most popular fantasy type."

"Really? Rape fantasies are that popular?"

"Force can mean all kinds of things, not necessarily rape, but as a broad categorization yes, dubious consent is popular. So, if you had forced Penelope in your fantasy, that would be nothing to be ashamed of. There's a significant difference between a fantasy and reality."

Rowan nodded, starting to believe that, for whatever cold comfort it provided. "What are the first and second most popular?"

"Group sex and BDSM."

"Huh." Rowan wanted to ask if Genna fantasized about either of those. Or did the opportunities *all the other people* afforded her mean she didn't have to fantasize? Rowan wished it were possible to just forget about the history Genna refused to give up. She needed to file that under *don't ever think about it again if you want to be happy.* Genna was here with her now, that's what mattered.

"Back to Penelope," Genna said.

"Right. So logistically the fantasy isn't complicated. We're kissing, and I sort of maneuver her toward the deli counter and fuck her on it. It's a hate-sex sort of thing. She's hot and I'm into her, but I'm also angry and rough and she treats me like a kid, telling me what to do, telling me to be good."

"You're angry because of her role in the closing of the deli?"

"Majorly. That was a difficult time in my life." Understatement of the century.

Genna looked thoughtful. "In your prison break fantasy, is the person you're rescuing a family member?"

Rowan had to hand it to Genna. Whatever they taught in psychology research school had a way of getting to the truth. "Yes." Rowan took a leap of faith. "My sister."

Genna took Rowan's hand, somehow knowing that Sara being in prison wasn't make-believe. She squeezed.

A sour mix of anger, sadness, and guilt wove through Rowan like a prickly vine.

Sara. Who'd tried to help her parents in all the wrong ways.

Sara. Who'd gotten caught too many times on the other side of the law.

Sara. The prisoner.

Genna's expression flashed with raw sympathy, and she ran her thumb along the back of Rowan's hand. "That really sucks for her, and your family."

Genna didn't ask what Sara had done, whether she was guilty, whether Rowan visited her, or any number of questions other people felt they had a right to know. Her undisguised tenderness hit Rowan in the solar plexus and twisted, making it hard to breathe for a second. It *did* suck. There wasn't anything to make it better, no magic solution she hadn't thought of yet. It just was. Genna got that.

"Do you want to talk about it?" Genna asked.

Rowan shook her head. She supposed it said something that when given the choice between her fucked up family and her fucked up fantasies, she was happy to be thinking about Penelope and her gravity-defying breasts.

"All right." Genna gave Rowan another moment before asking, "Think back on other fantasies you've had, especially the ones you repeat on a regular basis. Are they related to your family?"

Rowan felt her ears go hot. *What?* Her brain might not have too many boundaries, but that was a rock-hard no. "My fantasies are a problem, but they're not about my family, that's…Jesus, no."

Genna shook her head. "Not *with* your family. But your family is peripherally related to all three so far. You breaking Sara out of prison. You being stalked by your parents' landlord's wife. You have sex on the counter of the family deli. Is there a connection?"

Rowan pressed her lips together to keep the *hell fuck no* on the tip of her tongue from coming out her mouth. Her family had nothing to do with her sex life. "Honestly, it sounds like a stretch. At best it's a coincidence. Maybe I take elements from life and weave them in, but that's it. I've fantasized about you, and you've haven't met my family." Rowan took a risk and added, "Yet."

Genna smiled. Maybe Genna really *did* like her back. Maybe this could work.

"Well, I won't know if that fantasy is peripherally related unless you tell me about it." Genna's tone was teasing.

Rowan shrugged, more than a little relieved the confession had steered them away from family. "It's not embarrassing. We hug."

"We hug?" Genna frowned. "You fuck Penelope's brains out, but we *hug*?"

Warmth filled Rowan's chest. By-the-book Genevieve never would've asked this question in such an affronted tone. Rowan liked not being Genna's study participant a whole lot. "It was a very sexy hug?"

Genna shook her head in mock sadness. "I see we have some catching up to do."

That sounded…promising. Rowan wanted to kick her own ass for spending her time talking about sex instead of getting naked with Genna. Hadn't they done enough talking? She was certifiable for requiring monogamy when they weren't even dating. Well, okay, they weren't dating *because* of the monogamy thing now. But what if Genna ultimately said no? The possibility extinguished the warmth their conversation had created. When it came down to it, if Genna didn't choose her, then Rowan didn't really want sex. Her fantasies might be morally gray, but in reality, emotion played a big part for her. She couldn't just turn that off, especially when she secretly more than liked Genna.

"Hey, I'm sorry. I was teasing." Genna took Rowan's silence as offense.

Rowan smiled. "I'd happily sign up for remedial lessons to catch up."

"Something just happened. Tell me." Genna took her hand again.

She didn't want to bring it up. Genna knew what she needed, and Rowan knew she had to figure herself out. "Just feeling a bit vulnerable. You know so much about my fantasies. About me."

"And you want to know mine?" Genna asked.

"No. I mean, yes." Of course, she wanted to know what turned Genna on, especially if it involved her, but it wouldn't ease the ache in her chest. "One day, when you're ready to tell me. But I need something else."

Genna's gaze never wavered. She had a way of giving Rowan her full focus, as if nothing and no one else mattered. In the age of commoditization of attention spans, such concentration was rare. She hadn't realized how much she craved it until Genna gave it to her.

"Tell me. If I can give it to you, I will," Genna said.

Rowan took a breath and opened the *don't ever think about it* file. "Tell me about all the other people that Grace was referring to."

A trickle of ice water ran down Genna's spine. Of all the things Rowan could have asked her, *that* was what she wanted to know? Why? To torture herself? Torture them both with sex that didn't matter? The old part of Genna that ran away from her emotions wanted to refuse, but somehow Rowan had changed that. Changed her. So instead, she said, "This is what you need?"

Rowan nodded. "I want to know you, to *be with* you, and this is holding us back."

Genna swallowed, the words *holding us back* settling in her brain like boulders. Rowan couldn't have been clearer. She either gave up the only thing that had saved her mental health for a decade, or they'd stay stuck in place.

When she didn't immediately reply, Rowan said, "I know it's hard. It's hard for me too. I don't *want* to know. But I need to, so I understand you."

"What do you need to know?" Genna asked around the lump in her throat. She'd give Rowan as much as she needed, but not a detail more.

"Why is it important to you?" Rowan asked.

Genna closed her eyes for a second. There was zero chance Rowan wouldn't think she was a philandering harlot. "Variety doesn't suck. Why have one when you could have dozens?"

She could tell the number surprised Rowan from the way her spine stiffened. Genna bit her lip, regretting the flippant defensive response.

"How long have you been doing this?" Rowan asked.

"The first time, I was nineteen. Same age as the twins." Intellectually, Genna knew she had zero to be ashamed of. There was nothing wrong with casual sex. But that didn't stop her wanting the ground to swallow her whole when the surprise on Rowan's face turned to pity.

"Where do you meet them? Online?"

Genna shook her head. "A lot of people do that, but it works better for dating, for sex it can be dangerous. I don't take risks."

"It's dangerous?"

"Rarely, but it can be. I'm fucked up enough already without adding that to the mix."

"You're not fucked up," Rowan said.

"Oh, I am." Genna laughed humorlessly. She didn't want to leave Rowan in any doubt on that score. Wasn't it obvious she came with a boatload of boring pedestrian childhood trauma manifesting as promiscuity? And wasn't talking about it fun?

"You said the sex wasn't about sex. Can you explain that? I don't understand."

How could Genna explain something she didn't really understand herself? Something she actively chose not to examine. She waved a hand at Rowan. "You spend way more time in a gym than average. Why?"

Rowan rolled with the segue. "I enjoy it. It helps me feel centered and relives stress."

Genna nodded. "It's the same for me. We both use our bodies to help our heads, just in different ways." This wasn't the answer Rowan wanted, but she couldn't do any better when she'd been avoiding *why* for a decade. *Please don't push me.*

"It relieves stress." Rowan's tone was so dubious it made the statement sound like a lie.

"I could say it's narcissistic to care so much about your body, to dedicate time to it. And while that might be true for some people, it's not for you. I pick up people at McKinney's for the same reason you go to the gym. The experience helps me deal with life."

"The gym isn't dangerous," Rowan argued. "It doesn't prevent me from having a meaningful relationship."

Genna hoped she hadn't actually flinched at that dagger to the heart. "I'm not saying they're equivalent. Just that they serve the same purpose. You asked why. That's why."

She could tell Rowan wasn't at all satisfied with that answer.

"What's McKinney's?"

"It's a bar halfway between here and Mom's place. That's where I find the *other people*."

"I didn't think pick-up places existed anymore, now that everyone meets online."

Genna shrugged. "It's just a bar that happens to be across the street from a Holiday Inn with great one-night rates. It's developed a reputation as a hook-up, hot spot. I prefer to meet people in person first, get a sense of them, and the hotel has decent security."

"I hate that it's dangerous," Rowan said.

Genna shrugged again. "Walking down the street is dangerous. I take precautions. I don't do any bondage, and I only sleep with women, or guys who are regulars. They're less likely to become violent."

She watched Rowan's throat work as she swallowed. "People tie up strangers?"

"A surprising number. McKinney's reputation attracts a lot of first-timers and swingers who don't know any better."

"That's scary," Rowan said.

Genna didn't disagree.

"I want to go to McKinney's with you."

Oh, hell no. Absolutely not. No fucking way.

"No." Genna kept her tone casual but firm. If Rowan wanted details, she could give them, even if doing so chipped a few chunks out of her self-esteem. But she wasn't taking Rowan there. There were some things you could never unsee.

"I don't want us to pick anyone up. But I need to understand," Rowan said.

Genna shook her head in frustration. "This isn't *me*. McKinney's is something I do. It's not who I am."

"Then give it up," Rowan said. "If it's not important, if it's not part of your identity, just let it go."

Godfuckingdamnit. Genna said nothing. They didn't speak for a minute. A silent battle of wills. Rowan out-stubborn-ed her.

"Fine," Genna said. "If you want to go, we can go. But I don't like it."

Rowan nodded. "I don't like it either, Dr. Sex. But I like you."

The hopefulness in Rowan's tone unraveled the anxiety that had built as they talked.

"Still?" Genna asked, the word coming out very small.

"More every day. I want to move forward with you."

Sigh. Only Rowan could make a trip to McKinney's sound romantic.

"I would rather show up at my high school reunion naked, but no one has ever tried to understand me before. I know how rare and special that is. It means a lot."

"I care," Rowan said, taking her hands again and kissing each knuckle.

"I care too."

And that was ten times more dangerous than anything she'd experienced at the Holiday Inn. If she couldn't *move forward*, she was going to have her heart smashed to smithereens.

CHAPTER EIGHTEEN

911. PLEASE come to McK tonight. I need backup.

Genna dumped every item from her closet on her bed looking for something to wear. Something demure and conservative that said kindergarten-teacher, or regular churchgoer, or "I'll be delighted to meet your mother." Her only-for-funerals dress? The pastel J. Crew number her mom had given her five birthdays ago that still had the tags attached? Should she just forgo a dress and show up in jeans like the guys did? Did she have a clean pair?

Travis: *No can do, Casanova. The game just started. 49ers are playing the Ravens.*

Seriously? Weren't friends supposed to be there for you when you needed them? She had an actual crisis, and Travis was going to stay home to watch a bunch of overpaid dudes chase a little ball. Time to play mean.

OK, that's cool. Remember that time you asked me to pretend to be your jealous girlfriend so you could get away from Cute but Clingy and Cries? I was so good AND I sat with her for an hour while she cried.

Fuck it. She didn't have time to dither any longer. She grabbed the black midi dress with the conservative neckline and cap sleeves. Morticia Adams as funeral director didn't say looking-to-get-laid.

Travis: *Hey, you two got along alright in the end. Girl power.*

Genna rolled her eyes. *You owe me. Be there by nine.*

Travis: *Where's the fire?*

Genna stepped into the dress and started working on the zillion tiny buttons. *I'm bringing Rowan. Not my idea. Don't want to talk about it.*

Travis's reply came so fast Genna didn't even have time to find her heels.

Travis: *Emotional masochist or virgin polyamorist?*

Genna stepped into her shoes and threw a few essentials into a purse so tiny it barely qualified. She headed for the door, stopping a second by the mirror in the entryway to apply some token lipstick. *She's trying to understand me. Bad idea.*

Travis: *Uh oh. You're gonna need all the help you can get. ETA* 9.

Uh-oh was right. The intercom buzzed, and Genna couldn't help thinking it heralded the beginning of the longest night of her life.

❖

Rowan held the door open for her when they got to McKinney's.

Genna resisted the impulse to turn and run in the other direction. Were they really doing this? "Wait. Can we just wait a minute?"

Rowan let the door swing shut, and they stepped to the side to leave the entryway clear. "Of course. Is everything okay?"

All Genna's emotions stumbled and ran into one another like dominos. "I need a minute."

Rowan went to take her hand.

Genna wanted to shove it in her pocket but the infernal dress didn't *have* pockets.

"Genna. You're trembling." Rowan caught her fingers and pressed them between her palms. "What's wrong?"

It was the way Rowan said her name. Not Dr. Sex, but her real name that brought home the enormity of allowing Rowan to see this side of her. A side Rowan was so not okay with. "I don't want to lose you."

The words had slipped out before she'd thought them through, and she cringed at how pathetic she sounded.

Rowan rubbed Genna's cold hands. "I don't want to lose you either. That's why we're here."

Until they went inside and twelve different people hit on Rowan in the span of a half hour. She would feel like a cow at auction. Prime meat. Rowan was *romantic,* and McKinney's was about as romantic as a strip club and a good deal less honest. Would Rowan still respect her?

"Talk to me," Rowan said quietly.

Genna blew out a breath. "You're going to think less of me if we go in there, and you're already so much better than I am. You're bound to realize dating me is a stupid idea."

"I'm *better* than you?"

Genna shrugged. "You're nicer. Kinder. Sweeter. People like you. I'm just...someone who fucks strangers. How can you not think being with me is stupid?"

Rowan cupped her jaw, bringing their lips together in a kiss. Then she gave her an okay-you're-stupid look. "Not everyone wants sweet. You're braver. Smarter. More empathic. I'm just someone who has god-awful sexual fantasies. Do you think being with me is stupid?"

Genna smiled. "Of course, I don't. I think you're amazing."

Rowan pulled her in for a hug, and Genna stepped into the comfort of her body.

"You can do this," Rowan told her. "I'm not leaving, and I think you're amazing too."

Genna pressed her cheek to Rowan's shoulder for a second to soak up the warmth. "Okay. Okay. Back it up. I'm not reenacting your hug fantasy for the whole world to see."

Rowan laughed and with Rowan still holding her hand, they walked into McKinney's together.

The sports game Travis was missing was muted on a flatscreen too small to entice actual fans, but big enough to give the people crowding the bar something to pretend to watch. Unfortunately, the place was packed. The crowd ran the gambit from woke, alternative bohemians to good ol' Southern Republicans. Genna didn't know if "sex sells" was always accurate, but it sure has hell crossed the cultural divide. She managed to spot Travis between the hordes of people.

"Come on, looks like Travis saved us seats."

They had only taken two steps when a tall skinny man with an absent-minded college professor vibe made a beeline for Rowan, hand already outstretched. Genna gave the guy her best back-the-fuck-off-before-I-castrate-you stare. Professor dude veered away. She kept her basilisk glare in place all the way to Travis's table.

Travis stood to shake hands with Rowan. "Hi, I'm Travis. I've heard a lot about you. You'd better sit before the women over there make off with these chairs. They've been eyeing them for the last ten minutes."

They all sat, and Genna caught Daryl's eye as he shook one cocktail after another at the bar. She held up three fingers, and he nodded at her. "Daryl knows they're underage, right?"

"He's already carded them. They're twenty-one." Travis shrugged.

"God." Genna said. "They look as if they're barely out of high school."

Travis smiled. "If memory serves, *you* were younger."

He turned to Rowan. "The bartender before Daryl refused to card anyone, and I had my hands full keeping her out of trouble."

Genna stared daggers at Travis until he pressed his lips together, the brainlessness of his statement apparently dawning on him. "So Genna tells me you're a student too? What are you studying?"

And so went the polite chitchat. Their beers arrived. Travis could befriend just about anyone with his eyes closed, which gave Genna way too much room in her brain to panic. Not that there was anything to panic about. Her arm resting along the back of Rowan's chair was enough of a deterrent for most people, and Rowan seemed relaxed enough.

Until Sam crashed the party like a nightmare fairy godqueer.

"Casanova! Introduce me." Sam, managed to infuse the words with enough *hello, sailor!* for an entire Navy fleet. And just when it had been going so well…

"Rowan, this is Sam, another regular. Sam, this is Rowan." Sam smiled so big all their teeth showed, and they doffed their bright yellow beret like a Parisian lost in Shakespearean times.

Genna couldn't help but smile. Sam had a way of pulling at her heartstrings, and her limits for annoyance in equal measure.

Then, since they seemed immune to the Basilisk, she added, "Hands off."

Sam smirked at her. "Or you'll what? Glare me to death?"

"We're not here to hook up. Can you just—"

Rowan squeezed her knee under the table and leaned over to kiss the side of her neck. She whispered in her ear, "Chill. It's okay."

Yeah. That wasn't happening. Genna was as chill as an active volcano.

Rowan turned to Sam. "I'm Genna's girlfriend. It's nice to meet you."

Genna's jaw dropped, and she saw Travis laugh into his beer. Her *girlfriend*? When had this happened? Her heart was doing a crazy dance, the "I Heart Rowan" flag waving in mad circles.

"Well, well." Sam's grin got so wide their cheeks all but disappeared. "Has our very own Casanova finally fallen victim to a *relationship*?"

Genna wondered how difficult it was to get away with murder, and if she really cared about life in prison.

Rowan smiled. "A victimless crime, I assure you."

Sam nodded slowly, looking back and forth between them like they were playing at Wimbledon. "Better you than me. Anyway, I just wanted to say hi, and if you need any help deciding who's an asshole and who isn't, hit me up. Most people are okay, but some get weird around those of us who don't present the binary."

Sam held their fist for bumping, and Rowan's face lit up as she returned the gesture. "I appreciate that. I worry a bit in new situations, you know?"

Sam nodded. "I get you." They tilted their head toward Genna. "Nova's aces with the gender stuff and hot as fuck in bed too." They winked at Rowan, clearly thinking this was something they could bond over.

Genna felt the world tilt under her. This was a terrible idea. An absolutely terrible fucking idea. Did Rowan really just say she was her girlfriend?

Rowan squeezed her knee again before replying to Sam. "I haven't had the honor yet, so I'll have to take your word for it."

Sam looked dumbfounded at that and started to speak, but before they could say anything else, Genna said, "It was nice seeing you, Sam, but we're on our way out in a few minutes." *Please go away before I kill you.*

They'd been here less than an hour, but Genna might actually implode from stress if they had to stay any longer.

Sam hightailed it, shooting Genna a look that radiated *we're going to talk about this later*.

"That was nice." Rowan traced a soothing pattern on Genna's knee. "It can be tough when you present differently. If I *was* here to find someone, I would've appreciated the assist."

"But this place isn't your style." Travis's tone was casual, but it wasn't a question.

"Nope," Rowan agreed good-naturedly. "It's fun though. There are so many people. It's entertaining to watch everyone."

Genna couldn't think of anything less entertaining than sitting like a fucking tourist in McKinney's with Rowan surrounded by people she'd seen naked. Sam was the least of her sins.

As if Rowan could read her thoughts, she asked, "So how does it work? You just find someone attractive and try chatting them up, then ask if they want to book a room?"

Genna tried to speak but her tongue was Velcroed to the roof of her mouth. She couldn't *do* this. Not here surrounded by all of them. Humiliation opened its arms wide and welcomed her in.

Travis came to her rescue. "Pretty much. The ones looking for casual sex will let you know. With everyone else it's just the same small talk hoopla that you'd get at any bar."

Genna stood. "We should probably get going so Travis can do a bit more than people watch. I'm just going to stop at the restroom. I'll be right back."

When Genna walked stiffly away, Rowan let out a breath. "I did not expect her to be quite this uptight. I thought she was about to bite Sam's head off."

Travis smiled. "She's into you, and this isn't your kind of place. She's embarrassed."

"I'm not judging her. Or you," Rowan added. "I just don't get the casual sex thing. I'm trying to understand what she sees in it."

Travis sipped his beer, his amused expression in place. "She liked it. You don't. Who cares?"

"Likes," Rowan corrected him.

Travis gave her a "go on" motion.

"I want monogamy. She doesn't." Everything was a bit more complicated than that, of course, but Rowan didn't feel like laying it all out to someone who was clearly on the side of non-monogamy and didn't think it was worth caring about.

Travis whistled softly. "This joint is in her blood. That's not going to be easy."

"Is it in her blood?" Rowan asked as her heart plummeted.

Travis shrugged noncommittally. "Casanova isn't known for being an open book. If she brought you here, then she's trying to make it work. In her own way. It's cute to see her so protective of someone who looks like they could snap her in two. Not that you would," he added generously.

"Protective of *me*?"

"Of course, you. She's trying so hard to be sure you're not uncomfortable that she's making it uncomfortable for everyone. Isn't love grand?"

Travis grinned.

Love?

Rowan didn't know what to say to that so said nothing and sat people watching. Sam was talking to the barely legal wannabee chair stealers, and it looked like they were sharing makeup tips.

"Am I really old, or is that a strange way to pick someone up?" Rowan asked Travis, nodding toward the group.

Travis studied them as they started trading cosmetics. "Sam isn't trying to hook up with them." He gestured to a corner closer to the bar. "See Balding Jude Law talking to the woman who keeps looking over his shoulder? *He's* trying to pick her up."

Rowan could see it. The way Balding Jude Law was leaning toward her, talking faster than a used car salesman. Her body language shouted her disinterest.

"Does he think he won't get rejected if she doesn't have the opportunity to speak?" Rowan asked.

Travis gave the pair a fond look. "Have a heart. He's nervous. He hasn't learned his league yet and started talking to the second most beautiful woman in the room just because she makes his dick hard. Rookie move."

"Genna's the first most beautiful." Rowan didn't miss Travis's insinuation.

Travis shrugged. "She'd laugh her ass off if I said it, but yeah."

Rowan couldn't exactly argue. She'd tried not to have expectations walking through the door, but she hadn't been prepared for how *normal* the place was. Just regular people enjoying a night out. Some of them pairing off and heading across the street, but many, like Sam, hanging out. Making connections. Like Genna and Travis had. Rowan wanted to ask Travis if he'd been kind to Genna when they'd hooked up. She hoped so.

"It's hard to picture Genna fast-talking someone into bed."

Travis took a minute to ponder that. "Casanova is a seducer. She's very direct. If you tell her what you want, and she's willing to do it, then she'll give it to you."

"So, she just asks people what they want?" Rowan asked.

"Yep. Novel concept, isn't it? Wish I had the confidence. But for her it's all about them, and I guess she's used to asking personal sexual questions."

"Is that how it went with the two of you?" Rowan asked. For some reason, the answer was important. The bar was full of pleasure-seekers but none of them interested her. She couldn't help but focus on the one person Genna clearly liked as more than an attractive composite of body parts.

Travis coughed. "I didn't mean to imply anything. We've never been together like that."

"You haven't? You just said she's beautiful."

Travis shook his head. "She's nice to look at. But her 'no touch' policy is a pass for me."

Rowan frowned. "No touch?"

"You know. How she refuses to let anyone touch her. Rumor has it she rarely even undresses. That's why we all call her Casanova. Legendary seducer. Personal enigma."

Rowan's breath caught. Genna didn't let anyone touch her?

Her surprise must have shown, because the color rose in Travis's cheeks. "Fuck. I just stepped in it, didn't I? You didn't know."

"I didn't." How could Genna not have told her? Was she never going to be able to touch her? Ever?

Travis looked pissed. "I'm sorry. I thought you knew, or I wouldn't have said anything. It seems like she would've…"

Travis trailed off uncomfortably.

Rowan said, "Like she would've told me something this important? Yeah. It does, doesn't it?"

"Maybe she was waiting for the right time."

Travis looked as miserable as Rowan felt, and she realized Genna had set this meet and greet up for her. Travis and Genna didn't usually sit about making small talk. He was probably counting the minutes until they left. The thought made her sad. They'd imposed on him long enough.

Rowan stood. "It was nice meeting you. I don't think I'll be back."

She waited for Travis's polite reply and then walked out of McKinney's alone.

"What the fuck is *wrong* with you?"

Genna took in the scene. Travis at an empty table looking murderous. Rowan nowhere to be found. "That'll take a while. Would you accept an abridged version? Where's Rowan?"

"She walked out," Travis said coldly, looking at Genna like she was pond scum.

Genna's heartbeat climbed into her throat. "What? Why? Where did she go?"

She grabbed her stupid little purse off the table.

"Sit. Down." Travis enunciated the words carefully, like a drunk acting sober.

If Rowan had left, Genna had to find her. The why didn't matter. She took a step toward the door and Travis grabbed her wrist. "Don't, Casanova."

Genna shook him off. "What's your problem? What did you say to Rowan to make her leave?"

"Something *you* should have said well before tonight," Travis replied just as hotly.

Genna sat. The line for the ladies' room had been ridiculous and she didn't know how long Rowan had been gone. She was probably in her truck and halfway home by now. "Tell me what happened. What was I supposed to have told her?"

"That woman is so head over heels for you that she comes *here* to figure out why you do it, and you haven't even told her that you don't like to be touched? Were you waiting for the wedding night?" When Genna didn't reply he shook his head. "I repeat, what is wrong with you?"

Genna's brain was blank. Travis's words not fully penetrating the dread that engulfed her and swept her out to sea like a tsunami. "You *told* her?"

Travis waved a hand at her. "Don't ask me that like I'm some schoolyard tattletale. I *assumed* you'd told her, that's the kind of thing someone mentions before getting serious. I assumed too much."

Clearly.

"What did she say?"

"Not a lot."

There weren't any curse words strong enough for this situation, and Genna's brain hadn't come back online yet. Travis didn't understand. And now Rowan didn't understand. Genna wasn't sure she understood herself anymore.

Rowan had left without even asking her about it.

Travis stood. "Whatever is going on with you, you should start seeing a shrink about it before you lose her. Rowan deserves better."

Travis walked away leaving Genna to wallow in the mess she'd created.

Chapter Nineteen

Genna walked toward the Uber pickup location like she had lead feet. She'd tried calling Rowan, but it was too loud in the bar to hear if she'd answered. God. What a disaster. Travis had told Rowan about her rule, as if it were fact, as if…

"Where are you going?"

Rowan leaned against the side of her truck and smiled.

Genna walked straight into her arms and held on to her as if she'd just come home from war, weak at the knees with relief. "You're here."

Rowan's arms wrapped around her, and nothing had ever felt so good.

Rowan lowered her head until their lips were almost touching. "Of course, I'm here. I told you I wasn't going anywhere."

Genna couldn't get words out, so instead she kissed her. She cradled Rowan's jaw as she poured herself into the kiss. All her anxiety about tonight, her pleasure at Rowan calling her her girlfriend, her desperation to find her and explain herself. Everything went into the kiss until there was nothing and no one but them. Rowan gasped and Genna kissed her harder, deeper, hot and hungry like she was making a point. When Rowan slid her hands up her back and into her hair Genna broke the kiss. "I love the sounds you make when I kiss you."

Rowan's eyes were a little blurry. "What sounds?"

"Good sounds. Like I'm the best ice cream sundae you've ever had."

"I've never had anything as good as you." Rowan nipped at her lips.

"Thank you for not leaving. Travis said you had."

"He felt bad that he'd accidentally spilled the beans on your secret, and I was unintentionally interrogating him before that. I realized that none of this is any of my business, and I should give him some space. I'm sorry I forced you to bring me here."

Genna sighed. "It's not what you think."

"So, you don't have a rule that people can't touch you?"

"Well, I do."

"But you take your clothes off."

"Not usually."

"Then they don't call you Casanova because you're great in bed but hold so much of yourself back?"

"The nickname isn't my fault."

"Travis obviously cares about you, but you never made an exception, even for him?"

Genna winced as Rowan hit a home run. "I can explain."

Rowan pressed her lips against Genna's in a kiss as delicate as butterfly wings. "Good idea."

"Let's go across the street. Find a place to sit."

Rowan gave her a *come on now* look. "I'm not going to the Holiday Inn."

Despite everything, Genna laughed "You won't catch casual sex cooties sitting in the lobby."

Rowan shook her head. "Not happening."

Genna took her hand. "I meant the coffee shop. Let's sit, and I'll tell you everything."

"You will?"

Rowan's expression was so open, so heartfelt, Genna simultaneously felt like a million bucks and the worst human alive. Stunned that Rowan cared for her enough to wear such an expression and horrified at herself for causing even a second of doubt.

"I will."

They found a booth in the back with a corner bench seat. Genna ordered decaf, and Rowan opted for chamomile tea. Unlike the bar, Brews and Chews was deserted this late. Genna waited to see if Rowan would say something, but she didn't. She blew on her steaming tea and waited.

"Have you ever had sex with someone you didn't know?" Genna asked.

Rowan wrapped her palms around the tall paper cup to warm them. "One or two I didn't know *well,* but no, not the way you mean. Not a stranger."

Genna nodded. She was a little surprised Rowan had sex at all outside of a relationship. "It's different. It's…" Genna fought for the right word. "Physical."

Rowan smiled humorlessly. "All sex is physical."

"This is *only* physical." She racked her brain to think of a way to explain it. "It's like getting a massage. It can feel good, great even, but it's a service. There isn't any emotion, and if there is, it's not about you."

"Okay." Rowan shrugged. "I'm trying not to judge, Dr. Sex, but you're not making this sound like something that's hard to give up."

"I need to explain why I don't let anyone touch me." Genna wanted to lay her head on the table and hide her face. Rowan didn't understand. How could she? How could anyone? But Rowan had had every reason to walk away tonight, and she'd stayed. So Genna stayed too. "I can't orgasm when it's just physical. There must be more than that, or I can't get there. I didn't know that about myself when I first started going to McKinney's. By the time I realized, it was easier to tell people I didn't want to be touched, so I didn't have to fake it. That's all. Over time people assumed I have some sort of aversion, but that isn't true. It just doesn't do anything for me to have someone I don't care about touch me."

Genna had always been embarrassed that she needed something different, something *more* than everyone else seemed to. She'd never intended for the thing to go viral and become her moniker. But with Rowan, who'd given more to her than anyone ever had, she could be honest.

"You go to a bar to pick up strangers, *dozens* of strangers, for years, but you need more than a physical connection to have an orgasm? It seems like the more I know, the less I understand."

Genna squirmed. It sounded dumb when Rowan put it like that. "I was nineteen. I started going to let off steam. Something I did just for me. I like sex. It didn't matter that I didn't come. Making them come was enough. Pleasure isn't just orgasms."

Rowan blew out a breath like she'd been holding onto the nation's air supply. "That's the line you're sticking with? It's fun? It's for your mental health?"

"It is!" What, this wasn't enough? She'd opened up. She'd told Rowan something that was frankly just a bit humiliating, and her confession wasn't good enough?

"Are you polyamorous?" Rowan asked.

Genna shook her head. She was already fucking up the one maybe-relationship she had on the horizon. There was a less than zero percent chance she'd be able to handle multiple relationships at once, even if she'd wanted to. Which she didn't.

"Okay," Rowan said. "So, it was fun. Fine. Give it up. Let it go. Walk away from it. A relationship is good for your mental health too. It's an easy swap, and you'll get pleasure and orgasms because I *do* care."

Genna burst into tears.

Rowan swore under her breath. She pulled Genna toward her until she was half sitting in her lap. "I'm sorry. I shouldn't have said it like that. Don't cry."

Genna just sobbed harder. She cried into her shoulder, shaking, making guttural ugly, involuntary sounds the way people who'd lost everything sometimes did. A decade's worth of tears it seemed like.

Rowan wasn't the kind of person who panicked when someone cried. She'd make a terrible social worker if she was. But confusion wormed its way through her insides. Had she pushed Genna too hard? Maybe. But she'd asked her to walk away from all of that before, and she hadn't cried as if her soul mate had just died in a famine.

Rowan held her and would have for a minute, or an hour, or endlessly.

Genna pulled away slowly, wincing. "Sorry, I made a mess of your shirt. I didn't mean to do that."

Genna's cheeks were tear-stained, her mascara giving her panda eyes. Rowan handed her a napkin to blow her nose. "I'm going out on a limb here, but I don't think that was about me."

"No, I don't think it was."

She'd pushed too hard. She couldn't bring herself to apologize. She *needed* Genna to choose her, but if giving up McKinney's hurt her so much, Rowan couldn't ask it of her. "Let's go home. It's been a hell of a night."

Genna shook her head. "You deserve to know, and I think I had to"—she waved a hand at Rowan's chest—"do that first. You're right. It's *a* reason, but not *the* reason."

Rowan pulled her back into her arms.

Genna stayed that way for ten more minutes, breathing slowly, wrapped around Rowan in a way that was highly inappropriate for a coffee shop, even if it was deserted.

Finally, she said, "I go to McKinney's because what people want from me there, I can do. I can make them happy, bring them pleasure. Sexual need doesn't suffocate me. Having something that feels good, gives me connection with other people, and is emotionally safe? Well, that's fulfilling in a way the rest of my life isn't. That's why I'm afraid to give it up."

Rowan hugged her tighter and had to seal her lips shut to prevent all the useless reassurances from coming out her mouth. For Rowan, McKinney's wasn't just unfulfilling, but an affront to the emotional intimacy that elevated sex beyond pleasurable fiction. For Genna, though? Puddle-deep intimacy was the only kind that felt safe.

"What suffocates you?" Rowan asked, already knowing the answer.

"Everything," Genna mumbled into her chest.

"Your mom?"

Genna nodded.

"The twins?"

Another nod.

"What else?"

"Work. Sometimes. Life. Sometimes. It's not that any of it is very difficult on its own, not anymore. But as a kid it was overwhelming, and those feelings hang on like nasty little freeloaders. When things get tough, that's my default. It's all too much, and I'm ten years old again. At McKinney's, it's simple and satisfying. It's not easy to give up the one thing that *isn't* hard and that actually helps."

Rowan kissed the top of her head. "You sell yourself short. You're so much more than that place."

"I don't have anything else to give."

"What about love?"

Genna snorted. "What has love ever done except suck me dry? I don't have any love left. Strangers don't ask questions. They don't expect too much of me. It might not be love, but at least it's not burying me alive."

Rowan just held her, at a loss for what to say. Some part of her had already known Genna felt this way. That the weight of everyone else's needs lay heavy on her shoulders and crushed her ability to even figure out what she needed. Genna's needs had never been a priority for anyone.

Until now.

Rowan cradled Genna's face and looked directly into her eyes. "When you touch me, you fill places inside I didn't even know were empty."

Genna shook her head so vigorously her hair fell into her eyes. "You don't need me."

"Yes, I—"

Genna pressed a finger to Rowan's lips. "You don't need me. You never have. You're the steadiest, kindest, most capable person I know. You could have anyone. That's why I feel safe with you."

"I still don't understand."

Genna sighed. "You know how in some romance novels the hero is possessive, with *I need you*, and, *you complete me*, and *here's a handy past life, or fated magic spell, or blood bond, or whatever, that ties us together for life, so you'll never leave me,* quasi-Stockholm-Syndrome?"

Rowan smiled. "Stockholm is a stretch."

"That stuff *is* suffocating. I've never understood what's so romantic about a love that leaves you no choice. But someone like you, who could have anyone, and chooses me? You have options and somehow, I'm the one you want not because you *need me*, but because you *want me*."

Rowan bit her lip as she thought about that. "I like the past life, fated magic spell, blood bond stuff, but I get your point."

She didn't say the rest. That sometimes you did need, and sometimes the other person needed too. That love was a give and take of feelings, and friendship, and sometimes, yes, even duty. Genna didn't know the kind of love that filled you and drained you in equal measure, so you stayed steady. But that was okay. Rowan would show her.

"You don't need me," Genna said again. "We don't have anything tying us together. Not marriage, or family, or finances. Not anything except what we feel for each other. That's why I trust you. You don't depend on me for anything, and if I walked away tonight, you'd be okay."

Now wasn't the right time to tell her that if she walked away, Rowan's heart would break.

"Do *I* suffocate you?" Rowan asked. "I ask a lot of questions and expect a lot from you too."

Genna laughed. "No shit."

Rowan didn't laugh. "Is giving up McKinney's one more have-to?"

"No."

Rowan searched her eyes, not entirely sure, and Genna repeated, "No. I promise. Falling for you has obviously brought up some stuff I need to deal with. But it's not a burden. *You* aren't a burden. You're the opposite. You make everything easier, and harder too, but harder in a necessary way. You make me want to change. I'm sorry I've made you uncertain. You shouldn't be. I brought you here tonight because I'm sure of us."

"Are you falling for me, Dr. Sex?" Rowan asked gently, her heart soaring and exploding like a firework.

"I think so," Genna replied. "That's what girlfriends do, right?"

She'd been wondering when Genna would tease her for that comment. "I should've run the girlfriends thing by you before making a general public announcement."

"You don't have to stake a claim. There's no reason to be jealous of Sam. They're oblivious to that kind of thing, anyway."

"They think you're hot in bed."

Genna raised her eyebrows haughtily. "I *am* hot in bed."

Rowan laughed and kissed her. She didn't deny that Genna was easily overwhelmed after a lifetime of responsibility. But she had a foundation of pure steel and faced life in all its complexity. Rowan had never known someone so strong. If Genna really was falling for her, she was sure Genna would have the mental muscle to see McKinney's in the rearview at some point. She could wait.

"Let's go home now," Rowan said.

If the universe had dropped Genevieve Feilding into her life to be her soul mate, then she'd do whatever it took to avert disaster.

Including famine.

CHAPTER TWENTY

"Have I told you lately that I love you?" Alice slid the stack of printer paper Genna had just handed her into a large and immaculate Chloé tote bag that she used to carry her laptop and other essentials around.

"Does your adoration come with a day off? Because I need one."

Alice laughed. "Take it. I really appreciate your reworking all of this. I can't wait to dig in."

"Those notes are preliminary. I'm a long way out at sea, but I think I see land." Genna yawned. She was glad she'd made Teach happy and was starting to see that she'd been right all along when she'd said her research would be stronger with an avenue for practical application. But damn she was tired. She'd locked herself in her office and done nothing but see study participants and work on the grant info for Alice for the last ten days. She'd wanted to get the monkey off her back, and once she got going, she found the task wasn't as paralyzing as she'd expected. She was excited to see how her research could be used as context and perspective to help people like Rowan who had fantasies that confused them. The psychosocial implications were endless.

Genna stifled another yawn as she and Alice walked out of the Gender and Sexuality Division building and made their way across campus.

"Did you decide to take an all-night break again?" Alice asked.

Genna grinned. "Is that your way of asking me if I was up late fucking?"

"I hope that one day you respect yourself enough not to use such derogatory language. You of all people should know it's based in shame and patriarchy." Alice thinned her lips.

"Fucking isn't derogatory," Genna said.

"Fucking," Alice enunciated the word like she didn't want it too far inside her mouth, "is most commonly used as an expression of annoyance or frustration. That you, and so many other people, use it as a synonym for sex is problematic, don't you think?"

Genna had never thought about it before. "I guess you're right. But God help me if I have to start calling it making love."

"One day, you'll meet someone who will make it *feel* like making love and then maybe you'll be able to call it sex like the rest of us."

"Okay, Ms. Take a Break."

Alice laughed. "Touché."

"I went home yesterday afternoon to help Mom with some errands. Her lawnmower is broken, and the grass was two feet high by the time she called me about it. I didn't get back until late."

"What was wrong with the mower?"

Genna shrugged. "It didn't start. That's the extent of my expertise. We ended up borrowing one from Bob Brown next door."

Rowan would probably know how to fix a lawn mower.

Rowan. Who'd taken up space in the back of Genna's mind even though she'd told her she needed this whole week to work. They'd texted every day, sometimes sweet, and sometimes sexy, but texts weren't enough, and she'd carried a little ache in her chest. Last night she'd dragged her tired butt home at close to midnight to find a DoorDash delivery on her doormat. Rowan had insisted she eat something that didn't come out of a vending machine.

Genna had called her, and they'd chatted about nothing while she ate and Rowan fell asleep, her soft rumbling tones wrapping around Genna like a warm hug.

Alice and Genna reached the intersection between staff and student parking. "Go home and get some rest. You've earned it. I'll see you in a few days."

"I'm on it." As Alice walked off in the direction of her car, Genna's phone vibrated.

Rowan: *How's work, Dr. I'm Thinking About Your Fantasies? I miss you.*

Genna smiled, not as wiped out as she'd been a minute ago. Rowan was thinking of her.

Where are you?

Rowan: *Central quad. Under the big oak.*

Genna turned and headed back the way she'd come.

She found Rowan just where she said she'd be, sprawled on the grass under the oldest tree on campus with her textbooks. When Rowan saw her, she jumped to her feet with more athleticism than any person should be allowed and scooped her into her arms, twirling her around before setting her back on her feet. "She lives! I thought you'd never surface."

Something inside Genna cracked open and spewed warm fuzzies at the uncomplicated delight on Rowan's face. She'd done exactly nothing to inspire it except show up. Rowan really had missed her. Not giving a damn that they were in the middle of the busiest section of campus, Genna stepped into Rowan's personal space and kissed her long and hard and deep, cupping the back of her neck in what was becoming *their* way when they kissed. Reluctant to stop but aware they were being watched by more than one undoubtedly horny coed, Genna pulled away, her breathing a little ragged. "I missed you too."

"You're killing me, you know that, right?" Rowan's voice was rough as bricks.

Genna smiled. "I love that kissing turns you on."

Rowan flopped back onto the grass and pulled Genna down beside her. "Being within twenty feet of you turns me on, kissing amps up the, what do you academics call it, response and duration of my arousal?"

Genna leaned over and kissed her again, long and lingering, to measure said response and duration. "Keep that up and I'll have to find a way to sneak you back into the study."

Rowan shuddered. "Not on your life. I have a very unethical crush on the researcher."

"Do you?"

"Yep." Rowan grinned at her. "And she has a crush on me too."

Genna laughed. "You're confident of that, are you?"

"I am," Rowan said, her eyes turning serious.

"Good." Genna was unable to look away. "You should be."

Rowan's phone pinged. "Sorry, let me just wrap up this conversation I was having before you arrived."

She texted a reply.

"Maria?" Genna asked.

"Gabby." Rowan sent another text then put her phone on top of her books.

"You're texting Gabby?" Genna asked.

"Yeah. She has a paper due next week and wanted my help with the research. Is that okay?"

Genna wasn't sure what was more startling, that Gabby was doing research for a paper, or that she and Rowan were texting. "It's fine. I'm just surprised. She usually asks me that sort of thing. I *am* a professional researcher."

Rowan smiled. "Well, I'm sorry to step on the toes of a pro, but it's an undergraduate paper, not a submission to a prestigious journal. She knew you had a lot going on at work and thought I might be able to help instead."

"That was thoughtful of her, and you." Gabby had needed help and she'd texted *Rowan*. "Are you sure you don't mind?"

Rowan brushed her lips casually over Genna's in a quick kiss. Apparently, neither of them could seem to stop. "Not at all. I just wish she wouldn't keep asking me when we're going on our date. She's relentless."

"What did you tell her?" Genna asked.

Rowan looked at the grass. "Nothing."

Genna leaned into Rowan. "If you're free tomorrow, I have the day off. That would be a perfect day for a date. Text her back right now and tell her. We can't leave her in suspense."

Rowan didn't pick up her phone. "I know you need time, and I'm happy to give it to you, but don't make promises you can't keep right now. That's not fair."

"Who says it's a promise I can't keep?"

Rowan gave her a look that said *you're kidding, right?* and silently squeezed her hand.

"The Silver Creek Cranes are playing the next few weekends. I don't know shit about basketball, but Travis loves anything with a uniform and a ball. I was thinking of inviting him to a game. We could all grab some food after if you want," Genna said casually.

"I didn't get the sense you and Travis really hung out," Rowan said. "But if there's food, I'm in."

"We've got to figure out some way to stay in touch, now that I won't be seeing him at McKinney's."

Rowan froze like a deer in headlights. "What?"

"Plus, I owe him an apology for how I left things. Boy, he was pissed at me." Genna would be hearing him say *What the fuck is wrong with you?* in her nightmares for a while.

"Genna." Rowan put a finger to her mouth, shushing her, and then used it to brush along her bottom lip. "Why won't you see Travis at McKinney's?"

Unable to keep up her easy-breezy act, Genna wrapped her arms around Rowan. "I'm not going back."

"Are you sure?"

Genna nodded.

"Is it because I texted Gabby?"

Genna laughed. "That doesn't hurt."

"Why?" Rowan asked again, tucking Genna's head against her shoulder as they leaned back against the tree trunk.

"Because I'm happy," Genna said, realizing it was true for the first time in a long time. "McKinney's gave me what I needed to survive, but I want more now." She played with a button on Rowan's shirt.

"If you say you needed it, I believe you," Rowan said.

Genna sighed. "I'm scared."

Rowan pulled her closer. "Of someone touching you?"

Genna shook her head. "Of *wanting* someone to touch me. Wanting more. McKinney's was low stakes. I didn't have to risk anything."

"And now?" Rowan asked so softly Genna almost didn't hear her.

"Now, there's more." Genna slipped between the buttons on Rowan's shirt, so her fingertips could rest against skin. Warm and solid. "You make me want, which is basically a giant flashing danger sign for me to fuck things up. This is all your fault."

Rowan pressed her lips to the top of Genna's head. "I'm falling for you too, Dr. Sex."

"We might be in for a crash landing," Genna mumbled.

"You won't fuck things up. I won't let you."

Genna closed her eyes and let herself believe it. The shade of the tree felt good with Rowan warm along her side, and the sounds of campus life a faint murmur in the distance. "I'm so tired."

Rowan settled Genna's head more securely on her shoulder and propped her textbook on a bended knee. "Get some sleep. I have plans for you tomorrow night."

Rowan set the grocery bags on the ground to press the intercom outside Genna's apartment building. Static, and then Genna's voice. "Rowan?"

"I come bearing heavy gifts. Let me in."

"What gifts?" The suspicion in Genna's voice made Rowan smile.

"Nothing that you'll feel awkward about accepting, I promise."

The buzzer sounded and Rowan made her way upstairs.

Genna stood in her doorway, waiting. "Hi."

Rowan almost dropped everything. "Holy shit."

Genna's smile was ten different kinds of pleased. "You wouldn't let me plan any of the date, so I planned my outfit. Poppy helped."

"Poppy?" Rowan asked, like she had no clue who that was. Heat pooled low and fast in her belly.

Genna tugged on a strand of hair. Whatever Poppy had done made it tumble around Genna's shoulders in glossy waves that didn't quite curl. "I'm not very good at the hair and makeup stuff. Poppy's an artist though."

"You got all dressed up for me."

Understatement. Genna looked absolutely gorgeous in a fire-engine red dress that hit at mid-thigh, showing off an endless expanse of leg ending in bare feet. Genna framed in the doorway looked every inch a siren temptress, and Rowan was a sailor caught in her song. She stared, engraving each detail into her memory.

"I wouldn't go that far. I'm supposed to be wearing fuck-me shoes, and Poppy wanted to do that smokey-eye thing that's attractive on other people but makes me look like someone socked me one. We compromised." Genna wiggled her bare toes. "I hope you don't mind I'm only half-dressed up."

Rowan swallowed, her heartbeat beginning to pound in places a long way from her chest. "Half-dressed is great."

She stepped inside and carried the bags to the counter while she still had control of her motor functions.

When she turned around, Genna was right there, not giving her room to breathe. She pressed up on her toes and brushed her lips against Rowan's. "Hi, you."

Rowan couldn't help herself. She dragged Genna against her, slanted her mouth over hers, and kissed her like her life depended on it. Genna wrapped a hand around the back of her neck, and Rowan groaned, the fire of Genna's touch making her blood rush in a thousand directions. Rowan pulled Genna's hips into hers until she could feel the burn of her body heat. "Fuck, I want you."

Not the most seductive words in the world, but there were none more honest.

Genna slipped her fingers under Rowan's shirt, a look of naked hunger on her face. "I hope you're not too traditional. I might cry if you're too much of a lady to sleep with me on the first date."

Rowan pulled Genna's bottom lip into her mouth and sucked. "If you're not careful, there won't be dinner at all."

Genna laughed against her mouth. "I could be very careless."

Genna in her arms, teasing her, sent off a spark of rightness within Rowan. *Hers.*

"You're just worried you're going to lose the mashed potato grand championship."

Genna pulled back. "Is *that* what all the groceries are for?"

Rowan nodded. "I'm making you shepherd's pie."

"You're…" All the breath seemed to whoosh out of Genna. She cupped Rowan's cheek. "You are?"

"If we can encourage enough blood back into my head so my brain starts up again." Rowan let her go and rummaged around in the bags, pulling out ingredients. "You, my sexy little sous chef, get to peel the potatoes."

Genna shook her head. "You really are the sweetest person I have ever met."

Rowan ripped open a bag of frozen vegetable medley. "You like sweet, right?"

Genna smiled. "I love sweet. Thank you."

I love sweet. Rowan was too tongue-tied to respond, but happiness suffused her and rippled outward. She handed Genna a potato peeler. "Times have changed. Not so long ago you'd have insisted on paying me back."

Genna grinned wickedly. "I intend to pay you back."

Rowan swallowed, ignoring the impulse to throw the food out the window, hoist Genna up on the counter, and slide that bright red barely-there dress up her thighs. A bullfighter's cape, testing her control, taunting the animal inside.

She placed the pot of water on the stove. "I'll add it to the invoice."

Rowan pulled two four-inch cast iron skillets out of the oven, the mashed potato contenders fluffy white with perfect golden-brown peaks. "Moment of truth. Will it be the sour cream or the butter and milk that rocks your world?"

"God." Genna stood close behind her, sampling the scents. "That smells amazing. I don't even care whose are better."

Rowan shooed her away. "Pour us some wine. These need to sit for a minute, or you'll burn your mouth."

"Can't have that. I'll need it later when I use my tongue to make you beg."

Rowan uttered a breathy curse and fumbled the second skillet. It crashed the last quarter inch onto the countertop.

Genna feigned wide-eyed innocence. "Was it something I said?"

Rowan shot her puppy dog eyes. "Have mercy. I'm trying for a little romance. You're not making it easy."

Genna pouted, but she poured the Pinot they'd left to breathe and brought the glasses over to the small two-seat dining table in the open-plan space between the kitchen and the living room. Determined to meet Rowan halfway, she'd rustled up some lumpy candles from her emergency power outage kit and had set one of her woebegone African violets in the middle of the table for ambiance. She studied the place settings critically. "This looks like a forty-year-old virgin who only shops at Hometown Hardware is trying to do romance, but it's all I had."

Rowan set the shepherd's pie on trivets in the center of the table. "You definitely did not buy that dress at Hometown Hardware."

She slid a chair out for Genna.

"True. I bought the dress this morning."

Rowan picked up her plate and started dishing out portions while Genna watched. "You didn't have to buy anything. I love the dress, but I'd love you in anything."

Genna chewed on her bottom lip. She hadn't wanted to wear something she'd worn to McKinney's. "It's a good thing because all this girl crap is way too hard without Poppy directing my every move and even then, it takes *forever*."

Rowan piled a fork with beef, vegetables, and mashed potatoes. She leaned across the table and held it out for Genna. "This is mine, see what you think."

Genna got lost in the way the candlelight flickered in Rowan's eyes and almost forgot to open her mouth. When the flavors exploded on her tongue, she closed her eyes and made a low humming sound that was lascivious even to her own ears. "Oh my God. You're a master chef."

Rowan laughed. "It's a recipe from *Good Housekeeping*."

Genna almost choked. "You read *Good Housekeeping*?"

"Well, no. I found the recipe online. But I do have an apron, if that turns you on."

Genna imagined Rowan in a long white chef's apron bent over the stove, and she wanted more nights just like this one so much her breath caught. "Hot as fuck, sweet as pie, knows her way around an engine, *and* she cooks. Is there anything you can't do?"

"I never could master the purl stitch no matter how many times Mom tried to teach me to knit," Rowan looked genuinely sorry for it. She loaded her fork with Genna's potato recipe and sampled. "They taste like potatoes."

Genna snorted. "Were you expecting filet mignon?"

Rowan took another bite, then one from her own recipe. "Yours are more potato-y. The milk and butter add a bit of richness to the natural flavors."

"Which are already superior." Genna dug in with her own fork. She savored a mouthful of beef and vegetables. "Yours have a kick. The chives are a nice addition. It's fancier than mine."

"Who wins the grand championship?" Rowan refilled their wine glasses.

Genna batted her eyelashes shamelessly. "If I let you win, will you make it again?"

"I'll make it for you as many times as you'd like, even if you don't let me win."

"Considering you bought all the ingredients, hauled it all here, and did most of the cooking, you deserve to win. I could get used to mashed potatoes with sour cream."

When the conversation moved from Genna's study and Rowan's classes to Gabby's latest man-boy, Genna said, "She has *terrible* taste. I almost wish she was like Grace. If they were both hot for you, I wouldn't have to worry."

Rowan winced. "I'm glad she's not."

"Grace is not going to jump you. It's a harmless crush. You'd never sleep with either of them."

"I never would," Rowan agreed.

They smiled at each other.

"It's not like Gabby's had examples of healthy relationships," Genna said. "She just falls into bed with whoever pays her the slightest attention."

"Gabby's smart and good at reading people. Maybe none of them last because she knows when to move on," Rowan said.

"Probably when the validation wears off." Genna picked up their plates and headed to the sink.

"You can't fix everything. They'll make their own choices. Gabby isn't as naive as you think."

Genna started the water. "How long have you two been texting? Does she talk to you about boys?"

"Sometimes she mentions a guy, or something funny that's happened that involves one."

Hope began to spread, cloning itself and attaching to any possible solution. "Do you think you could—"

"No," Rowan cut her off, laughing. "She doesn't talk to *you* about guys because you get all judgey when you have no right to be. I'm not giving her advice unless she asks me."

"They'll always be my baby sisters. All I've ever wanted is for them to be safe and happy."

Rowan blew out the candles and brought their wine glasses into the kitchen. "They *are* safe and happy. You gave them everything you could. Trust it's enough, and let them live their lives."

Rowan opened the dishwasher, but Genna waved her away. "You cooked." She pointed to the peninsula. "Sit. Drink your wine. I've got this. I'm awesome at dishes."

"We make quite a team." Rowan sat.

By the time the dishes were loaded, Rowan had wandered into the living room and settled on the couch. The opening credits of *Buffy the Vampire Slayer* were paused on the TV. "She who wins the mashed potato grand championship gets to choose the entertainment."

"Are you sure that's your choice?" Genna infused the question with so much innuendo it smoldered.

Rowan smiled. "I remember sitting in your office imagining cuddling up with you on the couch to watch *Buffy*. It was a nice thought then, and it's a nice thought now. Indulge me."

Genna could do a whole lot better than *nice*. She turned out the overhead light, leaving the glow of the TV as the only illumination, and draped herself sideways in Rowan's lap, making sure to take her time getting comfortable.

"Genna." Rowan said her name like she'd drawn the word up from some deep and secret place inside herself. "That's not playing fair."

"Who said anything about fair? If you'd wanted me to watch, you should've put on *my* favorite show."

"I cannot watch *The Batchelor*. My brain cells will shrivel up from all the scripted pseudo-dramas."

Genna kissed her, dipping her tongue into Rowan's mouth, already starved for her. "And you call me judgey. Go on, start your show. I'll give the hundred-pound unconvincing vampire slayer a chance."

Genna lasted about ten minutes before she got bored. She started undoing the buttons on Rowan's shirt.

"You're supposed to be watching," Rowan stage-whispered as if they were in a crowded movie theater.

"You watch. I'm busy." Genna couldn't bear not touching her a second longer. She parted the shirt and sucked in a shallow breath when she revealed Rowan's breasts in a black sports bra, her abs just visible in the light from the TV.

"Way too much time in the gym really works," she murmured and put her lips to the hollow of Rowan's throat the way she'd imagined doing a thousand times. She felt Rowan's breath catch when she flicked her tongue against the soft skin.

"You're missing all the best lines," Rowan said with no conviction, shifting to give Genna better access.

Genna slid out of her lap and onto the floor, kneeling between her legs.

Rowan deserted Buffy as heat swept through her, igniting every cell, setting ablaze all the parts of her that had been cold for so long. "You're terrible at cuddling."

"Don't worry." Genna slipped the shirt from Rowan's arms and pressed her mouth to the ink on her shoulder, bringing their bodies together. "I'm very good at a lot of other things."

Rowan's libido surged, hot and reckless when Genna's lips traced the ink down her arm. Genna tugged on the sports bra and Rowan pulled it off, smiling when Genna stopped kissing to ogle her breasts.

"I never got the point of the chest press. It always seemed like there wasn't a whole lot of muscle there anyway. But wow. I get it now."

"If you like it, then I'm happy."

Genna cupped Rowan's breast and stroked the nipple with her thumb. Rowan's clit pulsed like they were connected by Bluetooth. She closed her eyes, inhaling a sharp breath.

"You're supposed to be watching TV," Genna teased her, stroking her nipples until Rowan was so wet she worried she'd leave a damp patch on Genna's couch.

"Impossible." *Please fucking touch me before I come in my pants like a teenager who has never been laid.*

When Genna trailed a string of hot wet kisses over her breasts, circling her nipples with her tongue, Rowan's hips jerked, and she buried her face into Genna's hair. The tart apples of her shampoo blended with the scent of desire. There had never been a sexier combination. When Genna kissed a path down her abdomen, Rowan groaned. She fumbled with the zipper on Genna's dress. She needed skin on skin.

Genna batted her away, kissing a blazing path along the waistband of Rowan's pants. "Don't distract me."

Heat radiated from every place Genna pressed her mouth, and Rowan's blood hummed with need. She threaded her fingers in Genna's hair and tilted her head up until their eyes met. "Let's go to bed. I want you out of that dress."

Genna shook her head from side to side in Rowan's hold. "You've planned everything. Now it's my turn. I want to explore."

Rowan groaned. Everything felt so fucking good, and Genna's mouth was inches from her center. The mouth Genna had promised to pay her back with, to make her beg with. No way could she handle the barest touch with that thought dancing in her head. Unless she countered it with the less-dancey thought that was staging a surprise attack. She tried to ignore it, but a shard of worry cut a thin line through her lust. Would Genna take off her dress? Would she let Rowan touch her? "If you think I'm going to sit here passively while you Casanova me, you're wrong."

Genna froze.

Rowan wanted to pick the words up, shove them back inside her mouth, and then tape her lips shut. *Fuck, fuck, fuck.* "My brain's not working right just now. I didn't mean that the way it sounded."

Genna stiffened, but she didn't move away. "How did you mean it?"

Rowan stroked Genna's forehead with a fingertip. Between her brows. Down to the tip of her nose. Along her cheekbones. Mapping her face. "This is your comfort zone. I want you to touch me, but I want to touch you too. I want you to want me to."

"I do want you to touch me."

"Then let me."

Genna pouted. "Anyone ever tell you that you're sort of bossy?"

Rowan smiled. "*Please*, let me touch you?"

Genna rose and slid back onto Rowan's lap. "Unzip my dress."

Genna held her breath.

Rowan's fingers were so gentle as they undid the zipper and slipped the dress from her shoulders. When it pooled around her waist. Rowan moaned softly. "You're gorgeous."

She was a horny, clumsy teenager was what she was. If she wasn't careful, she was going to devour Rowan in one bite, the endless wait catching up with her. She pressed against Rowan, skin hot against skin, and kissed her. Rowan's lips parted under hers and their breath mingled, tongues exploring. Rowan cupped her breast over her bra, and Genna groaned into her mouth.

Rowan's hips pushed into her, and she broke the kiss, her breath exploding from her. "I've never wanted anyone in my life as desperately as I want you."

Genna pressed kisses along her jaw and slid a hand into the waistband of Rowan's pants. "Maybe we can be clumsy and desperate together then."

"Fuck, yes, we can." Rowan pushed up her dress and slipped a hand between Genna's thighs.

Genna's head snapped back when Rowan pushed aside her panties and ran a finger along her folds. Everything inside her tightened. "Whoa."

Rowan rested her forehead to Genna's shoulder, hiding her face. "I can't wait, I'm sorry. I've wanted you for so long."

Genna lifted Rowan's head and kissed her, pressing her back into the couch and plundering her mouth. "Don't apologize. It's not your fault I'm so turned on I could come from that." She paused, looking into Rowan's eyes, a mirror of her own desire. "Actually, that *is* your fault."

Rowan stroked her again and Genna's blood rushed, her entire body clenching like a fist. With superhuman effort, she untangled herself from Rowan and stood, barely noticing when her dress fell to the floor. She offered her hand. "I can do better than clumsy on the couch. Come to bed."

Rowan took her hand like it was the most precious offer she'd ever received.

CHAPTER TWENTY-ONE

"Touch me, please," Genna said.

She felt a little silly standing by the bed in only her underwear, even if it was the special-occasion have-your-wicked-way-with-me kind. She hadn't been naked with anyone since she'd gotten unexpectedly tipsy with her one-time high school boyfriend Tommy Remirez at her cousin's wedding over a year ago. But the way Rowan was looking at her made any awkwardness dissolve. If a stare could talk, Rowan's would be saying filthy things. "Please. I need your hands on me."

Rowan had bent over backwards to get to know her, to understand her. Had all but courted her like a proper English duke. And what had she done except make things harder? She'd caused Rowan to doubt how much she wanted her.

That ended now.

Rowan didn't obey her. Instead she caught Genna's hands in hers and leaned in to kiss her again, deeply, thoroughly, leaving her breathless. "Lie down, baby."

Genna stretched out on the bed gratefully. Rowan had a way of melting her bones. She held out her arms. "Come here."

"You're not in charge right now." Rowan's tone was soft but booked no argument. "I'm going to touch you everywhere, so you feel me deep inside."

Everywhere?

Genna swallowed, vulnerability teasing at the edges of the sink hole of bottomless lust that was her desire. She didn't let go like that.

Rowan stripped off her shoes and pants, but before Genna could get her fill of just *looking* at her, she sat on the bed between Genna's legs and ran her hands up the back of Genna's calves. "I've been thinking about doing this all night. You're quite the seductress in that red dress."

Genna levered up on her elbows, her mouth going dry at Rowan's nakedness. She swallowed to start up her vocal cords. "I had to do something to counterbalance the romance. You're so good at this, you're basically a walking Valentine's Day card."

Rowan slid her hands higher, dragging her fingernails along Genna's thighs. "Is that right? Not sexy enough for you?"

Genna gasped when Rowan's fingers found the crease where her thigh met her backside and stroked there. "Valentine's Day is my new favorite holiday."

Another few seconds of that and Genna wasn't sure she remembered what they were talking about anymore. Her center pulsed with need, and she squirmed, hoping to encourage Rowan's hands where she wanted them.

Rowan's lips parted, as if she was mesmerized by her effect on Genna. She stroked her again. "Do you like it when I touch you here?"

Genna nodded, suddenly shy. Being asked was a whole new experience. The truth was she loved Rowan touching her absolutely anywhere and would she please hurry up and stroke her again so the need clawing at her insides could be sated?

Rowan dragged Genna's panties down her hips and off, then slid her hands under Genna's backside and squeezed. "How about here, Dr. Sex? Do you like that too?"

"Rowan." Her name was a prayer. A benediction. "I need you to touch me."

"I am touching you." Rowan squeezed again.

"You know what I mean."

"I want it to last so you feel every moment. Every stroke. Every sensation. You said pleasure isn't only orgasms, right? So, just feel."

Genna flopped backward against her pillow in surrender. "I might hate you right now."

Rowan slid her hands outward until they were cradling Genna's hips. "Let's save hate sex for another time."

Genna all but levitated trying to shift Rowan's hands between her legs. "Please, please stroke me again. I need you inside me."

Rowan made an unintelligible sound and *finally* cupped her where she needed it most. Shivers exploded from her center. Then Rowan stayed absolutely still while Genna cursed all the gods in heaven.

"You're sopping wet, Dr. Sex."

Would it be a faux pas to grab Rowan's hand and start grinding against it like a gold medalist in the dry humping Olympics? Not that she was remotely dry.

Rowan pressed at her opening, stroking the sensitive folds. Sensation sparked at her touch, everything hot and wet and aching. There was no more room for thinking when Rowan's touch had every nerve vibrating.

"Is this what you need, baby?" Rowan pressed her fingertips inside.

"Yes." Genna arched off the bed. "Please. Inside."

Rowan filled her and moved languidly, torturously slowly. Inside, but not deep enough. Firm, but not hard enough.

"*Please.*" Genna gasped the word, barely able to get it out through the ocean-like roaring in her head.

Rowan leaned forward and over her, stretching out on top of her kissing her more thoroughly than anyone ever had. "You won't hate me in a minute."

"*Please*, fuck me."

That seemed to tip Rowan over some invisible edge and her fingers went rough and hot, sliding with sensuous intent, thrusting into her with long strokes, burying deep, over and over again. Deeper inside than anyone had ever been.

Genna clenched with need, her hips rising, everything going tight and ready. "God. I'm going to come."

Rowan held her gaze, and Genna lost herself in the depth of her eyes. Rowan didn't have to say anything. She could hear it all.

Feel me. Want me. Come for me.

The power in those words scared her, but with Rowan inside her, her fingers a maddening rhythm, she couldn't hold on to the fear. Her body throbbed with every touch, and she had to close her eyes to stave off the climax.

"Don't fight it," Rowan said against her ear. "Give in to the pleasure."

Rowan's fingers curled inside her, pushed in deep, and her thumb brushed over Genna's clit. Claiming her.

Sensation exploded through every cell. Every touch magnified a thousand times—the cool bedsheet beneath her, the heat radiating from Rowan's body over hers, the penetration of Rowan's ceaseless fingers.

Rowan kissed her and a million stars burst behind her eyes. Every inch of her became electric, turning hyperaware.

Genna clung to Rowan as if she were a life raft when the room began to spin and her body splintered into a dozen pieces. Her cries mixed with the slippery wet sounds of Rowan fucking her, and she came in a wave of jolting orgasms, pleasuring piling on pleasure, over and over, until she tugged at Rowan's wrist to stop.

"You're beautiful." Rowan kissed her.

Genna pulled Rowan down on top of her. "I think I might have lost some limbs I came so hard."

Rowan went to roll onto her side. "I'm heavy."

"I want you on me. I like it."

Rowan cautiously let her weight rest on her until Genna sighed softly in her ear. "Perfect. You sexy human weighted throw."

Rowan stilled as Genna caught her breath.

"You okay?" Rowan brushed Genna's hair out of her eyes. Genna's eyes were hazy, a bit dreamy. The way Genna held on to her, as if she'd never let go, was better than any fantasy she'd ever had. Now she *did* feel like Thor.

The trust in Genna's eyes undid her. She was so used to frustrated, independent, by-the-book Genna who distrusted all emotion like she distrusted love. But the raw vulnerability of their lovemaking left her breathless. She'd been worried Genna would resist her. She'd imagined needing to wear down her defenses. Seducing her with their physical connection until Genna just plain wanted her too much to hold back any longer. Rowan would've been okay with that. Hell, she'd have been delighted. But this was so much better. Genna asking her, begging her, so damn wet for her Rowan's mouth had watered.

I love you.

Rowan could admit it to herself, safe in the cocoon of their passion. In the knowledge that Genna wasn't only falling for her but opening up and trusting her as well. Giving herself. Truth was the deepest form of intimacy, and when Genna had come in her arms, all Rowan heard was *I'm yours.* Genna would tell her it was all kinds of possessive to think of someone as *hers,* as if she owned them. But she didn't want to own her. She wanted Genna to be hers because Genna gave herself, and as Genna had come with Rowan inside her, Rowan had given herself over to the love that lurked on the edges of her consciousness.

Genna wriggled her hands between them and palmed Rowan's breasts, stroking her nipples. The arousal that had simmered since their first touch roared back. Rowan gripped Genna's arms and dropped her forehead to Genna's shoulder. She sucked in an unsteady breath as pleasure rippled. "I'm not going to last."

Genna hummed teasingly. "What if I want to take my time? Savor every delicious moment. That plan sounds like revenge."

Rowan shook her head, hating that she wouldn't be able to give Genna what she wanted. Unable to stop, she pressed her center to Genna's thigh, her lower body going hot and liquid. A needy sound ripped from her throat. "I can't wait."

Genna's fingers teased her breasts, down her stomach, stroking fire along her pelvis. "Are you hot for me?"

Rowan was going to spontaneously combust. It wasn't humanly possible to be that hot for so long and not go up in flames. Making Genna come had her so on edge, the gentlest breeze would send her over. Genna's fingers grazed her center and Rowan cried out, pleasure swelling and twisting. She toppled over the precipice of control. "I'm sorry, I can't stop."

Genna muttered something too soft for Rowan to hear and wrapped her legs around her, holding on. "It's okay. I've got you."

Genna stroked Rowan's clit, and her touch was firm and fierce. No teasing now. Rowan moaned. She needed to come and Genna knew it.

Rowan thrust into Genna's hand. "I'm sorry. I'm sorry" she chanted as the pleasure enveloped her and she raced toward a finish she couldn't control.

Genna murmured nonsense in her ear. "It's okay. Let go."

Genna kissed her and there was so much in the kiss. Need, desire, compassion.

Rowan pressed Genna hard into the mattress and ground shamelessly against her fingers. "I can't stop."

"Don't stop. I've got you."

Rowan pressed harder, the hardness of her against the softness of Genna. Small hands roamed her body, one between her legs and the other everywhere all at once. Rowan all but growled, her body flushed warm and needy. "Fuck. I need…"

"Whatever you need, take it," Genna told her, her pretty dressed up hair stuck in sticky strands to her face, eyes a raging storm. "I've got you. Take it."

Rowan's need to come was frantic, as if all her nerve endings were on fire. Her breath came in short bursts, reality receding as passion overwhelmed her. She bucked against Genna, colliding. Genna's fingers slipped from her clit, but it didn't matter. Nothing mattered as a hard shudder went through Rowan. She squeezed her eyes shut as sparks shot behind her eyelids. Bliss stampeded through her, flinging her into an orgasm so intense her cries echoed off the walls.

"I'm sorry," Rowan whispered. "I'm so sorry."

Genna stayed wrapped around her as Rowan came down. When Rowan tried to roll off, Genna held on.

"No," Genna said, her voice loud in the otherwise silent room. "Don't even think about it."

"I'm crushing you." Rowan's body was satisfied and floating, but her brain started its predictable loop of self-disgust. She'd held Genna down, been too rough. She pushed up on her hands to take her weight off even as Genna hung on.

"I *like* it." Genna kissed her.

Rowan made a sound deep in her throat and pulled away. She couldn't. Genna was no match for her, and she fell onto her back, her skin clammy now that the passion fever had broken.

Genna touched her cheek. "Talk to me."

Rowan didn't want to open her eyes. She wanted to hunker down in a cave, live off the land, and never enter civilization again. She opened them anyway, unable to deny Genna anything.

Genna leaned over her, concern etched in every line of her features. Rowan went to assure her everything was okay but saw the fingerprints on her arms before the words made it out.

The bottom fell out of her world so fast she went dizzy. "Oh, God. I hurt you."

Genna followed her eyes and saw the marks. "They're nothing. Don't worry about it."

Rowan traced the perfect imprint of her thumb dug into Genna's bicep and stopped breathing.

Genna slid on top of Rowan, cradling her face in her palms, forcing her to meet her eyes. "I wanted that."

Rowan shook her head.

Genna kissed her. "I loved that."

"I'm sorry, I—"

"*No, Rowan.*" A hint of anger in Genna's voice now. "Stop it. Get out of your head and look at me."

Rowan looked, tears pricking her eyes.

"You have nothing to feel ashamed of. That was incredibly hot. You didn't hurt me."

"I bruised you."

Genna shrugged that off as if Rowan's fingers had been feathers. "They'll be gone by morning." She kissed Rowan lightly. "No one has ever come like that for me before. So wild."

Rowan groaned.

"So hot. So out of control. I loved it. The bed is soft. You felt so good. You didn't hurt me." Genna kissed her the way she had the very first time, a brush of lips, a tender caress, cupping her face and holding Rowan to her, as gentle as Rowan had been rough until she surrendered and opened for her. Rowan felt the kiss all the way down to her toes.

"Touch me again," Genna murmured against her mouth, rolling into her side, and pulling Rowan with her until they were heart to heart. "Feel how much it turned me on."

Rowan's stomach flip-flopped as she felt Genna's desire against her fingers. "You really didn't mind?"

Genna laughed, the sound disbelieving. "Does it feel like I minded?"

"I want to make you come again. Would that be alright?" Rowan asked.

"I can't get enough of you."

Rowan kissed her one last time and then slipped down the bed to press her mouth to Genna. They both moaned when her tongue found the slick center of Genna's need. But she didn't hurry. She slid her hands under Genna's backside and held her to her mouth, nipping and sucking, licking and stroking until Genna arched off the bed, fingers curling in her hair and holding Rowan's head right where she needed her for endless minutes. When Rowan sent her over, she felt Genna's orgasm as it if were her own, an arc of pleasure that washed away her doubts until there was only, always, Genna.

Chapter Twenty-two

Penelope breezed into Graham Marks's deli like she owned the place. Well, that was fitting. She did own it now. Rowan had seen her coming and didn't glance up from cleaning the equipment they'd soon sell to competitors for pennies on the dollar. Penelope's Louboutins smacked the tile in sharp threatening clicks. She marched to the counter and peered at Rowan. "Who are you?"

Rowan wanted to ignore her, but her mom had drilled manners into her head with textbook authoritarian parenting. She didn't look up as she answered, "Rowan Marks."

"The kid."

That whipped her head up. "I'm not a kid."

Thirty-two-year-old Rowan merged in a complicated tangle with her teenage self.

Penelope put a hand to her heart in a parody of distress. "My apologies. I need to speak to your father."

"He isn't here."

Penelope closed her eyes as if Rowan's obstinance was going to be the death of her. "I've already tried your residence. He needs to sign these documents. Today."

Rowan shrugged. Her dad was at the bar. The way he always was nowadays. She wasn't going to tell Penelope that. "That's not my problem."

Penelope huffed. "It's not my fault Graham was too stubborn to see past his own nose. We made him a good offer. He could've retired in luxury." She shrugged it off, as if the decisions of small people weren't worth getting hot under the collar about. "But it is what it is. Please have him sign these. I need to file them by Monday."

She placed the documents she'd brought with her on the counter.

"Dad didn't want to sell." Rowan was too young and untouched by life's razor edge to tamp down the righteous indignation that flooded through her. "You made sure he had no choice, and then offered him a tenth of what it's worth."

Penelope smirked. "That's what happens when you deny the inevitable and delay construction. It's not my fault he's stupid."

Rowan was around the counter and in her face before Penelope could so much as blink. "Dad is not stupid, you *cunt*." She felt herself flush the instant she said it. The worst word she knew. If her mom could hear her now.

Penelope's smile was pure evil. "Oh my. So much anger for such a young…" She looked Rowan up and down slowly, her raking gaze assessing. "…girl."

Rowan felt her perusal like fingers stroking her skin, and that it turned her on only made her angrier. "You destroyed everything. And for what? Money? What good is that?"

Penelope glanced at her Cartier watch, obviously growing bored of the conversation. "I need to go. Give Graham the papers, okay, kiddo?"

Before she could turn away, Rowan grabbed her by the shoulders. "I'm not done."

Penelope gave a windy sigh. "There's really nothing I can do about it now. You can say whatever you want, but the deal is done."

"You owe me," Rowan told her, though for what exactly was unclear.

"I don't—"

Rowan shoved her face into Penelope's and kissed her, hard, not caring if she hurt her. She was no fucking *kiddo*. Penelope had ripped that from her when she'd stripped her parents of their livelihood.

Penelope went very still. Rowan pulled away, ashamed. She'd never force herself on a woman. Not even this one.

She started to turn away, but Penelope caught her arm. "Do that again."

"What?" Rowan froze too, filled with equal parts contempt and arousal.

"Kiss me," Penelope commanded her, looking at Rowan with new eyes. Not a kid at all, but a conquest.

Rowan did as she was told and kissed Penelope so fiercely her head rocked back, her lip swelling from Rowan's teeth scraping along it. Penelope jerked Rowan closer, not seeming to care that Rowan's grungy work clothes were smearing God only knows what all over Penelope's designer suit. Rowan sure didn't mind messing her up.

Rowan gripped her hips and lifted her onto the deli counter, right on top of her stupid papers. She thrust a hand into Penelope's salon blond hair and crushed another bruising kiss to her mouth, plundering her in hot angry strokes while she ripped at the buttons of Penelope's four-hundred-dollar blouse. When the shirt opened, Rowan groaned. Such substantial breasts in purple lace, enough to blow her mind. She buried her face in them while Penelope cooed and stroked her hair, urging Rowan to suck her nipples.

Rowan moaned, turning over in Genna's bed, between sleep and waking. Her hand drifted between her thighs, and she stroked herself as Penelope urged her on.

"Hey, are you okay?"

A soft voice faintly in the background. Rowan knew that voice. Longed for it. She tugged at the hem of Penelope's skirt, sliding a hand up silken thighs.

A warm body pressed along her, spooning her, and Rowan's thoughts blurred. Her clit beat a drum under her fingers. She moaned again, pressing into the heat at her back.

"You're dreaming," the soft voice said in her ear as Rowan found Penelope wet and ready. Took instruction like a good girl when Penelope told her how she wanted to be fucked. Rowan squeezed her clit, and the breath burst out of her.

She opened her eyes.

Genna pressed her lips to the back to Rowan's neck. "You okay? You were making those sexy sounds."

Rowan kept her eyes open to ground herself in the present, the last vestiges of her dream fantasy fading into memory, her clit still pulsing. “Fuck. Sorry.”

“If you say that one more time tonight, I’m going to get a complex.” Genna nibbled the shell of Rowan’s ear.

Completely involuntarily, Rowan pushed back against Genna, wanting more, wanting to be closer. Genna snuggled into her, hands sliding around Rowan’s waist, wrapping around her forearm. The one that ended in a hand between her legs. Rowan shifted, removing her hand, going cold all over. *Jesus.* She was in bed with Genna and dreaming about Penelope. Could her psyche be any more fucked up? Or was pressing Genna into the mattress and leaving marks on her not enough for one night?

“Was it Mrs. Sutton?” Genna asked in a jokingly lewd tone.

“What?” Rowan held her hands over Genna’s so they wouldn’t wander and pressed her thighs together, trying to diffuse her arousal.

“Your dream. Was Mrs. Sutton being especially evil?”

Despite the precariousness of her predicament, Rowan smiled. “I think *you* might have a thing for Mrs. Sutton.”

“You might be right. Tell me more.”

Rowan held her still when Genna tried to move her hands. “Not right now. Go back to sleep. I’m sorry I woke you.”

“Rowan.”

“No.”

“You’re turned on. I can feel how tense you are. It’s okay. It’s just a dream.”

“I know,” Rowan said, to shut her up. “Go to sleep.”

Genna was quiet for a few minutes, and Rowan waited for Genna’s body to go loose and pliant behind her, signaling sleep.

“Was it really Mrs. Sutton?”

“*Genna.*”

Genna laughed at Rowan’s aggrieved tone and the sound reminded her of the way Genna had laughed at flummoxed. She’d never not love making her laugh, even when it was at her own expense.

With her hands captive, Genna made use of her mouth, kissing Rowan’s shoulder. Sucking hard enough to leave a mark of her own.

Biting into her flesh. Rowan's clit throbbed, and she groaned. "Stop it."

"Keep touching yourself," Genna whispered, "it's really sexy."

"It's not sexy."

They lay there together for a few minutes before Genna sighed and slipped her hands from around Rowan's waist, kissed the back of her neck chastely, and turned over. "Good night."

The hopelessness that crowded into the bed between them was the only one to get any sleep.

The generic ring tone of Rowan's cell woke Genna. She rolled over, saw the time, and bolted upright. Ten a.m. She hadn't slept past seven since…well, since she'd spent all night at the Holiday Inn with Hot Soccer Mom a lifetime ago. The memory had the tinge of nostalgia. She shook Rowan's shoulder. "Hun, your phone is ringing."

Rowan opened bleary green eyes, and Genna's heart did a slow, lazy summersault. First thing in the morning Rowan was damn cute with her messy blond hair and a pillow crease on her cheek. Even if it was practically the afternoon. Rowan snagged her phone from her pants on the floor, looked at the screen, then answered. "Mom. Hi."

Genna stretched and rolled out of bed. Damn. Moms really did have a radar for sex. Did she have anything worth feeding Rowan for breakfast? The cinnamon and brown sugar Pop-Tarts she usually ate standing over the sink while reading her email wouldn't cut it with someone who made food from *Good Housekeeping* recipes. She wasn't all that great at being an adult sometimes, and it was another thing Rowan excelled at.

Maybe she could trade sex for pancakes.

"What? When?" Rowan's voice shot up a few octaves, and Genna turned back before she got to the bathroom. "How long has he been missing?"

Who was missing? Genna sat on the bed next to Rowan, who'd gone white as the sheets. She squeezed her hand, but Rowan didn't seem to notice she was there.

"I'm on my way. We'll find him, Mom, don't worry."

Rowan leapt out of bed and grabbed for her clothes, her hands trembling. "I have to go."

"Who's missing?" Genna dove into her dresser for something that wasn't a sexy red dress.

"My nephew. Fuck. He's only three." Rowan shoved her hands in her hair, looking around the room wild-eyed, as if the boy might be hiding under the bed. Rowan yanked on clothes, shoved into her shoes, and almost tripped on the untied laces when she started to run for the door.

Genna grabbed her own shoes and ran after Rowan, no time to put them on. "Fort Donavan, right? Take the interstate. It'll be faster this time of day."

Rowan raced down the stairs so fast Genna's breath seized, If Rowan didn't slow down, she'd take a header.

Rowan jumped the last two steps and hit the bottom with both feet. "I'll call you. I'm sorry about this, but I have to go."

Genna pushed through the security door. "You're not going to call me. Don't be an idiot."

Rowan unlocked her truck. "I don't have time to argue."

"Good." Genna swung herself in. "I'm coming, so just deal with it."

Rowan shot her an exasperated look but started the truck and peeled out at a speed that would surely piss off law enforcement if they were caught.

"Give me your phone," Genna said.

"If Mom calls—"

"I'm not going to use it," Genna said calmly.

Rowan handed over her phone without looking at her, all her concentration on breaking the sound barrier without getting them killed.

"Do you have your mom's landline in here?"

"I think so," Rowan said. "No one uses it though."

"Exactly." Genna scrolled Rowan's contacts until she found "Mom" and two numbers. She typed the one under "home" into her own phone, leaving Rowan's free in case someone called with news.

"What's your mom's name?"

Rowan looked at her then. "Doreen. What are you doing?"

Genna didn't have time to explain.

When Doreen Marks answered, Genna could hear the hysteria in her voice. "Doreen. My name is Genna. I am a friend of Rowan's. We're on our way. I need you to send me a photo of the missing child. What's his name?"

Doreen didn't ask any questions. "Sawyer. Oh God. His name is Sawyer Marks. He's three. He's only three."

Doreen was losing it, and Genna needed her to keep it together just a bit longer until they got there. "I'm going to give you my number. Send me a photo. We'll need it when we canvass the neighborhood. Can you do that?"

"I think so." Then a bit more confidently, "Yes, I can do that."

"Tell me what happened. Where was Sawyer before you noticed he was missing?"

Genna spoke calmly, gently but firmly gathering all the critical details. What was Sawyer wearing? Did he have anything with him? Where would he go? Where had they already looked? Were there any neighbors who might have seen him or taken him inside?

"The police are here," Doreen blurted and hung up.

She closed her eyes for a second, giving herself one minute to think. Where would a three-year-old go?

Rowan merged off the interstate, and they got stuck behind a lumbering RV almost instantly. Rowan cursed colorfully, and Genna rubbed her thigh. "Getting into an accident won't help. You're doing everything you can right now. The police are with your mom. People are looking."

That seemed to help the tiniest smidgen because Rowan blew out a breath. "What happened? I didn't have time for details."

"Your mom and your neighbor Talia were playing with both children in the front yard when someone named Bertie asked your mom to help her down the porch stairs. Doreen handed the youngest child to Talia and went to help."

"Cameron," Rowan told her.

"Cameron started to fuss when your mom left, and Talia was distracted tending to him. Sawyer wandered off."

Rowan went so still Genna knew she was trying not to explode. "How could she be so stupid? He's *three.*"

"Kids move like lightning. It could've happened to anyone." Genna used the same tone that had worked on Doreen. "What's important now is finding Sawyer."

Minutes later, Rowan's phone rang and Genna answered it immediately.

"The police want the two of you to search eastbound from Talia's house and fan out toward the wildlife preserve five blocks away," Doreen said rapidly.

Genna typed the details into her phone while Doreen talked. When she broke down sobbing Genna did what she could to sooth her. "Everyone is out looking for him. He's only been missing a short time. Talia noticed right away."

They would find him. Of course they would. They had to.

Rowan broke the speed limit again when they entered Fort Donavan, but fortunately Doreen lived right on the edge of town. She parked sloppily at the curb of a large yellow Victorian, that from all the mailboxes out front had been cut up into a multifamily at some point.

"Tell me everything," Rowan said.

Now that Rowan wasn't driving, she didn't seem to know what to do with herself and sat shell-shocked.

"Come on. Let's get started," Genna said.

She met Rowan on the sidewalk and took ten seconds to throw her arms around her in a fierce hug. "Here's what's happening."

She talked her through the plan the police had laid out. Rowan headed toward the search area, and Genna stopped to speak to an officer, confirming what Doreen had told her.

Every neighbor on the street was scouring yards and garden sheds, calling Sawyer's name. If he was in the vicinity, they'd find him.

They didn't.

As the minutes ticked into an hour, Rowan grew paler, her face an ashy gray.

"Come to the house," Genna said. "You need some water."

She'd expected Rowan to refuse, but Rowan followed her pliant as a kitten and that made Genna worry even more. When they got back to the Markses' front yard, a headquarters of sorts had been set up. Doreen was perched on the edge of a lawn chair with a kid halfway between baby and toddler, who could only be Cameron, in her arms. Doreen was holding him so tightly Genna wouldn't have been surprised if he turned blue. She took Cameron so Rowan could hug her mom. Both their faces were tearstained in seconds.

"He's gone," Doreen repeated over and over into Rowan's chest. "It's my fault."

Genna grabbed bottles of water for all of them, knowing better than to mention food. She passed them off and left Rowan and her mom to comfort each other. She wanted nothing more than to wrap herself around Rowan and comfort her as well, but that wasn't what Rowan needed most right now.

The best thing Genna could do for Rowan was find Talia.

Cameron found her. His eyes lighting up with pure delight, his chattering garble at full volume when he spotted the brown-haired teenager in black tights and bright pink running shoes surrounded by about a million adults. A man and a woman flanked her like sentinels. Her parents probably. Genna didn't have time for parents. She pushed through the crowd, Cameron on her hip giving her an all-access pass.

Talia was as gray as everyone else, but she was wringing her hands instead of crying. Cameron squealed and Talia gave them a wobbly smile. "Hey there, CamCam."

Cameron held out his arms and Talia scooped him out of Genna's, hugging him to her. When she looked at Genna, her eyes were devastated. "I'm so sorry. I don't know what happened. One minute he was there and the next…"

Genna folded both Talia and Cameron into a quick hug, her heart breaking for the poor kid. "You don't need to apologize to me. These things happen in a split second."

She managed to muscle some of the overprotective adults out of the way and sat with Talia and Cameron on the curb. "You know him better than almost everyone here. Where would Sawyer go?"

"I don't know."

"I bet you do. Think," Genna said patiently. "Does he like cars? Would he have followed a car?"

Talia shook her head. "He's afraid of the road. Mrs. M. drills that into him." Talia's eyes brimmed. "She's never going to forgive me."

"She will if you help us find him." Genna hoped it was true. "Does he spend time at your house? Do you take him anywhere?"

Genna battered Talia with questions until the girl looked ready to crumble. "Relax for a minute. Close your eyes. Tell me about a day with Sawyer."

"I don't know," Talia said. "I don't…" Her eyes flew open. "We go to the dog park, sometimes. He loves dogs."

Every cell in Genna's body set its hopes on the dog park, just outside the initial search parameters. The only place Sawyer knew that no one had searched yet. Could a three-year-old walk that far? If he were following a four-legged friend, hell yes. People always underestimated the stamina of small but determined children.

She jumped to her feet and pulled Talia up. "Come on."

They handed a squirming and overwhelmed Cameron back to a still-tearful Doreen and took off at a run.

Genna and Talia found Sawyer in less than five minutes, asleep on a man's blanket, his head on a black-and-brown spotted mangy mut that clearly belonged to his new landlord. Talia didn't appear to notice the man and fell to the ground, burying her face against Sawyer's chubby cheeks.

"Check him over," Genna told Talia. "Make sure he's okay."

Genna approached the man cautiously. "I'm sorry to bother you, but you seem to have found a child half the town is searching for. Thank you so much. Would you mind if we took him home now?"

Genna showed the man the photo of Sawyer on her phone to confirm she wasn't a stranger.

The guy had a beard that rivaled Gandalf and a cap pulled down low. He looked as worn down as his dog and smelled worse than Genna had ever imagined a person could. Sawyer though showed no obvious signs of having been harmed.

"I didn't take him. He came and sat down and fell asleep. That's it."

"He's fine," Talia said eyes shiny with tears. "Not a scratch, and he's not even upset."

Genna swallowed a sigh of relief and smiled at the man. "I understand he just wandered over. He was chasing your dog? Sawyer loves dogs. What's its name?"

The guy looked over at Talia and Sawyer, now both petting the dog who was flat on its back and loving every minute of it. "That's Dumpster. Dumpster the dog."

Genna swallowed a hysterical laugh, the panic and relief catching up with her. Dumpster probably had a colony of fleas, some of which would be in Sawyer's hair, but that was the least of her problems. "And you are?"

The guy said nothing, looking at her in that empty-eyed way of someone who'd answered that question before and lived to regret it.

Genna searched her pockets and gave him all the cash she had. "I have to call the child's family now. There are police out looking for him."

At the word *police* the man struggled to his feet and Genna took a step back, understanding why he hadn't gotten help when a small kid had run over and plonked himself down on his blanket in the middle of the day. The police weren't the good guys for everyone.

Before the man could leave, Genna took his hand. He jerked at her touch. How long had it been since anyone had bothered with such a small gesture? "Not everyone would have looked after him to make sure he didn't get hurt. Thank you."

The man looked at her for a long moment, then nodded, called his dog, picked up his stuff, and slowly shuffled away.

Genna called Rowan. "Talia and I have him. We're at the dog park. He's okay."

Rowan gasped. "You have him? He's okay? Mom! Genna has him."

"He's okay," Genna repeated, her heart finally beating a steady rhythm.

She called the police for good measure and sat down in the grass with Talia and Sawyer waiting for the mob to descend. Talia occupied Sawyer by showing him how to make a dandelion bracelet.

"You're good with kids. Younger siblings?" Genna asked.

Talia shook her head, ruffling Sawyers hair, unable to keep her hands off him. "I just love them. Their mom is in jail, and Mrs. M is kind of old."

Genna nodded. "You're an awesome big sister."

Talia ducked her head. "I dunno."

"You can get down on their level. You're patient. You love them. That's what kids need most, and some don't get it. They're lucky to have you."

"Thanks." Talia picked the fluff off a dandelion, her cheeks reddening.

Two cop cars pulled up as a swarm of people on foot poured through the gates.

"This is not your fault," Genna reminded Talia, getting up and hugging the girl to her side.

"It sort of is," Talia muttered.

Genna shook her head. "Nope. Kids get lost all the time. I lost my sister in a mall when she wasn't much bigger than Sawyer. We didn't find her for over three hours. She doesn't even remember it."

Talia's hazel eyes widened. "You? But you're amazing. You knew exactly what to do."

"You live and learn," Genna told her dryly, right before Rowan swept her off her feet.

Chapter Twenty-three

Rowan's hug cracked ribs. Genna held on, running her hands up and down Rowan's back in a soothing caress, finally able to give her exactly what she needed. "It's okay. He's safe. He was asleep. Completely unharmed."

Sawyer had burst into tears at all the attention and was screaming bloody murder in Doreen's arms.

"God. If you hadn't found him. No one else thought of the dog park. It's so far! Thank you," Rowan said.

"Talia found him." Genna eased back from Rowan as the police approached. She kept one arm protectively around Rowan's waist as she relayed the details to the cops.

"The man appeared to be living in the park? Did you get a name?" Asked an officer who looked so earnest and had such narrow shoulders Genna figured he was mint fresh from the academy.

"No. I asked but he wouldn't say."

The officer nodded like he had expected as much. "Which direction did he go?"

Genna waved behind her with deliberate vagueness. The man could've taken Sawyer and hurt him. Some would have. But this guy had watched over him, probably for more than an hour, and made him feel safe enough to sleep. Sawyer had been unspeakably lucky.

Once the police got a statement from Talia and departed, Rowan was next in line to hug Sawyer senseless. His screams had mellowed into pitiful hiccups. Being rescued was a whole lot harder on him than being lost. Rowan held him the way one would hold a fragile priceless artifact.

"You scared us, little man. Don't run off again, okay?"

Sawyer nodded miserably.

Doreen took Genna's hands. Her smile was sunshine through storm clouds. "Thank you, sweetie. Thank you for finding my boy. When I think of what could've happened to him…"

"Don't think about it." Genna's experience told her the advice was useless. "He's okay. He's safe."

Doreen hugged her. "I don't know who you are."

Genna laughed. "I wish we had met under happier circumstances. I'm Genna, Rowan's girlfriend."

Genna blushed a little when she said it, never having used the G word with Rowan before.

Doreen stepped back, took her shoulders, and looked at her properly for the first time. "Rowan's chosen well. I always knew she would, but I never expected we'd need you to save Sawyer."

"Talia found him, not me." The Markses ought to know who had really saved the day. It would help all of them. Chances are, if they hadn't found Sawyer someone else would have, and he'd have been perfectly fine, but she understood what it was to fear the worst.

Doreen looked at Rowan holding Sawyer on her hip, his little blond head tucked into the crook of her neck. "It was my fault he wasn't properly supervised. If anything had happened to him, I'd never have recovered."

"It's not your fault, Mom." Rowan said it in such a way that Genna knew this conversation had been on repeat. Rowan was right, but Rowan's eyes fell on Talia trying valiantly to blend into the scenery. Genna saw her shrink back even further as the relief in Rowan's gaze turned frigid. There was little question as to who Rowan had decided *was* at fault.

Genna wiped a hand over her face tiredly. What a day.

"I'll go now," Talia said quietly.

"That's all you have to say for yourself?" Rowan asked Talia, her tone barely controlled fury.

Genna put a hand on Rowan's arm. "You're afraid and stressed, and this has been a terrible day. There's no need to blame *anyone*."

Rowan didn't look at her, her attention lasered on Talia. "He could've been kidnapped. You understand that, right? He could've ended up a statistic because you were *distracted*."

Genna let go of Rowan and stepped directly in front of Talia. "She isn't your punching bag just because you need an outlet for your fear. It could've happened to anyone."

Rowan scowled, misery etched in every line of her features. "She's sixteen. That's too young to be looking after kids."

"I did it a whole lot younger," Genna said coldly. "And I lost Grace, in much the same way, for an even longer span of time. Do you want to take a few cheap shots at me too?"

Rowan's face crumpled. She squeezed her eyes shut for a long second, her shoulders sagging. "Of course, I don't." She looked over Genna's shoulder at Talia. "I'm sorry. That was uncalled for. Genna is right."

Genna stepped away now that Talia no longer required a human shield and hugged the girl to her side again, tamping down her own memory of paralyzing fear. "Talia was the only one to remember how much Sawyer loves dogs. If not for her, we'd still be looking."

Doreen nodded decisively. "Thank you, sweetie. We all know how much you love him."

"I do." Talia righted the tremor in her voice. "I'd never intentionally let him wander off."

Doreen hugged her, holding Talia to her like she was her own. "This day calls for brownies, what do you say? Want to come over and have some with us?"

Talia nodded and they all set off out of the dog park, Genna, Rowan, and a now exhausted Sawyer bringing up the rear.

"I'm an asshole," Rowan muttered.

Genna fit herself into Rowan's side. "No, you're not. You were scared. It's natural to want to blame someone."

"She goes out of her way to help Mom. The Miracle, Mom calls her. I had no business saying what I did."

Genna was too damn worn out to shove down her irritation. "Sometimes we all think things that aren't perfect. Welcome to being human. There's no need to beat yourself up every time it happens."

Rowan didn't reply, but the way she stiffened indicated that she understood they were no longer talking about Talia.

❖

Rowan reclined the passenger seat and closed her eyes. "I shouldn't have let you drive. You're just as tired as I am."

"Sawyer's not my kid," Genna said. "It's different when they're yours. Rest. We're almost home."

Rowan liked the way Genna said *home* as if it were hers too. She thought about a lost little Grace. Rowan would've been worried, frantic even, but not crushed into uselessness and rage by fear. "You really lost Grace? That must've been awful."

"One of the worst days of my life," Genna agreed. "We were at the mall and Gabby was throwing a tantrum. By the time I'd turned around, Grace was gone. Just disappeared as if she'd never been there. We looked everywhere for *hours* and couldn't find her. I wanted to die. I was too afraid to call Mom, so the police did. She got a call from the cops that her child was missing, and then had to *wait at home* wondering if she'd been found. Mom didn't speak to me for a week after that."

Rowan marveled and at how far Genna had come. The story rolling off her tongue, no difficulty talking about one of the worst days of her life. She reached over and took Genna's hand. "That wasn't fair. It wasn't your fault You were, what? Thirteen? Fourteen?"

Genna smiled at her. "I know. So did Mom. But fear makes you want to blame someone. We all got over it eventually."

From the way Genna had protected Talia earlier, Rowan figured it wasn't something she'd ever really gotten over. Who could? How much had Genna endured taking on responsibilities too big for her small shoulders? And how many of those did she shrug off today as if they were nothing? Losing her sister even temporarily, the blame, the silent treatment as punishment, and even having to deal with Grace's misdirected attractions, it was all too much, too young. And those things were probably the tip of the iceberg. If it were Rowan in Genna's shoes, she'd be in a lot worse shape than *a decent amount pissed off.*

Genna said, "Doreen could probably use some help. Talia is wonderful, but there are other options. Has she looked into services provided to the families of the incarcerated?"

Rowan's stomach twisted, reminding her she hadn't eaten more than a brownie all day. "I know they exist, but we haven't explored options. Sara only has a year to go. Mom figured she could handle it."

"She can handle it. But that doesn't mean she has to. Maybe once the dust settles, you'll use your social work skills and see what's available?"

"That's a good idea." Then, because she wanted to tell her, Rowan said, "Sara got busted for breaking and entering. She got two years."

Genna steered the truck into the residents' lot of her apartment complex. "Why was she breaking and entering?"

The question didn't feel intrusive the way it did when other people asked. Genna had waited until she was ready. If *she'd* been the one wanting to know, she'd have pushed. But Genna understood hard things that were even harder to talk about. Rowan fell in love with her all over again, more than a little humbled. "Let's go inside, and I'll tell you."

Chapter Twenty-four

Rowan showered, dressed in the fluffy robe hanging on the back of the bathroom door, and found Genna in the living room on the couch. Two steaming plates of shepherd's pie sat on the coffee table with Sarah Michelle Gellar frozen mid-stabbing with a pointy wooden stake buried to the hilt in a vampire's satanic heart.

"I'm ready for my cuddles now," Genna announced.

Rowan smiled. "If you're not careful, you'll get good at this romance thing."

"Microwaving leftovers isn't very romantic."

Rowan sat next to her and grabbed their plates off the coffee table, handing one to Genna. "Thank you for this."

They ate in silence until Rowan put her plate to the side and tipped her head back against the couch. "I can't believe today actually happened."

"I know." Genna put her plate down and curled into Rowan's side.

Even though it was the very last topic she wanted to talk about, Rowan said, "To understand why Sara did it, we have to start with Penelope."

She stroked Genna's arm, staring blankly at the TV. She'd spent so much of her life trying *not* to think about this. Pushing it down and shoving it away whenever it popped into her head. But it was always there, like a beach ball held underwater, struggling to rise. Now that she allowed herself to access it, the story burst from her grasp, jetting to the surface. "When I was fifteen, developers contacted my parents. They had plans to turn my family's deli and everything else on the street into an office complex. They offered Dad a lot of money. He didn't want to sell."

"Why not?" Genna stroked the back of Rowan's neck, along the edge of the bathrobe.

Rowan leaned into the touch, grounding herself in their connection, as the past rushed her. "Dad wanted to leave it to me. He'd wanted a son and got two daughters, but he never held it against me. Who I am gave my dad what he needed. Family was important, and we all thought he was doing the right thing."

Genna didn't say anything. Just kept touching her lightly, small gestures to let Rowan know she was there.

"Penelope worked for the development company. She wasn't really in charge, but acted as the liaison between the locals and the developers. She kept asking and asking, until it bordered on harassment. Dad took so much pride in saying no. He would've taken the money and retired, but he was waiting until I was out of school and could take it over. I'm the reason he didn't sell. Eventually, Penelope gave up, and they built around us. We didn't think it through. Offices hold people, and people need to eat, right? But over time, the noise mixed with all the other businesses selling out drove our regular customer base away. During the height of construction, downtown Fort Donavan was a ghost town. We couldn't pay the bills. By the time we realized Dad would have no choice but to sell, Penelope took great pleasure in spitting in his face."

Rowan hadn't realized she'd clenched her jaw until Genna's fingers stroked along it, unknotting the tension. Shame had wound itself around her, binding her in thick cords and sweeping her out to sea, defenseless. If not for her, they'd have sold immediately, and everything would've turned out differently. "They offered just over ten percent of their original amount, citing delays and the added expenses for having to work around him. All lies. They have enough money to feed a small country, but they knew we were desperate. Plus, Dad had turned Penelope down, so she enjoyed screwing him.

Dad took the insulting deal. The deli closed. Nothing was ever the same after that."

"I'm so sorry." Genna rested her head on Rowan's shoulder.

Rowan shrugged. That wasn't even the worst part. The memories were still as fresh as the day they'd happened, but now Rowan had to force the words out, the aftermath so much worse.

"Dad lost his way. Started drinking. Couldn't hold down a job. Three generations the deli had been in the family. He was the one to lose it for a tenth of what it was worth and destroy the legacy he'd hoped to pass on."

"It wasn't his fault," Genna said.

"I know." The only person who'd ever blamed Graham Marks was himself, and her dad never forgave his toughest critic.

"Mom found a job, but she'd only ever been a homemaker and made minimum wage. Sara was just finishing high school, and I still had two years to go. I wanted to drop out, get a job to help, but Mom said no. I'd done what I'd been told my whole life. I didn't question her."

Genna kissed the side of Rowan's neck. "You were a teenager. Staying in school was the best thing."

Rowan just shook her head, hearing the words but not believing them. It had been the wrong decision, but she didn't expect Genna to understand. "After Sara graduated, she fell in with a wild crowd. Started going out nights, not getting home until morning. Mom tried her best to put a stop to it, but she was so busy, and Sara was an adult. What could she do? Then the money started rolling in. Just a little at first, enough to cover some bills. Then more. Then enough that Mom didn't have to work so hard. Enough to get Dad into therapy, not that it worked." Why hadn't she seen what was happening sooner? Why hadn't Mom? Were they all just too damn tired? Rowan swallowed the familiar guilt. "Sara told us she'd gotten a job working nights. I'm not sure if Mom believed her, or if she was just so sad and overwhelmed that she didn't want to know. Dad wasn't doing well. Drinking and angry and making life difficult for everyone. And all the while I stayed in school and got good grades."

Like a good girl.

Genna wrapped an arm around Rowan's waist, and Rowan melted in Genna's hold, grief leaving her boneless. Useless. Just like before. Just like today.

"Sara was stealing for the money to help your parents?" Genna asked.

Rowan nodded. "She was in a gang who did B and E and carjacking. She was good too. Didn't get caught for years and funneled most of the money to Mom and Dad. She took care of us."

Rowan rested her cheek against Genna's hair. "I graduated. Did two years of college before Sara was arrested for the first time. She had no weapons, no priors, a sob story. The court went easy on her. I insisted on dropping out of school and getting a job after that. I thought if I contributed, then maybe Sara would choose a different path."

"I'm assuming she didn't," Genna said.

"No." Rowan almost laughed. "She said she owed *her guys.* I think it's more likely she was in so deep she couldn't get out. You don't just walk away from that life. But I worked overtime thinking it made a difference. It didn't."

Nothing had. Nothing would ever undo her mistakes.

"A few years later, she was arrested again, and then two years ago for a third time with a knife. By then she'd had Sawyer with one of her *guys*, was pregnant with Cameron, and was in so deep she'd be dead before they let her walk."

Genna made a small incoherent sound and held on to Rowan so tightly she could feel Genna's fingers digging into her side. The gentle pricks of pain were satisfying. She *should* hurt.

"Sometimes I wonder if she got arrested on purpose, to get away. To get the boys away. The men who'd made them didn't have any interest in them, thank God, but they wanted Sara and she was Sawyer and Cameron's mom. What could she do? She had so few choices."

Rowan sighed. "It took almost a year for her case to wind its way through the courts with Sara out on bail. We were all there when she was sentenced. Dad. Fuck. I've never seen anyone look so pummeled by life. He couldn't take it. He died a year later. Mom says it was the drinking, but I think Sara going to prison for supporting the family he was convinced he had failed broke him. He died of shattered dreams."

"What a tragedy," Genna murmured, "for all of you."

Rowan only knew the shame of failing to help before it was too late. Needing to be done with it, she hurried on, "After, there was life insurance money. I went back to college. Mom cared for Sawyer and Cameron. Sara has a year left. That's it, really."

It'd taken less than ten minutes to tell an avalanche of pain. Emptied out and a little lost, Rowan pulled Genna onto her lap. She would've curled up inside Genna's skin if such a thing were possible.

Genna whispered soothing words, slipping a hand around the back of her neck, and stroking her hair as if she were a child. "I'm so sorry. That's a terrible thing to have to go through. I wish I knew the right thing to say. Is there anything that would help?"

Rowan kissed her. "You're here. That's what I need most."

Rowan lost track of how long they sat there, wrapped around each other with the past like a third person squeezed on the couch. Telling Genna hadn't exactly felt good, but it did offer some small relief, like a puff of air from a balloon, allowing her to let it go just a little bit. She wished her story was different for a million reasons, but a new one worked its way to the top of the stack. Genna's own history had put so much on her that Rowan was loathe to add more. Genna would bear the weight of her past with the same resolve she bore everything, but Rowan wished she could spare her. Share happy memories instead.

"Your dream last night was Penelope, wasn't it?" Genna asked.

"Yes. Now you understand why it's fucked up. Why I couldn't last night when you said it wasn't a big deal. Penelope was the domino that destroyed everything, and she *turns me on*. What sort of horrible person does that make me?"

"You are *not* horrible," Genna said, her eyes steely with determination. "Don't say that. Sometimes our brains do strange things to help us cope."

Rowan did laugh then, the sound so bitter and hollow she scared herself. “Not everyone is so fortunate to have mind-blowing orgasms to cope when their family is destroyed. I’m so lucky.”

Genna’s eyes were so sad. The empathy radiating from her was almost tangible. Rowan instantly regretted the comment.

“I don’t know exactly why you have these fantasies,” Genna said, “but you are the kindest, sweetest, best person I know, and I can’t stand it when you talk about yourself that way.”

Rowan pressed her forehead to Genna’s. She’d give her anything, even lies. “Okay, I’m sorry.” If it hurt her, she’d never mention it again. But she’d never stop thinking it.

“You’re not to blame. Not for wanting to take over the family business and not for staying in school either. It’s not your fault,” Genna said.

“Whose fault is it? Some faceless corporation stuck in late-stage capitalism that puts profit over people? That’s so common, it’s boring. Dad for wanting to do the right thing and being unable to cope with the disastrous outcome? Sara for taking what was probably the only opportunity available to an eighteen-year-old that would support us? Whose fault is it? I have to blame someone, and I did *nothing* while everyone around me was drowning.”

Genna shook her head. “What could you have done?”

“I could’ve told Dad I didn’t want to run the deli and to take the deal. I could’ve left school and gotten a job, so Sara didn’t feel so responsible for us. I could’ve gotten Dad into rehab. Hell, even today I was useless. *You* were incredible, and you don’t even know Sawyer. I should’ve been there helping Mom with the kids, and maybe Sawyer wouldn’t have gotten lost.”

I’m useless, pathetic. I could have done a million things and instead I dream about Penelope and get off.

Genna cupped Rowan’s cheek and kissed her. “First of all, you *did* want to run the deli, and it sounds like everyone encouraged that goal. There was no reason to believe it wouldn’t happen. Second, you *did* want to get a job and your mom said no. You did as you were told, and that it turned out horribly is no more your fault than Doreen’s. Third, rehab doesn’t work unless the person wants to change. You know that already. Fourth, what happened today with Sawyer was an accident. If you'd been there, maybe it wouldn't have happened. Or maybe Talia wouldn't have come over and Doreen would have handed Cameron to *you,* and Sawyer still would have wandered off. You're not clairvoyant. *No one* knows how things will turn out. You make the best decisions you can at the time with the information you have. Do you think I was useful when Grace was missing? I was too afraid to call my own mother. A mall employee on a smoke break found her *outside* in the parking lot. All the ways that could've gone wrong played on repeat in my head for months. I hated myself, so don't think I don't get it. But, hun," Genna pressed her lips to Rowan's again, "you're human and shit happens. Some things are out of our control *especially* when you're young and just trying to make it through a bad situation. You need to forgive yourself for not having all the answers."

Forgive herself? Not likely. Rowan didn't want to talk about it any longer. She owed Genna honesty, but the fierceness in her voice, the way she'd made a list into a declaration, only made Rowan more ashamed. She looked away and took *Buffy* off pause. "Thanks for saying all of that."

No reason to tell Genna she didn't deserve to be defended.

Genna said nothing more, just settled comfortably in her arms while Rowan stared at the TV, seeing nothing, her eyes dry.

Rowan surfaced to the sensation of fingers drifting through her hair. She kept her eyes closed for a long minute, luxuriating in the intimacy of waking up with Genna. The soft caresses. The warmth of Genna's body close by but not touching. Total perfection. Sharing a bed, waking up and falling asleep together, bookending the day, comforted her. She barely remembered Genna leading her to bed, but she'd never forget waking up bedside her. She pulled Genna close. "Good morning. I could get used to waking up like this."

Genna kissed her. "Could you get used to waking up earlier? I've been impatiently waiting to ravish you. You have a distractingly naked and gorgeous body that the sheet is doing nothing to hide. I've been leering inappropriately for the last half hour."

Rowan pulled Genna on top of said body, enjoying the way they fit together all warm and snuggly. She stroked the small of Genna's back, wrapped her palms around the flare of her hips, pressed into her. "You could've roamed. A Genna-centered erotic dream would've started the day off right."

Genna stopped kissing down the column of her throat and looked at her in surprise. "No, I couldn't. That's sexual assault."

As cold showers went, *that* was an ice bath.

"Of course it's not. You have every reason to believe I'd want you to touch me."

"Person one may believe they have every reason to think person two wants them as well, even if it turns out to be untrue. What's the difference? Consent isn't optional."

Rowan frowned. "We're *dating*. We've slept together. It's completely different." The morning glow she'd woken up with was fading fast. What. The. Fuck.

Genna shrugged. "A court would disagree. A sleeping person cannot consent, which would make touching you intimately while asleep sexual assault. If I had penetrated you, that would be rape, legally."

Rowan stared. "You're serious? Just because I was asleep?"

Genna nodded.

Did Genna have to be so inflexible all the time? Grumpy, she said, "Are there any other long-held daydreams of mine you want to ruin before seven a.m.?"

Genna raised her eyebrows in that way Rowan loved. "Laws don't only apply to single people. I didn't mean to ruin anything. I was explaining why I didn't want to touch you while you were sleeping."

Single people. Genna didn't consider herself single. Did that mean they were in a relationship? Joy shoved aside her annoyance and jumped up like an overexcited puppy, wagging its tail. "That's fair. I just think there's a whole lot of context that you're not taking into account. Touching someone like that, turning them on before they're even fully awake, it's hot."

Genna nodded, fingers in her hair again. "That's fair too. What's black and white in a court can be shades of gray outside it. But I'm not comfortable unless we discuss it first."

Rowan kissed the tip of her nose. "Did we just compromise, Dr. Sex? We're getting pretty good at this girlfriend stuff."

Genna laughed. "I might never get good at your penchant for turning everything into a rose-colored romantic pipe dream."

"And I'll never get good at your cold logic that takes all the whimsy out of things."

"Whimsy?"

Rowan stared Genna down playfully. "Do *not* say it's like flummoxed. I'm no one's grandpa."

"*That* we can agree on." Genna did the leering thing.

Rowan slid a thigh between Genna's and pressed it lightly to Genna's center. "And what rule does staring brazenly at a sleeping woman break in a court of law? You're pleading guilty."

Genna tilted her head to the side, thinking, even as she pressed into Rowan, her eyes going hot. "I don't know. I'll have to look it up. Seems like there ought to be a precedent against lechery."

"Look it up later." Rowan slid Genna's pajamas and underwear off and settled her against her thigh again. "You're wet, and I haven't even touched you." Rowan brushed a kiss over her lips. "You really were having dirty thoughts."

"I really was." The statement came out breathy, caught on the edge of a gasp as she slid against Rowan's thigh. "Waking up with you all spread out for me, on display, so beautifully built, so blindingly sexy, I couldn't help myself."

Warmth filled Rowan's chest. They'd both enjoyed waking up together. She ran her fingers over Genna's small breasts, down her abdomen, cupping her hips and squeezing her backside. "Having a dirty mind isn't a legal defense."

"Maybe not. But it's fun." Genna closed her eyes and rocked against Rowan, slowly and sensually, a low moan escaping her. Genna's need was coating her skin, and Rowan's desire rose with it. She used her hands on Genna's backside to encourage her, but Genna kept the pace excruciatingly languid. Rowan ran her hands up and down Genna's body from shoulders to thighs, gliding over the plains and valleys, loving the way she felt beneath her fingers. "You're beautiful."

"The way you look at me makes me believe it." Genna held herself up with her palms on Rowan's pillow on either side of her head and ground against her. She leaned down until their lips were almost touching. "You make me want things."

Rowan's breath caught in her throat as her heart began to sprint and her vision narrowed. "What things?"

"All the things," Genna said cryptically.

Rowan didn't know whether to be pleased or disappointed with that answer, but it didn't matter because Genna's mouth descended on hers and thought was impossible. Rowan loved the way Genna kissed. So intentional. Like an archeologist exploring long-buried terrain. Genna swirled her tongue from one place to the next, one minute stroking, then sucking, nibbling, dipping and teasing, unhurried, as if kissing were the main event. Rowan shuddered.

Genna tore away, breathless. "Need you. Over me. Let me feel you."

The staccato commands threatened to obliterate Rowan's control. She held on by her fingertips. "Come for me like this."

Genna groaned, her body as taut as a bowstring and beginning to tremble. "Now is not the time to be pigheaded."

It clicked for Rowan then as their needs aligned. Genna *wanted* her on top. Rowan flipped her as easily as a pancake in a frying pan, slid a hand between them, and let all her weight fall on Genna. She stroked between Genna's thighs and found her clit. "Is this what you need, baby?"

Genna's moan turned into a cry as Rowan caressed her. Her eyes had been closed but she opened them and looked directly into Rowan's as she surrendered to her orgasm, her skin flushing powder pink. Rowan's heart swelled as Genna let go, eyes wide-open, unafraid, as she took what she needed to orgasm. Something of the heart that only Rowan could offer.

Rowan rolled onto her side and held her as Genna's trembles subsided. She breathed deeply, rubbing her nose playfully against Rowan's neck, and kissing the fragile skin with Rowan's breath, her life, a thin barrier away. "You've got skills, Thor."

Rowan kissed her forehead. "That was all you."

Genna shook her head. "You provided the inspiration. God. All I have to do is look at you, and I want to come."

"Could be dangerous," Rowan teased her.

"It's *definitely* dangerous." And that struck too close to home, so Genna followed it with, "If my orgasm hasn't liquified my memory, I believe you said that being woken up mid-ravish was hot?"

Genna watched Rowan's throat work as she swallowed. "I happen to be very awake right at the moment."

"What do you find hot about it?" The question reminded Genna of when she'd first met Rowan, all sweetness and reserved in a way she hadn't understood.

Now there was none of that as Rowan answered easily. "There's something about waking up to pleasure that's sexy. You're sleepy and relaxed and not distracted by the day's events. Maybe your lover is unaware you're awake so you can enjoy being pleasured in a very hedonistic way. There's nothing to do, nowhere to be, and your lover wants you so much they couldn't wait a second longer. That's the part I like most, I think. Being desired like that is a huge turn-on."

Genna swallowed back the rush of *let me have you, I can't wait either* and ignored the burn that spread through her, coalescing like embers between her thighs. "I think we need a preview of what *could* happen on a morning just like this one if we'd agreed beforehand that I was allowed to give in to temptation."

"I deliver you on the express train to evil?" Rowan asked.

Genna's brain worked through the reference until a laugh bubbled up in her throat. Here she was trying to seduce her, and Rowan had tossed her a catholic schoolgirl joke like the Lord's Prayer was sex banter. "*That* was like flummoxed."

Rowan groaned. "Don't grandpa me."

Genna shook her head. "You have no idea how sexy you are."

Rowan was relaxed, smiling and it was such a relief to see her happy after the sadness of the night before. Rowan kissed her, quick and easy, making Genna's heart stumble. A perfectly chaste everyday kiss. A flash of connection and reassurance that set the world right. Fuck. Genna was fine with dating, she *wanted* to be dating. But they were kidding themselves that they were exploring their potential.

This moment, sexy and cozy and laughing in bed.

That simplest of kisses.

Had *couple* written all over it.

CHAPTER TWENTY-FIVE

Genna stripped back the sheet all the way to the end of the bed exposing Rowan from head to toe. Rowan's hair glinted shades of straw in the morning light that filtered through partially open curtains, sunshine running golden fingers over tantalizing skin. "I'm going to make you feel so good."

Rowan reached for her, but she shook her head. "I know you want it to be mutual, and I understand why. But you've had your fun. I want to Casanova you."

Rowan winced like the nickname had smacked her in the face. "When I said that, I—"

"Was right," Genna finished for her. "It was my comfort zone. You want to know why it was so comfy?"

"Because of all the practice?" Rowan asked, dryly.

Genna sighed. Would Rowan ever get past the past, or would *all the other people* forever be squeezed between them twisting the knife? "I got the practice because I fucking love it. Touching you, especially when…" She bit her lip.

She'd always *liked* sex, but its importance had been in the connection that had helped her to survive. Now, with Rowan, sex was so much more. Rowan had been right all along. Genna *did* have more to give than the over-hyped seducer moniker suggested. Falling for Rowan had expanded her in ways she hadn't even realized.

Rowan smiled, and Genna found the courage to try again, "Touching you, especially when I care, brings me so much pleasure.

I want to take my time. To explore your body at my leisure. I'm not Casanova. I never really was. But I love the adventure of discovering what brings pleasure. Maybe I started out with other people. But you're the only one I want to touch now. Will you let me?"

Rowan swallowed audibly and uncertainty flickered in her eyes. "Do you really mean that?"

Genna leaned over to kiss her lightly, softly, her heart a physical ache in her chest. "I had a terrible time at McKinney's. Even the idea of someone coming on to you made me want to punch something."

"I noticed." Rowan smiled again.

"I understand how you feel. I don't want anyone else touching you, either. I can't change my past, and I wouldn't want to, but please, let me show you how much I want only you."

"I don't want to disappoint you. I might not be very good at lying back and being tended to. I don't have your patience. Waiting like that, it can be frustrating for me."

Genna shrugged, taking Rowan's hand and kissing her palm. "I'm not asking for patience. Come if you need to. There's no rule against it, and no reason to fight it. If you can't stop, don't. An orgasm doesn't mean it's over. I'll keep going and maybe you'll get aroused again, or maybe you won't. Being together and feeling good is the only goal."

Rowan gave her a look that said *feeling good* weren't words she generally associated with sex. Genna wanted to show Rowan that sex could be more than hurried, stolen moments of guilty pleasure. More than ripping each other's clothes off without having to try. Desire, passion, horniness, whatever you wanted to call it, was a bonus when it happened. But really good sex with someone you cared about? The not-at-all-spontaneous let me work at it until I figure out exactly what turns you into a trembling mess of need, marathon sex? That was a whole lot more satisfying than a temporary spike in oxytocin.

Rowan shoved a hand through her hair. "No one has ever presented me an offer like that."

Genna laughed. "Would it be wrong to say I'm pleased?"

Rowan rose on her elbows for a kiss. "It's not wrong at all. Ravish me, please."

They smiled at each other goofily.

"Lie on your stomach," Genna said. "Close your eyes and get comfortable. Relax like you're sleepy."

Rowan flipped over, and Genna sucked in a quiet breath at the beauty of her body. Hose her down before she went up in flames level gorgeous. Broad shoulders tapering to a narrow waist, hips just a little too wide to be masculine, a backside of pure muscle that made Genna's mouth water, and an endless expanse of naked skin she was dying to run her hands over. Passion wouldn't be a problem. The longer she looked, the more patience she had.

She started in Rowan's hair. Rolling her fingers through the short strands, pressing into Rowan's head. Mapping the shape of her, allowing the length to flow through her fingers. Genna closed her eyes, listening to the soft sounds her fingers made as she swirled them against Rowan's scalp, the featherlight slide of Rowan's hair. She held only the very tips, tugged.

Rowan sighed. "Why does that feel so good?"

Genna did it again and was rewarded with another sigh. She stroked along the outer shell of Rowan's ear, once, twice, slipped her fingers behind and down, caressing the impossibly soft skin.

When she tugged Rowan's earlobe, Rowan muttered, "I don't think I'm going to survive you doing this everywhere. The torment will be endless."

Genna smiled. "Imagine the coroner's report. Rowan Marks, thirty-two, succumbed in bed after slow and seductive torture stopped her heart. May she rest in peace."

Rowan's laugh turned into another long sigh when Genna transferred her attention to the other ear.

"My heart is yours," Rowan murmured.

Genna's fingers tucked behind Rowan's ear trembled, and she pressed them into the space where her jaw met her neck so Rowan wouldn't notice. She wasn't going to think about it right now. She would show her.

Genna ran the tip of her tongue over her lips and leaned over Rowan until her mouth was a millimeter from the back of her neck. She let her breath out slowly and gently across Rowan's skin, not touching but so, so close.

"Fuck." Rowan squirmed.

Genna smiled. "You're so sensitive here. I know you like my hands, but maybe a breath kiss would arouse you?"

Genna let her breath go again, blowing oh-so softly.

"Or," Genna continued teasingly when Rowan pressed her face into the pillow, "you might like my lips." She kissed Rowan's hairline, then trailed a string of wet kisses all the way down to her shoulders. When she reached the last vertebrae of Rowan's neck, she kissed her way back up again, alternating between sweet and sexy, the tip of her tongue flicking playfully. Then she breathed kisses all over her.

"I'm ready to die now," Rowan announced, voice muffled by the pillow.

Genna fluttered the backs of her fingers across Rowan's shoulders. "Buck up, Thor. I've barely started."

She kissed, licked, breathed, swirled, caressed, and traced all over Rowan's upper back, fascinated by the way her muscles seemed to flex and release at the attention like ripples in water. She pressed her thighs together as distracting sparks of heat shot through her body. That certainly never happened with *all the other people*. She'd just had an orgasm, for God's sake. Rowan made her insatiable.

Genna applied a little more pressure as she ran the heel of her hand down Rowan's spine from her hairline to her tailbone and back up again in long even strokes. "Does that feel good?"

Rowan groaned in response, shifting her hips. Genna used her palms in a flat-hand caress across her shoulder blades, down her sides, and meeting in the small of her back. She alternated between gentle and firm, paying attention to the sounds Rowan made, the way she pressed into the mattress, the cadence of her breathing. Learning what style and pressure Rowan liked.

Genna pressed with the heel of her hands, fanned her fingers outward, and then drew together to make a heart. "You really ought to get regular massages with all the workouts you do."

"If they feel like this, there's no way I'm getting naked on some random table with only a towel preserving my dignity." Rowan's breathing hitched when Genna cupped her hips and swept her thumbs back and forth.

Genna laughed. "Why not? A massage therapist sees naked people all day."

Modesty wasn't a make-me-melt virtue for her, but when you wrapped it in romance and sprinkled a little sweet on top, modesty was damn attractive on Rowan.

"Because." Rowan's backside lifted when Genna stroked a single fingertip lazily from hip to hip. "It's really turning me on, and that would be uncomfortable for everyone."

Genna made a low seductive humming sound and leaned over to kiss Rowan's tailbone, running her tongue in a slow circle. "Does this make you uncomfortable?"

Rowan groaned. Her hips rose again, testing Genna's patience now. "Not with you."

"What's so different about me?" Totally fishing for compliments, Genna was a little embarrassed to need reassurance. Touching Rowan, watching her respond, had her throat tightening in a way that had nothing to do with arousal and everything to do with all the other things she wanted and wasn't sure she could have without breaking both their hearts.

They'd moved way beyond caring. She trusted Rowan wouldn't hurt her. Their differences didn't make them incompatible if they worked to understand each other. Didn't all couples have to do that? Even if they discovered they weren't a great fit, Rowan would be gentle with her heart.

Genna didn't trust *herself*.

How could you trust someone you didn't know?

Rowan fell silent, her hips rising and falling in a pattern she seemed unaware of as Genna kissed and licked all the silken skin right above the swell of her backside. To get her attention, Genna bit down gently. Rowan jerked and Genna breathed in the scent of her desire only inches away.

"You're like no one else. You're everything. Please. Touch me." Rowan turned the words into a moan.

Everything? Genna swallowed. That was a lot to live up to. "Surely you have something more original in your back pocket than *like no one else*. Such a cliché."

Genna kept her tone teasing even as her heart raced with the need to give Rowan what she wanted.

"You tell me. You're closer to my back pocket than I am." Rowan sounded as if she couldn't quite breathe a full breath.

"You make a fair point." Genna licked slowly down from Rowan's tailbone and noticed she tensed almost imperceptibly. Someone else might've missed the subtle shift from *God, yes, don't stop* to *I'm not sure about this*, but Genna didn't. "Do you not like this? We can do something else."

Rowan's laugh was rueful. "I think we both know I like it. I'm ruining your sheets."

"But?" Genna wasn't willing to let it go. She was good at learning by touch, but sometimes you just had to talk about it.

"No has ever…you know, there, before."

Rowan sounded embarrassed, so Genna bit her lip to kill the smile that threatened at Rowan's use of *you know* as a synonym. So fucking sweet. She ran her palms back and forth across Rowan's backside, making no further move in the direction of her *you know*. "Do you like when I rub you this way?"

"Yes," Rowan said in a tone that was more abashed than uncertain, and Genna wondered if being embarrassed that she wanted it was part of the turn on for her. She ran her hands over Rowan again and again until Rowan parted her thighs and begged. "God. Please."

"Feeling frustrated?" Genna checked in.

"I want to come."

Rowan's tone had a hint of desperation, and it took all the patience Genna had not to fill her instantly. Genna squeezed her thighs together, almost as turned on as Rowan. To test her theory, she said, "Tell me exactly what you want me to do to you, and I'll do it."

Would having to say it out loud make Rowan want it even more?

Rowan pushed back against her hands, face so deep in the pillow Genna wasn't sure how she was breathing. "Please, touch me."

"Touch you where? How?" Genna stroked Rowan's open thighs, gently bending one of her legs at the knee for the access she needed.

"Slide my clit between your fingers." Rowan ground out the words. "Don't tease me. I have to come right now."

Heat flooded and pooled between Genna's legs. The push and pull of Rowan's desire lit her up like Christmas lights. Rowan's impatience and demand entwined in sweetness and embarrassment shouldn't have worked so powerfully to make Genna lose control, but she wanted to see how many times she could make her come. Right now. Would Rowan be satisfied after the first orgasm, the second?

Keeping her promise to give her what she needed, she brushed the backs of her fingers through the wet heat of Rowan's center.

Rowan groaned. "Please, baby."

Genna wanted to keep Rowan skittering on the knife edge of pleasure forever, but she'd been given very explicit and sexy instructions. "Lift your hips an inch for me."

When Rowan did, Genna slipped around her clit, stroking and swirling her fingers. Rowan pressed against her, trapping her hand. Genna was reminded of the first time they'd made love with Rowan's body heavy on hers.

One day you'll meet someone who'll make it feel *like making love*. Alice's voice surfaced from her memory and landed a semi-trailer on her chest. Fuck.

Genna ignored the way her stomach climbed up into her throat and focused on Rowan. She slid Rowan's clit between her fingers just as she'd asked. No teasing.

"I'm going to come." Rowan sounded as if she already was. "Don't stop."

"Never," Genna promised, stroking over and over, falling into the rhythm until Rowan stiffened and came on a low guttural groan. A gush of heat pulsed between Genna's thighs. Rowan leaned into her touch, riding out her pleasure. Genna didn't let up until her tremors subsided.

"Jesus, fuck," Rowan muttered into the pillow, shaking.

Struggling to ignore the tenderness that engulfed her, Genna dipped her fingers into Rowan's folds and caressed her up and down, staying away from her clit while she recovered. Stroking her to see if Rowan would push her away.

Rowan made a sound that was ten percent protest and ninety percent fuck-me-blind.

Genna smiled. She'd guessed right, and Rowan was capable of more. "Turn over."

Rowan turned with what seemed like a disproportionate amount of effort. Her cheeks were flushed and when she looked down at Genna nestled between her legs her eyes were bottomless. "Casanova might be my absolute favorite after all."

Genna laughed and was horrified to discover tears pricking her eyes. "Casanova is having a very good time." Sex had come between them, and sex was stitching them back together.

Genna kissed Rowan's inner thigh. The taste of desire on Rowan's skin made her crazy. She used the very tip of her tongue over Rowan's entrance, flicking back and forth and swirling in a lazy circle. Rowan tasted so good. Light and delicious. Hot and wet. Soft and inviting. Genna traced every inch, using only the barest touch, in no rush, building the anticipation for them both. Because it was for *both* of them. Rowan might be the one mid-ravish, but Genna felt as if they'd traded places. She had more than patience now. The whole thing was totally doing it for her in a way she'd never experienced before.

"How do you most enjoy oral sex?" Genna asked, coming up for air. "Can you describe it for me?"

Rowan half-laughed, half-groaned. "So many questions, Dr. Sex. No one asks this stuff."

Genna frowned, looking up at her. Was she in for another compromise? She knew she talked more than most people in bed. Rowan wasn't the first to mention it. But she wasn't sure she was capable of shutting herself up. She genuinely wanted to know. "Sorry. I guess I do ask too many questions. Maybe it would be easier to talk about it when we aren't in bed?"

Genna warmed to that idea. Talking about sex when you couldn't *have* sex was its own brand of slow torture. Compromising didn't suck.

Rowan slid fingers into her hair and tilted Genna's head up so their eyes met again. "I love that you love talking about this. Don't apologize. It's going to sound pathetic, but no one has ever paid so much attention to what I like before, and I don't think I'm an unusual case. You're pretty amazing, you know that?"

Light bloomed in Genna's chest so good it was scary. So, she did what she did best: deflected. "You're making a very dirty question about oral sex romantic. I'm trying to learn what turns you on."

Rowan used the hand in her hair to stroke the back of Genna's head. "With you, they're the same thing."

So much for deflection. The emotion in Rowan's eyes was a drug shot straight into Genna's veins.

"I have a question of my own. Would that be okay?" Rowan asked.

Genna's heart spun at how politely Rowan had phrased the request. "Of course."

"Tell me the things I make you want."

Apprehension misted like sweat on Genna's skin. Her mouth went dry. She looked away.

Rowan made a grumpy sound in the back of her throat and used her superior strength to haul Genna up and on top of her until they were nose to nose. Heart to heart.

"Two-player game, remember, Dr. Sex? You tell me the things you want, and I'll tell you how I want you to use your mouth. It doesn't have to be scary."

"It's *terrifying*." Genna's voice cracked on the word, and she closed her eyes, mortified, wanting to leave, wanting to stay. Wanting to hide, wanting to merge. Wanting to tell her but so fucking afraid of the future, her vision blurred.

She'd never felt like this before. She didn't know how to say it.

Rowan pressed her thumb to the dip in Genna's chin and kissed her nose. "I love you, Genna."

Simple.

Uncomplicated.

Heart-stopping.

Rowan took her lips in a kiss that was sensual and perfect and *right*. Genna closed her eyes, absorbing the words, filling herself with Rowan's scent, her warmth, her love. Willing herself to say what she knew in her heart was a *two*-way street.

The silence was so loud Genna's ears rang. Her eyes filled. "I'm sorry. I feel it too, I just…"

Genna went to pull away, disgusted with herself, but Rowan held her close and whispered into her hair. "Love doesn't have to be terrifying or suffocating. It doesn't always take from you. Love gives as well. It can be so good."

How could Rowan possibly know that? Genna willed herself to just say what was already true. She'd launched herself baggage and all into this love rocket ship and would have to deal with the ride whether Rowan was right about it or not.

Saying the words wouldn't change anything now.

Making the words real was like freefalling into a concrete pit of vipers.

Rowan kissed her, but Genna pulled back. "I don't mean to hurt you. That's the last thing I want. I *feel* it, I promise."

"I believe you." Rowan wiped away a few tears that had escaped down Genna's cheeks.

Genna stared. That was it? She hadn't said the L word and Rowan just *believed her*? For most people this would be a total deal-breaker. Her heart filled with so much emotion, the love was practically bursting from her and barreling toward Rowan, but the words still wouldn't come.

"Show me you're mine." Rowan pressed very gently on her shoulders to indicate her meaning.

A tiny contrary part of Genna wanted to argue the concept of *mine-ness,* but the truth was, she felt like they belonged to each other. Maybe Stockholm syndrome had been a little bit of a stretch. She slid down Rowan's body until she was between her thighs again and took Rowan in her mouth without hesitation. Slowly, lovingly, she built her arousal again until Rowan's back arched and Genna's name fell from her lips.

Genna submersed herself in sensation, using her tongue to take Rowan higher until she was panting and gasping. When Rowan gripped the back of her head and came on a sharp cry, Genna stayed with her, teasing out every last tremor of pleasure until Rowan went boneless.

She rested her cheek against Rowan's thigh and closed her eyes, content to stay there forever while Rowan stroked her hair and told Genna again that she loved her.

Pleasure and panic fenced in a delicate battle of one upmanship inside Genna's heart.

I love you too.

Chapter Twenty-six

Genna checked the clock on her phone as the Silver Creek Cranes set up for what she thought might be a two-point shot inside the important arc thingy, or was that the three-pointer? She couldn't remember. Travis leaned forward on the bleachers in the basketball stadium, literally squirming in place like a neurotic pet poodle struggling to stay. A grown man turned into a ball of anxiety over a game. Genna would never understand the allure, but she admired its power.

She *also* admired the athleticism of the women's team and enjoyed watching them race up and down the court. Travis had explained the rules, and she'd internalized about ten percent of what he'd said before shushing him. One did not attend women's sports for the *game*. Travis just sighed and declared her objectification of the very talented players to be her least outstanding quality. Judgey, judgey.

The basketball flew, skimmed the rim of the hoop, and dropped through the net seconds before the buzzer sounded signaling the end of the game. The crowd, already on its feet, stomped and roared. Yay. The Cranes had squeaked a narrow one-point victory against their arch nemeses the Johnstown Jaguars. Travis pumped his fist in the air and hugged her. "We won!"

"I guess we did." Genna laughed.

"*Pretend* to be happy."

"I'm happy, I'm happy." Hard not to be with everyone jumping up and down around her, the cheers deafening. She gave Travis two more minutes of whooping before motioning to the exit. "Let's try to beat the crowd out of here, or it'll take a year."

It still took them twenty minutes to hit fresh air. Genna took a big breath. The players might've been hot, but she could live without the sweat-soaked locker room smell of hundreds of bodies squeezed together. "Come on. Happy Hour is going to be *jammed* tonight. Rowan and Maria should already be there."

As she and Travis made their way across campus, Genna took the longer well-lit and more central route out of habit. Travis was still high from *his* team's win. A team he'd barely known until Genna had asked him to the game, and now swore his undying allegiance to. She smiled. She pretty much liked the guy.

"How's it going with Rowan?" Travis asked. "I'm surprised she didn't join us."

"If I want to torture her, I have other methods." Genna flashed back to the marathon sex of last week and shoved the thought away. Not a good time to get turned on.

Travis grinned. "Casanova strikes again. You two sorted yourselves out then?"

Genna bit her lip. Would Travis be pissed if she told him the truth ten years too late? "Let's retire the Casanova thing, okay? I'm with Rowan now, and it's mutual."

Travis stopped walking. "Shit. Really? After all this time, you just needed some buffed up female Ken doll to spin your wheel?"

Genna stopped too. "Some *what*?"

"Sorry. That was—"

"*Objectification*?" Genna suggested, loading the word with so much judgey it sagged under the weight.

"Down, Casa—Genna. I didn't mean anything by it."

Genna shot him a look and decided to let it go. "What I needed, I couldn't get at McKinney's, that's all. I'm sorry too. I should've told you and not let the assumptions escalate like they did. I'm working on being easier to get to know."

Travis gave her a sideways glance. "What you need is something you couldn't do with strangers, right? Gangbanged by twenty topless lesbians? Bound and tortured with sharp implements to multiple orgasms? Forced to wear a diaper and cry like a baby while you get off?"

Genna let him expound upon his theme, pleased Travis had decided not to be pissed. When he finally ran out of steam, she asked mildly, "Seen some pretty racy porn, have you?"

Travis laughed. "You're unshockable. That was my best effort too."

Genna just shook her head. "The real answer will ruin your fun."

"The truth usually does." Travis let it go, the way he always did.

Genna saw it happen and was determined *not* to be so evasive. "I need someone to care about more than my body but wasn't ready for a relationship until Rowan."

Travis raised his eyebrows. Probably shocked by what did it for her or by her opening up. Genna had to work not to shuffle her feet. Would she ever get used to this intimacy thing that seemed to come so naturally to everyone else?

"You're hardly alone in needing that." Travis squeezed her shoulder. "McKinney's wouldn't appeal to most people for more than a night or two."

"True," she said. The turnover was proof of that. But she was glad the place existed for people like Travis, who got true pleasure from it.

"You and Rowan," Travis said as they neared the center of campus, "an item. Wow. Good for you. I like her."

Genna's stomach lurched. She and Rowan were well and truly itemized. All she had to do was say I love you and they could live happily ever after like the rogue cop and too-stupid-to-live. Why did she feel like she was walking a tightrope between skyscrapers?

"She believes in soul mates."

Travis glanced at her. "Soul mates? Like 'I'm destined to grow old with you?' You don't sound thrilled about that."

"That's pretty much it," Genna said, surprised that she'd sounded so negative, but then the idea had always bothered her. "She thinks there's one person for everyone, and the key to a perfect life and perfect sex is finding that person."

"So, you're her soul mate," Travis said it with an insulting amount of dubiousness.

Genna swallowed, her throat closing. "She hasn't said that. But we all know I'm *not* her soul mate. No one is. And the minute she realizes I'm not worthy of the pedestal she's put me on, I'm toast. I'm the end piece on the loaf that no one wants."

"Rowan has stuck this far, and from the little I've seen and heard, you've given her more than one reason to leave. Maybe you're being a bit melodramatic? Just because she believes in soul mates doesn't mean she expects you to be perfect."

"Doesn't she?" Genna asked, miserably. "I'm so far from that there's no way I can live up to her lofty expectations."

"Ah," Travis said quietly as they rounded the corner toward Happy Hour. "You fear being a major disappointment."

"How can I not be afraid when she's so unrealistic?" Genna asked, more defensive than ever.

Travis sighed like she was wearing on his last nerve, and he was gathering all this patience. "I don't know her. Maybe Rowan has some prettied-up notions of love. Whatever. She's a grown woman, and if she's made it this far, soul mates doesn't mean eternal sunshine and daises."

"Gee, thanks," Genna said, miffed.

Travis shrugged. "You're making too big a deal out of this because you're afraid you can't give her what you think she needs. But it sounds like you don't have a clue what that is."

Genna frowned at him. "Why are you an expert on my life suddenly?"

"I'm not an expert on your life. But a blind chihuahua could see you're afraid. *Someone* has to tell you to pull yourself together."

"It's just…a lot of pressure. *Suffocating.* And okay, maybe that's a me problem. But what am I supposed to do about it?"

Travis gave her an exasperated look. "What would you tell someone who wanted to act on their fantasies but was afraid to share them with their partner?"

Genna considered this. "To take it slow. Ask their partner about their own fantasies to see if there are similarities and start with those. Show genuine curiosity without judgment and create a space for their partner to do the same."

"Well, there's your solution." Travis pointed at her. "You'd never tell someone to take the risk without doing the groundwork. You don't have to free-fall off a cliff without a rope. *Ask her* what she wants and expects from a relationship. You've assumed she expects the soul mates thing to fix every problem but that can't possibly be true, or she'd have moved on by now. She's still here. So, maybe soul mates mean something different to her."

"What if I ask and it's even worse than I imagine?" Genna asked.

"Take the risk." Travis opened the door of Happy Hour. "That's what falling in love is. Standing on the edge of the cliff looking over and being too chicken to put on a parachute *guarantees* you'll be unhappy. Is that what you want?"

Genna hated when Travis was right.

❖

Genna tried to fit the key into the lock on her apartment door, her body throbbing with arousal. She almost dropped it when Rowan crowded her from behind and slipped her hands under Genna's sweater, stroking along her waist. Genna shivered. *Fuck.* If Rowan didn't stop, she was going to rub herself all over her like a needy kitten begging for attention right here in the public walkway. "Mr. Hanson across the hall walks his pitbull Sweet Pea at nine sharp every evening. If you keep that up, we're going to give them a show."

As if her don't-you-dare-stop tone didn't belie the warning.

"Then you'd better open the door," Rowan whispered in her ear, her breath coasting along Genna's neck as she ran her fingers teasingly up Genna's ribs.

Genna resisted the urge to snug her ass into Rowan's front and almost cheered when the key finally slid into the lock. As soon as she pushed the door open, they stumbled inside like teenagers. The door had barely shut before Rowan had her up against it, pinning her hands above her head and pressing her entire body along the length of Genna's from shoulders to thighs.

Genna's foggy head spun, the display of dominance pushing buttons she didn't even know she had. "I make it a rule not to sleep with drunk people."

"I'm only a little bit tipsy, and I fully consent to ravishing you." Rowan slid her palms all the way up to cup Genna's breasts, pressing her hips into Genna's, making it very clear exactly what she intended to do to her.

All Genna's systems switched to green lights. *Go, go, go.* She did her best to keep her feet under her with Rowan's body, hot and hard along hers, making her knees wobble. When Rowan slid a thigh between hers, Genna groaned. If Rowan hadn't been holding her up, she would've melted into a puddle on the floor.

"We're too old to be doing it standing in the hallway."

"Let's test that hypothesis." Rowan's warm palms slid up Genna's skirt, hiking it up to her waist, and stroked along her outer thighs. When she reached her panties, she tugged them down, easing back just enough for Genna to step out of them.

"Not even going to undress me, huh? And here I thought you were so romantic." Genna's words came out choppy and breathless, as Rowan's blunt fingernails skated up and down her thighs.

"You can trash talk all you want," Rowan found Genna's center and swiped a finger through her wetness. "But we both know dirty up against the door is totally doing it for you."

Rowan's words were hot rain on her already sizzling skin.

"And you're unaffected, are you?"

"Baby, I'm so fucking wet spontaneous orgasm is a real possibility." Rowan shucked off her shoes, pants, and underwear before grabbing the back of Genna's thighs and guiding Genna's legs around her waist.

Rowan rocked against Genna's center, and everything inside her turned liquid. Her head dropped back against the door. More of that. More.

Usually, Genna abhorred drunk and sloppy sex. In her experience, it only ended in regret. But not with Rowan. Drunk, sober, standing up, lying down. The details didn't matter as their connection sparked and fizzed like static electricity. There was simply nothing to regret so Genna didn't mind that Rowan was feeling the effect of their celebration at Happy Hour, followed by a tipsy make-out session in the truck, then barely restrained groping all the way up to Genna's apartment.

"I want to fuck you," Rowan's voice was tires on gravel.

Genna could almost feel Rowan sliding inside her as she said the words. "Yes. God. Please."

Up against the door just made her top ten list of places she wanted Rowan to fuck her.

Rowan slid her hand between them and had just skimmed her center when Lady Gaga serenaded them from somewhere in the mess of clothes on the floor. They groaned in unison.

"Don't answer it." Rowan teased at her entrance, kissing down the length of her neck.

"Not an option until I see who it is." Genna untangled herself from Rowan, a hand on the door to support her knees, and crouched to open her purse. She looked at her phone screen. Gabby. Gabby had better things to do on a Saturday night than call her sister to chitchat.

Uneasiness crawled like ants across Genna's skin, killing her desire.

"What's wrong?" Genna asked instead of saying hello.

"Thank God." Gabby's tone was just shy of nails on a chalkboard.

Genna's stomach twisted. "Gabby—what?"

"I think Mom's broken her wrist. She says it's just sprained. It's all puffy and swollen. What if it's really broken, and she's just saying it's sprained because she doesn't want to go to the hospital?"

Gabby paused to suck in air, her breathing erratic.

"Gabby, what—"

"It's bad. You have to come. I can't stop remembering that time she slipped on a ladder and split her head open and didn't go to the hospital for *days*. There was so much blood everywhere. She still has that massive scar. She says she won't go now either. What do I do?"

"Gabby." Genna's heartbeat banged against her ribs at the sheer panic in her sister's tone. She used the middle-of-a-crisis-super-calm voice that'd been getting a lot of airtime lately. "Slow down. Is Mom hurt anywhere else? Are you?"

"No." Gabby's voice was tremulous with tears. "She tripped on the rug at the bottom of the stairs and threw her hands out to catch herself. It's her wrist and a few bruises. I'm fine."

Thank God.

"That's good news. Take a breath, okay? This isn't so bad. It's not like before. I need you to calm down for me."

"I'm scared," Gabby whispered, and the words epitomized the way Genna had felt every single time something like this happened when they were kids. No one had been there to help then.

A blind chihuahua could see you're afraid.

"I need you to go into Mom's closet and find one of her big winter scarves. Make a sling out of it. Mom needs to keep her wrist elevated and close to her body. See if you can find a bag of frozen peas for the swelling. Can you do that?"

"Yeah." The quiver in Gabby's voice lessened now that someone else was in charge. "Thanks, sorry to call you. It's just, what if it's really bad again?"

"You did the right thing," Genna assured her. "You've got this, and I love you. I'll be there as fast as I can. Put Mom on the phone, okay?"

"I love you too," Gabby said fervently, making Genna smile.

Genna waited while Gabby handed her phone to their mother.

"I'm perfectly fine. It's just a sprain," her mom said as soon as she came on the line. None of the Feilding women were very good at pleasantries.

Genna sat on the floor and tugged her panties up her legs with one hand. "I'm leaving now. I'll be there as fast as I can. You have to get an x-ray, Mom. It could be broken."

Her mom sighed. "Gabrielle is worrying about nothing. It's just swollen. You don't need to drive over here so late at night. There's nothing you can do."

Genna took a second. Just one second to remind herself that her mom's refusal came from mental illness. The way Genna, Gabby, and Grace experienced her mother's illness was entirely different from her mom's experience. She wasn't being a jerk on purpose. "Can you move all your fingers without pain?"

"Yes," her mom said like the question had been stupid.

"How much pain are you in on a scale of one to ten?"

There was a pause on the other end before her mom said, "About a three."

Genna figured that meant somewhere around five or six. "You're going to rest it, ice it, and if it's still a three in the morning, we'll make arrangements for you to be transported to urgent care for an x-ray."

"No, I—"

She cut her mother off. "*Yes*. Gabby is terrified and trying desperately to hold it together for your sake."

Genna took Rowan's hand and allowed herself to be hauled to her feet.

"It's a sprained wrist," her mom said again, exasperated.

"Yeah." Genna picked up her keys. "But the head wound you didn't get treated when she was six wasn't. You bled through every linen we had and were unconscious. Gabby remembers. So, do I. I'm going to be there with both of you while we wait to see if the swelling goes down and the pain lessens. If it doesn't, we'll use the backup plan and get it taken care of. Don't argue."

Her mom started to do just that. Fear of leaving the house made her mom unable to empathize. It sucked, but it wasn't her fault. Genna talked over her. "I love you, Mom. I'll see you soon. Elevate and ice your wrist."

By the time she'd hung up, Rowan was dressed, Genna's purse in her hands. "Let's go."

Rowan had her hand on the doorknob, but Genna reached out to stop her.

"Stay here and get some sleep. I'll be back as soon as I can."

Rowan stiffened. "You don't want me to come?"

"Of course I do," Genna said. "But you've been drinking, and it's a long drive. Plus it's late, and it's not an emergency. There isn't anything to do. I'm only going because the incident has reminded

Gabby of a similar, but much worse, situation years ago, and she's freaking out. Someone will need to strongarm Mom into going to be evaluated if her wrist *is* broken, and it's not fair to leave that to Gabby."

"But it's fair on you?" Rowan asked.

Genna shrugged. "Who else is there?"

"I'm going to worry." Rowan already looked more than worried.

"You don't need to worry. Even if the wrist is broken, it will heal, but Gabby needs me there. *You* need to drink some water and get some sleep. I want you rested so you can take care of me tomorrow when *I'm* tired and need you. Okay?"

Rowan still looked like she wanted to argue but nodded.

"Thank you for not making this harder." Genna hugged her.

She turned to leave but Rowan caught her arm. "I just want to be sure this isn't one of those things you need and find it difficult to ask for."

Genna smiled, unable to resist sliding back into her arms again. "I need you. I needed you to help me when my car broke down. I needed to borrow your truck. I needed you to withdraw from my study. I needed you to stick around at McKinney's even though I screwed up. I'm going to need you tomorrow when I'm dead on my feet. But I don't need you for this. This is a standard Saturday in my life."

Rowan kissed her forehead. "Will you text me when you get there so I know you're safe? I love you."

"I will."

Genna slipped out the door to go care for the other people she loved, leaving her heart rumpled and just a little bit tipsy in her hallway.

Chapter Twenty-seven

Rowan pressed her mouth to Mrs. Sutton's, eliciting a desperate needy sound that flipped all Rowan's switches. She groaned, dragging Mrs. Sutton against her, and succumbing to the desire rolling through her. They'd been running into each other serendipitously all week until Mrs. Sutton had finally, almost shyly, asked Rowan if she'd like to grab a drink at a restaurant that just happened to be Rowan's favorite. The conversation flowed effortlessly, they had so much in common. An evening so perfect it was as if Mrs. Sutton could read her mind. Now, they were back at her place so she could unwrap her one item of clothing at a time like the goddess she was.

"You make me crazy," Mrs. Sutton whispered coquettishly against her mouth. "I'd do anything to be with you."

Claudia was away on business, and Rowan backed Mrs. Sutton toward the bedroom before she could think too hard about what she was planning to do in Claudia's bed. She stopped kissing her long enough to unbutton Mrs. Sutton's soft shirt, noticing the monotonous blinking light of the camera out of the corner of her eye. What the fuck? Rowan stared confusedly into the lens anchored to the far-left corner of her living room. Who had installed a camera in her house? Her stomach dipped and shivers crept down her spine. Maybe Claudia was worried about intruders? Neither she nor Rowan were home much. That must be it.

Mrs. Sutton began to pout at Rowan's distraction and undid the button on Rowans pants. "I know how much you like it on top. You wanna hold me down while you fuck me? I'll come so hard."

This was their first time together. How could Mrs. Sutton know what she liked? But the thought dissolved when Mrs. Sutton slid a hand into her pants and squeezed her. Rowan groaned into her mouth, all the things that didn't make sense no match for lust-induced tunnel vision. Her brain stuttered in error mode.

"I knew the minute I saw you we were made for each other," Mrs. Sutton said. "You don't need that workaholic bitch."

They were through the bedroom doorway and halfway to the bed when Rowan heard another voice. "Look at the two of you putting on such a naughty show."

Rowan's blood froze in her veins. *Genna*. And there she was, lying on the bed in coffee-colored lace, lazily stroking herself as she watched them.

Oh God, what was she doing here? Rowan pulled away from Mrs. Sutton only to have her push Rowan toward the bed with a Mona Lisa smile on her lips.

"We all know you want this. We're everything you could ever need. You can't leave now."

The backs of Rowan's thighs hit the mattress, and she toppled onto the bed next to Genna.

Genna stopped touching herself long enough to glance at her with a knowing smirk. "She's right, you know. Group sex is the number one fantasy in America."

Mrs. Sutton pulled at Rowan's pants, tugging everything off until she was bare from the waist down. Before she could take a full breath, Genna rolled on top of her and straddled her hips, the rough lace of Genna's panties a teasing caress against her thighs. Heat suffused her from head to toe as Genna began to rock against her, levering herself over Rowan, kissing her as the curtain of her hair fell forward, blocking Mrs. Sutton from her view.

"Does that feel good, Thor?" Genna asked her, breathless.

Rowan could only whimper. A tongue teased her clit as Genna writhed on top of her. Wait. What? Was Mrs. Sutton between her legs? How could that be possible with Genna there too? But, fuck. It was so real. Rowan kissed Genna, drowned in her, as the tongue on her center swirled around her clit and then dipped lower, flicking at her entrance. Pleasure rocketed through her as fire chased across her skin. God. So good. She was going to come. Rowan groaned in protest when the tongue backed off.

"She such a tease, isn't she? I'm so glad I could be here. I have such a crush on Mrs. Sutton. She's perfect. Though, this time I seem to have stolen the show." Genna sounded like herself but…different. Detached and ethereal. Rowan's head was full of cotton wool.

"Smile for the cameras," Genna said, and only then did Rowan notice two more blinking lights on the ceiling. Why was she being recorded? Her skin flushed fever hot, her brain clouding with desire. What was happening?

"That's it. Let go. It's okay," Genna whispered in her ear. The tongue pushed inside her, and Rowan's eyes flew open on a gasp as her center clenched needily. "Oh, God."

Rowan tangled her fingers in Genna's hair. Sleep and wake crisscrossed as Genna's mouth moved over her, bringing her to the edge again. Worlds collided. Fantasy smashed into reality. The imagined scenario eclipsed by Genna's very real, very talented mouth on her. "Fuck."

Her arousal coiled deep in her center, her muscles tensed, and her vision narrowed. She was going to come.

Genna looked up. She must have seen something in Rowan's face because her expression instantly turned wary. "What's wrong?"

"Nothing. God. Don't stop."

A frown slowly formed as Genna studied her. When she shifted as if to move upward, Rowan pressed down with the hands she'd somehow tangled in Genna's hair.

Please. Don't. Stop.

Rowan lifted her ass off the bed, presenting herself wet and ready for Genna's mouth. She couldn't say it, couldn't actually beg to come with Mrs. Sutton still lingering like carbon monoxide, but God did she want to.

"We're going to talk about this later," Genna promised before wrapping her lips around Rowan's clit and sliding her fingers inside in one long stroke.

Choppy, choked sounds spilled from Rowan when Genna sucked her clit. Desperate need steamrolled her and she cried out, muffling the noise with a pillow as she squeezed around Genna's fingers. *Ohmyfuckinggod.* Light exploded, eclipsing the early morning dawn, as she gasped her way through her orgasm, pleasure an endless spiral.

She lay splayed on the bed, eyes closed, her limbs slowly filling with concrete as Genna slid up her body. She could feel Genna watching her. Those well-honed observational skills undoubtedly deducing more than she wanted to reveal.

Genna tapped a single finger against her nose, and Rowan opened her eyes.

Genna smiled. "There you are. Was sleepy sex everything you hoped it would be?"

Rowan tried to smile back, but the effort of lifting the corners of her mouth was gargantuan. "Definitely hot. When did you get in?"

"Twenty minutes ago. I was going to sleep after my shower, but you looked so gorgeous I couldn't help myself again."

Rowan wrapped her arms around Genna. "How's your mom?"

"She claims to be in less pain this morning. She's probably lying, but if she keeps it in the sling and it doesn't get worse, she'll be alright without the x-ray. Gabby's still having flashbacks. Talking it through seemed to help."

The pain in Genna's voice ripped Rowan in two. Six years old watching your mom bleed to unconsciousness from a head wound. Sixteen and having to call 911 after days of worry. "I wish I could've helped…both of you."

"You did—you're here. I'm okay. Text Gabby later, she'll tell you about it. She says, and this is verbatim, 'Rowan is cool as fuck.'"

Rowan laughed. "Is fuck cool now?"

Genna just kept looking at her.

Rowan wanted to crawl under the blanket, call the postal service to change her address, and not come out again. "I'm going to make us some breakfast. Have you eaten?"

When she tried to move, Genna placed a hand on her chest. No pressure, no pushing, but a firm *stay* signal. "What just happened?"

Rowan shrugged, feeling like scum for lying to Genna. "Nothing. You've had a long night. Stay here and rest while I make us some food."

"Rowan."

Genna didn't need to say anything else, her gaze slicing into her like a laser. Prying her open when she didn't want to be.

Fuck. Why couldn't she just be normal for once in her life? "I was turned on when I fell asleep last night after we were interrupted. So, when you touched me just now, I was primed."

Genna nodded.

Rowan sighed. "It got mixed up in my brain. It felt so good, and I was having a fantasy. Then suddenly you were there too. In my mind you were straddling me, but you were really between my legs, and it all got jumbled. I have sex dreams a lot. It's weird."

Genna stroked lightly up and down Rowan's torso from the base of her throat to her belly button. "It's not weird. If you resist the thoughts and fantasies when you're awake, it makes sense your subconscious works through them when that resistance is diminished by sleep. Your fantasy getting jumbled distresses you?"

"It was great." Even as Rowan said it, she winced at the lack of conviction in her voice.

Genna stopped stroking. "What happened just now, I can handle it. I can't handle you lying, so please stop."

"I'm not lying. It *was* great. I love coming in your mouth."

"Then why were you being evasive and running out of bed like your ass was on fire?"

Genna's bottom lip wobbled. She quickly firmed it, but Rowan saw. The stupidity of what she was doing crashed in on her.

"God. I'm sorry. Come here." Rowan pulled Genna toward her.

Genna rested her head against Rowan's shoulder, one leg thrown over Rowan's.

Rowan held her tightly. "I don't mean to rush away. It's just a bit of a mindfuck to have you make a guest appearance in that fantasy. I was hoping…"

Genna waited, the silence so heavy Rowan could hear a clock ticking in the next room.

Finally, Genna said, "You were hoping they'd be gone, and instead I make your half-asleep fantasy come true and end up inside your head with…?"

"Mrs. Sutton." Rowan was thankful that at least it wasn't Penelope.

"Figures. She *is* my favorite."

Rowan smiled. "You said that in the fantasy too."

Genna sat up against the headboard, and Rowan did too. "It's unlikely your fantasies will disappear."

Fear snaked through Rowan's veins. "I'm sure it was just an anomaly because I was so hot last night. Trust me, I don't normally fantasize about someone else when I'm with you. I *much* prefer only you between my legs."

"You might prefer it," Genna said gently, "but love doesn't make fantasies disappear. They're not a stand-in for a soul mate."

Rowan hissed out a breath as she absorbed the punch to the gut. "You don't know why I'm having them."

"I do, I think." Genna took her hand and held it to her heart. "I'm not a hundred percent sure. No one can be. But I have a solid theory."

An answer that might free her? "Tell me."

"Sometimes, trauma survivors have fantasies related to their trauma as a way of rewriting history, taking control, experiencing it in a safe way on their own terms. Rape survivors having force fantasies. Holocaust survivors fantasizing about Nazis, and so on. It's not especially common, but more than a handful process their experiences this way."

Rowan blinked, the words crashing like cymbals in her head. "But I haven't experienced trauma."

Genna squeezed her hand, holding it in both of hers. "Your family lost their livelihood. Your dad couldn't cope. Sara went to prison. You had to reimagine your whole future. Is that not trauma?"

Rowan swallowed the instinctive denial and tried to really think. Genna wasn't just her girlfriend. She knew more about sex fantasies than anyone. If she said this was why, chances were she was right. "Bad stuff happens to people all the time. What happened was hard, but it's not *trauma*. Certainly not on par with sexual abuse or genocide."

Genna tilted her head to the side, considering this. "If we see trauma as a spectrum, then what you experienced could reasonably fall somewhere along it. It doesn't need to be equivalent to the worst thing that's ever happened to anyone to have impacted you."

Yeah, but, *trauma?*

"So, you think my fantasies are me reliving what happened? I can't really see that. What happened back then had absolutely nothing to do with sex."

"Your fantasies give you an opportunity to help in a way that wasn't possible at the time. You offer yourself to the prison guard to help Sara escape. You're an obsession for Mrs. Sutton, the personification of your parents' financial troubles, and Penelope..."

"I'm Penelope's good girl," Rowan murmured, all of it clicking into place. "I'm a conquest, and maybe if I please her, she'll give the deli back."

Bile rise in Rowan's throat, and she had to close her eyes and breathe through her nose until her stomach decided to stay where it was supposed to. God. Genna was right. All her fantasies, the bad ones, anyway, could be traced back to that time. The helplessness she'd felt when everything fell apart. The guilt she dragged around like an anchor.

"Why do I make it about sex, though? Why *sex* fantasies?"

Genna raised her eyebrows and shot her the *really, cowboy?* look. "Oh, so you have other kinds of fantasies about your past?"

Rowan laughed because it was so clear Genna already knew the answer. "I tend to shove the thoughts down."

"When your mind is free to imagine, that's where it goes, probably because adults don't spend a lot of time having fantasies other than sexual ones."

The chains that had held her captive for so long finally fell and the weight lifted from her chest. She finally had an answer. Not one she liked, but there was a *reason*. It made sense.

"How do I make them stop?" Rowan asked.

Genna sighed. "I know that's important to you. Therapy might help. Processing the experiences another way may lessen the frequency of your fantasies. But you need to be prepared since it's just as likely it won't. You may have to accept them as part of how you cope with what happened to you and be okay with it."

Be okay with it? Could she do that? After hating everything about them for so long?

That first day in Genna's office, the answer would've been a resounding *hell no*. A lifetime of Penelope invading her dreams, sneaking unbidden into her mind, weaving through her body so she had no choice but to give in to pleasure she didn't want? The answer was still no. Would always be no. But now she wasn't alone. Now she had Genna, in her fantasies and in her life. With Genna, she could handle it.

"As much as I don't want to go see a therapist about sex fantasy problems, I'd like to try that route and see if it helps."

Genna smiled, looking more than a little relieved. "That's a good idea. For your fantasies and for yourself. I'm here if you need someone to lean on. We'll be together, whether or not they stop."

Together. "I like the sound of that."

"Good." Genna kissed her.

Rowan still worried, Genna might be promising more than she could deliver. "Says the woman who fantasizes about sweet guacamole kisses."

Genna shrugged. "Just because my fantasies are sweet doesn't mean I don't understand. I have some that are embarrassing to me as well, you know."

"I don't know—you haven't actually told me, but that's okay. Everyone is entitled to their secrets."

"Watching you sleep really turns me on," Genna said unexpectedly.

"Is that a common fantasy?" What was so sexy about sleeping?

"No. I just like you in my bed. Wrapped in my sheets. I like knowing you'll be there all naked and sexy when I wake up."

Rowan kissed her. "Me too. I like doing life with you, Dr. Sex."

Genna's eyes widened a little and she twisted the sheet into a ball. When she looked away, Rowan tried not to be too disappointed. Genna was doing her best to work through her own stuff. Trauma she'd been carrying longer than Rowan. She'd just have to be patient.

Genna took a breath, had a few stern words with the dozen monkeys wreaking havoc behind her ribs, and looked at Rowan dead in the eyes. "My horribly, terribly, embarrassing fantasy is falling in love."

The air around them seemed to sharpen—every detail of Rowan, of the bed, of the room was in hyperfocus. Genna's chest seized. What had she done?

"You don't fantasize about sex?" Rowan's voice was so quiet, Genna wondered if she was breathing.

"I do, but not the way you do. Not complete scenarios or stories. My fantasies are moments. A few seconds or a minute of this or that. Flashes in my mind. But they're romantic." Genna waved a hand in the air. She could feel her cheeks burning. "Lots of stuff about how you'll always be there. You'll always be mine. Like I said, horribly embarrassing."

"You fantasize about me being yours?"

"Mine." Genna closed her eyes. The idea was...*mortifying*. "It's *awful*. Do you know how many centuries of patriarchy and exploitation are wrapped up in that word? You're a person, not a possession. I *know* this."

Rowan laughed. "Wasn't it you who said people often fantasize about things they wouldn't want to really happen? I think I'm safe from becoming property because you want me to be yours."

Genna did her best to glare at Rowan while struggling against a smile. "Rule number one when someone tells you their fantasies: Don't laugh."

Rowan kissed her and Genna held on to the touch as if it was a treasure.

"I'm not laughing at your fantasy," Rowan said "I'm laughing that you're so hard on yourself when you shouldn't be. I *am* yours. Today. Tomorrow. In fantasies and in life. Yours."

Genna groaned. "Rowan."

Rowan cupped her cheeks and looked so deeply into her eyes, Genna felt the stare all the way to the back of her head. "You're safe with me. I'd survive without you if I had to, but I don't want to. I want to be yours and for you to be mine forever."

Genna rested her forehead to Rowan's and allowed the words to seep into her skin. Into her bones. Into every cell she had. *Hers*. She believed it. "No one has ever loved me the way you do. I didn't even know it existed outside of fantasies. I need to ask you something."

Rowan kissed her and then kissed her again when once wasn't enough. "Ask me anything."

"Am I your everything? I won't be able to give you what you're looking for if you're expecting me to complete you. I won't be your soul mate. I don't even *believe* in soul mates. I'm sort of fucked up as it is, and what you want feels impossible. So, is it what you want? A perfect life? A do-over to replace the one that was ripped away from you as a kid?"

Rowan leaned back, the shock on her face making Genna feel worse. "You think I want some too-perfect-to-be-real do-over?"

"I don't know what I think. So, I'm asking. What do you want this relationship to look like?"

"Baby, I want what we have." Rowan sounded as surprised as she looked. "You don't have to worry about meeting some impossible standard. You've already exceeded any expectations I might've had. What I need is what everyone needs, to be seen, admired, respected, loved. You challenge me, make me think, make me laugh. You've accepted every part of me, even the parts I want to change. I want our relationship to look exactly like it already does. Like we are. I know relationships take work, but some things come included. You don't need to *work* for my love. It's yours."

Genna had worked for love her whole life, but somehow Rowan had moved them beyond that hurdle. Had freed her. To love and be loved. To work at their relationship when it was needed, and to trust in all the things that came built in when you did life with the person who really saw you and loved you anyway.

Rowan was hers.

And she was Rowan's.

"I love you." The words came so effortlessly, Genna kicked herself for not saying them before. They filled her up inside, made her chest expand and her head light with happiness.

Rowan's smile unfurled like a flower opening to sunlight. She touched her lips to Genna's so tenderly, she stole the air from the room. "I know. You've shown me in a thousand ways."

I love you. Such simple words that meant everything. Love could give, and Genna could accept. Finally. For the first time. She'd given enough.

EPILOGUE

One year later

"If you don't relax, I'll tell Mom you're freaking out and she'll make you help her with the chocolate souffle." Gabby snatched away the napkin Genna was anxiety-shredding.

"You wouldn't dare. You like dessert too much to let me ruin it." She watched Gabby fold a stack of white dollar-store napkins into crisply edged swans and set each in the middle of a royal blue Fiesta Ware dinner plate.

The tablescape was an acquired taste. She and Gabby had spent the last hour setting it for what might be the most nerve-racking family dinner of her life. She'd picked up the bright centerpiece of multicolored roses and green hydrangea from the florist while Gabby crawled around in the attic to find the *good* wineglasses that looked just like the everyday wineglasses to Genna. The eye-searing coral flamingos on her mom's best table runner clashed horribly, and the paper swans were just the right amount of cute to give the finished look some cheer and zero cohesion.

But who cared anyway? Nothing said *welcome home* like Gloria Feilding's famous dessert and a face full of flowers, right?

"She's going to hate me."

"Who hates you?" Grace asked Genna, setting a mouthwatering charcuterie board overflowing with stuffed olives, various fruits, and what looked to be four kinds of cheese, on the table. As the only one to inherit their mother's magic touch in the kitchen, Grace was allowed to help with the appetizers while Genna and Gabby had been assigned menial labor.

"Sara." Gabby told Grace, turning the word into an exaggerated eyeroll.

"Stop worrying, Sara's going to love you. We all love you. You're a dork, but it suits you," Grace said with her attention on placing little knives at perfect ninety-degree angles to the hunks of cheese.

Genna wrapped her arms around Grace and reached up on her toes to brush a kiss over the top of her head the way she had when the twins were little. "I love you too."

Grace wriggled away, but Genna saw the smile she tried to hide. "Yeah, yeah. You love everybody."

Grace's subtext missile hit its target perfectly. *Especially Rowan.*

Genna bit her lip to stop from sighing out loud. Now that Rowan was family, Grace's harmless little crush had the power to hurt her. But what could Genna do? She *did* love everybody.

When the silence stretched, Grace switched to her favorite subject. "Fess up. Did Rowan's hottest fantasies melt your underpants off? What are they? I won't tell."

Grace tried to get her to spill the details at least once a month. It'd become a well-worn play and Genna fell easily into her role. She raised her eyebrows at Grace. "Not going to happen. You know we only had one session before she fell madly in love with me and had to withdraw to save my career."

"Aww." Gabby fell hook line and sinker for the sappy reply, the way she always did. "I love her too."

Genna smiled. "Rowan loves both of you like *sisters*."

Gabby's whole face smiled at that. "Yeah?"

Genna grabbed a swan and bonked Gabby on the head with it. "Yeah." She paused, considering. "I wouldn't be sad if you were into women, though. Ever had a hot sapphic fantasy?"

Gabby didn't have the decency to keep her sigh to herself. "I'm not going to get pregnant. I've been insisting guys use protection since I was fifteen."

Silence fell again as Genna struggled to hold back *who the fuck was deflowering you at fifteen?* And Gabby got busy with the silverware, avoiding Genna's gaze.

"Good," Genna managed, staring hard out the glass doors to the garden. She could listen to strangers fantasies all day long, but she wouldn't picture Gabby insisting *whoeverthefuckehewas* wear a condom. That line of thought was a whole big bucket of nope. Gabby hadn't trusted her with her how she lost her virginity. Genna bore the stab to the heart the way she supposed many guardians did as their kids grew up and stopped needing them. An everyday kind of death.

Table complete, they all looked toward the kitchen where their mom was in her element as reigning monarch of the eight-burner Viking.

"Rowan would look so hot in an apron," Grace said wistfully.

Genna threw a swan at her and watched it sail past Grace's head. "Don't make me hurt you."

Grace grinned. "*My* sapphic fantasy involves tying apron strings around Rowan's wrists and—"

"Rowan isn't your fantasy anymore. Why don't you tell Gen about maybe-call-me Paisley?" Gabby said in a tone perfectly pitched to mimic the one their mother used when trouble was brewing. Not for the first time Genna admired Gabby's ability to navigate a sticky situation.

Grace's eyes narrowed to slits. "You did *not* just go there."

Gabby shrugged, supremely unconcerned by Grace's outrage.

"Wait. Paisley? Like, the pattern?"

The twins nailed Genna with the same look that said she was being ten kinds of millennial right now. "*Paisley.*" Gabby drew out the word out so two syllables became fourteen. "Is this blond cheerleader in Grace's ceramics elective. She wants Grace to *maybe call her sometime*. She flips her hair and everything. She's so smiley it's sort of creepy."

"She isn't creepy!" Grace's ears went pink.

Genna tried not to go *aww* too, showing any kind of enthusiasm for a potential date would just make Grace clam up. "Smiley is cool. You going to maybe call her, Grace?"

Grace picked the now deformed swan up off the floor. "Maybe."

"That means yes," Gabby informed Genna.

"If you three are done with the table, go into the living room and tidy the mess you made in there. I swear it's like you all still live here," their mom called over her shoulder, bent over the oven the way another woman might over a baby's bassinet.

They did sort of all still live there. Genna and Rowan had been spending a lot more time at her mom's now that Doreen and the boys had moved a few blocks away. Her mom babysat Sawyer and Cameron as often as Doreen needed and the front door was a revolving barrage of muddy feet, shrieking children, and adults who never said no to souffle. Messy, perhaps, but it'd taken ten years off her mom's life to have the house full again.

Before they could troop into the living room to clean up the mess they'd made watching Netflix and eating popcorn, Rowan's voice carried through the front hall and into the kitchen. "Hi, we're here. I brought that casserole dish you wanted, Gloria."

Genna's heartbeat instantly climbed up into her throat. The Markses had arrived. *Sara* had arrived. What if Sara really did hate her? What if—Grace slung an arm casually around Genna's waist and poked her in the side. "Ridiculously loveable and don't you forget it."

"Thanks," Genna muttered.

The Marks family spilled into the dining area, Sawyer and Cameron running ahead to hug everyone in turn. "Gen, come meet her, come meet her." Sawyer tugged on her wrist ineffectually as Genna's feet glued themselves to the floor. But, like, seriously, for real, what if Sara hated her? Sara'd *been through stuff*. Way more than most people. What if she took one look at Genna and saw straight though her pretense at responsible adulting? What if she thought Rowan was too good for her? What if—

"Everyone." Doreen smiled when all eyes turned to her. "I'd like you to meet my daughter Sara. We're so happy to have her home." Doreen wrapped an arm around Sara's shoulders, more smiley than call-me-maybe Paisely could ever hope to be.

"Hey." Sara lifted a hand like she was going to wave and thought better of it at the last second. "Um, it's nice to meet you all." Sara was exactly as Genna had expected her to be, the million photos Rowan and Doreen shared with her giving her something to go on for a first impression. Her shades of sunlight hair was choppily cut to fall messily around her shoulders, too long bangs falling into her eyes. Green eyes just like Rowan's that crinkled at the corners when she smiled. Paler and skinnier than her out of date social media photos had led Genna to believe. Even though Sara was talking to them, she hadn't taken her eyes off her sons. Two years apart. Genna couldn't imagine the pain.

When the introductions train stopped at Genna, she cast wildly about for something interesting to say about herself. Something Sara could relate to. "I'm Genna. I love everybody."

Out of the corner of her eye she saw Grace wince like the introductions train had just come flying off the tracks. "I mean," Genna plowed on because what else could she do, "I'm Rowan's girlfriend and this is my family. Our family. I'm glad we finally have everyone here. I've wanted to meet you for so long."

Sara smiled. "I like people who love everybody. Lowers the bar, you know? I'm nervous enough already."

Relief flooded Genna. You could always tell nice people from how they handled an awkward situation, and clearly niceness was a Marks family trait. She unglued her feet and walked over to fling her arms around Sara, hugging her before pulling away. "I hope you're ready for more sisters because you just got three. There's no need to be nervous. We're all dorks."

Grace laughed but Gabby pouted theatrically. "Just because *you're* a dork doesn't mean I don't know how to behave like a normal person."

The twins hugged Sara too and Rowan pulled Genna into her side. "You're sweeter than you think."

Genna raised her eyebrows. "Keep that to yourself, please. I have a reputation to uphold."

Rowan kissed her cheek. "Not here you don't."

Genna smiled. With Rowan she could be herself, even if she was still figuring out who that really was. Genna watched as everyone descended on the table, Gabby helping the boys fill their kiddie cups with water, Doreen gushing over the charcuterie board, and her mom with her chin in her palm listening intently as Sara talked. The delicious scent of eggs, butter, and cocoa wafting from the kitchen and enveloping them all in a comfortable hug the way only chocolate could. With Rowan by her side, it really felt like home, safe in a way Genna hadn't even known to dream of. Sara the final piece of the puzzle. Rowan was right. She didn't have to pretend here. She didn't know if she'd ever truly *find herself* the way personal transformation sagas promised. But she'd found a new piece of her heart when her family had merged with Rowan's. Comfort. Familiarity. Acceptance.

"She's home," Rowan said quietly. "I almost can't believe it."

"She is." Genna reached up to brush her lips over Rowans. They were all home, and the best part was, Genna really did believe it.

About the Author

Sandy Lowe has a master's degree in publishing from the University of Sydney, Australia. In her capacity as senior editor at Bold Strokes Books, she reviews submissions and proposals, edits and develops content for publication, and oversees publication production. *The Naked Truth* is her third novel.

Books Available from Bold Strokes Books

All For Her: Forbidden Romance Novellas by Gun Brooke, J.J. Hale, Aurora Rey. Explore the angst and excitement of forbidden love few would dare in this heart-stopping novella collection. (978-1-63679-713-7)

Finding Harmony by CF Frizzell. Rock star Harper Cushing has to rearrange her grandmother's future and sell the family store out from under her, but she reassesses everything because Gram's helper, Frankie, could be offering the harmony her heart has been missing. (978-1-63679-741-0)

Gaze by Kris Bryant. Love at first sight is for dreamers, but the more time Lucky and Brianna spend together, the more they realize the chemistry of a gaze can make anything possible. (978-1-63679-711-3)

Laying of Hands by Patricia Evans. The mysterious new writing instructor at camp makes Grace Waters brave enough to wonder what would happen if she dared to write her own story. (978-1-63679-782-3)

Seducing the Widow by Jane Walsh. Former rival debutantes have a second chance at love after fifteen years apart when a spinster persuades her ex-lover to help save her family business. (978-1-63679-747-2)

The Naked Truth by Sandy Lowe. How far are Rowan and Genevieve willing to go and how much will they risk to make their most captivating and forbidden fantasies a reality? (978-1-63679-426-6)

The Roommate by Claire Forsythe. Jess Black's boyfriend is handsome and successful. That's why it comes as a shock when she meets a woman on the train who makes her pulse race. (978-1-63679-757-1)

Close to Home by Allisa Bahney. Eli Thomas has to decide if avoiding her hometown forever is worth losing the people who used to mean the most to her, especially Aracely Hernandez, the girl who got away. (978-1-63679-661-1)

Golden Girl by Julie Tizard. In 1993, "Don't ask, don't tell" forces everyone to lie, but Air Force nurse Lt. Sofia Sanchez and injured instructor pilot Lt. Gillian Guthman have to risk telling each other the truth in order to fly and survive. (978-1-63679-751-9)

Innis Harbor by Patricia Evans. When Amir Farzaneh meets and falls in love with Loch, a dark secret lurking in her past reappears, threatening the happiness she'd just started to believe could be hers. (978-1-63679-781-6)

The Blessed by Anne Shade. Layla and Suri are brought together by fate to defeat the darkness threatening to tear their world apart. What they don't expect to discover is a love that might set them free. (978-1-63679-715-1)

The Guardians by Sheri Lewis Wohl. Dogs, devotion, and determination are all that stand between darkness and light. (978-1-63679-681-9)

The Mogul Meets Her Match by Julia Underwood. When CEO Claire Beauchamp goes undercover as a customer of Abby Pita's café to help seal a deal that will solidify her career, she doesn't expect to be so drawn to her. When the truth is revealed, will she break Abby's heart? (978-1-63679-784-7)

Trial Run by Carsen Taite. When Reggie Knoll and Brooke Dawson wind up serving on a jury together, their one task—reaching a unanimous verdict—is derailed by the fiery clash of their personalities, the intensity of their attraction, and a secret that could threaten Brooke's life. (978-1-63555-865-4)

Waterlogged by Nance Sparks. When conservation warden Jordan Pearce discovers a body floating in the flowage, the serenity of the Northwoods is rocked. (978-1-63679-699-4)

Accidentally in Love by Kimberly Cooper Griffin. Nic and Lee have good reasons for keeping their distance. So why does their growing attraction seem more like a love-hate relationship? (978-1-63679-759-5)

Fatal Foul Play by David S. Pederson. After eight friends are stranded in an old lodge by a blinding snowstorm, a brutal murder leaves Mark Maddox to solve the crime as he discovers deadly secrets about people he thought he knew. (978-1-63679-794-6)

Frosted by the Girl Next Door by Aurora Rey and Jaime Clevenger. When heartbroken Casey Stevens opens a sex shop next door to uptight cupcake baker Tara McCoy, things get a little frosty. (978-1-63679-723-6)

Ghost of the Heart by Catherine Friend. Being possessed by a ghost was not on Gwen's bucket list, but she must admit that ghosts might be real, and one is obviously trying to send her a message. (978-1-63555-112-9)

Hot Honey Love by Nan Campbell. When chef Stef Lombardozzi puts her cooking career into the hands of filmmaker Mallory Radowski—the pickiest eater alive—she doesn't anticipate how hard she falls for her. (978-1-63679-743-4)

London by Patricia Evans. Jaq's and Bronwyn's lives become entwined as dangerous secrets emerge and Bronwyn's seemingly perfect life starts to unravel. (978-1-63679-778-6)

This Christmas by Georgia Beers. When Sam's grandmother rigs the Christmas parade to make Sam and Keegan queen and queen, sparks fly, but they can't forget the Big Embarrassing Thing that makes romance a total nope. (978-1-63679-729-8)

Unwrapped by D. Jackson Leigh. Asia du Muir is not going to let some party girl actress ruin her best chance to get noticed by a Broadway critic. Everyone knows you should never mix business and pleasure. (978-1-63679-667-3)

Language Lessons by Sage Donnell. Grace and Lenka never expected to fall in love. Is home really where the heart is if it means giving up your dreams? (978-1-63679-725-0)

New Horizons by Shia Woods. When Quinn Collins meets Alex Anders, Horizon Theater's enigmatic managing director, a passionate connection ignites, but amidst the complex backdrop of theater politics, their budding romance faces a formidable challenge. (978-1-63679-683-3)

Scrambled: A Tuesday Night Book Club Mystery by Jaime Maddox. Avery Hutchins makes a discovery about her father's death that will force her to face an impossible choice between doing what is right and finally finding a way to regain a part of herself she had lost. (978-1-63679-703-8)

Stolen Hearts by Michele Castleman. Finding the thief who stole a precious heirloom will become Ella's first move in a dangerous game of wits that exposes family secrets and could lead to her family's financial ruin. (978-1-63679-733-5)

Synchronicity by J.J. Hale. Dance, destiny, and undeniable passion collide at a summer camp as Haley and Cal navigate a love story that intertwines past scars with present desires. (978-1-63679-677-2)

The First Kiss by Patricia Evans. As the intrigue surrounding her latest case spins dangerously out of control, military police detective Parker Haven must choose between her career and the woman she's falling in love with. (978-1-63679-775-5)

Wild Fire by Radclyffe & Julie Cannon. When Olivia returns to the Red Sky Ranch, Riley's carefully crafted safe world goes up in flames. Can they take a risk and cross the fire line to find love? (978-1-63679-727-4)

Writ of Love by Cassidy Crane. Kelly and Jillian struggle to navigate the ruthless battleground of Big Law, grappling with desire, ambition, and the thin line between success and surrender. (978-1-63679-738-0)